THE RED BOOK

ALSO BY
DEBORAH COPAKEN KOGAN

Between Here and April

Hell Is Other Parents

Shutterbabe

The Red Book

DEBORAH
COPAKEN
KOGAN

HYPERION
New York

Library of Congress has catalogued the hardcover edition
of this book as follows:

Kogan, Deborah Copaken.
    The red book / Deborah Copaken Kogan. — 1st ed.
        p. cm.
    ISBN 978-1-4013-4082-7
    1. Harvard University—Alumni and alumnae—Fiction. 2. Class
reunions—Fiction. 3. Friendship—Fiction. I. Title.
    PS3611.O3654R43 2012
    813'.6—dc23

                                                    2011041830

Paperback ISBN 978-1-4013-4199-2

FIRST PAPERBACK EDITION

10 9 8 7 6 5 4 3 2 1

THIS LABEL APPLIES TO TEXT STOCK

We try to produce the most beautiful books possible, and we are also
extremely concerned about the impact of our manufacturing process
on the forests of the world and the environment as a whole. Accord-
ingly, we've made sure that all of the paper we use has been certified
as coming from forests that are managed, to ensure the protection of
the people and wildlife dependent upon them.

For the ghosts of my past:

dead or alive,

out of touch or on speed dial,

you remain.

CONTENTS

Author's Note   ix

Friday, June 5, 2009

1. Addison   13
2. Clover   29
3. Mia   61
4. Jane   89

Saturday, June 6, 2009

5. Morning   125
6. Afternoon   169
7. Evening   227

Sunday, June 7, 2009

8. The Memorial Service   293

Epilogue

Twenty-Fifth Anniversary Report   335

Acknowledgments   345

AUTHOR'S NOTE

Every five years, after graduating from Harvard, its alumni are asked to account for the previous half decade of their lives by filling out a form with basic biographical information (name, address, e-mail, job, spouse, kids) and composing a few descriptive summary paragraphs—three to five are suggested—for inclusion in a bound, crimson-colored anniversary report known, for lack of a better or actual title, as the red book. Many graduates write in, others do not, but whether one completes the assignment or not, at a minimum every name and address of the living are published, some prefaced only by *"Last Known Address"* for those classmates who've managed to elude the grasp of Harvard's mainframe: a feat, considering how diligently the shepherds in the Alumni Affairs and Development office work to keep track of their flocks.

The deadline for these entries is the last quarter of the year prior to one's reunion, so the class of 1989, who returned for their twentieth reunion in 2009, would have composed their red book entries in the fall of 2008. The books then land with a prereunion thud at the doorsteps of every graduate, whether they write in or not, whether they pay the suggested sixty-dollar donation to offset printing costs or not, whether they're impatiently waiting for it or not.

No data exist concerning the percentage of red books that are cracked open the minute their recipients arrive home from work, the playground, an adulterous tryst, what have you, but the author will go out on a limb here and guess one hundred.

*It's very difficult to keep the line between
the past and the present.
You know what I mean? It's awfully difficult.*

—Little Edie Beale,
GREY GARDENS

THE RED BOOK

Harvard and Radcliffe

Class of 1989

Twentieth Anniversary Report

ADDISON CORNWALL HUNT. *Home Address:* 85–101 North 3rd Street, #4, Brooklyn, NY 11211 (718-427-0909). *Occupation:* Artist. *E-mail:* ahg@addisonhunt.com. *Spouse/Partner:* Gunner Griswold (B.A., Yale '88; M.F.A., University of Iowa '92). *Spouse/Partner Occupation:* Writer. *Children:* Charlotte Trilby, 1995; William Houghton, 1997; John Thatcher, 1998.

Okay, so here I am, just like back in college, writing this thing with only forty minutes left to go before the deadline. *Plus ça change.* (She pauses briefly, for inspiration, to hunt down the Fifteenth Anniversary Report, which is wedged between all the other red books and her freshman facebook—the very facebook, she's been trying to explain to her offspring, which was the original model for their beloved virtual one, but they look at her as if she's crazy, something she's not so sure they're incorrect to assume these days, except of course in this instance.)

So. Where were we? Right. My life these past five years. And can I just say that when I accepted Harvard's invitation to join the class of '89, I don't remember agreeing that every five years, *for the rest of my life*, I'd be forced to complete another writing assignment. There's a reason I nearly failed freshman expos, people!

Just saying.

Ack! I got sucked into rereading the Fifteenth Report. You guys are fascinating. A tribute to your alma mater. I can't even understand half of the things you're doing, but I'm glad you're out there doing it. Someone has to figure out the secrets of the universe, and better you than me, and I guess this is where I should probably take a moment to formally apologize to the TA I called (Joe? John? Josh?) in a panic at 3 A.M. before the Science A final, but the funny thing is, it's been over two decades since that call, and I still don't understand dark matter or quarks, though you did a valiant job trying to explain them. Okay, twenty minutes left. Come on, Addison, you can do this.

Okay, so, I guess the biggest change since my last entry is that

I've finally entered the modern age: I have an actual Web site of my work (http://www.addisonhunt.com), I've hung out a shingle on etsy.com (http://www.etsy.com/shop/AddisonHunt?ref=seller_info), and I've been taking classes in QuarkXPress—finally! A quark I understand!—and PhotoShop to stay on top of the latest digital technologies. Still painting as always, but my process has evolved from a kind of neo abstract feminist expressionism into a photo realistic rendering of the mundane. That's artist-speak for "I used to throw paint on a canvas and use the palms of my hand to smear it here and there as a visual representation of unconscious female desires. Now I make intricate drawings of my hairbrush."

Wish I could drone on longer, but there are Christmas cards to send out, and I have to help Houghton build the Parthenon for social studies by tomorrow, and Thatcher needs to be picked up from guitar, and Trilby's boarding school applications are due in two days. As you might expect, I'm a little behind.

CLOVER PACE LOVE. *Home Address:* 102 East 91st Street, New York, NY 10128 (212-546-7394). *Occupation and Office Address:* Managing Director, Lehman Brothers, 1897 Broadway, 41st floor, New York, NY 10014. *Additional Home Address:* 4 Lily Pond Lane, East Hampton, NY. *E-mail:* clover_love@lehman.com. *Graduate Degrees:* M.B.A., Harvard '98. *Spouse/Partner:* Daniel McDougal (B.A., Boston College '95; J.D., Yale '98). *Spouse/Partner Occupation:* Attorney, Legal Aid Society.

I wish I had something more interesting to report other than that, aside from a brief detour at the B-school midcareer, I've been with the same company, Lehman Brothers, since the week after graduation. I sometimes wonder what it would have been like to have jumped around a bit more, but one of the reasons I've stayed with Lehman for so long is that I actually love both my workplace and my job. I find the challenges of managing both people and equity fascinating, and though I'm proud to be one of only a handful of female leaders in our company, it's still shocking to me that we're not better represented in positions of power on Wall Street.

I was named managing director of my group in July 2004. I lead a large and vibrant team focusing on mortgage-backed securities, our most profitable department in fiscal year '07.

On the love-life side of the equation, I finally found my soul mate, Danny McDougal, after I allowed my former roommates to create a profile for me on Match.com. They called it an "intervention," which they staged during the annual July Fourth weekend we spent together at my house. Addison took the photo, Jane wrote the text, and Mia tried to use her Meisner techniques to coax me out of what she called my "robotically corporate" communication skills. (Apparently asking a man on the third date whether he's willing to change an equal number of diapers as his wife is a Dating Don't; luckily Danny found both my honesty and the two-page, single-spaced document mapping out a future of equitably shared domestic responsibilities I presented to him on our ninth date slightly weird but charming enough to stay the course.)

Danny and I closed the deal, so to speak, six months later and found our dream house, an 1897 brownstone in Carnegie Hill, which we gutted and renovated over the course of the next year. If I'd better understood the various stresses of renovating a property while simultaneously living in it, I might not have insisted we do it during our first year of marriage, but when you get hitched at the ripe old age of thirty-nine, there's no time, as they say, like the present.

Meanwhile no children yet, but they are definitely high up on our list of goals for FY09, and we hope, with any luck, to bring a couple of them to our twenty-fifth!

MIA *MANDELBAUM* ZANE. *Home Address:* 45 San Remo Lane, Los Angeles, CA 90049 (310-589-0923). *Additional Home Address:* 17 rue des Ecoles, Antibes, France. *E-mail:* mia.zane@gmail.com.

Spouse/Partner: Jonathan Zane (B.A., University of Maryland '70; M.F.A., UCLA '74). *Spouse/Partner Occupation:* Film director. *Children:* Max Benjamin, 1992; Eli Samuel, 1994; Joshua Aaron, 1998; Zoe Claire, 2008.

As I sit here typing this, the newest member of the Zane Train—our tiny caboose, Zoe—has finally fallen asleep in her BabyBjörn, the only place she seems to want to engage in this kind of activity. Those of you familiar with the medieval torture device that is the Björn will understand what this means: I've had a baby glued to my middle-aged torso, without reprieve, every day since her birth. In fact, I think I must have been single-handedly responsible for the recent spike in Johnson & Johnson stock, as I've decimated the entire West Coast supply of Motrin to deal with the inevitable backache. Good practice, I suppose, for all the aches and pains we'll all be feeling soon enough. (Have twenty years actually gone by so fast? I walk around assuming I'm still twenty-two, then I catch a glimpse of myself in a store window or a bathroom mirror and am suddenly and brutally shocked back into reality. Who's that scary chick with the streaks of gray in her hair and the deep lines around her mouth? Oh, right. That's me.)

It's been, well, interesting, to say the least, to run around the country visiting colleges with my eldest while breast-feeding an infant. I've been so physically and mentally addled, in fact, that the other day Eli, my second, walked into the kitchen in search of a snack—oh my God, those boys can eat!—and I said, "Since when did you grow facial hair?" and he said, "Um, like a year ago, Mom? Duh."

Okay, so here's the part where I'm supposed to tell you about the total awesomeness of my career, followed by a rattling off of my awards and accolades, but the only award I have sitting framed on my mantel is a "#1 Mom" plaque my eldest, Max, made out of macaroni and clay for Mother's Day circa 1996. Max was born soon after I got married, which was soon after I graduated, which was probably too soon, but there you have it. Max was followed closely by Eli, who was followed four years later by Josh, and though I was still going out on auditions from time to time, suddenly I had three young boys and little time, energy, or desire to keep banging my head against that wall. Plus, the kind of work I was able to land as an actress—a Tums commercial here, a public service announcement there—never felt as fulfilling or stimulating as spending an afternoon on the floor with my children. I know that sounds like an excuse, and on some level I'm sure it is, but it's also as true a statement as any: What I'd planned as a short maternity leave turned into seventeen years. And while they might not have been the most mentally challenging or professionally rewarding years of my life, spiritually they were rich and full. So rich and so full that when my husband asked me what I wanted for my fortieth birthday, I joked, "Another baby." But then the more I thought about it, the less it felt like a joke. Hence, Zoe Claire, now stirring in her baby carrier, rooting around for some lunch.

That's not to say I spend every hour taking care of my kids, because until Zoe was born, there were many years when they were in school most of the day. I know I'm lucky to have been given the gift of time with them, so I try to pay it forward, in some way, every day. This past year and a half we've been particularly busy hosting fund-raising events at our home to help raise money for the Obama campaign. (G'Obama!) I'm also active in our local chapter of Planned Parenthood and in the soup kitchen committee at our synagogue, B'nai Israel. I've been running the Pinehurst School's annual fund-raising auction ever since our son Max was in kindergarten, and I do outreach in Watts to help locate scholarship students who might not otherwise have heard of the school. Pinehurst has been a great learning environment for our three sons: small classes, one-on-one attention, a focus on the whole child. Zoe seems eager to get started as a student there as well—

she often wails when her brothers leave in the morning—but for now, I'm hanging on to her lovely babyhood. Or, rather, her lovely babyhood seems to be hanging on to me. Constantly.

Jonathan, my husband, continues to direct romantic comedies. His latest, *Give and Take*, featuring Hugh Grant and Keira Knightley as former schoolmates caught on different sides of the law, should be hitting the theaters just before we head back for reunion, so definitely go see it if you get a chance!

Life, as they say, has been good to us, and my husband and I feel blessed and fortunate to be where we are. We have our health, four beautiful children, good friends, and a sturdy roof over our heads. A few years ago, we renovated an old stone house in the south of France, where we try to retreat every August, depending on Jonathan's shooting schedule, so if you're ever near Antibes during the summer, drop by! We'll open up a bottle of local wine and watch the sun set over the Mediterranean. That's a real invitation, so take me up on it. If you're lucky, you'll get to spend time with Jane as well, who always makes it down for at least a week with her daughter and her beau, Bruno. And if Jane ever makes an honest man of Bruno, we've promised to hold the wedding for them there as well. (Jane? Oh, Janie-pie? Hint hint.)

I look forward to catching up with everyone at reunion.

JANE NGUYEN STREETER. *Home Address:* 11 bis, rue Vieille du Temple, 75004 Paris, France (33 1 42 53 97 58). *Occupation and Office Address:* Reporter, the *Boston Globe*, 11 bis, rue Vieille du Temple, 75004 Paris, France. *E-mail:* jnguyen@bostonglobe.com. *Spouse/Partner:* Bruno Saint-Pierre. *Spouse/Partner Occupation:* Editor, *Libération*. *Children:* Sophie Isabelle Duclos, 2002.

I am a card-carrying rationalist. I do not believe in God or higher powers or anyone up there manipulating our puppet strings, but every once in a while I do wonder why some of us are targeted, seemingly more than others, to endure loss. I'm not complaining. In fact I'm grateful for my life every day. It's just that when I sit down to read these entries every five years—actually, more like *devour* them in a single, all-night, sleepless gulp—what strikes me most profoundly about the nature of our disparate paths is not the infrequent "I lost my spouse" or "My father died last year," but rather the fortuitous lack of life-altering tragedies in the majority of these entries.

I consider myself relatively happy, emotionally stable, and extremely lucky compared to many of the people I've met over my nearly two decades as a reporter, but examined closely, as this book forces those of us masochistic enough to send in these updates to do, my life reads more like a bad soap opera than like the life of a typical Ivy League grad, whatever *typical* means in this context.

As some of you know, I lost both of my parents and all three siblings to war before the age of seven. After making my way to Saigon, I was adopted by Harold Streeter, the army doctor who treated me upon my arrival in the city, and his wife, Claire. Then, a year after my new parents brought me home to their house in Belmont, Harold died of a freak staph infection he contracted at the hospital where he worked.

Then, thank goodness, there was a long lull, about which I've already written extensively in these pages, so I'll just summarize here to refresh our collective memory: After college, I moved to Paris, to work for the *International Herald Tribune* and to live out my Jean Seberg expat fantasies; this led to a freelance gig with the *Christian Science Monitor*, which got me out into the world beyond, where I began to specialize in covering global refugee crises. I met my husband Hervé on the back of a truck in Rwanda. I was asked to take over as the Paris bureau chief for the *Globe* a few years after that, until they shut down the bureau. They kept me on as a staff reporter, however, which basically means I work out of my home office when I'm in town, which suits both the *Globe* and me just fine, at least for now. I gave birth to our beautiful daughter Sophie, whom many of you met at the last reunion, in the summer of '02. Because of Hervé's humane French benefits, I never had to worry—as I often read in these pages that many of you do—about going bankrupt paying for Sophie's medical bills, schooling, or child care. (Although now that Obama just won the presidency, yesterday as I write this, I'm assuming the U.S. will finally get its act together on the health care front.)

I took predictable joy in these tragedy-free years, but as they began to accumulate, year by year, I started to get cocky, believing that the "curse" of bad luck that had plagued my earlier life was finally, thrillingly over.

Then, in late 2004, my husband's car was hijacked near Jalalabad, Afghanistan, where he was on assignment for the French newspaper *Libération*. Or at least that's what we think probably happened, as his body wasn't found until six days later, tossed into a ditch. For the next six months, our daughter, who was only two at the time, kept looking for him in all the places she remembered her father taking her: a restaurant in our neighborhood, the patisserie on the corner, the playground in the Place des Vosges. And then she stopped looking or even talking about him altogether. A year later, I fell in love and moved in with my current partner, the wonderful Bruno Saint-Pierre, who was Hervé's editor at *Libé* and the shoulder I often leaned on after Hervé's death.

Then, a few months ago, Claire, my adoptive mother, the most solid rock of my life, called to tell me she'd been diagnosed with Stage IV colon cancer. Her prognosis is not good. The doctors won't give her an exact time frame, but they said she's probably looking at six months tops. She still lives in her (our) old house in Belmont, so I'll definitely be back and forth between Paris and Boston this fall and winter, but I'm also hoping she sticks around long enough to see the buds on her rosebush in May and the smile on her grandchild's face in June when Sophie and I arrive for reunion.

Friday, June 5, 2009

1

Addison

I t had simply never occurred to Addison that the Cambridge Police Department not only kept two-decade-old records of unpaid parking tickets, but that they could also use the existence of her overdue fines, on the eve of her twentieth college reunion, to arrest her in front of Gunner and the kids. If such a scenario had struck her as even remotely possible, she'd be thinking twice about zooming through that red light on Memorial Drive.

But it hadn't, so here we go.

"Oh my God, look at these idiots," she says, slamming her hand down hard on the horn of her blue and white 1963 VW Microbus, which she purchased online one night in a fit of kitsch nostalgia. Or that's the story she tells friends when they ask what she was thinking buying a vehicle that takes weeks or even months to fix when it breaks down, for want of parts. "Take my advice: don't *ever* go on eBay stoned," she'll say, whenever the conversation veers toward car ownership, online shopping, or adult pot use. "You'll end up with a first generation off the master Cornell '77 along with the friggin' *bus* the dude drove to the show."

While the story is technically true, the impetus behind the purchase was much more about economic necessity, practicality, and appearances than Addison likes to admit. For one, she and Gunner couldn't afford a new Prius. They refused, on ecological principle, to buy a used SUV, or rather they refused to be put in the position of being judged for owning an SUV. (While they loved the earth as much as the next family, they weren't above, strictly speaking, adding a supersize vehicle to its surface for the sake of convenience.) A cheap compact, with three kids and a rescued black Lab, was out of the question. And they couldn't wrap their heads around the image of themselves at the helm of a minivan. To be a part of their close-knit circle of friends, all of whom have at least one toe dipped in the alternative art scene in Williamsburg, meant upholding a certain level of épater-le-bourgeois aesthetics. If a minivan or even a station wagon could have been done ironically, believe her, it would have.

Traffic in front of the Microbus has halted, an admixture of the normal clogged arteries at the Charles River crossings during rush hour compounded by the arterial plaque of reunion weekend attendees, those thousands of additional vehicles that appear every June like clockwork, loaded up with alumni families and faded memories, the latter triggered out of dormancy by the sight of the crimson cupola of Dunster House or the golden dome of Adams House or the Eliot House clock tower, such that any one of the drivers blocking Addison's path to Harvard Square might be thinking, as Addison is right now (catching a glimpse of the nondescript window on the sixth floor of that disaster of a modernist building that is Mather House), *There, right there: That's where I first fucked her.*

No, that wasn't a typo. Prior to marrying Gunner, Addison spent almost two years in a relationship with a woman. This, she likes to remind everyone, was before "Girls Gone Wild," before the acronym LUG ("lesbian until graduation") had even debuted in the *Times*, so she'd appreciate it if you wouldn't accuse her of following a trend, okay?

If anything, Addison has come to realize, thanks to a cut-rate Jungian who came highly recommended, Bennie was just one more way— like the roommates she wound up choosing—she'd been trying to shake off her pedigree, to prove to herself and to others that she had more depth and facets than her staid history and prep school diploma would suggest. Addison may have been one of the eighth generation of Hunts to matriculate from Harvard, but she would be the first not to heed the siren call of Wall Street. For one, she had no facility with numbers. For another, she'd seen what Wall Street had done to her father. He, too, had been enamored of the stroke of fresh Golden's on canvas from the moment he could hold a paintbrush, but he'd tossed his wooden box of acrylics into the back of the closet of his Park Avenue duplex—where it gathered dust until Addison happened upon it one day during a game of hide-and-seek—because that's what Hunts did: They subsumed themselves into their Brooks Brothers suits. The cirrhosis that killed him in his early fifties, when Addison was just a sophomore in college, was no act of God. It was an act, every glass-tinkling night, of desperation.

Bennie was the first person in her life to make that suggestion. Out loud, at least, and to Addison's face. And though both Bennie and her pronoun were aberrations in the arc of Addison's sexual history, what the two had together—although Addison would only be able to understand this in retrospect, per the cut-rate Jungian—was love.

"Is Bennie coming this weekend?" Gunner asks. He's been hearing about this mythical creature, Bennie Watanabe, ever since he and Addison bumped into each other that summer at a seaside taverna in Eressos, where Addison had gone with some vague and mostly unrealized notion of studying the poems of Sappho in their place and language of origin as inspiration for a series of abstract studies of the Isle of Lesvos she never ended up finishing, and Gunner had retreated to start what would become, ten years later, his first and thus far only published novel, a coming-of-age tale that would feature, after his run-in with Addison, a girlfriend/muse from a socially prominent family who dabbles in bisexuality with a Japanese American lesbian before marrying her old boyfriend from prep school following their chance encounter at a taverna in the Lesvos city of Molyvos (because something had to be fictionalized, and it had a picturesque port he could describe, knowing boats as he did, in intimate, Moby Dick-like detail).

The Walls of St. Paul's had been sufficiently well received—especially the boat parts, which the *New York Times* critic, an aquatic enthusiast himself, dubbed "Melvillean"—that Gunner was paralyzed by a decade-long writer's block. Though publicly he's always insisted that Tilly, his protagonist's self-delusional, bisexual wife, is nothing like Addison, privately Addison knows that the vaguely unflattering, unhinged portrayal of their early years together is a roman à clef in every sense of the phrase except for the inventively imagined scenes of three-way sex among the protagonist, his wife, and the random assortment of foreign women they picked up along the way during their first year of marriage, which was spent, as Addison and Gunner's had been, backpacking around the globe. For as much as Gunner had begged his new bride to bring another woman into their bed, Addison did not share this same fantasy, and, in fact, she resented her husband's preconceptions that such a scenario was possible. Bennie was an anomaly, she kept telling him. A momentary slip of the self.

"So what exactly is your regular self when it comes to sex?" Gunner recently asked, after Addison once again claimed exhaustion as an excuse against her husband's amorous onslaught.

"I'm just tired, okay? I deal with three kids and their endless pits of need all afternoon while you're off in Dumbo in your 'garret' writing the great American novel, and my paints go untouched. I'm sorry. I'm just not in the mood."

"You're *never* in the mood," said Gunner, sulking. "We need to talk about this, Ad. It's affecting my work."

Don't you fucking blame me, she thought. And while we're on the topic, what about *my* work? But wanting to avoid conflict at such a late hour, she said only, "Yes, sure, okay," and kissed his forehead. "Let's talk about this when I'm more rested. I'm sorry, I really am. When you finish your novel and sell it, maybe we can use some of the money to go away, just the two of us."

"That'd be great," his voice said, though the rest of him seemed less convinced.

And another night of lovemaking was once again averted.

It's been a year—no, fourteen months—Addison figures, since

they've had sex. All right, maybe fifteen or sixteen. She's kind of lost track. She understands this must be frustrating for her husband, but she can't will herself to feel passion where none lingers. She tells herself it's all because of him—his lack of a successful follow-up, his moping around feeling sorry for himself, his sullen moodiness, his financial impotence. But at night, when she finds quiet moments alone for release, it's images of ripe breasts and swollen vulvas that send her over the edge.

"Oh, please, I'm as heterosexual as they come, and I have an entire encyclopedia of breasts and va-jay-jays in my head," her friend Liesl recently told her when Addison wondered aloud, over a Red Stripe, whether her pregame masturbatory fantasies were within the realm of heterosexually normal. "There's no such thing as 'normal' when it comes to sex. You of all people should know that."

"But do you fantasize about other stuff, too?" Addison wondered. "You know, besides the lady parts."

"You mean like the scene where I'm lying on the pool table at a frat house? Or where I'm Kate Winslet on the *Titanic*, being sketched by Leonardo DiCaprio?"

"See? I don't have any stuff like that," Addison lamented.

"Oh, please," Liesl said, laughing. "You're welcome to borrow mine."

But later that night, when she tried to conjure the pool table scene, the undergrad boys turned into undergrad girls. And on the *Titanic* she herself was being sketched by Kate Winslet.

"I have no idea if Bennie's coming," she now tells Gunner, "although she did just send me a friend request on Facebook."

"Really? What'd she say?"

"Nothing."

No matter how many times her kids have made fun of her for feeling insulted by friend requests made without even an intimation of a greeting—a "Hello there!" or "Long time no see!"—Addison is pretty sure she'll never get used to the idea that modern online social interac-

tion completely eschews the laws of common courtesy, never mind
dilutes, forever, the meaning of the word *friend*. Her fourteen-year-old
daughter has 789 "friends." 789 friends! What can that even mean
when Addison, with forty-two years of nonvirtual social interaction
under her belt, has 139 "friends," all of whom sought her out like cancer cells in search of a new blood supply from the minute she created a
login and a password, half of whom she only vaguely remembers, if at
all, from this or that era of her life?

Sure, anyone who showed up in college with a typewriter, as she did,
then wound up purchasing one of those pathetically quick-to-crash first
Macs, was just finding her sea legs in the world of online social network-
ing, at first to monitor her still-technically-too-young-to-join-Facebook
children's profiles, then because, once ensconced and entrapped, it felt
mildly comforting to reconnect with those who'd disappeared from
one's Filofax-era life. Even if reconnecting meant simply scrolling down
an endless stream of mundanities—Joe Blow has the flu; Jane Doe is
contemplating eating the last Girl Scout cookie—and wracking one's
brain to come up with a comeback that was both restrainedly witty and
seemingly effortlessly so. "Blow, Joe, Blow!" "Courage, Jane."

When Bennie's message-free friend request suddenly appeared on
Addison's screen, attached to a profile photo containing Bennie, her
children, and her partner, Katrina Zucherbrot—aka Zeus, the German-
born artist whose ten-foot-tall sculpture of a phallic vagina had recently been added to the permanent collection at the Whitney—Addison
felt slight tinges of nostalgia (for time past), jealousy (over Zeus's success), and curiosity (to check out Bennie's photos), but she was otherwise unmoved. On the other hand she'd read, with breath-accelerating,
body-chemical-changing fascination, all about Bennie and Zeus and
their Petri-dish progeny five years earlier, in the Fifteenth Anniversary
Report, wherein Bennie had described, in raw detail, how each partner had given birth to one child using sperm from the other's brother.
And she'd been riveted by the recent Twentieth Anniversary red book,
in which Bennie announced her intentions to retire from Google at

the end of 2009 to begin the next phase of her life, in which she planned to start a foundation that would give scholarships to bullied gay teens and fight for the right of gay marriage.

Clicking through Bennie's photo albums on Facebook had been voyeuristically interesting, to be sure, but the act lacked both the context and enlightenment that Bennie's narratives were able to offer. Addison was struck only by the universality of the visual banality therein: Here's the happy family on vacation at the beach; and here they are opening presents on Christmas; and oh, look, here they all are standing in front of the Brandenburg Gate with Zeus's parents.

"That's bullshit!" Bennie had hurled at her, that frigid January of their senior year, just after finals, when Addison abruptly broke off the relationship. "You've never heard of a turkey baster?"

Addison had come to Bennie's spartan room in Mather House, dry eyed and rational, to explain that as much as she'd enjoyed the nearly two years they'd spent together as a couple, as much as she'd learned about herself and about her body's ability both to give and receive pleasure—skills she would, she assured Bennie, touching her lover's forearm, treasure forever—she'd decided that she simply couldn't wrap her head around the concept of spending the rest of her life with a woman. "I mean, experimenting in college is one thing, but I want to have kids one day," she said. "A normal family."

Hence Bennie's initial comment about the turkey baster, followed by more colorful castigations after Addison admitted to having joined the mile-high club with her male seatmate on the Delta shuttle home from break. "You bitch!" Bennie wailed. "You fucking two-faced, dick-sucking bitch! And if you touch my arm one more time in that patronizing way I will deck you." Which was soon followed by: "And what the hell do you mean by 'experimenting,' you entitled piece of shit? What happened to *'I'm in this for real, Bennie, I promise. You're my soul mate. My snuggle bunny. I want to make love to you forever'*? Jesus fucking Christ, Ad, I'm not some tab of acid you ate in prep school to gain 'experience' or cool points. I'm not your Dead show phase or a stranger you fuck in an airplane restroom because *it's on your list of things to do.* I'm a person! I have feelings! And up until five minutes ago, I was stupid enough to have given you the benefit of the doubt that you were an actual human being with feelings, too."

"Nothing?" says Gunner.

"Not a word," says Addison.

"So did you accept or ignore?"

"I haven't decided yet. I mean, do I really want to read, 'Bennie Watanabe is drinking coffee' or 'Bennie Watanabe is taking her daughter to school' or 'Bennie Watanabe just cashed in the remainder of her Google stock, and now she has more money than you, Warren Buffett, and God combined, so suck it'?" She honks the horn anew, motioning wildly and fruitlessly to the driver in front of her. "Jesus, go through! Go through! We're going to be late for the—"

"The *luau*?" Gunner laughs. He'd agreed to come this weekend, but only after Addison had pointed out that she'd attended his twentieth reunion the prior year without whimper or complaint. In fact, she'd continued, unable to stop herself, she'd even gone onto the Yale Web site herself, using Gunner's login, and made all the reservations and purchased the tickets for him. "I do *everything* for this family," she'd mumbled under her breath, "so just do this one fucking thing for me," but either Gunner didn't hear this last part, or he decided not to take the bait.

Gunner's stance on all things domestic has remained somewhat militant since Addison broached the idea of having children with him when they were still, according to Gunner, too young to spawn. He wanted the chance to write unencumbered for a decade or so, until they were into their mid-thirties; to have the freedom to sleep late and work whenever the muse struck. Addison tried explaining to him that since her art was gynocentric, she needed to experience childbirth and motherhood in order to be fully conversant in her field. More saliently (she showed him a chart of female fertility, with its gradual downward slope between eighteen and thirty-five, after which the line made a sudden nosedive toward zero), if they were going to have children, she ideally had to fit it in before she turned thirty-five.

"Fine," Gunner said. "You want kids now, you deal with their mess." He was the eldest of five. He knew from whence he spoke. Addison was an only child who'd never lacked for the kind of pocket change that drives adolescent girls to babysit.

So while Gunner sat frozen in front of his computer, searching for his muse, Addison produced a series of squalling Griswolds in rapid succession, taking on the full responsibility, as preordained, for their care. She fed them, first from herself, then from a jar, then off a plate. She changed their diapers and taught them, with varying degrees of success and trauma, to use a potty. She handled the grocery shopping and the doctor visits and the straightening of toys and the baths. She did the dishes and the laundry and the bills, she read them their bedtime stories. She dealt with school forms and playdates and Halloween costumes and sneakers and Valentine's cards and birthday parties and fingernails and snow boots and vomit. Oh the vomit! How had she never realized how much vomit three small humans could produce over the course of their childhood?

In between all this, she squeezed in time to paint, and she continued to answer the question "What do you do?" with "I'm an artist," even though personal assistant or short-order cook would have been more accurate. Then one day, just after her thirty-fifth birthday, she was stooping to pick up her dog's poop, another chore from which Gunner recused himself, when she spotted a flyer advertising the solo show of a girl from her childhood building who'd still been in diapers when Addison was in middle school. It suddenly struck her, like an anvil to the skull, that a whole decade had passed without so much as an exhibition or a sale or even a group show at one of the lesser homespun galleries in her neighborhood. So she pulled Gunner aside and said, "Enough." He was now officially the age at which he'd originally said he wanted to have kids, so she expected his equal participation as a line worker in the family factory. But by then Gunner had grown so used to the status quo, his domestic muscles had atrophied.

"Outsource it," he said. "I'm on the brink of something great."

He was able to suggest this solution, when neither spouse was bringing in money, because both he and Addison were the beneficiaries of small trust funds left to them by their grandparents. Gunner's parents also paid both for the children's tuition at St. Ann's and for their North 3rd Street loft, which was purchased in their name—in cash and in full—back in 1995 when the then-young couple decided to trade up from their one-bedroom in Alphabet City to 3,400 square feet of raw space in the then up-and-coming but still transitional neighborhood in Brooklyn when Addison was pregnant with Trilby. "A great investment," Gunner's father had declared, his voice echoing off the walls as he placed his hand firmly on the sturdy column supporting what would become his son and daughter-in-law's living room, a statement that both time and the Williamsburg real estate market had proven prescient. Their $250,000 loft was now worth, well, who knew with this crazy market? But before the collapse, the apartment below theirs, which was slightly smaller and didn't have a balcony, sold for $2.1 million.

So Addison hired more help. The housekeeper started coming in three times a week. A college kid was employed to help with after-school pickups and children's activities. Groceries were purchased online and delivered straight into their kitchen. A tutor was located to help Trilby with her dyslexia and Houghton with his math. A therapist was hired for the many months it took to help Thatcher work through his night terrors, and a dog walker showed up every day at midday. But still Addison felt frustrated by Gunner's lack of participation on the home front. "Gunner, please," she said. "What about if you cook dinner, and I'll clean the dishes? You were always a much better cook than me anyway. Or maybe you could take the kids to school on Tuesdays and Thursdays. Or to a birthday party now and then. Or I could deal with the pediatrician and you could do the dentist. You get the better deal there, trust me, because they only have to go to the dentist twice a year."

But Gunner held his ground. "My parents never took me to the doctor," he said. "The nanny did."

"That's not the point," said Addison.

"Please, Ad, I'm on the verge of a significant breakthrough in my work."

"What about my work, huh? What about my breakthroughs?"

"Nothing's keeping you from making art but you," said Gunner. A strange sentiment coming from a stalled writer, but also—Addison was loath to admit—partially true. Ever since Thatcher had entered kindergarten, she had five to six hours a day during which she could have chosen to ignore the ambient noise in her head, but for whatever reason, she couldn't.

And try as she might, both alone and with the Jungian, she could not figure out why. "I'm so angry at my husband!" she'd yell from the couch. Or, "Maybe I'm too stupid to figure out what I want to say with my work. I often wonder if every branch of my family tree hadn't all gone to Harvard whether I would have even been admitted." Or, "Most of the artists who succeed have some sort of gimmick. Keith Haring with his cartoon babies. Matthew Barney with his Cremaster Cycle. I need a gimmick. Or a penis. Or whatever." Or, "Fuck it. Maybe I should just throw in the towel and get a normal job like everyone else."

This last part she added in for the benefit of her shrink, so he would think his patient was making progress—yeah, right, she thought as she said it, like anyone would ever hire me to do a regular job—but for several weeks afterward she dreamt she was a graphic designer working in a cool glass and steel office in SoHo, wearing horn-rimmed glasses and the leather jacket Bennie had picked out for her at that thrift shop just off Bow Street near Adams House. She would wake up from these dreams with intense longing.

"It's not the luau I care about, sweetheart." She pronounces *sweetheart* harshly, like an epithet. "It's the *people* at the luau. My old friends from college. The ones I haven't seen in twenty years?"

"Oh, please, Ad," says Gunner, laughing. "Stop being such a drama queen. You see them all the time."

"I'm not just talking about Clover and the gang." Aside from the random dinner in the city with Clover once or twice a year, Addison, Clover, and their other two roommates, Mia and Jane, have been making a retreat, every year for the past ten, to Clover's weekend house in East Hampton, from which Addison always comes back to the city both refreshed from the multiple massages, mani/pedis, and yoga classes Clover insists on providing gratis but also agitated, in some unnamable way, by being waited upon so overtly. At the Hunt summer house in Deer Isle, Maine, in the compound that's been in Addison's family for six generations, most of the help disappeared after her father's death, and the woman who stayed on made herself scarce whenever the family was around. Gunner's family's retreat on Block Island, which his great-grandfather established in 1896, still employs a few caretakers and cooks, whose salaries are paid out of the family trust, but they are the kind of help who come and go undetected, save for the freshly folded towels stacked in the linen closet or the magical disappearance of the grit and sand from the bottom of the bathtub or the freshly baked blueberry muffins left to cool on a wire rack every morning at dawn. The idea of an eager fleet of young Filipinas arriving at 10 A.M. each day to file and buff everyone's nails, to rub oils into their skin, to wax their pubic hairs so *openly*, so *interactively*, is anathema to the way Addison was taught the help should help.

But Clover, who grew up several inches below the poverty line, could be forgiven for not understanding such nuances and for wanting to make grand shows of largesse. She'd had an image in her head of what extreme wealth looked like, she once told Addison, born of watching TV shows such as *Dallas* and *Dynasty* on the sly as a child—on sleepovers where the parents allowed TVs or, soundless, in front of the appliance store in Novato. And she'd decided she wanted every glittery drop of it, shoulder pads and all.

"There are at least thirty or forty people I was really close to, yes, including Bennie, if she decides to come," continues Addison, "most of whom I haven't seen since we all left Cambridge right after Bush *Senior* took office. That's a long time ago, Guns. The Berlin Wall was still up. I'm looking forward to this weekend, so let's drop the cynicism, okay?"

The driver in front of her hesitates, and she misses the light once more. *"Move the fuck out of the way!"* she screams. *"What is WRONG with you people?"*

"Mom, Jesus, chill," says Trilby, behind bangs she recently dyed pink. "It's a friggin' luau." She'd wanted to stay back in Williamsburg to go to a horrorcore rap show on Saturday night, but Addison had insisted she come with the family. "I don't care if Dismembered Fetus is playing at Pete's Candy Store, you're coming with us, and that's final," she'd shouted at her daughter, sounding so much like her own mother that time momentarily collapsed on itself—it had been doing that a lot lately—although really, *horrorcore*? At least the Dead shows that accompanied her own years of teenage angst and rebellion were not actually about Death with a capital *D* but rather about Peace and Love and, okay, yes, altered states of consciousness, but the good kind.

As far as she could tell, having done some primitive research online after her daughter became infatuated with the genre—her firstborn daughter! who used to cry and bury her head in her blankie whenever the Wicked Witch appeared on *The Wizard of Oz!*—horrorcore was, at its horrible core, a celebration of murder, rape, Satan, mutilation, and cannibalism, replete with loud, atonal music and a dash of crystal meth. Hence Addison's insistence that Trilby apply to St. Paul's, her and Gunner's alma mater. At least there, she figures, the type of drugs she'll ingest will expand her mind instead of rotting her teeth.

"Trilby, please. I don't need your snarky commentary right now, okay?" She glances into the rearview mirror to catch her daughter's kohl-outlined eyes, and the two stare at one another with mutual incredulity. In the row of seats behind Trilby's, she notices that Thatcher has fallen asleep on Houghton's lap, while Houghton is using his younger brother's head to prop up Addison's iPhone. "Houghton, don't drain the battery too much longer, pumpkin, okay? We might need it."

"Five more minutes?" he asks.

She and Houghton have always had an uncomplicated, easy rapport, the kind she'd always assumed she'd have with her daughters. But with Trilby playing the goth, and Thatcher's anxiety and innate shyness requiring medication, of late, to help him sleep, stay in school, and navigate even the most banal social interactions, Addison is left with just one child who even remotely resembled the type of offspring she'd imagined pre-them. "Sure, five more minutes, my sweet. What are you playing?"

"Mayhem," he says, shooting a Nazi zombie in the heart.

"It's not one of those shooting games, is it?"

"It's educational, about World War II," says her son, not wanting to lie to his mother outright.

That's when she spots it, just as the light turns yellow: a hole in the traffic. She guns the engine, as the light turns red—cue the siren—and plows through.

ARCHIBALD BUCKNELL GARDNER IV. *Home Address:* 450 Morgan Place, Oyster Bay, NY 11771 (516-672-8976).

ARABELLA *DEBEVOISE* GARDNER. *Home Address:* 450 Morgan Place, Oyster Bay, NY 11771 (516-672-8976). *E-mail:* arabella gardner@aol.com. *Spouse/Partner:* Archibald Bucknell Gardner IV (B.A., Harvard '89; M.B.A., ibid. '92). *Spouse/Partner Occupation:* CEO, Gardner Industries, Inc. *Children:* Archibald Bucknell V, 1994; Eloise Mason, 1996; Caroline Pearce, 1999; Charles Case, 2001.

Bucky and I will be celebrating our nineteenth wedding anniversary this spring. We live in Oyster Bay with our four children. I serve on the board of their school.

2

Clover

Clover never met an excuse to dress up she hasn't embraced: weddings, the opera, Halloween, toga parties, Christmas, black-tie benefits, white-tie benefits, New Year's Eve, that time she was out in LA for work several years back, and Mia told her to wear all white and join her family for the closing ceremony of Yom Kippur, the one that sounded like a Russian cabdriver pronouncing the Nilla in Nilla Wafers, and they both held hands and teared up watching Mia's three sons walking down the aisle of the synagogue carrying their flashlight candles—Mia because even though she was a bacon-eating, twice-a-year Jew, she was thinking about the generations of Jews that came before her, and how centuries of hatred had nearly wiped them out, and yet just *look* at her three living, breathing sons in their baseball-themed yarmulkes, carrying the torch into the future with all those other pint-size offshoots of the tribes of Israel, but also because absent from that twinkling parade was the one thing life had denied her: a daughter; Clover because she was getting to that age when the window for having a child of her own was growing narrower, and witnessing such a flagrant show of her contemporaries' productivity flooded her with a toxic brew of desire and jealousy, which was tempered only and somewhat pathetically, she knew (she *knew!*), by the realization that none of the women in that synagogue looked as physically striking in their white frocks as she. Even now, at forty-two—with her giraffe legs, her gym-toned arms, her still-smooth skin, her salon-straightened hair framing a fine-boned jaw, and the oddity of those cerulean eyes parked in the middle of a dark-skinned face—she was still asked, on occasion, if she modeled.

All this to say that when Clover signed up for the reunion online and saw not only that the Friday night cocktail party in the Kirkland House courtyard had a luau theme but also that Bucky Gardner would be in attendance, she headed straight to Calypso to find the perfect tunic. Something in light blue, she asked the salesperson, to bring out the color in her eyes. Bucky's wife Arabella, or so she'd heard, had not aged well. Rumor had it that she was an alcoholic (no surprise there) and that the decades of smoking and meal purging had taken their toll on her skin and teeth. Clover, though newly and relievedly married, wanted Bucky to see, really see, if only on the most superficial level possible, the depths of his mistake.

"Clover Love. How the heck are you?" says Bucky, nearly bumping into her after emerging from the Kirkland House bathroom in what seemed like a random encounter but wasn't. Clover had seen him heading to the men's room and had planted herself directly in front of the door, pretending to be deeply engaged with her BlackBerry. A ridiculous ruse, as she and her device were no longer the Siamese twins they used to be, back when Lehman was still a bank, and she still had a job.

She suddenly wishes Danny were here with her, instead of traveling for work, if only to show Bucky that she, Clover Love, has been deemed reworthy of her last name. "Bucky! Oh my God. Is that you!" The two embrace in the type of respectful-but-familiar hug practiced by those who were once on a first-name basis with each other's reproductive organs.

"Yeah, it's me." Bucky points to the plastic-covered name tag—ARCHIBALD BUCKNELL GARDNER IV, a name that still astonishes Clover with its audacity—hanging around his neck, its cheap, elastic lanyard caught in the lapel of Bucky's luau-inappropriate blue blazer. Unlike Clover, Bucky has never met an excuse to dress up in anything other than a coat and tie he has embraced. And nearly always begrudgingly at that.

Clover catches herself reflexively reaching out to free Bucky's lanyard from the V-shaped trap as the two finally stand face-to-face, examining the scuffs and hollows of time and gravity on each other's surfaces. "Sorry," she says. "I can't help myself. If it makes you feel any better, I walk up to random strangers on the subway and fix their shirt collars."

"Hmm," says Bucky. "I wonder what Freud would have to say about that?"

"Tons," she says, thinking, since when has Bucky Gardner ever given a passing thought to the unconscious?

The electronic beat of the Psychedelic Furs' "The Ghost in You" bounces from wall to wall as Bucky chuckles, politely, and stares for just a beat longer than appropriate at the wreath of plumeria resting in the delicate valley of Clover's chest. "Nice lei," he says.

Clover nearly chokes on her half-swallowed sip of wine. "Speaking of Freud."

"No, I meant"—he reddens—"the flowers. You know, *l-e-i*, not *l-a-* . . ." He quickly scrambles to dig himself out. "Look at you. You haven't aged a day."

"Thanks. And—" Clover nearly returns the compliment but knows Bucky would immediately sense her disingenuousness. Bucky Gardner has not only aged more than a day, he's aged more decades than the four he's weathered. His once lean midsection has grown a small paunch, noticeable in the pull of the bottom buttons of his blue oxford. His skin has a grayish, sallow hue, as if he'd spent the past twenty years in an underground bunker. The dense forest of strawberry blond hair that used to flop just beneath his left eye, such that the whipping of his head back to clear his vision could become tic-like if he went too long between haircuts, looks as if it has been razed by a fire and replaced with the scorched nubs of gray twigs. "You look good, too," she says. This, at least, is not *un*true. He does look good. Really good. For a sixty-year-old man.

"And you're a phenomenal liar, *Pace*." He emphasizes the last word and presses his lips between his teeth to try to keep a smile at bay.

"Man oh man, Gardner, you're never going to let me live that one down, are you?" She crosses her arms and shakes her head before shoving him, playfully.

"Nope. Never . . ." Bucky finally frees his mouth to smile, and rays of his buoyant young self push through the slate brume. "Pace."

★   ★   ★

Pace became Bucky's de facto pet name for Clover after he mispronounced it the night they met, rhyming it with *race*, as it appeared on
the page, instead of pronouncing it double syllabically, Italian-style—
pah'-chay—as her peacenik parents intended. "So, Pace . . . ," Bucky
had said, pointing to the middle name printed under her photo in the
freshman facebook after having planted himself on the lumpy couch in
her Canaday dorm room to wait for Addison. Jane was out at a comp
meeting at the *Crimson*, Mia was off at an audition for *The Cherry Or-
chard*, so Clover was left, once again—not that she minded—entertaining
yet another spoke in the endless circle of Addison's East Coast prep
school friends and acquaintances, all of whom kept dropping by the
room to see if she was in, which, due to the intense intermingling of
said circle during those first heady weeks of school, she hardly ever
was. Bucky's sockless, blucher-shod feet were propped up on a tapestry-
covered board atop two LP-filled milk crates, which Addison had
fashioned into a coffee table, when he asked the question that would
forever define for Clover both the future of their relationship and everything about Harvard that made her feel like a visitor from Planet
Kumbaya. ". . . Any relation to the Pace Gallery?"

This was at the end of the first week of freshman year, which Clover
had spent like the rest of her classmates: overdrinking; undersleeping;
surveying classes; making midnight runs to Herrell's for coffee ice
cream sundaes or to Tommy's Lunch for lime rickeys and fries; partici-
pating in a Rocky Horroresque screening of *Love Story* in the Science
Center, where those in the know lobbed the most oft-quoted lines of
dialogue back at the screen; taking a French aptitude test and writing a
primitive program in BASIC to get out of various intro-level language
and computer science requirements; passing a swimming test; setting
up the living room of the three-bedroom suite she shared with Addison, Mia, and Jane according to Addison's exacting prep school standard

that, because they adhered to the same 1967-California-opium-den aesthetic favored by Clover's parents, felt both nostalgically familiar and flagrantly inappropriate for 1985 Ivy League New England.

"Of course we get the one freshman dorm in all of Harvard that looks like a jail," Addison had lamented when they'd first arrived, looking around at the freshly painted cinder block walls that, to Clover, felt more civilized, safe, and bright than any walls that had previously housed her. "Well, I guess we'll just need to buy more tapestries."

The Pace Gallery? "I'm sorry?" Clover had said, pretending she didn't hear Bucky's question, not wanting to admit she had no idea what he was talking about. What Pace Gallery? A secret chalice of proper nouns seemed to exist from which everyone except her—or at least everyone who hailed from states between Pennsylvania and Maine—had imbibed before arriving on campus: Dorrian's;[1] Spee;[2] Brearley;[3] Limelight;[4] Shady Hill;[5] Andover;[6] Fly;[7] Siasconset;[8] Buckingham Browne & Nichols;[9]

---

1. Dorrian's Red Hand, the bar on the Upper East Side of Manhattan where underage private school students would congregate to drink, later made infamous by Robert Chambers's premurderous partying there in 1986.

2. The Spee Club, an exclusive all-male club (aka Final Club) at Harvard where John F. Kennedy was once a member.

3. The Brearley School, a selective, academically rigorous, private girls' school on the Upper East Side of Manhattan.

4. A nightclub located in an abandoned church in Manhattan's Chelsea district.

5. Shady Hill School, a top-notch private day school in Cambridge, Massachusetts.

6. Phillips Andover Academy, aka Phillips Academy, aka Andover, one of the oldest boarding schools in the United States.

7. The Fly Club, an exclusive all-male club (aka Final Club) at Harvard where Franklin Delano Roosevelt was once a member.

8. A village in eastern Nantucket, an island off the coast of Cape Cod, pronounced *skon'-sit*.

9. Buckingham Browne & Nichols school, aka BB&N, a private day school on the Charles River in Cambridge, Massachusetts.

Knickerbocker;[10] Colony;[11] St. Albans;[12] St. Barths;[13] Farmington;[14] Cotillion;[15] Sidwell;[16] Narthex;[17] Signet;[18] Deerfield;[19] Area;[20] Locke-Ober;[21] Porcellian.[22] And those were just a few of the ones she'd overheard that first week.

---

10. The Knickerbocker Club, aka "The Knick," an old, exclusive, all-male social club in Manhattan.

11. The Colony Club, an exclusive women's club in Manhattan modeled on all-male New York clubs like the Knickerbocker, the Metropolitan Club, and the Union Club.

12. St. Albans School, aka STA, a selective, all-boys college preparatory school in Washington, DC, whose Latin motto translates as "For Church and Country."

13. The Caribbean island of Saint Barthélemy, an overseas collectivity of France and a popular vacation spot for the barefooted well-heeled.

14. The in-the-know name for Miss Porter's School, an exclusive all-girl's preparatory school in Farmington, Connecticut.

15. The International Debutante Ball, held every December in New York's Waldorf Astoria Hotel, to formally present young, impeccably bred women to society.

16. The Sidwell Friends School, a selective private school in Washington, DC, described as the "Harvard of Washington's private schools."

17. A position of distinction (just under President and Ibis) on the masthead of the *Harvard Lampoon*, a humor magazine that has been the training ground for scores of television writers and comics. Narthex also refers to the entrance area of the Lampoon castle (just as Ibis refers to the sculptural bird that sits atop it, stolen by *Crimson* writers and sent as a gift to the government of the Soviet Union).

18. The Signet Society, a literary society at Harvard whose new members have to be invited by current members to join. T. S. Eliot, John Updike, James Agee, and Norman Mailer were all members.

19. Deerfield Academy, formerly an all-boys (when Clover was in college) but now a coeducational, selective preparatory school in Deerfield, Massachusetts.

20. A nightclub in Manhattan from 1983 to 1987, known for its bathroom stalls, where the glitterati would snort cocaine and fuck.

21. An old Boston Brahmin restaurant, where wealthy parents of Harvard students would dine with their progeny during school visits.

22. The Porcellian Club, aka the Porc, aka the P.C., the most exclusive and storied all-male Final Club at Harvard. Its interior rooms, unlike those of other Final Clubs, are off-limits to both non-members and women.

Then there were the verbs. "To punch," from what she could gather, when used in connection with one of the nine exclusive men's social clubs on campus, called Final Clubs, was the Harvard equivalent of rushing a fraternity. "To comp" meant "to compete," as in to compete for a place on the student newspaper, the *Crimson*, or on the humor magazine, the *Lampoon*. Archrivals, those two, again from what Clover could gather.

"You know, the Pace Gallery? In New York?" Bucky smiled mischievously. "Actually, I was just—"

But she interrupted him too soon before the second half of his sentence, "yanking your chain," to detect his undercurrent of jest. "Oh, of course, the Pace," she said. "I think we're distant cousins."

And there it was. Her first lie at Harvard. Set loose into the world via a spasm of insecurity released, in that brief moment of confusion, because Clover had also spent freshman week soaking up more than she would ever learn, either before or since, about her country's caste system. Not that she was naïve enough to have believed, prior to matriculating at Harvard, that all men were created equal—growing up as a nappy-headed girl in the late sixties and seventies, even in as liberal and tolerant a setting as northern California, had shattered that myth long before—but she'd had no idea how many strata and substrata the social soil her country contained until she met Addison. Where she came from, people either had enough money to have sufficient reserves of canned food and dry goods to meet their basic needs, or they were struggling, like her parents, to survive.

But Addison could take one look at any entry in the freshman facebook—that hardbound crimson volume containing the tiny black-and-white faces, names, home addresses, and schools of each one of their 1,600 classmates—and make shockingly accurate snap judgments about that person's net worth, politics, footwear, breadth of travel, recreational drug use, and proficiency with Latin verb conjugation.

"Okay, what about him?" Clover would say, pointing to a random photo, a candid shot taken outside, against a large oak, of a kid named Jedediah Brooks Pearson III.

"Easy," Addison replied. "721 Park. Hard building to get into. Father's a Republican, has a Town Car pick him up every morning for work, the mother used to be a kindergarten teacher at Spence or Nightingale before she left her career to shop, but I'm betting she secretly votes Democrat. Milton Academy: That means he probably went to an all-boys school that ends in eighth grade on the Upper East Side, I'll say Buckley, where he wore a coat and tie every day, like a miniature version of Dad, but now he wears one of those navy blue sweaters from L.L.Bean with the diagonal white dots, Norwegians I'm pretty sure they're called, although he definitely has a coat and tie in his closet, freshly pressed and ready for punch season next fall at one of the Final Clubs like the Fly or Porcellian, but definitely not the Owl, which his mother will have suggested, firmly, is NOKD."

"NOKD?"

" 'Not our kind, dear.' Or sometimes we'll say NOCD, 'Not our class, dear.' " Addison must have caught the look of horror on her face. "I mean, *I* wouldn't say that, of course, but you know, it gets said. By others. Moving on: He smokes pot, maybe snorts some coke now and then if someone at the party has some, but he does not buy. Buying is the domain of the Eurotrash and Choate kids. There was that one dude, oh my God, I forget his name, a year older than us who went down to Venezuela to make a buy and tried to smuggle $300,000 worth of pure coke into JFK only to be caught—duh!—at customs. Turns out like half the class had given him $5,000 each. Out of their own pocket money. And none of their parents even noticed. Anyway, back to our pal Jedediah, who most likely is not called Jedediah but goes by his middle name, Brooks, because, well, just because. You give your kid the odd or stuffy or necessary-to-please-the-family first name, and then give him a silly nickname like Boots or Bops or better yet call him by his second name, which is always some historical family name that has significance only to the people who care about such things. In Jedediah's case, the family didn't even have to think, since he's a III. I guess he could go by Jed or Trip or Tre—you know, like 'the third'—but

Jed's a bit pedestrian and Trip's overdone and Tre's more of a southern thing, so I'd put good money on Brooks. And what do we know about our new friend Brooks? Well, he speaks fluent French, *Maman* made sure of that, and his Latin is proficient enough that he could figure out all the Latinate roots on the words he didn't understand on the SATs, just like his tutor taught him to do when he got stuck. He's been listed in the *Social Register* since he turned thirteen, which was the same year he started taking formal dance lessons at that place on East Sixty-fifth, where the girls, at least when I had to go to classes there, are still required to wear white gloves. He's been to Europe. Many times. Probably lost his virginity to some girl from the *seizième* he picked up at the Bains Douches that spring break in Paris when he turned sixteen, or to an Italian chick he met in Crete the following summer, after checking out her tits on the beach. The Italian girls always go topless, so he would have known exactly what he was getting. He spends his winter breaks in the Caribbean, his spring breaks skiing, either in Aspen or the Alps, and his summers either in the Hamptons, Nantucket, the south of France, or Tuscany, and I can't be more specific than that, because sometimes his family does one place one year and another place the next year, you never know. They might have even done a big educational trip to Nairobi or China or Nepal or Thailand, if the parents were feeling like the kids needed some culture or good material for a college essay, but it really depends on the family. Some of them won't go to places where there isn't a Four Seasons. Okay, so, he ate dinner with his nanny until he turned, oh, let's say ten. Then he had three years of family meals in the formal dining room, prepared by the cook and served by the housekeeper—until he was shipped off to boarding school at fourteen."

"Jesus, you can tell all that from a name and an address?" said Clover.

"No. I need to see the photo and the name of the school as well. If I don't know the name of the school, the photo itself helps me nail it down. Public school kids always have those stiff formal school portraits, and the girls wear makeup. Day and prep school kids go bare faced and lean up against trees."

"What's the *Social Register*?"

"Come on. You've never heard of it?" Addison seemed genuinely shocked.

"No, never."

"It's just this . . . book. This kind of, you know, stupid book that no one cares about anymore, with the names of people from the same circles. Just a bunch of WASPs, really. Who all either know each other or know about one another or summered together or served on boards with one another or organized benefits together or . . . whatever, it's so pointless and boring." She paused, still seemingly flummoxed at having to explain a concept she'd grown up knowing about since as far back as she could remember, like the fact that rain comes from clouds or doormen open doors. "The only people who really care about being in it are the ones who marry into it. Those of us who are in it by default don't give a shit."

"I'm guessing there aren't any people who look like me in it?" said Clover.

"No. No blacks yet. But there aren't any Jews either. Or there could be a few, but if there are, they've changed their last names, so you can't tell, or, like I said, they married in. And there aren't any Catholics either, so it's not really, you know, about race or anything. It's about, well, I was going to say ancestry, but it's more about like . . ."

"Exclusion?"

"Something like that."

Clover had to pause while she processed this information and the cavalier, matter-of-fact way in which Addison presented it. "Does anyone ever get taken off the list?"

"That depends."

"On what?"

"On whether or not they do something 'unbecoming,' like having an adulterous affair that makes it into print or committing a crime. Or if they take up a career in the arts, like the theater or the circus or really anything that might be considered showy or where they might reveal too much of themselves. I mean, I'm planning on becoming a painter, which I'm pretty sure is okay so long as I don't go all Mapplethorpe on them or anything."

Clover was still trying to get her head around the idea that a book—an actual printed *book*—existed listing the names of people belonging to some secret society to which she could never aspire to belong, even if she wanted to. "So, wait. Taking a job as a circus clown and stealing cars are considered equally bad?"

"Something like that."

"Huh." Clover opened the facebook and flipped through the pages until she reached the *L*s. "What about my entry? What does it say about me?"

"Your entry's harder to read," Addison admitted. "I mean, I love the fact that you took the photo in a drugstore photo booth—it's like a real fuck-you to the whole process—but I've never heard of your school, and your name is confusing. Like, okay, you have what would be a typical WASP last name for a middle name, but your first name and skin color throw the whole thing off, and your last name, Love, I mean, I just have no idea where that comes from. But Novato, your hometown, I've heard of that. Isn't that like where a lot of East Coast kids fled in the late sixties? The Dead used to hole up there when they weren't on tour, right?"

"You're good," said Clover, without revealing anything further. For how could she explain the particularities of her origins—the commune; the homeschooling; the orgies the adults did little to hide; the traveling musicians, yes, like the Dead and Jefferson Airplane and many others, who came and went and played music and soaked up nature and cavorted, openly, with the residents; the copious amounts of LSD, pot, mushrooms, mescaline; the freeloaders who once got so high they set the Barbie Dream House she'd bought at a tag sale, with her own lemonade-stand money, on fire ("You'll thank us for that later," they said); the total lack of clothing, decorum, and boundaries; the breakup of the commune in the late 1970s, when the roof caved in, and there was no money for repairs, and too many of them had overdosed or slept with each other's lovers or *lost children*, for Christ's sake, to neglect and an unprotected swimming pool—how to explain all of *that* to these people who'd had normal lives? (Back when Clover still believed there was such thing as a normal life.)

Her mother Lena, a descendant—Lena would remind everyone—of southern slaves, called herself a civil rights feminist activist poet but had never published a poem, at least in any traditional way. Frank, her father, was one of the visiting musicians who wound up staying. Nine months after they met, blue-eyed, mulatto-skinned Clover was born, further proof, Lena would often remind her daughter—or anyone who commented on the unusual hue of her dark-skinned daughter's wolf eyes—of the rape of black slaves by their white owners.

"Lena, please don't say the word *rape* every time someone says something nice about my eyes," Clover would say to her mother, starting when she was eight.

"I don't have to bring it up," Lena would respond. "It's there in your eyes, for everyone to see. The violence not only in your history but in the history of mankind. It's nothing to be ashamed of, muffin. It just is."

But Clover didn't want her eyes to serve as metaphoric proof of mankind's imperfections, or of his banishment from Eden, or for any other horrid truth for which her mother claimed their synecdoche-like powers. And she certainly didn't want anyone peering that intimately into her background. Not then, and not that first week at Harvard, a place she'd applied to without informing her parents, because she'd assumed (correctly) they would not have approved, even if they'd had the money to pay for it. So she lied to Bucky Gardner, and he immediately called her on it. "You're distant cousins of the Paces?" he said. "I'd always heard Arne Glimcher named the gallery after his father's first name. Pace Glimcher. Unless I'm wrong?"

Clover, hot with embarrassment, suddenly realized it was going to be a challenge, to say the least, to spend four years pretending to be someone she was not. She didn't have the proper tools yet. Or the anthropological understanding of the tribal customs and bylaws. You couldn't just stare longingly into the window of the Tip Top TV Shop as a teenager, watching *Dallas* and *Dynasty* without sound, and get it. She would have to start from the ground up, observing this species in its natural habitat, so that one day, if her offspring were lucky enough to be admitted to a school like Harvard—for she understood, even then, that luck, timing, and a good overcoming-of-extraordinary-odds story were of equal if not greater consequence than skill in the game of college admissions—they could arrive in Cambridge armed with the vocabulary and touchstones and background she lacked, such that when they opened up the facebook to the page containing Archibald Bucknell Gardner IV, aka Bucky Gardner, who hailed from 940 Fifth Avenue and Phillips Andover Academy, they would know, instinctively, what that meant. And they would not be overly impressed or unnerved by it, like their mother had been that night she and Bucky first met. Clover stood up, swiped two beers from the minifridge, and handed one to Bucky. If she was going to set the record straight about who she was, where she came from, and how she got from there to here, she might as well get started. With a little help from her new pal—she examined the beer's label—Miller Genuine Draft.

"Okay," she'd said, suddenly emboldened. "Let's start again." And she began, haltingly at first, then with genuine draft gusto, to tell Bucky the story of her life.

"Oh, *I* get it, like the Italian word for peace," said Bucky, when she got to the part about her middle name, chosen by her father as a sly complement to the last name, Love, adopted by every member of their commune. "And Clover? Where does Clover come from?" Bucky, far from recoiling from Clover's story, she noticed to her relief and surprise, had taken his feet off the coffee table and was sitting, literally, on the edge of his seat.

Clover felt her face grow hot. "Um, well, apparently I was 'created' in a field of clover."

Now Bucky blushed, revealing, as his jaw dropped and his lips parted into a half smile, the most perfectly aligned set of teeth Clover had ever seen. "Dude. No way," he said. "No way!"

"Way," said Clover, and she downed the rest of her beer in one gulp.

"Good thing they didn't do it on a pool table."

"Don't laugh!" said Clover. "I had a friend named Back of Truck."

"You're shitting me."

Now Clover smiled. "I am. How'd I do?"

Bucky bobbed his head back and forth, accepting defeat. As his smile widened, there seemed to be no end to his shiny teeth. "I'd give you a solid A minus. But"—he took her hand and placed it on his knee—"I could bump you up to an A if you meet me after class for office hours."

Clover felt her insides turn to liquid with the speed of a stick of butter in a microwave, an appliance she'd never used before discovering its utilitarian joys in the freshman dining hall. "They have laws against that, you know."

Bucky lifted her hand from his thigh and kissed her knuckles one by one. "I have excellent lawyers." Then he leaned over, planted his lips proprietarily onto hers, and carried her straddle-legged into the bottom bunk of the bed she shared with Addison, which would soon be cordoned off, for the sake of the new couple's privacy, with a primitive canopy fashioned from two of Bucky's old tapestries from prep school.

That Clover and Bucky became inseparable that fall surprised Addison, who'd been friends with Bucky ever since their days as King Bucky and Queen Addie in the dress-up area at Episcopal preschool, when they locked up that poor kid Thurber, whose father was later indicted for securities fraud, in the supply closet. Addison had known each of Bucky's girlfriends since seventh grade, blond ice queens all, so either guileless, sepia-toned Clover was Bucky's new type, in which case Addison was ready to eat her hat, or—and this seemed more plausible—Clover was an experiment.

When the couple broke up four months later, after a disastrous Christmas with Bucky's parents in New York, Addison finally admitted her earlier doubts about the union while driving a sobbing Clover, who was supposed to have been sitting in Bucky's passenger seat, back up to Cambridge for January reading period. "Oh, come on, Cloves, it's not as if we didn't see this coming," she said, putting on her blinker to take the exit onto Route 84.

"Speak for yourself," Clover said. "I didn't see it coming at all." She stared out the passenger window, her eyes struggling to make sense, in the fading dusk, of the bare branches, the icy air, which Addison would be escaping mere hours after her last final exam, via a week in St. Barths with a posse of old friends. *We?* What *we?* Even though Addison had urged Clover to join her in the Caribbean ("There's plenty of room in the house, it's already paid for, so you'd just have to deal with airfare, and the cook is *awesome* . . ."), Clover didn't have a spare twelve hundred dollars lying around to purchase a roundtrip ticket. In fact, she was already falling behind on her tuition bills, which she was paying out of her own pocket through a work study program called "dorm crew": a deliberately vague, inoffensive, sports-team-like term for the twenty to thirty hours a week she spent scrubbing the fecal streaks off her classmates' toilets and mopping their floors.

Clover had once tried to describe the humiliations of dorm crew to Addison, to paint a picture of that strange paradox of feeling simultaneously invisible and publicly nude while pushing one's shame, in the shape of a mop, bucket, and broom, through a Harvard Yard choked with central casting freshmen playing Hacky Sack. Addison, attempting to be nice, had replied, "Oh please, Clover, no one's paying any attention to you and your mops."

Rummaging through her purse for a tissue, Clover found only an old tampon, barely clinging to life in its torn wrapper. Which is when it struck her that her period was nearly two weeks late. She took mental inventory of her four months with Bucky, trying to recall one sexual congress during which she had not used some form of birth control. No, they'd been safe, definitely. That new epidemic the newscasters were calling AIDS made certain of that. ("Be careful, baby," her mother, whose phone had been shut off, had written her on a postcard. "They're saying on NPR that you can die from sex, that it's not just a gay men's disease. Death from sex, I can't even wrap my mind around that one. Love, Mom.")

Maybe it was the cheap condoms she bought, she thought, the ones in the half-price bin that were well past their expiration date. She was so sick of having no money, of the less than wise decisions it forced her to make. Old condoms, what was she thinking? But the question was, of course, rhetorical: She was thinking, I need birth control, and the pill is too expensive, and I can't find my diaphragm, and if I buy these at half price, I can use the money I save to buy a few pages of next semester's books. Ironic, really, because now, it struck her hard, she was going to have to use the money she'd saved up for books and put it toward the cost of an abortion, there being no way she'd ever ask Bucky or his family for a dime.

"Do you have any tissues?" Clover asked.

"Check the glove compartment," said Addison.

Clover opened the glove compartment, and a thick stack of parking tickets came tumbling out of its mouth. "Holy shit, Ad, these all yours?" Addison had Scotch-taped several dozen of her tickets in a brick pattern on the wall behind her desk—"Wallpaper," she'd answer, whenever anyone pointed to the expanding enigma and asked, "What's *that*?"—but out from that glove compartment, as far as Clover could tell, fell literally hundreds if not thousands more dollars in fines, all for minor infractions ranging from parking in front of a hydrant to unpaid meters.

"Ugh, those Cambridge police are *ruthless*. It's like you can't even park without getting a ticket."

"What do you mean? You just have to pay the meter and not park in front of hydrants."

"Oh, please. Who has time?" Addison's tone was dismissive, entitled, and Clover, at that moment, hated her for it. If she ever climbed out of her hole of debt and started making some real money—and she would, she was determined she would—she promised herself that she would never become one of those people whose piles of cash are stacked so high that they presume themselves to be above the law, above following rules, above, for Christ's sake, sticking a fucking quarter in a parking meter.

Bucky stirs the ice in his gin and tonic with his forefinger and takes a swig. Clover examines the pallor of his skin and wonders if, given enough years spent floating in whatever toxic miasma has pickled Bucky's life, her husband Danny—whose physical resemblance to Bucky's younger self had not gone unremarked, either by her or by friends who'd met both—would be similarly transformed. Bucky, it saddens her to realize, has become any one of those besuited shadows one sees on the LIRR platform, staring vacantly down the tracks, waiting with equal indifference for both train and death. She was disappointed—but not surprised—that he'd neglected to write an essay for the Twentieth Anniversary Report, since his fifth and fifteenth reunion entries were similarly vacant. As for his wife Arabella's cipher-like entry, which was about as revelatory as Arabella herself, she might as well have not even bothered.

Not that Clover's entry was much of a window into her soul either. The day she filed it, that crazy Sunday in September before Lehman's collapse—when she rushed down to Midtown to join her colleagues, and the CNN trucks were outside, fueled by schadenfreude and the ire of a nation—it was already a foregone conclusion that her name, address, and marital status might be the only pieces of information in that report that would remain factually accurate come Monday morning.

But she'd gotten a jump start on the essay during Labor Day weekend, finishing it one night after work that same week, knowing she'd soon be receiving some sort of communication from the Harvard alumni office asking her, once again, to define the past five years of her life in three to five paragraphs or less. She always tried to stay on top of her various responsibilities, anticipating the work before it hit her inbox: a trait each of her superiors had praised during performance reviews over the years. Clover Love, everyone at Lehman knew, was your go-to person when you wanted something done yesterday, because by the time you asked her to do it, she'd already anticipated it, dealt with it, and moved on to the next task, some hanging thread you hadn't even realized would need trimming.

But what happens, she wondered, when the entire fabric of your life unravels? Her answer, in the short term, was to log on to her work computer, which she assumed she would not have access to come Monday morning, and quickly open the file for her reunion essay in one window and the Harvard alumni Web site in another. She copied the former, pasted it into the latter, and hit "submit" before her life no longer resembled the cheerful, carefree summary of it she'd composed two weeks earlier. Then, loaded down with banker's boxes, she stepped out into the blinding glare of the news cameras.

"So, tell me," she says to Bucky. "What have you been up to?"

"For the past twenty years?" he says, smiling.

"For a start."

"Eh, the normal stuff," he says, considering his gin and tonic. "Made a few kids, did a few deals . . ." He tosses the rest of the liquid back into his throat like water. At which point a former classmate, one of two who'd repurposed herself as a himself, crosses his line of vision and into the men's room. "I mean, nothing as exciting as her," he says.

"You mean him," says Clover. Joe McMahon, née Josephina Mc-Bride, was one of the first people Clover had met at Harvard, while waiting in line for the keys to their dorms. "Do you consider yourself black or white?" Josephina had asked her. It was the first time in Clover's life that anyone had turned what was normally a binary question in search of a single objective answer—*Are you black or are you white?*—into a subjective, open-ended, gray-scaled discussion about the mutability of self. "Some days I feel black, others I feel white," she'd said. "Depends on the context." This was her one and only interaction with Josephina McBride, but it had stayed with her.

"It's kind of brave of her, I mean him, isn't it?" says Bucky.

"What?"

"Tossing everything that defines you away like that and starting from scratch."

Clover cocks her head to the side in mock confusion. "I don't know, Bucky. I can't really see you in a dress."

Bucky laughs. "I wasn't talking about a sex change, Pace. More like a . . ." He pauses. Then punts it. "What about you? Everything good with you, too?"

Good with me, too? Clover thinks. What is he talking about? Anyone with a subscription to the *Wall Street Journal* knows that Archibald Bucknell "Bucky" Gardner IV was not doing well, having driven Gardner Industries into the ground years before the great recession of '08. Yes, they were heavily invested in both the printing and newspaper industries, which accounted for some of the recent turmoil, but Gardner's international real estate holdings alone should have kept the company afloat, had Bucky not made the kind of amateurish missteps he'd made, like overestimating occupancy rates of his vast rental properties, and underestimating the building costs on that skyscraper in Dubai. The company's stock price was a joke. They'd had to lay off nearly three thousand employees since 2005. The bankruptcy lawyers and the LBO experts were circling the rotting carrion, salivating.

Fine, Clover thinks. If that's the way he's going to play it, I'll lob the same bullshit right back. "Yup!" she lies. "Everything's perfect! Danny's good, work's good, you know, same old same old," she says, leaving out minor details such as losing her job and the lack of motility of Danny's sperm.

"Any rug rats yet?" says Bucky.

Only yours, she thinks, and I killed him. "No, no kids yet . . ." Clover has no regrets about her decision to terminate her pregnancy freshman year, but it suddenly strikes her, standing here with Bucky, that had she found herself in the same situation just a half a generation earlier, she could have ended up as the Radcliffe dropout single mother of a twenty-four-year-old. Or dead from a botched abortion. Or the wife of Bucky Gardner, which might have been—she realizes it only now—the most soul-crushing option of all. ". . . but we're working on it."

Her infertility specialist, Dr. Seligman, after a full battery of tests, ranked Clover's chances of having a baby with Danny via IVF as modest to good, provided they did ICSI, wherein the sperm is inserted directly into the egg. Danny, who'd grown up as the middle child of nine, in a big Irish Catholic family from Southie where babies simply materialized every eighteen months like clockwork, was initially opposed even to meeting with Dr. Seligman. After the consultation, however, he promised to think about the various options, although many months had passed since then, and he still wasn't ready to revisit the issue. ("This may be less about his Catholicism, as he claims, and more about his ego," Seligman conjectured privately to Clover one day. "We have excellent psychologists on our staff if your husband wants to speak to one.") "What about you?" says Clover, trying her best to sound blasé, uncovetous. "You have four kids now, right?"

"I know. It's crazy, right? Four kids, what were we thinking?" says Bucky. "And the oldest one's off to college soon. I mean, it blows my mind to think he's nearly the same age as us when we . . ." He pauses, midsentence. His tone—even his facial expression—changes from cocktail party breezy to serious. "You know, Pace, I've been meaning to apologize to you for being such a douchenozzle back when we were, you know, back at the beginning of freshman year. I mean, I was *such* a frigging douchenozzle. I've been thinking about it a lot lately, what with this weekend coming up. And I was hoping I'd run into you so I could tell you in person. And, well, I just, I hope you can forgive me."

"A *douchenozzle*?" Clover laughs nervously, disarmed. An apology she's been waiting over twenty years to receive has finally been proffered, and she hasn't a clue what to do with it.

"Tell me you've never heard of that word."

"I've never heard of that word." She feels relieved to have turned the conversation away from uncomfortable mea culpas toward linguistics.

"Come on. Not even at work? I thought those traders were the biggest potty mouths on the planet."

"They are, but . . ." She realizes she has no desire to be caught by Bucky Gardner, twenty-plus years later, in another face-saving lie, and this strikes her as revelatory. She's suddenly too old to care what he—what anyone, really—thinks. If nothing else, the passage of time has allowed her the thrill of this liberation. "But it's been a while since I've been on the trading floor." Clover stares at her feet, spotting a chip in the nail polish on her right toe. "I lost my job, Bucky. A few months ago. I stayed on when Barclays took over, but my department didn't survive the second round of layoffs in January." Now she finally addresses him directly, her eyes meeting his. Smiles in a way that she hopes conveys the bravery of which she's in sudden, surprising possession. "So if you hear of any openings in mortgage-backed securities . . ."

"Oh, Pace, I'm so sorry. That sucks big time."

"Yeah, well . . ." Clover is touched by what appears to be genuine concern in Bucky's voice. "We're okay for the moment."

This was a bit of a white lie. What with the purchase of the brownstone on East Ninety-first Street at the top of the market and its head-to-toe renovation, she and Danny, whose job as a public defender paid only a modest wage, were quickly tearing through their reserves. Danny thought they should sell the new house when it was finished and trade it, and their tony address, for a similar property up in

Harlem, using the difference in cost to provide a bulwark against an uncertain future. "Think about it. You've always said you don't want to be a banker forever," he'd said. "Harlem has such a rich history. Plus it's part of your heritage." Clover had become so used to defining herself as un-black, for a split second she had no idea what he was talking about.

"If it makes you feel any better," says Bucky, "Gardner Industries is kind of . . ." He turns his hand into a deep-sea diver.

"I know. I read all about it. I'm sorry. I'm sure you've been doing your best to try to keep it afloat."

Bucky shrugs and shakes his head in defeat. "Not really. I mean, I *am* trying, and I definitely put one hundred percent into the business at the beginning, no doubt, but, well, in the end, I think it's just not my thing. I'm not . . . *good* at it. Twenty years of my life, Pace. Buying this, selling that, always on the wrong cycle. I bought high, I sold low. It's a frigging joke, my lack of business acumen. Just not my thing." Bucky's expression hovers somewhere between embarrassment and the shell shock of a kid in a mall who's in that transitional stage between having lost sight of his mother and starting to panic.

"So, what is your thing?"

"What, workwise?"

"No, anything-wise. Go for it. If this was your last day on Earth, what would you do?" A career counselor had asked her the same question a few months earlier, right after she'd lost her job, and she hadn't been able to respond. An hour of yoga had come to mind, as had making love to Danny and eating a nice dinner at Taillevent in Paris and getting a massage at that place she loved in Tribeca, but those weren't the things the counselor was looking for, plus they were wants, not needs, and anyway what Clover really wanted *and* needed, more than a massage or a good meal, was to go back to work. Her work centered her, gave her (she knew) the illusion of control, in a way nothing else in her life had ever done. Yoga, sex, eating, relaxing, none of those yins would ever be nearly as enjoyable without the concomitant yang of her job.

And yet, even before the job loss, particularly in the wake of the death of her friend Sharon, whom she was scheduled to eulogize on Sunday (shit, she thinks, I really have to finish writing that), she was feeling antsy, in need of change, so in some ways her unemployment was the kick in the pants she should have given herself, had she had the nerve to do so. She more often than not *liked* her job and was good at it—some would even argue brilliant—but her professional satisfaction, her superhuman productivity, the enormous piles of cash she once earned for Lehman were never about the thrill of the gambling itself, never about bragging rights or beating out others for the same slice of pie, but rather about what the fruits of her eighty-hour weeks could buy her: peace of mind, relaxing vacations, light-filled homes, soft bedding, beautiful art, generous charitable donations, and Christmas gifts that left their recipients speechless, like the time she collected as many of her mother's poems as she could get her hands on into a hardbound volume and presented Lena with a thousand copies to do with as she pleased; or the time she paid for her housekeeper's mother's chemotherapy; or the time she sent each of her roommates and their family members first-class round-trip tickets to France, so they could all spend New Year's Eve at Mia's new house in Antibes.

"My last day on Earth?" Bucky pauses for a minute, his lips pursed, his eyebrows furrowed in thought. "I'd unhook my boat from the dock," he says finally, "and go sailing."

Clover, who's never once shirked a request to mentor a kid or a colleague falling through the cracks, becomes animated. "So start a sailing business! Take tourists like me who love to be out there on the ocean but have no idea how to sail on excursions. Or become a teacher! Move down to, I don't know, the Bahamas or something and open up a sailing school. Or, hell, yank the kids out of school for a year, hire a tutor, and take the family on a trip around the world. They'll learn more on that trip than they'll ever learn in the classroom." How easy it is, she thinks, to fix other people's problems.

"Very funny, Pace. I see you haven't lost your sense of humor."

"I'm being totally serious." Gardner Industries may have been driven into the ground by its lackluster CEO, but Clover knew from the most recent issue of *Forbes* that Bucky himself was still worth enough. Which combined with Arabella's chunk of the Debevoise family trust meant, theoretically, that Bucky could spend the rest of his life circling the globe, and not only would his bank account not feel the difference, but it would also continue to grow, recession notwithstanding. "Really, what's to keep you from sailing off into the sunset today?"

"My wife. She hates boats. She hates anything having to do with the water."

"Arabella hates the water? But wait, don't you live on Long Island Sound?"

"Yeah. She hates our house, too. And quite possibly everyone in it."

"Huh. Well, what *does* she like?"

"That's a loaded question, Pace. I'm not sure you want to hear the answer." The effort of keeping the outside edges of his lips turned up into a smile lends his face an air of desperation and melancholy that Clover finds more haunting than a circus clown's.

"Try me," she says.

"Okay." Now Bucky stares down at the nick in the nail polish on Clover's left toe, remembering the pleasure of having once sucked on it. "She likes our portfolio manager, Brad."

"Huh?" Clover feels her BlackBerry vibrating in her purse. She ignores it. "As in *like* like?"

"As in God only knows, but a few months ago I accidentally picked up her phone instead of mine and found reams of full-on sexts between the two of them. He calls her—I mean, it's so crazy—his little Bac-o-bit. I think he's like an Orthodox Jew or something, for Christ's sake! Or for, well, you know, whoever's sake. Yahweh I guess they call

him. I'm sure she's with him right now. Brad, that is, not Yahweh."
Bucky's face shows neither sadness nor anger. Numbness, if Clover had
to pinpoint the emotion, but she can't get a proper reading. "She said
she didn't feel well this morning as we were packing to leave, that I
should just go to the reunion without her, but I called the house to
check in after my plane landed, and the housekeeper told me she was
out playing tennis."

"Oh, boy." Clover isn't sure what she finds more surprising, the
fact of the affair itself or the part about Arabella Debevoise having sex
with a Jew. "So what are you going to do?" Her BlackBerry buzzes
again. This time she quickly checks the screen and sees a 617 number
she doesn't recognize. She hits "ignore" again.

"Nothing. At least for now. I mean, a divorce would be really complicated and messy. And I have no idea if she even wants one. Or what
she wants, period. I guess part of me is relieved that she's actually getting out of bed in the morning. Arabella, well, let's just say she hasn't
been a picnic to live with, and I certainly haven't been able to make
her happy, and if this guy wants to take on that kind of burden, I say
be my guest. The irony of course is that I was the one who insisted on
hiring *Brad*"—he says the name mockingly—"to manage our money.
This guy I knew from the Fly Club recommended him. Said he's ethical to a fault, and when I met him I thought perfect. That's exactly
what I need. An ethical Jew. Which is funny, considering the circumstances, but on the mark, money-wise at least. I mean the guy's so
unbelievably good at his job—his regular job, that is, managing our
assets, not, you know, fucking my wife—that I don't want to fire him.
Especially in this climate, you know? I mean, some days I'd like to
shoot him in the balls, but . . ."

"Oh, Bucky, I'm so sorry."

"Don't be. I'm not." He smiles wearily. "By the way, nobody else
knows about this, so, you know, keep it on the down low, okay? I
don't even know why I just told you."

Clover touches him lightly on the sleeve. "Don't worry. I'm a good keeper of secrets." There must be something mentally liberating, she thinks, about unloading to a person who once knew you intimately but would probably never see you again until the next reunion, if ever. A kind of tabula rasa without the blankness of the rasa.

"Thanks. What about your husband?" says Bucky. "Is he—"

"Oh, we're practically newlyweds," says Clover, cutting him off. "I still find all of his faults endearing, and as far as I know, he's not fucking his secretary."

"No, I meant"—Bucky laughs out loud, eliciting the first burst of color in his cheeks that Clover has noticed all evening—"is he here with you?"

"Oh, sorry. Sadly, no," she says. "He's down in Guantánamo with a client." The client, Abdullah Amir, owned a profitable chain of grocery stores in Islamabad before his incarceration as a suspected terrorist in 2002. His captor, a Pakistani border guard of meager means, was paid twelve thousand dollars by the U.S. government to turn him in. Abdullah's children had not seen him for seven years. Danny had been working pro bono, during his weekends off, to try to rectify this, so that Abdullah Amir Jr., now a teenager, would not be so fueled with rage at the U.S. justice system that, unlike his father, he might actually (and somewhat justifiably) resort to terrorism in vengeance.

"Good for him. Somebody's got to defend those dudes." Clover detects a trace of disingenuousness in Bucky's voice, reminiscent of his mother's offhanded remark about Clover's eyes that ill-fated Christmas—"Isn't that just the most marvelous shade of blue! Are those colored contacts?"—but she can't be sure. She is reminded, once again, that she dodged a bullet. "Hey, do you want to get out of here?" says Bucky. "I'm dying for a roast beef sandwich."

"Elsie's is gone," says Clover, practically smelling the dank woodiness of the sawdust on the linoleum floor of that tiny hole in the wall whose siren call lured the young couple whenever it was flounder night in the freshman union.

"Really? Okay, then, how about the Tasty Diner?"

"It's now a Citizens Bank."

"You're kidding me."

"I wish."

"Man, fuck Adam Smith." Bucky had majored in economics, retaining little beyond the basics of what he learned. "What about a cheesesteak at Tommy's?"

"It's a pizza joint now. I think Bartley's is still around, though, if you need a side of nostalgia with your fries."

"Great," says Bucky. "Burgers and beer on me. Let's go." He throws his arm casually around Clover's shoulder and leads her toward the exit.

"No," says Clover, although she allows the arm to stay. "On me." Saying this gives her an intense jolt of pleasure. Back when they were dating, it was a foregone conclusion that Bucky would fund all meals out, since Clover had no wiggle room in her meager budget for nonessentials. Or even for nonluxury items like condoms. Because Bucky's stomach, always achingly empty after his daily crew practices, required frequent ingestions of off-campus food between regular meals, he was more than happy to foot the bill.

"Fine." Bucky smiles. "On you."

The two head up Dunster Street past the new Malkin Athletic Center and the Signet Society, the arts and letters club where Jane, who spent the bulk of her college years writing for the *Crimson*, and Mia, who spent the bulk of hers starring in school productions, had been denied admission, while Addison, who spent the bulk of her years partying instead of painting, had been tapped for membership sophomore year by an old prep school friend who thought she'd be fun to have around. "I don't get it, guys," Addison had said to Jane and Mia, when the club nixed her suggestion to have the two of them join at the end of sophomore year. "I told everyone how great you both are. How good your writing is, Jane; how good your acting is, Mia, but I have no idea what happened!" Jane brushed off the rejection without a second thought. Mia, who was dying to spend her lunch hour digesting both the Signet's reputedly good food and Ibsen's transformation of the theater with like-minded souls, looked completely crushed. "No big deal, Addison. Thanks for trying," she said. Later that night, Jane came into Clover's bedroom, where Mia was nursing her disappointment in an ice cream sundae, rolling her eyes, claiming she'd just heard from another member that it was actually Addison, whether intentionally or not, who'd quashed any chance of her and Mia's membership, when she was asked to describe her roommates in a single word. "Suburbanites?" Addison had answered, adding a delayed, "But really fun and nice!" too late to matter. And that was the end of that.

"You know," Clover now says to Bucky, after settling down in a booth at the burger joint, "people work through the kind of stuff you and Arabella are dealing with all the time. Take my parents. They spent *years* sleeping around with other partners—with permission, but still—and now the two of them are off living by themselves up in the woods of Oregon, totally at peace and seemingly happy together in their little self-sustaining yurt."

"Oh my God, a yurt?" says Bucky. "I always loved all those crazy stories about your family."

"Yeah, well . . ." she says, thinking: You had your chance, and you blew it. And by the way, I hated most of the stories about your family— "they're definitely colorful." She states this without the shame or disdain she once felt for her parents; if anything, the older she gets, the more she's grown to appreciate their adherence to a particular set of guiding principles, as far as they might be from her own.

"I remember the one about your mother getting arrested for, what was it again?"

"Defacing government property." Lena had taken an anthology of poetry out of the Novato Public Library, the kind where all the poems are written by white men, and scribbled her own poems in the margins.

"That's right! I remember now! That was such a badass story . . ."

Clover's BlackBerry buzzes for a third time, from the same 617 number. "Sorry, Bucky, I have no idea who this is, but whoever it is keeps calling me. Let me just get rid of it . . ." She holds the phone up to her ear. "Hello?"

The voice on the other end is crying, gasping for air. "Clover? Is that you?"

"Yes," she says. "Who's this?"

The woman sounds so distraught, she's barely able to speak. "It's Addison."

"Addison, baby. What's wrong?"

At the sound of Addison's name, Bucky's ears perk up, like a dog's.

"I'm . . . I'm in jail!" she says.

"*Jail?* What the fuck . . . for what?"

Bucky grabs the phone from her unceremoniously. "Ad, it's Bucky. Where are you?"

Okay, Clover thinks, so the two were friends since preschool. So they went on mind-expanding binges in the Ramble in Central Park during school breaks when they were teenagers, and they took formal dance lessons together when they were twelve. Does that give him greater claim to her cell phone or to a friendship she's now stoked and nurtured for twenty years? Where was Bucky when Addison was recovering from her appendectomy; when each of her children was born; when her postpartum depression after the second was so intense she was threatening to kill herself? Where was he when Addison's daughter Trilby fell off the monkey bars and broke her leg, and someone had to pick up Houghton and Thatcher at preschool and bring them to the lobby at Mount Sinai? Where was he when—

"Which police station?" says Bucky. "I'm sorry, where? Sixth Street? Near Kendall Square? Yes, okay, don't worry. We're on our way." He throws three crumpled twenties on the table, despite his earlier deal with Clover, and grabs his ex-lover's hand, as if it were once again November of 1985, and they were rushing off to the Fly Club to rescue Addison, who this time had eaten so many mushrooms before a game of strip poker that she was standing on the roof of the club wearing only her panties (this last part much to the delight of the Fly's members, many of whom had dreamt about seeing Addison Hunt's breasts thus unleashed), flapping her arms like a bird and squealing to the young buck trying to coax her back inside, "It says the *Fly* Club, silly! I'm just following the rules!"

VIVICA SNOW. *Address:* Creative Artists Agency, 2000 Avenue of the Stars, Los Angeles, CA 90067.

LUBA ANDREYEVNA SMOLENSK. *Home Address:* 2238 S Street, NW, Washington, DC 20008 (202-335-9334). *Occupation and Office Address:* Attorney, Covington & Burling, 1201 Pennsylvania Avenue, NW, Washington, DC 20004-2494. *E-mail:* lsmolensk@ cov.com. *Graduate Degrees:* J.D., Yale 2001.

I finally gave in and decided that not writing one of these things is as revealing, in its own way, as writing one. The way I see it, those who don't write in do it for one or more of several reasons: (1) They're dissatisfied with where they are, and they don't feel like broadcasting it to 1,600 former classmates; (2) They consider themselves above such nonsense; (3) They're bad with tasks and/or deadlines; (4) They dislike(d) Harvard and have no desire to be reminded of those four years; or (5) Writing three to five paragraphs on any subject, no matter their innate knowledge of the topic, is still as painful for them now as it was during freshman expos. I used to lie to myself and claim #'s 2 and 5 for my own, when in fact, it was really #1 all along, with a small smattering of #3.

So, now that I'm here, where do I begin? The assignment says I should describe the past half decade of my life, but I can't really do that without referencing all the other stuff that came before, which I haven't yet reported on. But I'll be brief, as instructed, I promise.

Okay, so first five years out of school I pounded the pavement in New York City trying to get a role on Broadway. Bartended, waitressed, tutored kids for their SATs and worked periodically as an office temp to pay the rent. Got a few off-off-Broadway parts here and there, but suddenly I was twenty-seven, and I wasn't any further along to making my Broadway debut, and my hair was turning prematurely gray. So I dyed my hair blond and moved to

LA to try to make it in film before it was too late. Landed a few minor guest appearances here and there on soap operas, dramas, and whatnot (I played a corpse in a Fox Tuesday night movie and a waitress on *Mad About You*) but suddenly I was thirty and broke and tired of living with roommates. I thought about trying to get a job in the film industry behind the camera—writer, producer, agent, what have you—but I realized it would be too painful for me to be on the periphery of acting.

I'd like to say I went to law school after that because I had a sudden epiphany that I was always meant to be a lawyer, but my thought processes at the time were much more scattered and mercenary. I needed a job. Preferably one that would give me good health insurance, and where my weight, age, hair color, and bra size had no bearing on my future earning potential. I figured what I'd learned as an actor could not only be applied in the courtroom but maybe even be put to good use.

Turns out? I was right. Not only that, I've been told I'm actually good at my job. Clients hire me (I know, it shocks me, too!) to represent them because they've heard I'm a persuasive orator, that I win over juries, that I "put on a good show" in the courtroom. Which was and still is a welcome change from the daily rejections, the "Sorry, next!," the freak show and lack of control over my own destiny I felt when I was an actor.

I made partner at my firm last year. I celebrated by buying a house in Adams Morgan. There's plenty of room for guests, so next time you're in DC, look me up.

Still no husband or kids yet, but if life's taught me anything it's this: You never know what's just around the bend.

Mia

Zoe Zane, aged seven months, is starting to fuss for her night feeding when Mia receives the call from Clover asking her to drop everything and head to Kendall Square. So after a brief explanation to her husband—"Get this: Addison was taken into the Cambridge police station. Something about old parking tickets, God only knows"—she straps the baby to her chest, throws some extra diapers and wipes into a bag, and leaves Jonathan and her three sons to sort out the housing situation on their own. "Let her spend the night behind bars," Jonathan shouts after her, only half-jokingly. "It'll teach her a lesson." Jonathan can't understand how his wife and Addison were ever friends, though Mia claims that buried under Addison's rampant narcissism lies a tenderhearted kitten, scratching at the walls of her self-importance.

Jonathan sees no evidence of this, but he tends not to argue with his wife when it comes to questions of character and human nature, because it was Mia's ability to see both the good and the less-good in everyone (she doesn't ever use the word *bad*, which she claims is more judgmental than descriptive) that drew him to her in the first place, when she walked into his casting director's office, fresh off the boat from college, and performed a stirring rendition of his most villainous character with the type of multilayered pathos that was totally wrong for the part he'd written yet absolutely right for what he'd always envisioned—but hadn't yet found, after nearly two decades of searching—in a life mate. "Make sure the boys eat some dinner," Mia now shouts over her shoulder. "And keep your phone nearby, okay? I'll call when I figure out what's going on." She hurries out of the dorm room assigned to her family—the dorm room her husband and sons had called respectively upon entering, much to Mia's populist chagrin, "a fluorescent-lit hellhole" and "lame"—and heads toward the front entrance of Kirkland House, feeling guilty for telling Max to leave his laptop at home. "There's no Wi-Fi in the dorm rooms," she'd said when he asked if he could bring it, picturing the Adams House suite she, Clover, Addison, and Jane had shared their senior year, with its antique wood trim and primitive electronic infrastructure that could barely handle their answering machine and those first archaic Macs, which crashed whenever a term paper exceeded five pages. Meaning, always.

To which Max, nonplussed, said, "Are you sure? Like, sure-sure?"

"I'm double sure," she'd answered, doubly sure, rambling on about how hard it was just to get a phone line connected back when she was a student. "Now, hurry up and finish packing."

When, several hours and three thousand miles later, the friendly junior manning the reunion check-in table handed the Zanes six thread-bare white towels, a minuscule bar of soap, five keys to their room in C-entry, and a series of wallet-size cards, five of which opened the front door of Kirkland House, one of which bore a series of numbers and letters comprising the guest Wi-Fi password, Max turned to her, mouth agape. "Mom! Of *course* there was no Wi-Fi in the dorms when you were in college *because the Internet hadn't been invented*! Oh my God, I can't believe I listened to you!"

"You could read a book," she offered brightly.

"I didn't bring any because you said we had to pack light!"

"Homework?"

"It's all on the Web. Which I can't access. Because you said there'd be no Wi-Fi!"

"Well, I screwed up," said Mia. "And I'm sorry. Really, I am."

"Oh, Mom, it's just"—Max, who's been taller than her for three years now, leaned down to hug his mother, whom he could tell, she could tell, was experiencing a middle-aged person's time warp—"what are we supposed to do while you're out at your parties?"

Mia hadn't considered the answer to this question when she was booking their dorm room on a whim, instead of a hotel, out of a sense of nostalgia only she could appreciate. "You could take your brothers out for an ice cream?"

"Great. Then what?"

Jonathan told her not to worry. First he'd locate them a hotel room, then he'd take the boys into Harvard Square to find a bookstore before joining her at the luau. When Addison's call interrupted the latter part of these plans, Jonathan was secretly thrilled that Addison had always been such a fuck-up. He's always hated cocktail parties, especially costume-specific ones, and now he has the perfect excuse not to attend the Hawaiian-themed extravaganza, whose chattery buzz Mia can hear receding in the courtyard behind her.

She, too, is somewhat relieved to miss it. Not that she doesn't want to mingle with her former classmates. She's dragged her entire family across the country, after all, when they could all have been doing things they would rather be doing: location scouting (Jonathan); sucking face with his girlfriend (Max); playing Xbox (Eli); going to Ezra Lang's birthday party (Josh); pulling all the books out of the bottom shelves and teething on them (Zoe). But Mia's feeling a bit bedraggled after the flight from LA, and she has yet to lose the baby fat from Zoe's birth, and her jowls have suddenly grown jowlier, and her joints ache from carrying the baby around or age or probably both, and her hair would not be out of place on a cartoon character who's just stuck his finger in an outlet. In short, she feels sleepy, ugly, scruffy, and old. Or at least sleepier, uglier, scruffier, and older than usual, although a good night's sleep and a quick fling with her blow-dryer should be able to plug the dike in time for tomorrow's picnic.

Just as she's congratulating herself on a clean escape, Mia pushes the exit door open to find Luba Smolensk pulling it in. "Oh my God, Mia Mandelbaum?!" Luba played Arkadina to Mia's Nina in *The Seagull* and, in an instance of life imitating art, seduced Mia's then boyfriend, Clay Collins, who was playing Trigorin.

"Luba!" Mia doesn't bother correcting her last name, which hasn't been Mandelbaum since she married Jonathan, a year out of college. That was the same year she spent banging her head against every stucco wall in Hollywood, trying to catch a break, wondering if the Semitic thud of her maiden name might be partially to blame. So after she and Jonathan married, she pulled a Bob Dylan and changed it to the ethnically ambiguous, melodious Mia Zane. Although Mia Collins, she'd sometimes imagined, would have been equally euphonic. She was secretly relieved when Clay Collins came out of the closet in the tenth reunion red book. She'd suspected as much when they were dating, but she wasn't sure, and when he left her for Luba, she got so depressed, she spent a couple of days lying listless on one of the psych beds at the University Health Services; if nothing else, the revelation of his sexuality had allowed her to put to rest the sting of that rejection.

"You had *another* one?" says Luba. "How many kids does that make now? Four?"

"Yup. Four." There was something irritating to others about the addition of any child over the socially acceptable two, as if you'd hoarded too much candy from life's piñata. Sometimes it was subtle, like the widening of Luba's eyes as she formed the word *four*. Other times it was outright, like when Mia's mother responded to the news of her latest pregnancy, which she erroneously assumed was an accident, with a, "Wow, what a shame. You were almost home free."

"That's incredible," says Luba. "How do you do it?"

"Oh you know, the normal way," says Mia. "Missionary style." She loathes that question: *How do you do it?* As if women since the dawn of time haven't been birthing and raising litters of children far larger than hers.

"No, I meant—"

"Luba, I'm so sorry, but I'm sort of in the midst of a minor emergency. Let's chat tomorrow at the picnic?"

"What kind of minor emergency?"

Luba, Mia remembers, was both an unrepentant gossip and a social troglodyte who was—and still is, apparently—unable to read the subtle hints of verbal cues and body language. When she read that Luba had become a lawyer, she felt the same kind of relief she once felt when Eli, as a toddler, finally realized that the plastic pentagon, no matter how hard he pushed, would never fit into the shape sorter's hexagon. Everyone knew, even back in college, that Luba belonged on Broadway like a Mack truck belonged in a narrow alley. But no one had the guts to tell her, not even Clay Collins, who was cast in a small part on the New York stage straight out of Harvard, only to abandon both the bright lights and the Big Apple—and Luba, and several other women he tried and failed to love—for the cool mist and small core of the arts scene in Seattle, where he founded an experimental theater group in an abandoned milk-bottle factory. "The kind I'm not really at liberty to discuss," Mia says, dodging the whole Addison-in-jail issue. "But I'd love to catch up later. You'll be at the picnic?"

Luba was one of the chorus of people, no less loud than Mia's mother, who'd urged her to head for LA after college and try her hand at becoming a film star. This was awful advice in retrospect, and subconsciously she must have even known it back then, but everyone kept telling her, melodramatically, "You'll never know until you try," and the words rang in Mia's ears throughout the months leading up to graduation. She'd always succeeded at anything she undertook. Why should Hollywood be any different?

Of course she would have never met Jonathan had she taken a different path, or had the kids she had, and looking backward, she knew, was never useful, but she should have known better. Actresses like Mia were not valued in Hollywood. As an undergraduate, she was luminous: every role she performed—Nora in *A Doll's House*, Martha in *Who's Afraid of Virginia Woolf?*, Lady Macbeth—received standing ovations, incredible reviews in the *Crimson*, accolades from the likes of Robert Brustein, the director of the A.R.T. during her college years. But you can create the greatest Nora of all time and fall flat on your face in LA if you are short, of normal body weight, and have a head of recalcitrant, dark curls. Even if your face could hardly be called plain. In high school, she'd won Best Eyes, which was not Most Beautiful, but still. She'd also won Most Likely to Succeed, which while technically true up until her move to LA didn't stand the test of time as well as her eyes, which still shone as fiercely as they did back in twelfth grade, and had been passed down, despite Jonathan's brown eyes and the laws of recessive genetic probability, to three out of four of her long-lashed children.

"I'll definitely be at the picnic," says Luba. "So what are you up to these days? Are you working?"

Oh my God, Mia thinks, what is with her? Have I not made it clear I have to go? "Not at the moment, unless you count this." She points to the baby ironically but with a secret dose of pride at having raised what her children's teachers have consistently called good kids. She is under no delusions that her efforts on their behalf is work in any traditional sense of the word, or that her children would have been any less well adjusted had she hired a fleet of energetic, warm nannies and traded her dreams of stardom for a job that paid more than the nannies' salary, but she once calculated the amount of money it would have cost her to hire full-time help for each child since Max's birth, and she found, to her surprise, that during the past seventeen years she'd saved her family well over three million pretax dollars by doing the bulk of the child rearing herself: a small percentage of Jonathan's income during that same period, and somewhat beside the point, since her staying home was never about saving money and much more about the carpooling than she'd ever imagined possible, but it was not an insignificant number either.

Her college roommates, she knew, were baffled by her choices, though only Addison judged her out loud, albeit indirectly. "Don't you miss the stage? Miss being out there?" Addison had asked her last summer at their annual Fourth of July gathering at Clover's. Mia had answered as honestly as she could, knowing Addison's question was coming more from a place of insecurity of having not yet made her professional mark as an artist than from concern over Mia's welfare. "Sure," she said, "I miss the stage, but I live in LA, where it's all about film and TV, and no one ever wanted to cast me in their films or TV shows, either before I had the boys or after, when I lost the weight and tried again, and I could never figure out what else to do that would give me as much as it took away from my kids, and now I'm turning forty, and we're stuck living there because of Jonathan's career, plus the weather's great, so I really can't complain, and yes, Jonathan has offered me parts in his films, but I think that would create a weird nepotismy atmosphere on set, like when Francis Ford Coppola cast Sofia in *Godfather III*. Plus, frankly? I know it's not the most PC thing to admit, but I've really enjoyed staying home with my kids."

Her precollege life back in Syosset, for as far back as she could remember, had been consumed with getting into a good college. Her father, a graduate of Calumet, was a medical devices sales rep whose dreams of going to medical school had been shattered, he claimed, by having gone to a subpar college. Her mother passed the bulk of her days clipping coupons in front of the TV and seething. Together, they pushed their children to not make the same mistakes, carefully choosing for them only those after-school activities (debate team, cello, soup kitchen volunteer, candy striper, etc.) that would look good on a college application.

Their efforts with Mia's younger brother Jerry, who wanted to learn the electric guitar but was made to play the oboe, backfired. He quit everything, including high school, started smoking pot and shoplifting Hostess cupcakes from the 7-Eleven, and barely made it into a community college after taking his GED. Now he runs a successful biotech company in Palo Alto.

As for Mia, the classic oldest child, she did exactly as she was told, excelling at every activity. She skipped first grade, then third. She spent every afternoon after school finishing her homework and building her résumé. Then, one day in her early teens, after seeing an ad in the paper for weekend teen classes at Stella Adler, she asked her mother if she could take the train into New York on Saturdays to attend them. Her mother initially said no, having never heard of the school and thinking a frivolous activity such as acting would be frowned upon by Ivy League college admissions committees. Mother and daughter argued vehemently over it until, at Mia's urging, her father talked to the high school guidance counselor and was told that, on the contrary, colleges like to see child-directed interests pursued. Yes, even acting. For Mia those precious eight hours of intensive training every Saturday were a revelation, not only because she learned how to live—really *live*—a theatrical role, but also because it was the first time in her short life she not only excelled at an extracurricular activity but actually liked it. No, *loved* it.

She ended up writing about the birth of the Adler technique—how it differed from Lee Strasberg's method acting; how it was rooted in Stanislavski's teachings; how Sanford Meisner devised his own riff on it; how it taught her important lessons about authenticity in her own life, not just on the stage—for her college essays, going against her parents' wishes that she write about working at the soup kitchen instead. "Then what was the point of all those hours I drove you half the way to hell and back so you could ladle soup into those stupid hobos' dishes?" her mother asked, to which Mia responded, without actually answering, "Mom, we don't call them hobos. And a lot of them are just unlucky or chemically imbalanced, not stupid."

When she became a mother at twenty-three, again against her parents' advice, she had a similar—and somewhat surprising—revelation. She enjoyed what both her mother and the mothers of her own generation often referred to as the soul-crushing mundanities of the job; the cheering on from the sidelines; the waving hello to zoo creatures; the building up the blocks in order to knock them down. Mothering, to Mia, was simply a new role she assumed in front of an audience of four, and like all previous roles, she approached it with the kind of research, passion, diligence, and subtextual nuance her audience appreciated. She didn't just act the part of a good mother. She lived it.

"You're the best mom ever," her boys often told her, with genuine, unbidden hyperbole and frequently enough in front of friends and strangers that these witnesses to her children's admiration would ask for her secret. "Easy," she'd reply. "Whatever my mother did, I just do the opposite."

When she found out she was pregnant with Zoe, her insides did a little jig, not only because she was finally getting a little girl but also because now, instead of having to figure out what to do with this next chapter of her life, she would once again get to sniff the sweet ambrosia of fontanelle before immersing herself, at least for another decade, in the comfortable zen of her own deep-seated, maternal desire. This desire—for there was no other word to describe it—was one, she understood well within the first year of motherhood, when nearly every mother she met on the playground complained bitterly of sore nipples and sleepless nights, of careers sidelined and sex lives shattered, to which hardly anyone from her generation with her education ever admitted. Or if they did, it was always tempered by a long list of mea culpas and amorphous plans to get back out there once the youngest was in kindergarten.

Yes, every once in a while, Mia would feel a dull ache, an unnameable pang of dread, like that moment you walk out the door, and you know something's amiss, but you can't figure out what it is until you return home and realize you've locked yourself out. But she was such a good actress, she trained herself to ignore any negative undercurrents. Her life as a mother was full. It had meaning. It provided her with the same sense of purpose she'd first experienced in the soup kitchen. Everyone who knew her, who knew the children, could see this.

"I feel like Mrs. Stockman in a world full of Noras," she once said to Jonathan, after a back-to-school parent cocktail party at their children's school, during which the grumblings from her fellow mothers escalated with each glass of wine consumed. "Is there something wrong with me?"

"There's nothing wrong with you," he said.

"Shouldn't you resent me for not earning a paycheck? Shouldn't we fight more? Shouldn't I resent you when you're off on location for six weeks? Should I have more ambition? Are we doing this right?"

Jonathan, who still felt lucky to wake up in bed with Mia, as if his life were one long coda to his happily-ever-after films, simply laughed. "There's no right or wrong," he said. "There's just us and our kids, and if you feel good about our choices, I feel good about them, too." He appreciated everything his wife did both for him and the family, he told her. He knew his career would not be possible were he married to someone whose work also frequently took her away from home; or rather, it would be possible, but it would be hard on the kids, and the center of gravity would be off, and their house would not be a home in the way a home, he felt, ought to be.

Jonathan loved all the little compartments for buttons and shoes and toilet paper and pot lids his wife designed; he loved that anytime he needed to find a nine-volt battery or an international stamp or a yarmulke, Mia knew exactly where to find it. He loved the dinners she prepared, and the care she brought to the celebration of holidays, and the fact that he never had to worry about where the kids were or what they were doing or whether their time was well spent. Mia loved the fact that Jonathan's work brought in enough money to survive and then some, such that she never had to look at a bank statement to see whether or not the roof could be replaced or a vacation taken.

"I feel good about our choices, too," said Mia, who really didn't mind when Jonathan was off shooting, for it gave her time apart from him, which was part of the glue, she was certain, that held their union together. Plus—and this surprised her—as the kids entered their teenage years, they seemed to require the physical presence of a parent *more* than they did as babies. Not in the visceral way Zoe does, with her ravenous, minute-to-minute needs, but more like the overstuffed armchair in their attic, left over from the shabby chic era and placed inadvertently in the sole beam of garret light, such that on those rare occasions when one of her boys suddenly, without warning, needed a little sun and comfort in a secluded, soft place, she'd be there, thread-bare, steadfast, and glowing.

Zoe begins to fuss again, loudly. "Look, I'm so sorry, Luba, really. I gotta run," she says. "The baby's hungry, I have to catch a taxi, I wish I could stay and chat, but I can't." Just as she turns to head toward the taxi stand in Harvard Square, however, a black Escalade appears on Dunster Street, stopping on the sidewalk near enough to Mia and Luba that they're able to spy, as the back passenger seat door is opened, the profile of Vivica Snow, neck bent over her BlackBerry. Another woman—younger, anxious—steps out onto the sidewalk, clipboard in hand.

Vivica, who'd had to don a gray wig and a fat suit in order to hide her lambent tresses and sleek concavity when she played the Nurse to Mia's Juliet and Luba's Lady Capulet, won an Oscar several years back for her portrayal of Christopher Walken's dutiful daughter, who turns to a life of drug dealing, hard-core porn, and petty crime in order to pay her cancer-riddled father's medical bills. Jonathan had once con-sidered casting Vivica in one of his films, until a director friend of his told him the actress was a bit of a diva on his last set, demanding this kind of bottled water and that kind of hydroponic kale, a bendy straw for her green tea and a separate trailer for her bichon frise. This sur-prised Mia, who'd viewed gawky Vivica back in college as adorably insecure beneath her Breck-girl exterior, with a nice, even mousy per-sonality, horned-rim glasses, and a tall girl's don't-look-at-me slouch.

It's such a shame when the fame goes to their heads, Mia thinks. But she also knows, from having seen the girls Jonathan chooses for his films go from obscurity to household name overnight, how hard it is to stay grounded when your feet never touch the earth save to strut down a red carpet; when every latte you purchase, every pound you gain or lose, every person you fuck gets instantly chronicled by the Celebrity-Industrial Complex, the most recent rumor being that Vivica's baby had been fathered in a petri dish by Vivica's gay agent's sperm.

WHO NEEDS A HUSBAND? a recent *US* magazine caption had asked, over a photo of a smiling Vivica and her new baby, Madeleine Marcel, emerging from a trendy children's boutique on Melrose. The little girl, the rest of the text box explained, arrived in the world armed with an $895 receiving blanket, a $90,000 custom-built nursery, and a stroller equipped with both an iPod dock and a built-in cooler that was so new only those with inside connections were allowed to give them a test-drive. This though Vivica would be practicing attachment parenting with little Madeleine Marcel (named in honor of Proust, the French novelist, the article said, whom Vivica had admired ever since having majored in French literature and language at Harvard), using a $645 Peapod Pollywog organic cotton sling made exclusively for her and manufactured by fair trade weavers in Guatemala to cart her around the set of her new HBO miniseries, about a band of foreign correspondents working and sleeping together during the Vietnam War.

Vivica's assistant and/or nanny—it was unclear what role the woman with the clipboard was playing, apart from indispensable—leans into the backseat, after a quick glance at her paperwork. "Registration's just inside," she says, pointing behind her into Kirkland House. "I'll be right back with your name tag, and then we can head over to the hotel to get you dressed for the luau. You need to decide whether to wear the Marc Jacobs or the Derek Lam. I hand carried them so they should be fine. I'll have the rest of your clothes pressed as soon as we check into the hotel. Tomorrow's picnic is casual— I brought that ruffly green Stella McCartney plus a bunch of other shirts and capris, and your ballet flats—and the evening dinner dance is semiformal, which gives us a bit of leeway."

"Okay," says Vivica, lost in her texting.

"And then we fly back to Vancouver early Sunday morning, so we really have to go over your lines for Monday before then."

"Okay."

"Jake was adamant—"

"O-*KAY*," says Vivica, finally looking up before returning her attention to her tiny screen, marauding thumbs poised for the plunder.

"It's wild, isn't it?" Luba whispers to Mia. "Who would have thunk it would have been Vivica up there, thanking the Academy?"

"I know," says Mia, trying to sound as sincere as possible, for she felt that Vivica had overacted the part and that Oscar should have gone to Fran McDormand. "It's an incredible accomplishment."

Then again, Mia thinks, her graduating class is full of incredible, quantifiable accomplishments: There's that woman who used to live in Dunster House who was just appointed to the Obama cabinet; two Pulitzer Prize winners (one of them being her roommate, Jane); a Pritzker Award finalist; two MacArthur geniuses; a U.S. congressman; a guy who made a fortune patenting a new device used to treat diabetes; a gynecologist who fought hard to maintain an abortion clinic in Memphis where her work garnered praise from women's groups, daily death threats from the intolerant, and an eight-thousand-word homage in the *New Yorker*.

In fact, this particular edition of the red book seems to be bursting at the binding with the fruits of two decades' worth of dedicated labor by some of the keenest minds in the country: tenured professors, partners in law, brain surgeons, tech entrepreneurs, famous journalists, award-winning filmmakers, TV writers, rocket scientists, philanthropists, you name it, they not only do it, many of them have been doing it well enough to have become publicly known for doing it, which was always the implicit underlying promise held out to the 1,600 high school seniors a year the college tapped with its magic wand: You will shower, eat, study, and cavort with the future leaders and thinkers of America. Or so the theory went.

In practice, of course, just as a percentage of the high school fuck-ups, like Mia's brother, went on to conquer the world, a substantial percentage of the Harvard class of 1989 went on to live completely normal, ordinary lives. Others have had not-so-successful lives or, in some instances, tragic ones. Many, like Luba, got tired of reaching for the golden ring, or maybe they reached, like Mia, but fell, or maybe after having graduated from Harvard with a middling C average, their self-confidence was shot, and they aimed lower, or maybe their brain chemistry turned against them, or maybe once they finally nabbed that shiny ring with their outstretched hand, they realized it was just a piece of metal. One of her classmates owned a Subaru dealership in Pawtucket. Another was an organic farmer in Vermont. Both, in their red book essays, professed caveated contentment with the paths they'd chosen. "Do I love my job?" the Subaru dealer wrote. "You know what? Some days I do, and some days I don't, but what I do love, always, is that it allows me immense freedom to attend the kids' soccer games and parent teacher conferences, and it pays the bills, and for now and maybe forever, that seems to be enough."

And then there were those, also like Mia—and so many more than she would have assumed twenty years ago—who heard the siren call of motherhood (or, in only one essay she could find, fatherhood) and never looked back. Unstated but understood was the fact that you weren't supposed to become a Subaru dealer or an organic farmer or a stay-at-home parent if you graduated from Harvard. And nearly every woman in the class of 1989 who'd chosen the latter path and had a scintilla of self-awareness had either left their entries blank but for their address and children's names and birthdays, or had written some sort of mea culpa—a few witty, others more serious—acknowledging the paradox, understanding all-too-intimately that there would always be those out there in the world who would accuse them of having stolen their spots in the class of '89 from worthier candidates.

"I always thought you'd be the one holding one of those statues in your hand," says Luba. "Really, I did."

Thanks for that passive-aggressive vote of confidence, thinks Mia, raising her lips up in a faux smile she hope looks sincere while allowing Zoe to grasp her chubby little hands onto her forefingers, a private prize, she thinks to herself, as gratifying as any public one. Or so she has told herself often enough that it has oxidized into its own form of truth.

Mia is anxious to join Clover and Addison at the police station, but now that Vivica has arrived, her feet suddenly feel glued to the pavement. Silly, really, as she spends so many of her hours at home entertaining boldfaced names without ever getting starstruck. Then again, she never knew any of those stars when she outshone them.

A nanny-type now emerges from Vivica's Escalade, comforting Vivica's screaming baby, followed by a billboard-ready young buck, all sinew and sangfroid, holding Vivica's bichon on a leash as it promptly takes a dump on the Kirkland House lawn. "I guess it really does take a village," says Luba. The dog walker heads back to the car, leaving the pile of excrement behind.

Mia is distracted both by the audacity of the misdemeanor and by the man himself, whom the tabloids have reported to be Vivica's current beau, a model named Nico Carmichael who began his career cleaning celebrity pools. "He's not just going to leave that there on the grass, is he?" says Mia.

Both young man and dog turn around and swagger back, chest first, to the Escalade. "Yup, he is," says Luba.

"Well that's just unsanitary and wrong," says Mia, fishing around in her diaper bag for one of the blue plastic Nappy Sacs that made the leap from being marketed, unscented, to owners of pets to being strategically placed, powder-scented and for twice the cost, at eye level on the shelves of Babies "R" Us. When she finds one, she marches straight into Nico's path, forcing him to engage before he can sidle back into the car. Few things upset Mia more than those who don't pick up after their charges. One should not be allowed to reap the psychic rewards of small creatures if one is not prepared to deal with the concomitant responsibilities of their care. It goes against everything she believes. Everything! "Here," she says, holding up the Nappy Sac inches from Nico's face.

"Excuse me?" says Nico, feigning ignorance.

"I thought you might be able to use it," says Mia, waiting for Luba to back her up, but the actress-turned-lawyer has been corralled by another classmate. Zoe is rendered momentarily mute by the sight of Nico Carmichael's face. Babies are complete suckers for symmetry. All the recent studies on physical beauty attest to this fact, but Mia wasn't convinced herself until she saw the phenomenon in action one morning at around 3 A.M. when *The Way We Were* popped up on Showtime as she was trying to calm Zoe. Only when Robert Redford's angular, symmetrical mug appeared onscreen would Zoe grow instantly silent. Mia noted, with a jolt of familiar, postaudition pain, that neither the sight of Barbra Streisand's face nor of her own slightly asymmetrical physiognomy had the same soothing effect on her child.

"For what?" says Nico.

"For the crap your dog just took over there." The venom in Mia's voice, the severity of the point of her outstretched finger directing the man's gaze toward the offending pile on the green expanse, surprises even her. It's at moments such as these when she has to admit that, no matter how hard she's labored to break away from learned behaviors, part of her will always be her mother's daughter.

"Jesus, okay, chill out, lady," says the man, heading back to deal with the mess.

"I am chill!" shouts Mia.

Then, stooping to pick up the excrement with Mia's powder-fresh sac, Nico mumbles something that sounds to Mia like "Fucking cunt," but she can't be sure.

"What did you just call me?" says Mia, loud enough to rouse the attention of Vivica.

"I'm sorry, ma'am," says Vivica from the backseat of the Escalade, looking up from behind a pair of giant Chanel sunglasses. "Is there a problem here?"

Ma'am? Mia knows she's aged since college, but is she really that unrecognizable? No. She can't be. Luba recognized her right away. What is it with these movie stars? Every once in a while, she'll show up on one of Jonathan's sets, and an actress she's met twenty times—an actress who has, in fact, supped at her table and drunk her wine—will

still reach out a slender, manicured hand, as if this were their first encounter, as if Mia's face were truly as unmemorable as she once feared
it might be, and say, "So nice to meet you." Mia doesn't even bother to
correct them anymore.

But Vivica? "Sorry, Vivsy," says Mia, using Vivica's college nickname. "Your friend here and I were having a small disagreement about
whether it's okay to leave dog feces on the ground, but now everything's fine. How are you, anyway? It's been forever!" She could have
just as easily stated her name to spare Vivica the embarrassment of failed
recall, but Mia enjoys the momentary disparity in power. She also
knows her acting skills are still sharp enough not to reveal this.

"I know, right?" says Vivica, her smile camera ready, her brain still
clearly at a loss as to Mia's identity. "Two decades just . . . poof! Gone.
And who's this adorable drooling creature?" She reaches her hand out
to touch Zoe's fingers as Nico whispers something into her ear that
elicits an enigmatic smile before disappearing back into the car.

Good stalling, thinks Mia. Touché. "This is Zoe," she says, and the
two engage in several minutes of mother-to-mother banalities—baby
age, offspring number, type of delivery, lament over extraneous ab-
dominal skin, the inevitable do-you-still-have-hemorrhoids question
(Mia yes, Vivica no, of course), breast or bottle, dramatic sighs over tits
that will never be the same—until Vivica's synapses, Mia can tell, finally hit upon the buried name.

"Mia Mandelbaum!" Vivica says, with obvious relief. "Oh my God,
it's so nice to see you again! Wait, I heard you married Jonathan Zane,
right? He's such an *amazing* director. Everyone I know is *dying* to work
with him."

Of course they are, thinks Mia. Jonathan has a knack for making
rich tabloid stars out of struggling, pretty young things. Which Vivica,
Mia notes with a dollop of schadenfreude that makes her feel ashamed,
no longer technically is, time-frozen (botulism-smoothed) face notwithstanding. "Yup, he's pretty great."

People are always much nicer to Mia once they clue into her

husband's identity. It's an inevitable if somewhat annoying by-product of their union.

"So are you acting these days?" says Vivica.

Mia wonders whether Vivica has read the reunion book and is pretending not to have done so in order to be kind, or whether she *has* read the book and is asking the question for the thrill of watching Mia squirm. "No, not anymore. I moved out to LA after graduation and tried, but, you know . . ."

"Believe me, I know. Hollywood can be *so* brutal."

Oh, please, Mia thinks, don't lie for my sake. We both know it's been nothing but generous and kind to you. But she gives Vivica the benefit of the doubt. At their age, it might very well be turning brutal. She feels Vivica's eyes straying just over her left shoulder, a not uncommon sensation when you're the nobody wife of a somebody.

"Isn't that your husband over there?" Vivica has had several meetings with Jonathan, Mia knows, that have gone nowhere.

Mia turns around and spots a familiar sight: Jonathan, boys in tow, offering his assistance to a couple engaged in the awkward if increasingly common postdigital-era act of self-portraiture. The couple in question, both lassoed with class of 1989 name tags, look vaguely familiar. Everyone here looks vaguely familiar, but Mia can't place either one. Jonathan takes the camera from the woman and directs her and either her husband or an old friend, it isn't clear what the relationship between the two is, to move farther back, closer to the Kirkland House entryway, out of the unflattering rays of direct sun. Then, shielding the lens from stray beams with an outstretched arm—Mia calls this his *Triumph of the Will* pose—he shoots off several images of the couple from different angles while the Zane boys stand uncomfortably off to the side, waiting for the interaction to be over.

It's become a family joke, Jonathan's incapacity to pass anyone—on the street, in front of a monument, wherever he happens to spot people holding cameras out in front of their faces—without offering to shoot the picture for them. It got to the point, when they were in Paris last summer, where Max had to physically restrain his father when they were on the Champs de Mars, in front of the Eiffel Tower. "Dad," he said, trapping Jonathan in a wrestling choke hold and laughing, "you can't take everyone's pictures! We'll never get to the top."

"Oh, let him," said Mia, untangling father from son. "It gives him so much pleasure."

"Yeah, that's my husband," she now says to Vivica, waving to Jonathan and shaking her head, playfully, at his antics. He waves back, lifts his shoulders in a couldn't-help-myself shrug, and blows a kiss in her direction. Vivica waves, too, but Jonathan waves back noncommittally, eyes squinched, not recognizing the starlet chatting with his wife. "Don't be insulted," says Mia, sensing Vivica's deflation. "He's blind without his glasses."

"Oh my God, me, too, these days!" says Vivica. "It just happened. Overnight. A few days after my forty-second birthday. Boom. Blind as a bat. You, too?"

"Nope," says Mia, secretly pleased to still have this one tiny edge over her contemporary competitors in the game of decline. "Still twenty-twenty. For now. But I just turned forty. I skipped a couple of grades when I was in elementary school, so, you know, any day now . . ."

"You're only forty! Wow. I would have never guessed." Vivica doesn't intend this as an insult. Consciously.

"Oh?" says Mia, eyebrows raised in cartoon arches. "What age *would* you have guessed?"

Vivica, processing the gaffe, begins to backpedal. "No no, I just meant that back when we were in college, I had no idea! You were so . . . mature. You know, *emotionally* mature. Not physically. Not that you weren't physically mature, too, I mean, you had boobs of course and all that, but"—Vivica looks stricken, unable to stanch the flow of awkwardness—"you know what I mean. You look great, Mia. Really great, and so . . . *young!*" Her eyes fall on Zoe. "Like a baby!"

"In the thighs, maybe," says Mia, squeezing the ample, squishy flesh of her daughter's dangling legs. She doesn't have to check out the various carapaces of her female classmates to know hers has not aged as gracefully. Then again, her mother always appeared a decade older than her actual age, so Mia comes by her raisining, cratering, and thickening naturally. Forget karma, she thinks. Genetics are the real bitch.

"Oh, come on! You're not fat," says Vivica. "You just had a baby. Cut yourself some slack."

After several painful seconds of silence, during which Mia mines her brain for any comeback that doesn't sound disingenuous or bitchy, she says, simply, "Well, good to see you, Vivs. Will you be at the luau later?"

"Definitely," says Vivica, visibly relieved to put a clamp on the conversation.

"Cool, I might see you there," says Mia, leaving it noncommittal, because it's too complicated to explain why she won't be there or why (should she by some miracle make it back from the police station in time) she has no intention of exposing her fragile ego to Vivica Snow's again anytime soon. After waving good-bye to her sons and husband a second time, and kissing each of Vivica's Juvéderm-injected cheeks, she pivots on her feet, gripping Zoe's little fingers just a tad too tightly, and marches her jiggling thighs up Dunster Street toward the taxi stand in Harvard Square.

"I'm looking for Addison Hunt?" Mia says to the cop manning the front desk at the police station, swaying from side to side to try to calm Zoe, whom she started feeding in the backseat of the taxi until she realized the driver was a reckless maniac. "Shh, baby, shhh. You'll finish your dinner soon." She'd been given only the vaguest instructions from Clover, other than to bring cash. ("How much cash?" she'd asked. "I have no idea," said Clover, "but I guess as much as you can withdraw?") So before jumping in a taxi, she stopped at an ATM and took out the maximum withdrawal, $800, which she figured, with whatever cash Clover and Gunner were able to scrounge up together, should more than cover Addison's unpaid tickets.

"You mean the parking ticket lady?" says the cop, checking Mia's ID. "She's in the holding area. But you can join the rest of the party down the hall." His Boston *rs*—*pah-king ticket, pah-ty*—give Mia a frisson of nostalgia. Mia is still a wicked impersonator, a lifelong student of dialect; her impression of Sarah Palin on Ecstasy was the hit of the Obama-for-president party circuit.

"The holding area?"

"Yeah," says the cop, rolling his eyes. "It's an area. Where we hold."

"Can I see her?"

"Not a chance."

"But . . . you'll release her tonight, right?"

"Sheesh, what is it with you Harvard people?" (You *Hah-vahd* people, thinks Mia. So fantastic, that accent. It takes her full powers of concentration to keep her mouth from subconsciously forming the syllables.) "Don't you ever watch cop shows?" (No she doesn't watch cop shows. In fact, the bulk of what Hollywood produces, yes including some of her husband's own films, does not interest her.) "She's here for the night. Judge will set bail in the morning. Now, go join your friends, and tell them there's nothing more any of you's can do, so you can all go back to your party." (*Yoh pah-ty*. Mia could listen to that accent all night long.)

"But I brought cash to pay the fines." Mia pulls out the thick wad of twenty-dollar bills in an ATM envelope.

"Unless you got a hundred grand in that envelope, don't even bother. And I wouldn't go flashin' that around here neither."

"A hundred grand!?" Even taking into consideration the exponential ballooning of compounding interest, Addison must have racked up a hell of a lot of parking tickets to owe that much money. The sheer madness of the number causes Mia to choke on gulped air.

"Actually, no. My bad. It's only $99,436.53 to pay off the fines plus whatever fees the judge sets as bail for twenty years of nonpayment," says the cop, reading the number off a sheet of paper in front of him. "But who's counting?"

"Jesus." Zoe starts to fuss anew. Mia looks around, trying to figure out where she can feed the baby. Discreet doesn't matter, but germ-free would be nice. "Sorry," she says. "Okay if I nurse the baby in the waiting room?"

"If you want to flash your titties to a bunch of yahoos, be my guest."

"That depends," says Mia, smiling. "How many yahoos are we talking about?"

"Not including your friends, let's see . . ." The cop checks his paperwork. "We got the boyfriend of the junkie, the prostitute's girlfriend, the shoplifter's mother. That makes three."

Three yahoos, Mia thinks, despite herself. The restroom she rules out as a nursing station, sight unseen. "No perverts?"

The cop smiles and shrugs. "The night's still young." Then he points her in the direction of the waiting room.

"One hundred *grand*?" Mia exclaims when she spots Clover, and—oh my God, is that Bucky? He looks so pale and . . . old. And it can't be only because of the fluorescent lighting, because Clover looks as young and luminescent as ever. "Shh, baby, one more minute, one more minute . . ." She finds a lint-covered binky in her purse, cleans it off with her spit, and shoves it in Zoe's mouth. Fourth kid. What are you going to do?

"Mia!" Clover exclaims, embracing her friend. "Oh my God, I'm so sorry I made you come all the way out here. I didn't understand she had to have a bail hearing tomorrow first. I thought we could just pay and call it a day, but Jesus, I know. A hundred grand."

"Wass'up, Mia," says Bucky.

"Hey, Bucky. Long time no see," says Mia, wondering if Bucky experiences life differently now that he's no longer Adonis. It's a shame, really, his physical transformation; the latent actress in her automatically envisions the emotional privations of his backstory. "So do they have it?"

"Does who have what?" says Clover.

"Do Gunner and Addison have that kind of money to get her out of here after the bail hearing?"

Clover shrugs her shoulders. "Gunner said there might be an emergency fund in the family trust, but he's not sure." Gunner's great-grandfather, Tobias "Barns" Griswold, founded and sold a small merchant bank back in the 1800s whose profits have been feeding, housing, and clothing each descending generation of Griswolds since, although because no one else in the ever-expanding family has ever shown Barns's knack for wealth building, the principal has been dwindling.

"But even if Gunner can get his hands on that much liquid," says Bucky, fidgeting with his BlackBerry, "it's not as if anyone will cut them a check that size over the weekend. Trust me, I know. My wife has a habit of falling in love with antiques on Saturdays." His latest text message from Arabella, in fact, reads: "Found perfect new sideboard 4 dining rm. 65K. Will call Brad to arrange wire transfer." An absurd addendum, that last bit, or even a tell, Bucky thinks, because he assumes Brad the accountant was with his wife when she wrote it. For all Bucky knows, Brad's the one who picked out the frigging sideboard, not that their dining room even needed a new one. He probably convinced Arabella that the purchase could be written off as a business/entertainment expense. Oh, those two are just made for each other. Fuck them both.

"I know I'm a horrible person for saying this," says Mia, "but it feels like . . ."

". . . the chickens have finally come home to roost?" says Clover.

"Something like that," says Mia, remembering, with a shudder, the night senior year when Addison drove Jane and her into Boston to see a Pixies concert. (Clover was in the library that night, studying as usual.) "Are you stoned?" Mia had asked from the backseat, after the first stop sign on Athens Street was ignored. To which Addison responded, "No, better! I just ate a whole bagful of mushrooms!" Jane

issued a stern ultimatum: Stop the car immediately, or she'd take dras-
tic measures to make it stop. "Oh, come on, you guys!" Addison
whined, without stopping either for Jane or for the next stop sign.
"Don't be such wusses. We're having fun! Woo hoo! The Pixies!"
She reached down to crank up "Debaser" on the car's tape deck and
started singing out loud. Jane, who was in the front passenger seat,
pressed sharply on the brake with her left foot, snatched the keys, and
ordered Addison into the back. The cost of such recklessness back then
could have been three lives; by comparison, Mia thinks, a hundred
thousand dollars is a veritable bargain, although really, *a hundred thousand
dollars*! Mia wonders how much cash she and Jonathan could scrounge
up in twenty-four hours, if her freedom depended on it. "Where is
Gunner anyway?"

"He drove the kids to Belmont to get them settled at Jane's," says
Bucky. "He should be back any minute."

"They saw everything," explains Clover: Addison getting hand-
cuffed; Addison trying to bribe the cops with a hundred bucks to let
her go; Addison having a nervous breakdown when her head was
pushed down into the squad car. "They're totally freaked out."

"Yowza. That's awful." Mia tries to picture her own kids staring
out at their mother's arrest, the look on their faces as she is escorted
away. Max freaked out the one time years ago she got a speeding
ticket, for going 33 in a 25 mph zone. It took him months to recover.

"Oh, please. You want awful, I'll show you awful," says a frayed-
looking woman of indeterminate age, sitting off in the corner of the
waiting room in her housecoat and curlers, as if she'd been summoned
away from her nightly TV catatonia with little warning. The shoplifter's mother, if Mia had to guess.

Mia glances around and finally takes in the tableau of the other
friends and family of the newly incarcerated as the woman lifts up her
sleeve to reveal a large bite mark on the loose flab of her arm. "Who
did that to you?" Mia asks, half horrified, half enthralled with the
spectacle.

"A fucking prick, that's who," says the woman.

"Wow, I'm so sorry," says Mia, for what else is there to say?

The other woman in the waiting room rolls her eyes, as if she can't stand the sight of any of them. She has purple, spiky hair and a tattoo on her neck that says CLITS OF STEEL, with an arrow pointing downward. Mia wonders if the *s* at the end of CLIT might have been a typo. Two buns, one clit, she thinks. It doesn't make sense to have it in the plural tense. She feels a sudden, bizarre need to defend herself to this pierced, graffitied eye-roller. *I'm not who you think I am,* she would like to say, but maybe she actually *is* who the woman thinks she is, which might be more pathetic. Plus if dealing with her mother all these years has taught her anything, it's that rational logic rarely plays in the Peoria of Borderline Personality Disorder. She tries to imagine what Clits of Steel's childhood home might have looked like, picturing clumps of hair in the bathroom drain, mismatched socks in the drawers, mold-speckled ceilings.

In the far left corner sits a skinny man with train-track arms, scratching involuntarily at his thighs. Mia once had an audition to play a junkie, and she spent an entire afternoon in front of an outpatient drug treatment center, studying the way the addicts stooped and scratched and leaned into the wind, pulsing with need. She read primary-source psychological studies of addicts in treatment, noting that the two issues many of them shared in common were genetic histories of addiction along with neglect and/or abuse at the hand of a parent. "No one ever loved me," one addict had said to his shrink. "And no one ever will."

"You were great!" the casting director told her. "Completely believable. But we're looking for a blonde."

Clover bends down to look into Zoe's eyes. "Hi there, Zo-Zo. Remember me? We met when you were just three weeks old." Zoe spits out her binky and bursts into another loud wail that rattles the walls and causes Clits of Steel to roll her angry eyes afresh.

"Good job, Cloves," says Bucky, leaning over to pick up the binky off the floor before squeezing Clover, Mia can't help noticing, tenderly on her upper arm.

"Babies hate me. I'm serious." Clover is making a joke, but her expression, Mia notes, belies the pain under its surface.

Danny, she figures, probably still isn't onboard with committing to IVF. And Clover refuses to adopt. Someone has to budge, Mia thinks, but neither of those two is the concessionary type. Each marriage is so different. Jonathan always concedes. It makes things easier. "Don't take it personally. She's starving. I'm just going to feed her right here, right now." She addresses her next question to the room at large. "Everybody cool with that?"

"Knock yourself out," says Clits of Steel. The junkie doesn't even look up.

Mia unhitches the baby carrier, snaps open her nursing bra, feels her left breast then her right to assess which is fuller, then expertly latches her ravenous daughter onto the left nipple.

Housedress Lady refuses to honor the unwritten rule of averting one's eyes from the areola. "I bottle-fed mine," she says, with equal dollops of revulsion and self-satisfaction. "No muss, no fuss." It takes every ounce of will Mia has to keep from saying, *And look where they are now.*

Just then, the normally unflappable Gunner rushes in, looking as if he's just witnessed a beheading. "We're screwed," he says. *"Totally screwed!"*

"What are you talking about?" says Clover.

"I just called my dad . . ." He can barely unearth the words. "And he . . . he . . . he said . . ."

"Dude, take it slow," says Bucky. "Breathe."

"I am fucking breathing!" snaps Gunner, who knows Bucky mostly only as a recurring figure in his wife's childhood photo albums and as a recent addition to her growing queue of Facebook friends. ("Bucky Gardner is drinking a cold one"; "Bucky Gardner is now friends with Gacky Saltonstall and Bitsy Biddle.") "We're . . . we're . . ."

It takes Mia, Clover, and Bucky several long minutes after Gunner spits out the word *fucked* to ascertain what has happened, as they first have to find him a paper bag to keep him from hyperventilating. Two of the cops get into it, too, talking him down, asking him if he needs the oxygen tank they keep in the storeroom just in case. Clits of Steel offers to call an ambulance. Housedress is repeating, loudly and inexplicably, "Get him to stand on his head! Get him to stand on his head!" The junkie scratches his thighs with intense vigor.

"I'm fine, I'm *fine*!" Gunner says. And when he really is fine, or at least fine enough to emit sound, he explains to the assembled crowd, his voice, lips, and knees trembling, that what little was left of the Griswold fortune had been yanked from its steady-as-she-goes resting place at Smith Barney and handed over to what a trusted friend's son-in-law promised was a skyrocketing, surefire-bet hedge fund, Andover Associates, which turned out to be a Madoff feeder fund run by, "Get this," says Gunner, "two dudes named Danziger and Markoff": an unfortunate string of events that Gunner's parents, in their shame and embarrassment at having placed so much blind trust in a name like Andover, had quietly hidden from both him and everyone else. "Can you believe it?" Gunner says. "Those fucking Jews!"

The room suddenly grows so quiet you can hear the junkie's needle drop. "Shit," he says, falling on his knees to retrieve it from under his seat.

Mia, who felt moved enough by Gunner's anguish that she was about to offer to write a large check on the spot, keeps both her mouth and purse pointedly shut.

4

Jane

Jane spots one last empty beer bottle on the living room window-sill and sighs. Almost done. Six of the seven offspring of her former roommates, along with her own daughter, Sophie, have been tucked away into four beds and three musty sleeping bags. The air mattress in the basement has been located, inflated, and covered with mattress pads, sheets, and pillows for Jonathan and Mia; her daughter Sophie's old Pack 'n Play has been unearthed for their daughter, Zoe, a crib sheet tucked neatly inside it with the word CLEAN scribbled in her late mother's handwriting on an attached Post-it, the sight of which caught Jane, unexpectedly, by the throat. It was so like her mother to have anticipated a binary uncertainty (clean or dirty?) before it arose. Meanwhile, her childhood bedroom has been handed over to a solo, distraught Gunner, for whom she also located an Ambien with a still-valid expiration date in the downstairs medicine cabinet. "Claire Streeter?" Gunner had said, reading the name off the pill bottle. "Your mom's."

"What, does that creep you out?"

"No, not at all. I'm just grateful she left a few behind."

"Yeah, well, by the end, she didn't really need them to help her sleep. She just . . . slept. All the time."

Now Jane makes one last sweep of the kitchen, wiping down surfaces, recycling bottles and soda cans, and scrubbing the caked-on remnants of the giant vat of spaghetti she whipped up when it became clear that they would all be skipping the luau. Addison's eldest, Trilby, who was supposed to have babysat Sophie while the adults were out,

was understandably too upset by her mother's incarceration to have
been left in charge of her own breathing, let alone an eight-year-old's
welfare. And by the time the Zane boys and their father arrived, after
having abandoned all hope of ever finding an unoccupied hotel room
in Cambridge during a reunion weekend, cost be damned, it was too
late and too inappropriate, considering the circumstances, to get all
gussied up for a party.

This is my core group anyway, Jane thinks. Minus Clover, but still.
"No way," Jane said, when Mia told her that Bucky had been at the
police station before driving Clover back to the Charles Hotel. "Bucky
Gardner? How'd he look?" Jane had enjoyed the short period when
Clover and Bucky were dating freshman year, if only for the oblique
matinal thrill of watching Bucky amble shirtless across the common
room, on his way to a morning piss.

"A little like he'd been run over by life's truck," said Mia. "But
yeah, he's still attractive, in a sort of faded pretty boy way." Then she
excused herself to nurse Zoe again and pass out. The fruitless night at
the police station would have been physically draining enough, she
said, even if it hadn't come on the heels of a cross-country trip. "I
mean, really, *dayenu*," Mia said, but Jane didn't catch the reference.
"It's a Passover thing," said Mia, with a bizarre, pointed glance toward
Gunner, which Jane noticed but could not read and which Gunner,
lost in the miasma of his own immediate concerns, missed.

Jane runs a final wet rag along the kitchen's center island, her
thoughts spiraling inward. She tries to imagine what it would be like
either to wipe down the surface of this island every night for the rest
of her life or to never see it again. Her *Globe* editors have said they
want her back in the States anyway, now that they've shut down most
of their foreign bureaus; international stories, they've been arguing,
hardly ever make it onto the most e-mailed list, and the wire services
do a perfectly adequate job of it. Jane's been trying to make the coun-
terargument that she brings years of experience and firsthand knowledge to her work; that the wire services do a lousy job at producing

thoughtful features on any subject, let alone on the particular plight and daily struggles of the international refugee; and that she can produce stories relatively inexpensively out of her home office and still cover foreign news in ways that the wire services can't and won't.

And yet. And yet. Maybe it wouldn't be such a terrible thing to do the whole cosmic wipe-down again, she thinks, adding a touch of elbow grease to a splat of tomato sauce. To obliterate one life and begin another. Leave Paris and all those corners and bistros holding memories of Hervé behind. Reclaim her childhood home. Sophie's English would improve. And rent checks, written out in euros to a Monsieur Jean-Marc Dufour, would become just another ancient artifact of her past. Like speaking Vietnamese. Or making love to her late husband. Or feeling the warmth of her late mother's hugs. *Late*, she thinks, her mind catching and snagging on the word, like stockings on a splintery board. As if her collection of dead were simply hanging out in some warehouse for the perpetually tardy, just waiting to step back onto life's stage. What a stupid word to place before the dead. *Vanished* would be far more appropriate. Or just plain *gone*.

Hervé has been gone for five years. The enormity of this hits her at the oddest moments.

In the midst of these inner rumblings, Jane finally notices Mia's husband, Jonathan, standing at the edge of the kitchen in his pajamas, his mouth forming sounds that begin to approximate words once she focuses on them. "Jane? Um, Jane?" he is saying. When he sees he has finally captured her attention he continues. "You got any herbal tea?"

"Can't sleep?" she says.

"Hazards of old age. I've become a terrible insomniac." When Mia and Jonathan married a year after college, he was already middle-aged. Jane does the calculation in her head: Jonathan must now be pushing sixty. Though he still dresses in the Levi's-and-Sambas style of film directors everywhere, he is definitely showing the usual signs of wear and tear: What little hair he has left is now completely white; his crow's-feet scrape deep; the tops of his hands are turning mottled, ropy.

Jane's mother was only sixty-seven when she died. She wonders whether Jonathan will live long enough to see Zoe graduate high school. She does another calculation in her head, eighteen plus now, hitting on a number well into Jonathan's seventies.

"I can give you an Ambien," she says. "I just gave Gunner one, and he was out like a light in five minutes. I think there are a few more left in the medicine cabinet, if you want one."

"Nah, tea's fine. If you have some. I try to stay away from the hard stuff."

The hard stuff? she thinks. Odd response. Nearly every insomniac she knows in Paris takes a little something before bed. Which they buy over-the-counter with their aspirin and their codeine and, if they're female, their inexpensive birth control pills. She chalks up Jonathan's hyperbole to a typical American, Puritanical, litigious approach toward pharmaceuticals. If she moves back, she'll have to relearn all those attitudes and social mores from which she freed herself by settling in Paris. "Tea it is. I'm sure we have some in here," she says, opening the pantry. "My mom practically lived on the stuff toward the end."

Claire Streeter has been gone for less than five months, but the house is still stuffed with her presence, her odor, her clothing, piles of her bills, her bottles of pills, her tea bags. Jane told Bruno she planned to spend the week or two after reunion dealing with all of it, now that Sophie's finished with school. The task, which felt insurmountable in the weeks following her mother's death, cannot be put off any longer. "Here you go," she says, locating the stash of tea in the exact place the hospice worker had left it. "Do you want Passion or Sleepy Time?"

"Oh, I want Passion, but I'll settle for Sleepy Time, thanks," says Jonathan, with a wink. Then he turns serious. "Jane, I'm so sorry about your mother." He looks down at his feet. "Mia said the funeral was really moving. I wish I could have made it, I really do. I was in the middle of a shoot in Michigan. I feel bad about not having been here for you."

"No worries. Really. I totally get it." Jane forces a smile and puts on the I'm-okay face she mastered as a child, the one the adoptive father in whose love she basked for less than two years found compelling enough to bring her home with him as a gift to his infertile wife after his tour of duty in Saigon as an army medic. Jane has always prided herself in putting others at ease, in keeping her emotions firmly in check. Bruno, her current partner, is the only one with whom she allowed herself (once, just once) to fully collapse, with a throat-rattling, gut-clawing wail, after Hervé's body was found in that ditch.

That same night, she and Bruno made love for the first time, which in retrospect felt like a bit of a desecration but at the time felt like the only proper response to the news, for both of them. Now she wonders whether Bruno fell in love with her for the person she actually is or out of a mutual sense of shared grief. Or maybe he felt it was his professional duty (he was, after all, the editor who sent her husband to his death) to step in and take over. Or perhaps it was just your average garden-variety pity for the pathetic, young widow.

"And yes, Mia was right. The funeral was really kind of lovely," she says to Jonathan, "insofar as any funeral can be lovely. One of Mom's friends, a musician, put together a quartet to play a few of her favorite pieces by Bach. You know, the one that goes . . ." She sings the first few bars of the Bach Double, and Jonathan nods. "Then her cousin Frank delivered a really funny eulogy, telling stories about Mom when she was a girl I'd never heard before, like this one about a tadpole she caught which, when it finally turned into a frog, had a missing hind leg, so Mom tried to staple on a leg made out of fabric and cotton without killing him. A lot of her patients showed up as well. Most of them were total wrecks, but I guess that's not saying much."

"She was a shrink, right?"

"Yup."

"So how the hell did you turn out so normal?"

"Oh come on, Jonathan. First of all, I was adopted. Second, I'm hardly normal. Especially these days."

"Jane, you amaze me with how normal you are, considering every-thing you've been through."

"Oh, please. We all have to deal with grief sooner or later."

"True. But you've had to deal with a hell of a lot more sooners than laters."

"Dumb luck, dude." *Dude*? Where did *that* come from? Do people in the States even say it still? Jonathan doesn't look as if he's experienc-ing a vernacular time warp, so maybe they do. Jane wonders if she'll ever feel truly at home anywhere. "Here, I'll put the kettle on."

Jane has always held a special place in her heart for Jonathan. When the other roommates were questioning whether Mia was making a huge mistake, getting married so young to a middle-aged man, Jane's was the sole voice of support. "He's a good man," she kept saying. "A *really* good man." Even then she understood the rarity of such creatures. Yes, okay, so Jonathan didn't seem particularly deep or multilayered, and his films were box-office-generating fluff, but unless he was a better actor than the hunky studs he hired for his films, he actually believed in the happily-ever-after snake oil he was selling. Last summer in Antibes, Jane and Bruno were lounging with Mia and Jonathan on their deck, sharing a bottle of Domain Sainte Croix against the flaming orange Mediterranean sky, when Jonathan grabbed his wife's hand to caress it as if the two were newlyweds. With his other hand he rubbed Mia's belly, swollen with the soon-to-be Zoe, and said that had the rights to the Beatles' "All You Need Is Love" not been so outrageously prohibi-tive, he would have used it in the sound track of at least one of his films. "That song, in a nutshell, is my life's philosophy," he said, his eyes tear-ing up, his mouth kissing Mia's hand, then her belly, tenderly.

(When he said this, Jane couldn't help wondering, cynically, de-spite herself, whether Jonathan would still claim that all he needed was love minus the villa in Antibes, the infinity pool spilling out over LA, and the small army of Mexican women who kept Jonathan and Mia's life running so smoothly, there was nary a dish to be done or a towel folded. Ever. Then she felt guilty for harboring such thoughts.)

"How's Bruno?" Jonathan asks, plopping himself onto the couch, propping his feet up on the coffee table. "I was hoping he'd be here so we could ditch all you eggheads and go watch some old movies together at the Brattle. I love that guy, you know? You should marry him before he gets tired of asking."

"Marriage is overrated," Jane says, keeping it vague. "And I'm sure he sends that love right back at you, but you know, it's a long way to travel for a reunion."

"Tell me about it. I kept trying to convince Mia she'd have much more fun coming here by herself. She could have flirted with her old boyfriends! Stayed out 'til dawn."

"And you'd be okay with that? Her flirting with old boyfriends?"

"Are you kidding? I have enough confidence in my own aging good looks and bedroom expertise to know she would never, in a million years, leave me for some young stud she once bonked on a beer-stained sofa."

"You crack me up, Jonathan, you know that? You're one of the good guys. I've always said so."

"Ha! Then I tricked you, too," he says with a wink.

Hervé, she thinks to herself, had been a good man, too, steadfast and loyal, albeit in his own particular way. Yes, he got off on the highs of his job like all of their war-seeking colleagues, and there were times, especially after Sophie was born, when Jane would berate him for taking unnecessary risks now that he'd become a father. And, of course, like most of the working women she knew, she wound up bearing the brunt of their daughter's care, which was thankfully miti-gated somewhat by Hervé's mother, who picked up the slack when both Jane and Hervé had to be on the road at the same time or when Grandmère Duclos simply sensed that her daughter-in-law needed a night out, away from the baby, during one of her son's long absences. And yes, if Jane were being *really* honest with herself about the period before Hervé's murder, there were definitely times she'd wished she'd married someone steadier, like Bruno.

And yet lately it has seemed as if the whole idea of a steady man is just a mythical fallacy, a collective delusion foisted upon women for the sake of human continuity.

A man might appear to live a conventional life—to adhere to the standards of what her French colleagues call "*métro/boulot/dodo*" (subway, work, sleep)—but his thirst to break free, she fears, can never truly be slaked. It lies waiting for an errant hair tucked behind an ear, a tender word. Under certain conditions, it may even take action. And then, if the conscience feels bad enough for setting the beast free, the subconscious might even do what Bruno's did six months earlier and send an e-mail meant for his young Irish *stagiaire*'s box into Jane's.

My dear Siobhan,
I write to tell you, simply but perhaps without eloquence, that I must to not see you once more. This time with you, during the absence of Jane, was been full of tenderness without doubt, and you maked the difficult period bearable, but the fact stays that I still love her. Enormously. And yes, I know that we have spoken of this, my libertarian beliefs concerning monogamy, but these beliefs are in battle counter to my emotions as I have been feeling like an asshole fucking you while she is elsewhere caring for her mother. It is cliché, this behavior, embarrassing also and not correct to Jane. In plus, it is irresponsible professionally, especially on my part. So I say, it is sufficient. It must to end now.

With all my affection,
    Bruno.

"With all my affection? *All* my affection?" Jane screamed, transcontinentally, into Bruno's cell phone, the day she opened the e-mail with its ironic subject header, "*La fin inévitable*"—the inevitable end—which she assumed would be another one of her partner's eloquent missives, in French, on death and dying: the kind he composed without fail every morning before dutifully walking Sophie to school. "You couldn't have just written '*Bises*' and been done with it?" Jane knew that "*Avec toute mon affection*"—with all my affection—was simply a standard, informal closing in a French letter, but somehow, translated into English and placed at the end of such an e-mail, the words appeared sinister, cruel.

"It means nothing. I was breaking it away from her!" said Bruno. "I was telling her to go for a hike."

"To take a hike," Jane corrected him.

"*Peu importe!* I was telling her I loved *you*! If you read it again, without the shock of the news, you will to see that clearly. Look, I know, it was a terrible mistake. *I make* a terrible mistake, and I am really very sorry about it, very sorry, but can you not see beyond the words themselves to the sentiments they express?"

"*Why?*" Jane cried, the closing diphthong stretching well past its normal length then breaking into a staccato and purposefully muffled sob. Muffled, because she wanted to keep her mother's path to death free from the kind of debris a daughter's sudden marital crisis might engender.

"Sweetheart, *ma biche*—" Bruno tried to say, but Jane cut him off.

"Fuck your sweetheart!" she said, realizing the double entendre only after she spat out the words.

Since then, they've been sleeping in separate beds, though Bruno has often begged her, on his knees, to reconsider.

"Jonathan?" she now says, handing over a cup of steaming tea and collapsing into her mother's Eames chair, the one Claire moved from her office into the house when she realized she was too sick to continue seeing patients. "Let me ask you a serious question. What would you do if you found out Mia had started sleeping with one of those old boyfriends you claim you don't fear?"

"Wait," says Jonathan, blowing into his teacup. "Do you know something I don't know?"

"No, no, no," says Jane, smiling. "Sorry, nothing like that. I'm just . . . curious. Theoretically, what would you do?"

"Well, I guess that would depend on how I found out about it. Does she tell me or do I discover an errant text on my own?"

"You discover a text. Or maybe, you know, she accidentally sends you an e-mail she meant to send to her lover. And that's how you find out."

"Jane, your mother was a shrink. You know there are no accidents when it comes to this stuff. If Mia sent me an e-mail meant for her lover, some hidden part of her must have wanted to confess. So let me ask you . . ." He takes a quick sip of his tea. Allows the silence between them to linger, for to break it will inevitably take his heretofore un-complicated relationship with his wife's friend to a more intimate level. "Have you been cheating on Bruno? Is that what this is all about?"

"No, not at all," says Jane. "It's . . . it's just that he . . ." Her bottom lip, which has for the greater part of her life remained—as friends point out with mild concern behind her back—virtuously stiff since childhood, begins to quiver.

"Oh, Jane. Janie. Come here. Oh my God, I've never seen you like this before. Get over here." He pats the spot next to him, and Jane moves from Eames exactitude to Pottery Barn comfort. She sinks deep into the sun-faded cushions and accepts the weight of Jonathan's arm. They remain in this position for what feels like an hour but is probably only five minutes, both of them silent save for the sound of Jane's sobbing and the almost imperceptible rustle of Jonathan's hand rubbing small circles on the shoulder of her blouse. "Talk to me, Janie," he says finally. "I'm as discreet as they come, I don't charge by the hour, and trust me, I've dealt with this same situation with my friends a million times."

Jane cracks a small, quivering-lipped smile. "Come on. A million?"

"Okay, maybe nine hundred, ninety-eight thousand, but you know, at my age? In my line of work? There's a ton of extracurricular hanky-panky. If there weren't, no one would ever buy *US Weekly.* In fact, one friend of mine, this actor who, back in the day before he became a bloated, aging caricature of himself, used to get laid left and right, just said to me recently, he said, 'Enjoy all of the tortured stories of lust, betrayal, and divorce while you can, because soon enough all you'll be hearing about are doctors' visits and death.'"

Jane can tell, by the way Jonathan's face falls, that he immediately regrets bringing any reminders of death into this house. "No worries," she says, patting his knee. "It's good advice. Keep talking."

"Right, so, okay, just think about it for a minute. I mean, I don't know the exact statistics regarding the incidence of infidelity for the general population, and I doubt anyone does, but if you think about it, it's a self-selected group who are brave enough to rat themselves out to the scientists who count such things, right? But let's just assume that if fifty percent of all marriages end in divorce, there have got to be *at least* fifty percent of married people schtupping partners they're not married to, don't you think?"

"I don't know. I guess. But Bruno and I aren't married."

"A technicality. Besides, whose fault is that, Miss I'm Never Getting Married Again, hmm?"

"Okay, fine. Mine."

"He's been wanting to make an honest woman of you for *years.*"

"I know, I know."

"So strictly speaking, whatever happened—him, you, I don't give a shit whose body part went where—is kosher, right? Except of course we both know it doesn't feel that way. Now spill."

So Jane tells Jonathan the story of the errant e-mail; how she received it the afternoon of her mother's death; how the grief from these concurrent events has been so traumatizing, she hasn't been able to eat, to sleep, to work, to be a present mother to Sophie (Jonathan *had* noticed the extreme jut of Jane's clavicle bones and the circles under her eyes, he tells her, but he'd chalked it up to grief over her mother); how Bruno has all but thrown himself on the ground to try to win back her love, once even hugging her calves as she was putting on her shoes to beg for her forgiveness.

After the recitation of these facts, Jane recrumbles back into the crevice of Jonathan. And though the embrace is not sexual, by any means, its comfort strikes her in the same deep, primal place where love lives. She wonders to herself, as she has wondered many times before, why so few men are able to exhibit this level of empathy, to grasp the inner workings of the female psyche so effortlessly. Before the stray Siobhan e-mail, Jane thought she'd won the empathy jackpot with Bruno. He even does the dishes and folds the laundry. Without being asked.

"Jane," says Jonathan, pulling back, taking another sip of his tea. "I'm going to tell you a story, but I will simply assume, knowing you, that this stays between us, okay? I just think you should hear it, because I know Bruno, and I know how he feels about you, and I can't imagine it's been easy on him while you've been traveling back and forth this year, never mind how hard it is, period, when a spouse loses a parent. But first you have to promise, I mean really promise, that this stays between you, me, and the lamppost forever."

"Of course."

"As in forever forever. As in, I've never told this story, except to my shrink, and I don't plan on telling it again, probably for as long as I live, unless someone else as near and dear to me as you finds themselves in the same situation, okay?"

"Got it. I won't say a word to anyone, I promise."

"Okay, so . . ." He clasps his hands together, starts to absentmindedly knead his palm. "Anyway, it was a while back, when the boys were still pretty young . . ." Now he grabs a pile of old magazines on the coffee table, holds them upright, and taps them lightly on the surface to straighten them before transferring his attention to the next pile.

"Don't worry about it," Jane says. "I'm just going to recycle them on Monday."

"Huh?" Jonathan says. Then he smiles. "What, you mean you don't want your magazines anally organized by title and date while I sit here stalling?"

"No," Jane laughs. "I'm good." *I'm good*: another freshly unearthed addition to the American idiom that strikes Jane with its utter American-ness, with its elevation of virtuosity over indulgence, denial over satiation. Hungry? No, I'm good. Thirsty? No, I'm good. Randy? No, I'm *good*. As if goodness were even a rational counterpoint to need.

"Okay, so . . ." Jonathan takes another sip of his tea and finally dives in. "Fuck it. Here we go, Janie. It was back in 2001, okay? September. Yes, that day. I was in New York. In the middle of shooting *Jack and Jill in Clinton Hill*, but we were actually doing a scene in Manhattan that day. Mia was back home in LA with the kids. The planes hit the towers, all hell breaks loose. Cell phone service went out for a long time. Hours, at least, I don't remember exactly how long, but it was a significant enough chunk of time that I felt completely cut off, from my family, from reality, you know, from everything. I mean, it was only five A.M. in LA, so really Mia had no idea what was going on yet, but I needed to talk to her. As in, I *needed* it, probably more than I've ever needed anything. Ever. I kept trying to reach her, you know, just to hear her voice. To tell her I loved her and that I was okay, everything was going to be okay. I can't tell you how crazy it was there, how completely unhinged I was just being there. I mean, I know you're used to this kind of stuff with your job and all, but I'm not. As in utterly, completely not. I get unhinged when Whole Foods runs out of my granola, okay? Big sissy here.

"Anyway, we'd been setting up an exterior shot in SoHo at the time, not close enough to get covered in ash, but you know, close enough that people around us were either booking north or crying or walking around in a daze or thinking about hoofing it up north or panicking. We heard this woman screaming. She wasn't hurt, she was just, I don't know, traumatized. We could smell the fire. I mean, you could smell it all over the island. You couldn't escape it. I swear to God, all I kept thinking—in the way your mind goes to its craziest places when the shit hits the fan—all I kept thinking was, huh, this must have been what Auschwitz smelled like. And then that song, what's the name of it—shit, the one by R.E.M. about the end of the world as we know it—that song kept going through my head in a loop. I couldn't shake it. I couldn't shake anything. My mind kept folding in on itself, like a bad acid trip, only it was real. So I finally get a signal on my cell phone, I finally reach Mia, and I blurt out, before she even knows anything—she hasn't even turned on the TV yet—I say to her, 'Oh my God, I love you I love you I love you,' and she's out there, totally disconnected from what I'm experiencing, unaware of the news, and she tells me she's so glad I called because we needed to make a decision about which color tile we wanted for the backsplash in our kitchen."

"Yikes."

"I know. Total yikes. But okay, understandable, since she hadn't yet heard the news. But then? Even after I told her what happened, even after she turned on the *Today* show and had absorbed the basic timeline of events, the fact that I was safe and breathing was enough for her. She still wanted to know what color we should use for the backsplash tiles. She even used the word *urgent*, as in 'The contractor said he needs to know today. It's urgent.' I snapped at her, and she couldn't understand why. I said something like, 'Whatever the fuck color you want!' I mean, I never talk to my wife that way. Or, hardly ever. I hung up the phone, and I was just numb. Completely numb. I'd had this unbelievable urge for an emotional connection with the one woman in the world who's contractually obligated to be that go-to person for me, and she'd failed. As in utterly, completely, miserably failed. So there I am, alone in my hotel room, disconnected, feeling imprisoned by New York and desperate for . . . well, I don't know what to call it other than love. Clearly I wasn't the only one feeling that way, because, you know, nine months later, the hospitals were overrun with 9/11 babies, so you know, it's not like I was a statistical anomaly. Not that I'm rationalizing or anything. Okay, yeah, maybe I am rationalizing. Fine."

"Oh my God, quit stalling. So, you were in your hotel room and . . . ?"

"I'm not stalling. I'm just . . . meandering. Like I said, I've never told this story before. I don't have the narrative down pat the way I do with, say, the time Max pooped in the bathtub and Eli tried to eat it. Have I ever told you that story? Now, that's a funny story."

"I'd rather go back to the shit you were already shooting."

"Nice one, Janie!" He looks genuinely surprised at her joke. "I didn't know you had it in you."

"Jonathan! So you were in your hotel room *and* . . . ?"

"Right. I was in my hotel room and—oh, I should probably preface this with the fact that we had to stop production for nine days, because the city was basically shut down, and we couldn't get our trailers in or out of Manhattan, it was a logistical nightmare, the whole thing—anyway I was in my hotel room, and I called up my producer, Shari. I told her she needed to come up so we could powwow about contingency plans: you know, what to do with the crew while we waited to get back into production, how to proceed, what to tell the studio, what to tell accounting about projected budget overages, etc. But really? I just wanted someone to watch the news with me. I couldn't face sitting in that empty room all by myself seeing those planes go into the towers, over and over and over again. And so Shari came over . . ."

"Yes?"

"She came over and . . ."

"*Shari?*" Jane whisper-shouts. "The one with the . . . ?" She taps on her upper lip.

"Oh it's not *that* visible. Wait, how do you know Shari?"

"I met Shari. Remember, when she came to Paris a few years ago to work on that film? You gave her my number. I had a coffee with her at the Flore. Can't remember a word of what we talked about because I kept getting distracted by the cappuccino foam hanging from her mustache."

"She does *not* have a mustache."

"She so does." Jane pauses. "You fucked *Shari*?"

Though Jane is whispering, and it's well past midnight, Jonathan looks over his shoulder anyway, fearful of prying ears. "I don't think I consciously thought we would actually go there, physically . . ."

"So what, it just *happened*?"

"Come on, Jane. Don't be naïve."

"I'm not being naïve."

"Yes, you are. And willfully at that."

"No, I'm not. I'm just . . . shocked. I mean, we're talking about you. You! The man I always hold up as the pinnacle of all that husband-kind can be. I'm sorry. I just need a few minutes to digest it, that's all."

"Look, I'm sorry for bursting your bubble, Janie. I know it was 'wrong.'" He makes air quotes around the word. "I mean, trust me, I know. But . . . well, Shari and I have known each other a long time. She's produced six of my films, we go way back. She had a boyfriend in LA at the time, too—they're married now, Mia and I actually went to the wedding a few years ago—but that night, I mean . . ." His voice trails off.

"That night what?" Jane hears the undertone of anger in her voice—anger toward Jonathan, toward Bruno, toward any neat and orderly surface masking an underbelly of chaos, desire, greed, hunger, need. Is nothing ever as it seems? (*Of course!* she answers herself. *Jonathan's right. I am being naïve. Good is never a shield against need.*) A laissez-faire attitude toward adultery, it strikes her, is the one European convention she has yet to assimilate. Hervé, she was certain, would have never cheated on her, under any circumstances, and this certainty created a sturdy hammock into which she sank and waited whenever he was on the road.

"I don't know, Janie. I mean, I know it's a bit of a cop-out to speak about sex in the passive tense, as if I had nothing to do with it, but it just kind of happened. She came into my room to watch the news on TV, and we were both sitting there on my bed, stunned, you know listening to Brokaw, channel surfing from CNN to MSNBC to Fox and back again, trying to make sense of all that sound and fury, which of course was impossible, and Shari knew a guy who worked in one of the towers, I mean, not well, but she knew him from college, or maybe high school, I can't remember exactly, and before you could say *step away from the curb,* I muted the TV—I just couldn't take another minute of those talking heads, no one had a flying fuck of an idea what was going on—and I hit the clock radio, and this gorgeous Mozart piece came on, I don't even know the name of it, but it was just one of those things that grabs you by the gut and won't let go, and we were holding hands and crying, lost in our own lonely bubbles, and then we were holding each other more intimately and crying, and then we were kissing, and then one thing led to another, and well, whatever. It all sounds so tawdry in the retelling, but . . ."

"Jesus."

". . . I still can't explain it other than to say it happened. I had sex with this woman who wasn't my wife, and I asked her to stay the night because I couldn't face sleeping alone, and the next morning, Shari was in the shower, and for a minute, before I remembered where I was or what I'd done, I assumed I was back in LA, and that Mia was the one in the shower, and when I finally came to and processed what had happened . . ." He trails off again, but this time Jane doesn't interrupt him. "Anyway, it ended as soon as it started. We didn't even really have to discuss it. I could just see it on Shari's face, when she came out of the bathroom, shivering a bit, with her towel wrapped really tightly around her, that she was feeling the same, so I turned my back to give her some privacy to get dressed. Symbolically, you know? As if to say, we're back to where we were before last night, and we sort of shook hands awkwardly before she left, but that felt kind of weird, too, so I kissed her one last time, you know, not passionately but tenderly I guess you'd call it, just to kind of put the proper punctuation mark on what had happened—because there was beauty in it, too, there really was, and it felt wrong to deny that aspect of it—and she kissed me back, and there were a few tears in her eyes, and I'm sure in my eyes, too, and neither of us have ever spoken about it since."

It takes Jane a few seconds to digest the story properly before speaking. "Not once?"

"Never. I mean, there was this one time we were both at the same dinner party, and this friend of ours was telling a story about where he was on 9/11—a boring story, about being stuck at the airport in Chicago, I don't even remember the details—but anyway, he was telling this uninteresting story of that night he spent at the airport, and Shari and I exchanged, you know, this brief glance, and then I had to stare at my arugula salad for a few seconds, just to regain composure, but there's been no intimate contact since, and I can't imagine there ever will be, and she still produces my films, and she remains my closest, most trusted colleague. 'My work wife,' Mia has always called her. Even before 9/11. And—here's the real kicker—though I feel a *little* guilty about what happened, and I was obviously worried what would happen if Mia ever found out, if I'm being really honest with myself, I don't regret it. When I think about it, which of course I wind up doing whenever that day is mentioned—I mean that's my cross to bear, I guess, cheating on my wife on the one day of our generation's lives that will go down in infamy—it feels like its own, I don't know, little pocket of craziness. But also like a pocket of tenderness, too. A crease in time, if you will, which, were I given the same set of circumstances again, even with the benefit of hindsight, I'm pretty sure I would still take exactly the same actions I took. I *needed* to have sex that night, Janie. To feel loved. It happened to have been with my producer, which in retrospect was really dumb and could have been a total disaster, both personally and professionally, but really? I'm pretty sure either of us would have schtupped anyone reasonably attractive, kind, and traumatized enough."

"Nice."

"You know what I mean."

"I'm not sure I do."

"You're not sure you know, or you're not sure you *want* to know?"

"The latter, I guess."

"Janie, all I'm saying? You were gone, both physically and mentally, for what? Six months while your mother was dying?"

"Seven."

"Fine, seven months. That's a long time to be checked out from life's hotel. That doesn't excuse Bruno's actions, but it does offer a decent explanation as to why he might have done what he did. And sending you that e-mail by accident? Stupid, definitely, as in really fucking dumb, and I'll kick his ass for it in August when I see him, assuming you guys are still coming down to Antibes again, but maybe it was also a subconscious plea on his part. Don't leave him just because he screwed up. Humans are fallible. You should know that from your work, but it also applies to everyday life."

"Jonathan," Jane says, feeling like a shipwrecked sailor on a jerry-rigged raft, "thank you for this conversation. I think. But I'm too tired to process all of this right now. I need some sleep." And with that, she stands up, gives Jonathan a chaste peck on his adulterous cheek, and heads for her late/gone/vanished mother's bedroom.

A couple of hours of tossing and turning later, Jane realizes she'll have to take advantage of either the three Ambiens left in her mother's stash or these *nuit blanche* hours, while everyone else is asleep, to conquer one or two of the myriad domestic tasks requiring her long-overdue attention.

She opts for the latter, yanking a moving box from the pile of thirty she'd purchased earlier that day, transforming it from two dimensions to three with the satisfyingly noisy thrust and rip of packing tape along its seams. She figures she'll start with the least personal, most chaotic room of the house—the attic—and steadily move downstairs through bathrooms, the garage, random cupboards, and bookshelves until she's left with disposing of the clothes in her mother's closet, an activity she's been anticipating and dreading since her mother's diagnosis. Lately, she's been fixated on the image of all those dresses, all those years and memories, languishing on wire hangers at the Salvation Army. The thought of it creates an instantaneous if short-lived paralysis, but she refuses to go down the same path her mother did during the months after her father died, handing out all of Harold Streeter's shirts and shoes to the fathers in the neighborhood unlucky enough to possess similar measurements. "Thanks so much, Claire; and thank *you*, Ngoc," they'd say, unsteadily, when Claire showed up on their doorstep that Sunday morning clutching her newly adopted Vietnamese daughter in one hand, a carefully curated bag of Harold in the other.

It was during this morbid outing that Jane decided to change her name from Ngoc—pronounced "Na" but mispronounced by every family visited, every teacher and kid in the Buckingham Browne & Nichols school by its phonetic parts, "Nuh-gock"—to something both easier to pronounce and modestly unpronounced. She settled on Jane when her mother, when asked to procure a list of single-syllable American names from which she might choose, explained that people often placed the word *plain* in front of Jane. "What does *plain* mean?" Jane—who would answer to Ngoc for only three and a half minutes more, and was still mastering the fine points of English—asked.

Claire, never one to miss an opportunity for a teachable moment, said, "Well, it means simple. Not fancy."

Fancy Jane knew from one of the stories Harold used to tell her before bed, about a fancy princess locked in a golden room who longed for a dress of sackcloth and an honest job scooping ice cream. Books about princesses who were "saved" by rich princes and showered with luxury goods were not exactly banned but rather omitted from the Streeter family bookshelves. Both Harold and Claire, the first female in her family to go to college and pursue a well-remunerated career, felt quite strongly that it was their parental duty to instill the idea of self-reliance and a healthy suspicion of consumerist society into their child. That's not to say Jane didn't check out such books from the library of her elementary school on the sly, once she figured out how to read and use a card catalogue, but rather that she approached such stories, even then, with a cultural critic's cold eye. "That's the name I want," she told her mother. "Jane."

"That's an excellent choice, Jane," said Claire, addressing the former Ngoc instantaneously by her newly adopted moniker, smiling wistfully at what Jane realizes now, only in retrospect, must have been her first true declaration of independence, a boulder that, once dislodged, would slowly gather steam (Claire must have realized, hence the tears that welled ever-so-slightly in the corners of her eyes) until it rolled away down life's rocky hill forever. "I'm sure Daddy would have loved it."

Six months after the clothing handoff, when a now ten-year-old, fully fluent, fully Americanized, fiercely independent and bookish Jane had yet to spot a single button-down shirt or pair of shoes belonging to her father on the back or feet of any of the Belmont fathers, she asked her mother why.

Claire, similarly disappointed—she'd given her neighbors too much credit, assuming they could move beyond the idea of wearing a dead man's oxford to enjoy the fine workmanship and soft cottons— would shrug her shoulders and say, "I guess maybe it's too sad for them, sweetie. But what a shame. They're such nice clothes. Practically new, most of them."

"Come on, Janie," Jane now says to herself, out loud, opening up a drawer to an old metal file cabinet tucked under the attic eaves, "let's do this."

The files, organized loosely by subject, are labeled almost exclusively in her mother's handwriting—all caps with a Sharpie—with the exception of a few lighter-colored manila folders with fraying tabs whose labels were manually typed, back in the day, onto now yellowing stickers. In one of these, double labeled first with NGOC, then overstickered with JANE, Jane finds her adoption papers; a random assortment of report cards (all As with the exception of one B, ironically in eleventh grade French); her inoculation records; summer camp bills; clippings of her *Boston Globe* articles dating back to her very first, a profile she filed from Clichy-sous-Bois, a Parisian *banlieue*, about an elderly Nigerian woman who had been performing back-alley genital mutilations of undocumented Muslim girls; and a single black-and-white snapshot of Harold and her on the American base in Saigon, circa early 1975, when she was eight, just a year older than her daughter Sophie is now. She turns over the photo and reads, in her father's handwriting, "My dearest Claire, Meet Ngoc, our new daughter," and suddenly she is there, on that American army base in Saigon, clutching her father's hand so tightly, Harold said, he actually had to pry her fingers from his whenever he needed to use them to, say, perform surgery or eat.

Jane can no longer remember what impulse, other than shock and animal instinct, triggered her young, bare feet to pivot away from Nha Trang after she came back from a quick afternoon dip in the bay to cool off and witnessed, through the doorframe of her rapidly incinerating house, the six other members of her family immobile, limbs akimbo, eyes blank, on the bloodstained dirt floor, but pivot they did, away from the stench of burning flesh, away from those pierced torsos, her home, that first chapter of her life, falling in step with an enormous stampede of others for what she only years later, as an adult visiting the embers of her past in an air-conditioned Citroën with Hervé, realized was a journey of 275 miles.

She cannot remember what or how she ate or drank during that stretch, although she must have done both, and she has only vague memories of sleeping in the open air at night, under the stars, because of an argument she had one night with another child, a slightly older boy who'd also lost the other members of his family, over whether the Big Dipper was actually God's ladle (his assertion) or just a random pattern in the sky (hers). Her one vivid memory from that in-between period takes the form of the baby white mouse she found and captured on the side of the road, naming him Bao, a common male surname, which, as her mother's colleague, a Freudian analyst of Vietnamese

descent, would years later point out, is also the word for "protection."
She would either hold the wriggling creature in her palm, stroking the
downy softness of his pulsing back as she pushed southward through
the plumes into the city, or, when Bao would fall asleep in her hand,
she'd place him in the large apron pocket on the front of her dress for
safekeeping until one morning, just before dawn, she reached down
for a quick snuggle and discovered he was gone. "My mouse!" she cried.
"Bao! He's escaped!"

Her grief, locked up for the eighty-odd hours that had passed since
she'd assimilated the grisly scene on the floor of her arsoned home,
began to leak, in tiny rivulets, out of her face. "Someone! Please! Help
me find Bao! He's gone! He's gone!" Both pleas and tears—their flow
increasing in intensity with each passing second—were ignored by her
fellow refugees with the exception of one, an older woman missing
several teeth and two fingers on her right hand, who'd shown what
Jane had assumed was an unusually compassionate interest in her pet.
"It couldn't be helped," the woman admitted, with a burp and a pat-
pat of her belly with the palm of her maimed hand.

A couple of years later, when Claire presented her with a gerbil as a
Christmas present, thinking it would help ease her daughter's distress
over Harold's untimely death, Jane made her mother take him back to
the pet shop. "I don't have time for pets," she lied, unable to explain
that she couldn't fall in love with another creature who would one day
die, since she didn't understand it herself.

Jane removes the photo of her and Harold from the JANE folder and
places it in a large manila envelope she labels TO KEEP with—ever her
mother's daughter—a Sharpie in all caps, picturing her daughter Sophie happening upon it years from now when it's her turn to complete
the same macabre task of mother erasure. No, she thinks, Sophie's old
enough, at seven, to see this now. To start hearing the basic outline of
her mother's story, to understand why traces of her beloved grandmother's blue eyes are nowhere to be found on either Jane's face or

hers. She promises herself she'll frame it, place it out on some surface of, well, wherever she'll be living come the fall.

The rest of the contents of the folder she tosses into the moving box, which she labels TO BE RECYCLED, before turning to a frayed file labeled HAROLD containing her father's death certificate, his army records, and the last passport he held before he died. She briefly considers keeping the passport before tossing it, along with the rest of the folder, into the box. No sentimentality, she rebukes herself. Be brutal and swift. If she's lived perfectly well without her father's old passport for the past twenty years of adulthood, she can live perfectly well without it for the next. And the next. And, if life's kind to her, the next.

An entire hour passes. Then another as Jane digs through the archaeological strata of her mother's life. She does not feel the movement of this time. It passes by so seamlessly that were someone to ask her to guess how many minutes have passed since she left her bed and opened the newest folder, a jackpot of unseen photos from that blissful summer vacation at the Waldmans' house in Nantucket in 1975, the same year she arrived in the States, she would have said fifteen to twenty at the most, in the same way a child looks at a birthday party jar full of jelly beans and guesses 43 instead of the actual 796.

One of the photos from that August in Nantucket shows Lodge and Kiki Waldman and their two boys, Nate and Jack, sitting on the back deck of their house, overlooking the ocean; in another, eight-year-old Jane, still known back then as Ngoc, holds the toddler Nate in her lap while Jack, who must have been around six or seven at the time, makes a silly face in the background; there are several gorgeous photos of her mother and Lodge, sitting at an outdoor table, smoking cigarettes together and laughing, all sparkly in the dusk light, as Kiki, her back to the camera, fixes a cocktail in the background. Harold, before going to medical school, had considered becoming a photojournalist, and the images, Jane notes, are particularly well composed, the sole exception being a low-angle photo of Harold's torso, his head cut off, which she must have taken herself.

Jane wonders whatever happened to the Waldmans, her parents' best friends when she arrived in the States. She remembers them coming over for dinner one night after that trip to Nantucket—she'd spun Jack around on the tire swing so fast he wound up throwing up his macaroni and cheese all over the backyard, which caused Kiki to scold her, she now recalls as if it were yesterday, unnecessarily harshly, even though it was Jack himself who'd yelled, "Faster! Faster!"—but after that she has no memory of the Waldmans, either in her home, or at her father's funeral, or during any family event thereafter.

How odd, too, she thinks, that these photos never made it into one of the dozens of carefully curated family photo albums, documenting every moment of her mother's existence from her undergraduate years at Wellesley, circa 1959, until 2003, the year Claire Streeter acquired her first digital camera and never made another photo album again. ("But you can just make them on iPhoto," Jane explained to her, "or do it on Snapfish or on any number of the online photo services," to which her mother said, with the familiar sigh of the technologically challenged, "Oh, Janie, it's all too complicated. Just send me some regular photos of Sophie every once in a while on photographic paper, please, when you get a chance, so I can stick them on the refrigerator.")

A dozen or so files later, in a simple manila folder labeled RANDOM—Jane's first clue that the contents would be anything but, as her mother was nothing if not thorough in her pursuit of order and organization—she stumbles upon the reason for the Waldmans' omission from the Streeter family pictorial history in the form of a yellowing carbon copy of a typed letter, signed by her mother and addressed to Lodge Waldman:

September 15, 1975

Dear Lodge,

It is with the requisite, clichéd heavy heart that I write you this letter and hope to have the courage to actually slip it under your

office door come Monday morning. It goes without saying that I
don't want Kiki or Harold to accidentally stumble upon it, and
I'm assuming you'll rip it up and toss it into the trash after
reading it (or, at the very least, please hide it well, as I plan on
hiding its carbon twin in the bowels of my file cabinet), but when
I imagined calling you on the phone or talking to you in person
to respond to your question, I realized that, simply by virtue of
hearing your voice or seeing your face, I wouldn't be able to be
as brave and resolute as this situation requires.

Let me start off by stating the obvious. I love you. I love you
so much that I feel it as a constant physical ache. I love you both
with the heart of a teenager and with the mind of a woman who
has finally lived long enough, after four decades of stumbling
around in what feels like the dark, to understand not only what
she needs in a mate but also what she desires. This past year of
stolen moments with you has been one of the most blissful,
intense, and transcendent years of my life. I literally don't know
how I would have survived Harold's deployment without you, and
I know, with near certainty, that when the light is fading from
my eyes (hopefully) many years from now, images of us and all
that we shared will sneak back in, breaking through the dikes of
the subconscious, as they do now nearly every hour I endure
without your physical presence. Oddly, I'm treating an elderly
patient at the moment with a terminal illness who, week after
week, laments not having left his wife for his lover decades
earlier, and the ripples from the broken record of his thought
processes, as you can imagine, have only served to jumble both
my own thought processes and my resolve.

That being said, I want to make the right decision here based
not on how I'll feel at the end of my life but on how I want to live
and conduct myself now.

So. The answer to your question, in my heart, is an
unadulterated (ironic word, I know) yes. Oh my God, yes,

nothing would make me happier than to marry you. But as we
both know, in our capacity both as humans and therapists, we do
not live in a vacuum. We live in a community. We have families.
We work down the hallway from one another and refer patients
to one another, for heaven's sake. ("Do not shit where you eat,"
a wise colleague once told me, back when she suspected—even
before I did—that my feelings for you were heading beyond the
platonic.) We have spouses who not only love us—yes, okay, each
in their own highly imperfect ways, no need to go over that for
the thousandth time—but who would be devastated by both the
breach of trust and by imagining us, for the rest of their lives,
in bed together. You have two young boys whose psyches, as you
well know, you would damage, either slightly or irreparably, but
you have no way of predicting the extent of that injury.

Yes, I know everyone and his cousin is getting divorced
these days. That it's lost its stigma, that it's "no big deal." But
regardless of the current cultural trend, I don't believe we have
enough case studies of the lasting impact of divorce on children
to treat it so cavalierly. I have to imagine that if we took the
plunge and got married, and I became your sons' stepmother,
that over time, as they matured and began to understand the
origins of our relationship—even if they somehow grew to love
me—they would certainly grow to hate me as well. How could
they not?

It's not that I don't believe in divorce when it's called for. I
frequently encourage my patients to walk down that road if
there is emotional or physical abuse, or if they finally come
to terms with their homosexuality. If my situation with
Harold were untenable, if your relationship with Kiki was
unsalvageable—which I don't think either one is—then all of this
would be much simpler. But we both know that sexual frigidity
in a woman can be treated, and one doesn't divorce one's
perfectly adequate if slightly emotionally aloof husband simply

because a better, more passionate, more compatible version
appears on the horizon. People aren't cars to be traded in and
up. They're people. With complex emotional inner lives and filial
ties and psyches that are far too easily bruised.

This brings me to what I'm assuming you understand is one
of the more salient factors for refusing your hand, namely our
beautiful new daughter Ngoc. I can't help but feel that Harold
must have sensed me pulling away after all those years of
trying and failing to conceive, that Ngoc was his olive branch,
his way of saying he was ready for a new chapter in our lives as
a couple. Remember that letter of his I showed you, where he
wrote about his delight at having been transformed overnight
"into the father I always knew I was capable of becoming" after
having met her? I remember your reaction to that letter. You
looked positively stricken, because you probably realized, as I
did, that her arrival spelled the end of us.

Lodge, I will always love you, of this I'm 100 percent certain,
but I never knew what it felt like to have my own family, to be a
mother, until Ngoc came into our lives. Yes, I know she's only
been here less than a year, but the three of us, our odd little
family unit, deserve a chance to move forward in space and
time intact, unencumbered. Meaning, the relative freedom I
once felt vis-à-vis abandoning my own marriage to be with you
has been usurped, and not in a bad way either. Just in a way I
could have never expected or predicted, back when we first
started making love and uttering the kind of sweetheart
promises to one another that each of us probably knew, in
the back of our love-addled minds, would be difficult if not
impossible to keep.

In the spirit of our changed reality, knowing how torturous it
would be for us to pass one another in the hallway every day, I
have found a new lease on an office in Somerville, close enough
to my old one that my patients won't be inconvenienced but far

enough from yours that I won't be tempted to spend another
lunch hour with you on your fold-out sofa. It's for the best,
Lodge, and I know, in time, you will grow to feel the same way.
Even if you hate me for it right now.

I wish I had two lives. Hell, I wish I had three! I'd marry you
in a heartbeat in both of those other lives, and I am certain that
those other two lives would be filled with more joy and light than
either of us could ever imagine. But we're only given this one
shot, my sweet, this one narrative thread to weave, and it's
time for the chapter on Claire and Lodge to come to a close. I
will leave it up to you as to whether or not the idea of further
communication between us feels helpful or harmful. On my end,
I'm pretty sure I can handle it, so long as we're never alone
together. I'd like to talk to you on the phone every once in a
while, to hear your voice and listen to your stories. I think we
might even be able to meet for the occasional lunch, on neutral
ground, in public, given enough time to get used to the absence
of intimacy. But again, I can't know how you'll feel after reading
this letter. Or how I'll feel without your warm and steady hand
at the small of my back. I don't believe in God, as you well know,
but that has not kept me from dropping to my knees these past
few weeks to beg him/her/whomever to please give me the
courage to do what I know must be done. I'm going to miss you:
your touch, your smile, your brilliant, beautiful mind. Jesus,
you should see the tears falling as I type this. It's like Niagara
Falls around here.

You will always be an integral part of me, Lodge. A place
apart, a secret compartment in my brain I will visit as often as
my heart can handle. And I will be forever grateful for the love
and time we shared.

All my love forever,
    Claire

Holy shit, Jane thinks, placing the damning letter in her TO KEEP envelope. *Et tu*, Mama? *Is nothing sacred?*

She wonders if she and Hervé, had he lived, would have been the last monogamous couple left on Earth. Hervé was gone constantly. Constantly! And when he wasn't off covering some war or insurrection, she was off reporting on its collateral damage, all those wandering refugees with no place to sleep, to eat, to shit, to fuck, and yet she'd never once taken advantage of the surreal conditions and psychological stresses of her job, or of the frequent separations from her husband, to seek out comfort in another, as isolated and unhinged by her work as she admittedly often felt, and as easy—so easy!—as it would have been to do so. How many times had she been propositioned by those lonely male colleagues of hers, beautiful specimens of human flesh, nearly all of them, in hotel bars after-hours? Too many times to count.

She looks at her watch. 4 A.M. Too late, too early, to contemplate her late mother's early love life. To imagine Jonathan sticking his empathic, traumatized dick into his producer. To picture Bruno caressing the freckled breasts of that Irish whore. She settles into an armchair, clutching the TO KEEP envelope to her chest, and falls into a desperate, fitful sleep.

Saturday, June 6, 2009

BENEDICTINE ROSE WATANABE. *Home Address:* 1530 Grizzly Peak, Berkeley, CA 94708 (510–865–3357). *Occupation and Office Address:* Vice president, Product Development, Google Inc., 1600 Amphitheatre Parkway, Mountain View, CA 94043. *E-mail:* Watanabe@google.com. *Graduate Degrees:* M.B.A. Stanford '94. *Spouse/Partner:* Katrina Zucherbrot, known professionally as Zeus (B.A., Brown '88; M.F.A., Yale '92). *Spouse/Partner Occupation:* Sculptor. *Children:* Lucien Artemis Watanabe-Zucherbrot, 2000; Dante Leopold Watanabe-Zucherbrot, 2000.

It's hard to believe it will have been twenty years since we graduated college when you read this. I've never been much of a writer, but I have worked at Google now long enough to know a little bit about search, so what I can't express myself, I'll just steal. Here are a few of the things I found, typing "passage of time" into our search engine.

"Time will reveal everything. It is a babbler, and speaks even when not asked." —Euripides

"It is the time you have wasted for your rose that makes your rose so important." —Antoine de Saint-Exupéry

"They always say that time changes things, but you actually have to change them yourself." —Andy Warhol

"What a long, strange trip it's been." —The Grateful Dead

I chose that first quote by Euripides because, thinking back on college, when I was just a young, newly out dyke with a crazy dream of future nuclear family normalcy but no role models to follow, I wondered how I would get there and who would join me. But now when I come home from work and see my partner at the stove, her work clothes caked in plaster of Paris, and the boys sitting at the dining room table, doing their homework and gig-gling, well, time has revealed everything. I have my own version of that nuclear family dream, despite all the naysayers who told me it couldn't be done. Shouldn't be done. And guess what? It's better than I expected. Is it paradise? Of course not. We've all lived long enough now to know nothing is. But it comes close.

As for time wasted on my roses, I like to think I have several roses: my boys, my relationship with my partner, and my career. (Can you tell I'm an ace at PowerPoint?) These are the three main things I've been cultivating over the past two decades, and it's only now, looking back, that I'm able to see that it's the time spent watering these roses, the years of memories and history, that mat-ter in the end. As I wrote in our Fifteenth Report, Katrina and I decided to get pregnant at the same time, using sperm from each other's brothers, so we could raise our children like fraternal twins. Short term, when the boys were babies born three weeks apart, this was a lot harder than we expected, but long term, now that they're nearly ten years old, it feels like we made the right decision. Lucien and Dante are extremely close, both as brothers (technically cousins) and as friends, and their male pair combined with our female one has felt very balanced, family-wise, for lack of a better word. The boys' uncles/fathers are also in the picture, one of whom (my brother) is an A's fan who enjoys taking them to the ballpark, etc., with his wife and kids, the other (Katrina's brother) who takes them for a week every summer to help out on his farm in Oderbruch, a rural area southeast of Berlin, near the German/Polish border, where he works and lives with his wife, six kids, and God knows how many animals, we've lost count. We felt this was important, for them to have male role models in their lives, and very different ones at that. As for Katrina and me, well, we *feel* married, even though Proposition 8 just passed in Califor-nia, meaning the wedding we had in Provincetown, back in 2004, when Massachusetts first sanctioned gay marriage, does not count in our state of residence. (Try explaining *that* to your sons, who were the ring bearers.)

Which brings me both to my third rose, my career, and Andy Warhol's quote. As many of you know, I joined Google when it was still a tiny company with a great motto—"Don't be evil"— hoping to change the world. For many years, I think we stuck to this core principle, and we did change the world. We did! I will always be proud of the work I did and continue to do there. But now both the company and I have matured, and there are some days I wonder if a large corporation is ever capable of adhering to utopian ideals. Plus, let's face it, I've grown tired of the long commute from Berkeley to Mountain View, and I don't want to move our family to shorten it. Berkeley, being Berkeley, has been an unbelievable home for us, a place where families like ours are not only accepted but also celebrated. Our sons' school even has a gay pride day. All the kids come to school wearing rainbows or homemade T-shirts with things like MY FRIEND DANTE HAS TWO MOMMIES, AND THAT'S COOL. 'Nuff said.

So last week, fueled by my disappointment (or you could call it rage) over the passage of Proposition 8, I announced to my colleagues that I've decided to resign from Google at the end of 2009 to focus on changing what time refuses to change on its own: namely, the right for gay Americans to get married. To that end, I'll be starting a foundation, which I've decided to call Out and Out, whose mission will be twofold: (1) We will have an outreach program for teenagers, in which we will send gay families into middle and high schools to give lectures during assemblies in order to show, by direct example, that gay families are just like so-called normal families. We will also offer free counseling and college scholarships to bullied gay teens. (2) We will raise as much money as we can to lobby whomever we can, from local politicians all the way up to the White House, to create a national law granting gay couples the right to marry. We will also show our support, in the form of campaign contributions and volunteer manpower, to whichever candidates choose to run on a pro-gay-marriage platform. Suffice it to say, any of you who feel passionate about such topics and live in the Bay Area, hit me up. I'm going to need all the help I can get, and yes, a few of the positions will be salaried and include health insurance.

Which brings me to my last quote, even though I only had the pleasure of attending that one Dead show in Worcester back in 1987: It truly has been a long, strange trip. But now, with my chips cashed in, I can't wait to keep on truckin'.

5

Morning

Addison lies awake on the floor of her jail cell, her arms shackled, her bare back sweating against the plastic ticking of a thin foam mattress, whose sheets and bed frame were removed the previous night when it was determined that inmate #462879 needed to be placed on suicide watch. "I'm not suicidal!" she'd cried to the young female officer, fresh out of police academy, who'd made the determination, based on both the duration of Addison's tears and on paragraph 72A in the incarceration guidelines stating that, should an inmate cry for a period of time equal to or greater than ninety minutes, a suicide watch could, at the discretion of the corrections officer, be instituted. Once instituted, such a watch required that the inmates' arms be bound with chains and that any object with the potential to be used for auto-asphyxiation in the cell itself, or on or in the prisoner's body—including sheets, clothing, shoelaces, and tampons—be removed.

"I'm not saying you are suicidal, ma'am," said the officer. "I'm just following protocol."

"Oh, come on!" said Addison. "I'm just upset! Can you please try to understand that? I'm in here because of parking tickets. Parking tickets, for Christ's sake!" She leaves off the part about her family's financial crisis, a turn of events—relayed to her by Gunner last night, during the five minutes she was allowed to see him—that has triggered an arrhythmia in her heart so palpable she can feel the syncopation. How the hell will they survive? "You'd cry, too, if you were thrown into jail for goddamned parking tickets!"

"No, ma'am, I wouldn't," the young officer replied, still young and green enough to be filled with strong ideals and good intentions, "because I would have paid my parking tickets."

"Can I at least have one tampon? Just one!"

"No, ma'am, I'm sorry. You can't. Those are the rules. And rules are meant to be followed."

"Oh, to hell with your stupid rules!" Addison said.

Now, lying here, practically nude but for the shackles, which are digging into both her wrists and psyche in equal measure; feeling warm blood leaking between her thighs onto the government-issued paper gown she was forced to trade for her clothes, which she fashioned instead into a makeshift sanitary pad, she reconsiders this ingrained response. Perhaps a to-hell-with-your-stupid-rules attitude may not be the most prudent way to lead the second half of one's life. Or the first.

She'd always taught her children to think independently, to question authority. When Trilby had refused to take a spelling test in sixth grade, on the grounds that spelling was becoming unnecessary in a spellcheck world, she'd secretly beamed when she and Gunner were called in for a parent-teacher conference to discuss the matter. It was decided, by all parties involved, that Trilby could do an independent study on Greek mythology while the rest of the class toiled over their *their/there/they're*'s. But with Gunner's parents no longer able to foot the $108,000 a year bill for her three children's private education (and fuck those greedy fund managers, she thinks, unable to make the connection between their law-breaking and hers), this kind of creative rule-bending will become a thing of the past. New York City public schools will never put up with such nonsense. And, truth be told, Trilby's spelling is atrocious.

How, she wonders, will she even get Trilby into a public high school at this point? The nonspecialized one in their neighborhood is deplorable. Not to mention dangerous. She wonders if she can convince St. Paul's to cough up a dollop of emergency financial aid, even though she and Gunner own a $2.5 million apartment. Probably not.

Maybe she can take out a home equity loan to pay for school. But then how will she pay it back? How do people who don't have family help deal with this stuff? What kind of job could she even get at this point in her life? The whole thing spins her head.

"Ma'am," she hears. The voice has a southern twang. "Um, ma'am?"

Addison sits up, her arms crossed over her bare chest, to face a new cop who must be just starting her morning shift. "Yes?" she says.

"Ma'am, you're free to go. This woman just came in and paid your fines."

"You're kidding me." But who? she wonders. She dismisses Jane out of hand. Clover's still out of a job and worried about cash flow, so it can't be her. Which means it has to be Mia. Amazing, considering their somewhat rocky history. Jonathan must be doing better than she thought. She wonders how she'll pay them back. She imagines painting some massive piece to hang over their couch in LA. Lots of bright yellows and dark greens, echoing the lemon trees in her yard; then a slightly smaller canvas with muted grape and fig tones for their house in Antibes. Canvases that large and paints to cover them will be expensive, now that they're broke, but maybe Mia's wealthy friends will see her paintings and want one of their own. Maybe, Addison thinks, this is just the kick in the pants she needs. Didn't Mia once tell her that one of the mothers in her son's school was on the board of the Getty? Her brain races with the possibilities.

"Ma'am, I don't joke about such things." The cop opens the door and hands Addison a robe. "Here are your personal effects. I've given you a Tampax as well. You can go ahead and get dressed in the ladies'."

"But wait, wasn't there supposed to be a bail hearing this morning?" Addison wonders how a southern girl grows up to be a northern cop. How does anyone grow up to be anything? She tries to imagine herself cruising the streets of Boston in a black and white sedan, hunting down suspects, fighting crime. That wouldn't be so bad, as jobs go, she thinks. Except for the gun part. But the being-outside-in-the-world part? The breaking up domestic spats and arriving at the scene of the accident and busting down the drug dealer's door and following up leads and turning on the siren while *legally* speeding through red lights, all of that sounded kind of interesting, even thrilling. Theoretically.

She wonders how long it takes to get through cop school. Couldn't be more than two years, right? How crazy would that be, Addison Hunt, a cop? Yeah, maybe too crazy. Although she did once share a beer with that guy from Dunster House, the one a couple of years older than her who became a cop after Harvard and wrote that HBO series based on his experiences. Maybe she could become a cop for a few years and then paint a whole series of crime-inspired canvases.

Nah. Who's she kidding?

It pains her that she has never followed through on a single one of her (often seemingly) inspired ideas. How do people live?

"The judge said that since the fines were paid, and you have no priors, you're free to go."

"You're kidding me."

"Ma'am, like I said, I don't joke about such things. You're very lucky, I will tell you that."

"I guess that depends on your definition of luck."

The cop can barely contain her contempt for Addison's apparent lack of understanding that six-figure fines don't usually just get paid by most inmates' friends' AmEx Titaniums. "I guess it does."

"Is Mia still out there?"

"Who?"

"Mia Zane? The woman who paid my fines?"

"Ma'am, the woman who paid your fines goes by the name of Bennie. With some sort of Asian last name. At least that's what it said on the fancy piece of plastic she just gave me."

"Watanabe?" Addison gulps. Holy shit. Bennie? How'd she even find out about this?

"Yep, that's it. She's out there, waiting for you. Said she'll drive you wherever you need to go."

"Oh my God." She can't decide which is more impressive: Bennie

Watanabe's sudden reappearance in her life, her payment of the fines, or the fact that a credit card exists that can swipe through a hundred grand without blinking. Maybe she should go work for Google.

Not that she knows the first thing about the tech industry.

How do people *live*?

Ten minutes later, Addison is standing in the now empty waiting room at the police station with her head buried in Bennie's shoulder, soaking it.

"I always knew you were a bit of a rebel, babes," says Bennie, smoothing Addison's hair, holding her trembling body, trying to make her laugh, "but this is really taking it a step too far." When Addison's initial deluge finally gives way to calmer tremors, Bennie pulls back from the embrace and grasps her ex's slender biceps with her own arms parallel to the ground, like a parent examining a fallen toddler for bruises. "Look at you. I can't believe it."

"That bad, huh?" Addison smiles through trembling lips. Stares into Bennie's once-familiar brown eyes, which have survived the twenty-plus years since they were focused on Addison's with barely a furrow and still trigger that same snippet of Van Morrison. That's not to say her former brown-eyed girl hasn't physically aged or that her temples have remained unlined, but that where once, at nineteen, tiny Bennie could still pass for a middle schooler, now, at forty-two, she has the still-smooth skin and slight, tight frame of a woman in her early-to-mid thirties. By comparison, thinks Addison, especially after the night she just braved, she must look like death.

"I won't lie," says Bennie, who esteems honesty over all other human attributes aside from a diligence in delivering food to the bereaved. "I've seen you look better."

"Yeah, well, I guess a night spent shackled in the nude on suicide watch in a jail cell will do that to you," says Addison, still trying to wrap her head around too many elements of the past twenty-four hours, none more astounding than the fact that she and Bennie are standing face-to-face: the collapsing of two decades, like a slo-mo clip of an imploding building in reverse, in the blink of a brown eye. Followed in a close second by what she can only call a chemical reawakening. As if she even needed physical proof of the feelings she's been pushing down, willfully, for years. As if it were even possible to not feel something forever by mentally willing it from surfacing.

"You feel like talking about it?" says Bennie.

No trace of the anger Bennie hurled at her during their breakup remains. "Good lord," says Addison. "I feel like talking about a lot of things. So many. You got time?"

"Loads of it. I told Katrina I'd be back in an hour or so, but she took the kids out to breakfast at Au Bon Pain, and then they were going to head over to the Coop to buy sweatshirts, so we're good. I've got as long as you need."

"Bennie, why are you being so nice to me? I mean, I'm not just talking about paying my *absurd* fine—which I will pay back, I promise—and coming here and—"

"Addison! Are you kidding me? I loved you once. That stuff doesn't just go away. No matter how many years have passed."

"But I was such a bitch to you at the end."

"That you were." Bennie says this as a statement of fact, without judgment. "Ads, we were practically still kids. Babies!"

"It's been a long time, hasn't it?"

"Forever. Come on. Let's get out of this hellhole. I'll buy you a coffee."

"No way. At least let me buy you a coffee." Addison wonders, once again, how she'll ever pay Bennie back. A hundred grand. The number is staggering.

"Fine. Your treat. There's gotta be a Starbucks around here somewhere."

Sure enough, within minutes of leaving the police station in Bennie's Zipcar Prius, the two spot the ubiquitous green medallion with the black and white lady—shit, thinks Addison, I had that idea to start a bunch of coffee bars in the U.S. after Gunner and I came back to the States in 1990, why didn't I just do it?—and now Addison and Bennie are sitting at a corner table, the former nursing a lightly sweetened venti latte, with whole milk, the latter a grande shaken green tea, unsweetened. "Talk to me, Ad," says Bennie. "What's going on? I mean, aside from you being arrested for parking tickets."

Addison smiles and half-laughs, but she suddenly feels nauseated. She's jittery from the coffee on top of a sleepless night, no doubt, but also from the flash of insight she's having at this very minute, triggered by Bennie's presence. No, not that she wants Bennie, although it's the wanting that has flipped on the light. It's more that she has suddenly become brutally aware that she's been living, on nearly every front, a twenty-year lie.

"In all honesty?" Addison pauses, trying to figure out what an honest, Bennie-worthy answer to *What's going on?* might be. Twenty years ago, on her graduation day from a school whose very motto, Veritas, demanded truth, she would have written down, had she been asked to compose a laundry list of everything she wanted out of life, exactly what she currently has: three children; an enviably still-handsome husband; a sunlit home in a hip New York neighborhood; a community of friends who share her moral, aesthetic, and political outlook; the time and space to paint; enough money to get by. And that would have been as close to the truth as she then was able to process it, with her ignorance of adulthood's realities. But now that the enough-money-to-get-by part has been savagely torn from the Hunt/Griswold family portrait, its absence has revealed the more profound deficiencies and fissures of the line items left off her imaginary list, for lack of any prior mature grasp of their importance: love; passion; a desire to fuck her spouse. Without these, she thinks, the externalities not only don't matter, they are an indictment.

A short snippet from a Shakespeare sonnet she studied in English 10 flutters down from its storage branch and settles on the sidewalk of Addison's conscious thought: "Love is not love/Which alters when it alteration finds,/Or bends with the remover to remove." If nothing else, Harvard had been good for that: for stuffing the brain full of beautiful words, apt phrases, to be plucked out of the larder and thawed, decades later, as needed.

The family portrait she carries around as her iPhone's wallpaper suddenly turns, in her head, from vibrant color to a somber, grainy black and white. She has brought up three children, she thinks, by herself, in a mostly sexless, often-bickering household. The enviably still good-looking husband might turn others on—and she sees it, she does, whenever she and Gunner are walking down Bedford Avenue together on a Saturday afternoon, the way her husband still elicits longing stares from both the tattooed women and the slouchy men—but he does not turn her on, and maybe he never really did. Maybe only the idea of him did.

She thinks back to the start of their relationship, meeting up again at that taverna in Eressos, how the very rightness of their union—same background, same prep school, same well-scrubbed, flinty good looks, plus they'd deflowered each other at seventeen, so it made for a good story—had tipped them over into an ideation of couplehood. They had mythologized their origin story from its inception (high school sweethearts, the chance meeting, rekindled love) to the point where now, two decades later, it only made for compelling fiction, if barely.

She suddenly feels a strange wave of compassion for Gunner's writer's block: how impossible it must be to write the truth when both your own life and your sole published novel have been constructed on a scaffolding of half-truths and self-deception. From the small bits she's managed to gather, his new novel is supposed to be a modern meditation on the new frontiers of fatherhood and marriage in a post-feminist world. At least that's what he's told his editor, who gave up years ago on asking to see a manuscript, even a partial one. Gunner keeps claiming he has a good chunk of it done, but Addison wonders how he's managed to bang out a single word. Because when you outsource all of your parenting responsibilities to your wife and the household help, how much can you really know about fatherhood? And without sex, what's left of marriage?

"I don't know what's going on," she tells Bennie, a single tear leaving its streak on her cheekbone. "I suddenly feel like I'm disintegrating." For this is as close to the truth, for now, on this glorious June morning, as she is able to verbalize.

. . .

Trilby wakes up uncharacteristically early and slips into the home office in Jane's dead mother's house to log on to Facebook and check out what her friends are saying about last night's show at Pete's Candy Store. She opens Firefox, types *f-a-c-e* and sees that someone else in the house has been checking his page without logging out: Jonathan, Mia's husband, that old guy with the young sneakers. "Jonathan Zane is Cambridge bound" his update reads, underneath which runs a list of equally boring, old people chatter: *Lauren Green is yanking out the weeds and thinking about baking a rhubarb pie; Zach Frankel's four-year-old, after being apprised of the Big Dipper's existence, wanted to know where God keeps his forks and knives; Elaine Cutbill is OMG, Madmen marathon!; David Zelnick pulled out his back again, reaching for the Advil.*

Jesus, she thinks. If that's the kind of boring crap she has to look forward to as an adult, then no thank you. She wonders if there is an exact moment in life when they make you stop having fun or whether it's a more gradual slide into pie crusts, toddlers, TV, and Ibuprofen. She clicks on the message folder and quickly skims through a bunch of boring exchanges: people congratulating Jonathan on Zoe's birth; a fan, who grew up in Brooklyn, writing to say how much she loved *Jack and Jill in Clinton Hill*; a two-sentence missive from Max, saying, *You know I love you, Dad, but please stop commenting on my photos. It's kind of a buzzkill.* To shake things up, Trilby types *loves me some underage poontang* into Jonathan's status update, hits "return," and logs on to her own newsfeed.

Seven—seven!—of her friends had been to the show she missed.

Dismembered Feeeeeeeeeeeeeetussssss!, wrote her friend Maya. *epiccccc*, wrote Isadora. *Yo, I'm five feet from mad drummer Max Mattis, hit me up*, wrote her best friend, Jackson, under which his friend Christopher had commented *behind you, bro, ten o'clock.*

Trilby feels a new rush of fury and indignation. What right did her mother have to keep her from the most important event of her entire life? Dismembered Fetus! At an intimate venue *around the corner from her fucking apartment.* And she, fourteen years old and the proud owner of a new pair of breasts, which finally emerged from their excruciatingly long hibernation like slow-cooked Jiffy Pop to the point where they could now be expertly encased and cantilevered at a ninety-degree angle from the rest of her, thanks to the new Victoria's Secret push-up bra (black, lace) she bought with the money her mother gave her for a school trip to the tenement museum. Never again, she thinks, will the stars align so perfectly: Dismembered Fetus, Pete's Candy Store, the end of eighth grade, new tits. It would have been so easy for her to have stayed behind in Brooklyn at Maya's, instead of coming here to this boring fucking Harvard crapola memory-lane bullshit festival of oldsters with their moobs and back fat, trying to recapture what was once theirs but now, rightfully, hers. Or at least it should have been hers if her lame-ass mother hadn't insisted on dragging the whole frigging family here with her.

Trilby suddenly remembers that Addison spent the night in jail and feels a slight tinge of remorse. Her father had woken her up when he and Mia came home from the police station to promise he'd get her mother out this morning. But she knows her dad's promises. They're always loose interpretations of the word, like the time he promised her they'd go skiing at Mohonk, just the two of them on a special father/daughter bonding trip, but then he suddenly had an epiphany about his male protagonist, whom he realized would never take his daughter skiing, so for verisimilitude's sake, they stayed home. That being said, Mia is in on this one, and Mia (or so her mother once told her, in so many less-than-flattering words) is the official, responsible den mother of the group, so there's hope.

Trilby harbors more than passing jealousy of the Zane boys for growing up in a home with real adults as parents, the kind who always get the school medical forms in on time and don't sneak off to smoke pot on the balcony when they think their kids are already asleep. She wonders how different her life could have been with mandatory family meals, limits on television viewing, ironed underwear, organic smoothies, Christmas soup kitchen duties, chore charts, hot breakfasts. The Zane boys are definitely on the nerdier side of the people she calls friends, but they also don't seem as plagued with the same bouts of nihilism and depression into which she and many of these friends have recently found themselves plunging, like quicksand or tar.

Last night, for example, she nearly cried watching a seventeen-year-old Max Zane reading *Le Petit Prince* to Jane's seven-year-old, Sophie. She could see, as if in time-lapse photography, the entire arc of his fatherhood stretching before him, just in the comic inflection of his "Draw me a sheep!" Those lucky kids, she thought, hearing Sophie's giggles, choking back a surprising burst of tears. They'll never have to wonder whether their father's attention is motivated less by love than by a need to experience a situation—the reading of Saint-Exupéry to a child, Daddies 'n' Donuts Day at a child's kindergarten (during which her own father took notes—notes!—in his Moleskine instead of scarfing down the crappy donut holes like everyone else)—in order to write about it.

Hopefully, she thinks, imagining the kind of woman Max might one day marry, his children will also never have to watch their mother get taken away in handcuffs. She briefly considers writing something like, *OMG my mother spent the night in jaillllllll!!!!* in her status update but then realizes that'll take too much explaining, and really, who has time? It's pretty punk, she has to admit, but it's also totally embarrassing.

anyone in cambridge hit me up, she types into the status rectangle instead, fairly certain she'll get no response. But then, miracle of miracles, her friend Linus Angstrom from sailing camp in Maine writes, *nooooo waaaaaaaaaayyyyyyyy!* underneath it, and her chat window pops open.

u here in cambridge?

yep. mom's 20th reunion. fml

harvard lesley mit or tufts?

harvard

omg went to my dad's 25th last year.
so fucking boring

ikr

except for the moon bounce

lolz

moon bounces rock
u around tonight?

idk y?

cuz some friends and me r going
to the vaginal discharge show at
the roxy

omg i love vaginal discharge!!!!!!!

who doesn't?

hahahaha
i was supposed to see dismembered
fetus last night in brooklyn but obviously
i couldn't :(

omg, that sucks . . . come tonight tho

what about tix?

no problem, we can scalp

oh shit
wait
i said i'd help babysit . . . fuckkkkkkkk!!!!

the show's not til 10
just sneak out my brother can drive us

rly? he got his license?

yup

omg i want to go so bad

so come!

ok i will. so where shud we meet?
what time?

um, wait, lemme ask

kk

9, in front of the coop

where's that?

harvard square

im in belmont. is that far?

kind of
wait lemme ask my bro
if we can pick u up
he says if u r hot yes

ummmmmm . . . .

hahahaha jk whats the address?

idk ill find out and inbox u

cool

wait
how much are tix?

> $65 i think, but maybe more for scalped ones
> bring $100 to be safe

 ok

> c ya tonight!!!!!!

Trilby feels an intense internal quickening at the thought of the evening's plan, her lack of funds, and Finn Angstrom, Linus's older brother, whom she'd heard had gone all the way with Allison, their twenty-year-old sailing instructor, but that could have just been a rumor, you never know, although everything about the story when she heard it sounded completely plausible except for the part about the boat wax. Her planned escape seems relatively foolproof—the few times she ever babysat, not one of her young charges had ever woken up after she put them to bed—but how will she find $100 in cash to buy tickets? Trilby doesn't need to check her purse to know she has only a five-dollar bill and a one-dollar bill crumpled up in the bottom. And obviously she can't ask her parents.

Just then, like manna from heaven, she spots a thick wallet on the desk next to the computer. She opens it and pulls out the driver's license. Jonathan Zane. Ha! she thinks. He was probably shopping online or purchasing porn or something and needed his credit card number and forgot he left it here. She counts the bills, all of them—with the exception of three twenty-dollar bills and four singles—bearing the likeness of Benjamin Franklin. Twelve hundred-dollar bills? Who the fuck carries around $1,200 in cash? Then she remembers Jonathan and Mia's house in Antibes, where her family stayed two summers ago, and realizes people like Jonathan and Mia must carry around $1,200 cash without even blinking. Which means, in all likelihood, they won't miss a bill here or there. The mother of one of her friends from St. Ann's was bilked of nearly $47,000 before realizing that the nanny, who had access to the family bank card and pass code, had an overly generous interpretation of "take out whatever you need for groceries, cleaning supplies, and taxis." She can't imagine the Zanes would be any different.

She snatches a single Ben Franklin and slips it into the pocket of her pajamas. Then, reconsidering, she steals one more Ben and an Andrew Jackson, just to be safe.

．．．

Clover lies in a tangle of Egyptian cotton sheets and sticky thighs, staring at a zit that has come to a head on Bucky Gardner's back, which rises and falls with his exhalations. If it were Danny's, she'd just pop it.

At the unintentional conjuring of her beloved, she's pierced by a small but sharp stab of guilt and remorse, until she reminds herself that what happened last night with Bucky must be psychically processed, forever, within the context of fertility, not fidelity. Yes, technically she broke one of the more central marital vows, but she consoles herself with the thought that she did not do so in pursuit of carnal pleasure or out of boredom or with malicious intent but rather with the most lofty intentions possible. Danny has always said he'd be perfectly willing to adopt a baby, or even an older kid who was already fully formed but in need of a home, while Clover feels (admittedly selfishly, but one has to be honest with oneself) that she can only marshal the patience required to parent a child born of her own seed and womb. She wants to experience pregnancy, birth, the whole nine yards and months. Is that too much to ask?

No, she answers herself, it is not, Danny's feelings on the matter— yes to adoption, no to donated sperm, because what kind of freak donates sperm, he asks, huh?—notwithstanding.

In a sense, if it works, her plan will embody, literally, the perfect compromise between her desires and her husband's: The baby will be formed from her egg; it will look like a close-enough fusion of her and Danny—Bucky's doppelganger, everyone says so—that no one will ever question its paternity; she and Danny just had sex two days earlier, so she's covered on the temporal front; Bucky's sperm cannot technically be considered "donated"; and yet, should the truth of the child's genetic makeup ever come to light (she imagines bone marrow transplants, car accidents requiring blood transfusions, oh my God so many things can go wrong with a child, how do people bear it?), it shouldn't theoretically bother a vehemently proadoption Danny that he'd been unwittingly lavishing his time and resources toward the raising of a child that did not share a single nucleic thread of his DNA.

Wasn't that what marriage was all about anyway? Compromise? Yes, okay, so usually both parties are privy to the compromises being made, and extramarital sex, generally speaking, doesn't exactly fall under the umbrella of reasonable give-and-take, but in this instance, she decides, ignorance is not only bliss, it's a necessary element for the plan to succeed.

Plus, she rationalizes, in the way all people engaging in morally ambiguous activities must do—her former colleagues at Lehman ("We're bolstering the economy . . ."); prostitutes ("My kids have to eat . . .")—should the previous night's carefully calculated coupling result in an actual human, it would symbolically redress the uncalculated carelessness of Clover and Bucky's past: the almost child who was nearly theirs. Who would have today been twenty-four and most likely fucked-up in some profound, intractable way, just by virtue of illegitimate birth into the Gardner clan.

She crosses herself and gives thanks to the holy trinity of Roe, the Supreme Court, and the Harvard University Health Services.

Out of habit, she has been buying and peeing on ovulation test sticks every month, without fail since her wedding, for seven-day stretches during the most fertile week of her cycle. Yesterday morning's window had the darkest pink line of all, meaning her LH level was at its peak, meaning if ever the blessed event were to happen, it would be happening right now. Bucky has four children, in addition to the one she and he could have had together back in college, along with another cellular mass she'd heard had been eliminated from another uterus their junior year, formed from sperm that was, at least back in the day, potent enough to find its way around both the spermicide and the diaphragm worn by that girl from Lesley College.

The plumbing, in other words, works not only well but spectacularly so. (A kind of Supersperm, Clover thinks: faster than a seeping condom, able to leap small diaphragms in a single bound . . .) And though Danny still hasn't worked up the fortitude to ejaculate into a specimen cup—how dare he, she thinks, growing suddenly furious and self-justifying at his willful inaction—both Clover and her fertility doctor are certain it is Danny's sperm count, or lack thereof, that is the missing ingredient in their baby batter.

"Your eggs are still good," said Dr. Seligman, on more than one occasion. "But until we get a specimen from Danny, we don't have the whole picture."

She tries to envision the internal division of cells, mentally goading the mitosis projected in her mind's eye into actual existence: 2, 4, 8, 16, 32, 64, 128, 256, so baffling and miraculous, those first few hours of life! No question, she mourned that amorphous, eight-week-old Clover/Bucky blastula way back when, even though she firmly believed both in her right not to play host to it and in its right not to be born to an immature mother and father.

Ironic, really, that the one responsibility she knows she could have never assumed back then—and she's had no doubts, ever, that she made the right decision at the time to push off motherhood until she had the means and mental wherewithal to do so—is now the sole role she is desperate to play.

She and Bucky should probably have one more go of it, she thinks, just to be certain.

She kisses the back of his neck, which smells of sour sweat and gin.

An old man's odor, the kind that permeated the wood-paneled library where she once met Bucky's father, and he was unable to hide his shock at the caramel-colored sight of her.

"Hey there, Pace," Bucky says, waking, turning, smiling. "Jesus. Look at you." He touches her face then pulls down the sheets to uncover the dark areolas of her breasts, whose centers immediately rigidify the minute they make contact with the cool air and Bucky's gaze. It always amazed him, he once told Clover, the different sizes, shapes, and colors an erect nipple could take. It had made her self-conscious at first, knowing from the random locker-room subset to which she'd been privy how hyperelongated and dark hers were when erect, in comparison to others, but then Bucky had added the delicious addendum that her nipples, once touched, were the most beautiful peaks he'd ever scaled. "Holy shit, just *look at you*. They lied, you know."

"Who lied?"

"All those people who said it's inner beauty that counts, not outer. You wouldn't understand. You still look like a . . . oh, man, like a friggin' gazelle. But I know how I was treated way back when, versus how I'm treated now, as a much nicer, homelier old fart, and I tell you, life is easier for the physically blessed. It just is."

Clover agrees with this but won't cop to it, as she wishes it weren't true while simultaneously understanding, from personal experience, that it is true, not to mention that admitting it would be the equivalent of praising her own beauty. There's a viral video, "Pretty," that keeps popping up in her Facebook feed every couple of months, posted by female friends, most of them with daughters, featuring a poet who is furious at her mother for making her get a nose job in her teens. The poet then extrapolates from her own personal experience with the pain of beauty and the indignity of maternal coercion and applies it to a universal disdain for all forms of beauty, claiming she wishes for anything *but* beauty for her future daughter, which Clover finds disingenuous at best, hypocritical at worse. All other things being equal—intelligence, creativity, the ability to love, a zest for life—why wouldn't a mother want her child to be blessed with physical attractiveness as well, when study after study has shown that prettier people command higher pay, are given greater respect, feel more joy, and achieve more quantifiable success in life, not to mention having a larger population of potential mates from which to choose? But she doesn't say any of this to Bucky right now. She knows he just wants to be reassured that he's still worthy of love, despite having lost the luster of his outer plumage. "Oh, Bucky. First of all, you're not homely. You've just aged a bit, that's all."

"I'm not fishing for—"

She cuts him off. "Second, we're all going to be ugly, old ducklings soon enough. But thank you for the compliment anyway. I didn't mean to step on it."

"No worries, but I don't buy it. You'll always be a swan. Seriously, Pace, you're going to be one of those old ladies whose eyes light up a friggin' room. My grandmother was like that, I know." He lies on his back now and stares up at the ceiling, his expression pinched, pained. "Why did I . . . I mean, Jesus, can you imagine how great we could have been together? What the fuck were we thinking?"

We? Clover thinks. She doesn't remember having had any say in the decision. It was just handed to her like the Christmas presents Mrs. Gardner offered to everyone gathered around that tree except her. She shrugs. "Don't even go there. It's useless. And we were right to break it off. It would never have worked. Your family would have shunned me, and I would have crumbled under the strain of trying to please them, and, worst of all, I would have never made my own way in the world." Plus, she thinks, but does not say out loud, there was that whole other issue, which she only understood in retrospect, while in bed with her next lover—an expert, avid, hungry practitioner of clitoral stimulation— of Bucky's lack of aptitude in that department, something he's clearly worked on in the interim with, she has to admit, a decent degree of success, though she faked last night's orgasm in the name of guilt re-duction. Procreation she could allow herself; recreation she could not.

"Yeah, maybe," he says. "I don't know."

His expression is so open and vulnerable, so steeped with regret that Clover feels a simultaneous rush of pity, lust, nostalgia, and something approximating the chemical rush of love, the latter of which she tries to counteract with reason. This is a business transaction, she reminds herself. A delinquent repayment of debt. "I have an idea," she says. "Let's do it one more time, for old times' sake, and then we will never talk or think about this again."

"Dude!" he chuckles, preppily. "I'm totally up for another round, and I would *never* think of saying anything to anyone, but come on! I'm gonna *think* about this. How can I not?"

"Okay, fine, you can think about it."

"I wasn't asking for your permission." The skin around Bucky's eyes crinkle so deeply when he smiles that his pupils appear to be swallowed amid the folds. "Jesus, feel this." He puts her hand on his erection. "Just looking at you . . ."

"We always had good chemistry."

"Good? *Good?* Fuck, Pace, I've lived long enough now and screwed enough lonely Stepford wives to know we had *unbelievable* chemistry." Bucky reddens. "I probably shouldn't admit that part about the other women."

"It's okay. Really."

"No, it's not okay. But . . . well . . . I haven't had sex with my wife in three years. A man has needs."

"Three *years?*" No wonder Arabella's schtupping the accountant, Clover thinks.

"I know. Crazy, right? I was just, I don't know, never really that into her in that way."

"You're kidding."

"Nope."

"Never? Not even when you first met?"

"Not even when we first met."

"So—and please excuse me for prying—but, I mean, why did you marry her then?" If nothing else, even under the very real strain of fertility-issue-tainted procreation in the recessionary wake of a job loss, she and Danny continue to have more-than-decent sex. It's married sex, to be sure, but it has done the trick, so far, of holding their barren dyad together. (Please, Clover thinks again. Please let this baby be forming right now. It will solve so many problems, relieve so many marital stressors.)

"I thought she'd make a good partner."

"A good partner? That sounds so"—Clover searches for the right term—"clinical."

"I know. I don't know what I was thinking, other than, you know, we're cut from the same cloth, our families have known each other forever, we'll make cute blond babies together, blah blah blah." (Clover winces at this last one, but Bucky's too caught up in his admission to notice.) "Love never even came into the equation. I mean, not that I *don't* love her. I think I actually grew to love her, but by then I was already fooling around on the side, and then she followed suit, and then, wow, what a mess we've made . . ." He lies on his back again and stares up at the ceiling. "I wish I could have a do-over, you know? We should all get one, like a second serve in tennis. That way if we fuck up our first shot with our idiotic notions of how things should be, we'd get to take another with full knowledge of our mistakes and actual needs. Can you imagine? How cool would that be? Down forty love? No problem! Here's another ball." He hands her an imaginary tennis ball.

She takes it and pretends to study it in her hand. "Oh, I don't know. I think we'd probably still hit the net sometimes, even knowing everything we know."

"I guess." He turns back on his side to face her, his gaze intense, needy. "But at least we'd mess up with our eyes wide open, you know? Come here, you." Bucky pulls her torso close to his until they are once again touching, his erection, with its potent brew, smashed between them. "You sure I don't need to run downstairs to the drugstore to get a condom? Really, I'm happy to do it."

"No, really, it's okay," she says, careful to keep it vague without out-and-out repeating her drunken fib from the previous night. ("Don't worry about it, I'm on the pill," she'd lied, when Bucky asked, just prior to penetration, if she had a spare condom. "Oh, good," he'd replied, mercifully too drunk himself to question why a woman with fertility issues would be in the business of taking birth control pills.)

"Perfect," he now says. "I hate rubbers."

"I remember," she replies playfully, kissing his nose, pulling the base of his shaft toward her, recalling, as if it were yesterday, the first time they'd used a condom, back in 1985, when the letters HIV and AIDS were rapidly slamming the door on the two decades of sexual liberation that had preceded them. The Harvard *Crimson* had arrived at her doorstep that bright autumn morning with the thump heard 'round the campus, as it contained a condom insert attached to a shiny, black cardboard flyer heralding either the end of free love or the beginning of mass panic, depending upon its recipient's viewpoint. *Oh my God*s escaped nearly every mouth of every unsuspecting *Crimson*-fetcher that morning, followed almost immediately by some version of, *Check THIS shit out.*

Clover, who'd had a diaphragm at her mother's insistence since the age of fourteen—though she was not actually sexually active until her senior year of high school—had never actually held a condom in her hand or placed it on a boyfriend's penis, so for fun she'd asked Bucky to indulge her curiosity with the free sample.

"No way!" he'd said. "I hate those things."

"Oh, come on!" she'd insisted. "I just want to see how it works." So she opened the package with her teeth and tried to roll it on, but in her haste and embarrassment, she put it on backward, so it wouldn't unroll. When she finally flipped it over and unfurled the sides downward, something didn't look right, what with that small sac of extra space at the tip. "Okay, I'm hopeless," she said. "What did I do wrong?"

"Nothing, except putting it on," said Bucky. "Can we take it off now?"

"But what about this part?" She pointed to the reservoir at the tip.

"That's to collect the sperm, you doofus. You've really never used one of these things before?" Bucky seemed flabbergasted. A tenth grader on his squash team at Andover, a shy virgin whose virile father's third wife had been ordered to send him a care package of a thousand condoms, had hidden the Tupperware-encased stash in the crawl space above the ceiling in his dorm's common room. Bucky told a couple of friends about the stockpile, and then those friends told others, and then the whole thing snowballed into that Fabergé organic shampoo commercial, so popular that year on TV, until by spring, when the red blush of shame on the young man's cheeks had finally faded to a barely perceptible pink, and he was ready to embark on his awkward if sweet initiation into adulthood, the container was empty.

"Nope, never in my life," she'd said. When Bucky entered her, encased in latex, Clover immediately envisioned the world coming to an end as a result of AIDS. "Ugh, that doesn't feel good at all," she said.

"No shit," said Bucky.

"But what about AIDS?" she said.

"Don't worry," said Bucky. "They'll find a cure. They always do."

Now, with Bucky on the verge of penetration, Clover feels a new flash of concern, wondering about all those other women with whom he has been cheating on his wife these past twenty years. She knows it's become somewhat of an unpublicized rarity for someone in Bucky's and her socioeconomic strata to come down with HIV as a result of heterosexual sex, but still. "I probably should have asked you this last night, but . . . you're clean?" she says.

"As a whistle. Promise."

So Bucky enters her, for the second time in twelve hours, with the one part of him that does not seem to have aged at all, moving slowly at first, then building to a rhythmic, breathtaking crescendo. Clover grabs onto his gluteal muscles, her mind focusing on the word *procreation*, like a mantra, while her body heads in another direction altogether.

No, she chides herself, stop relishing the pleasure! This is not adultery. It's childery.

But her flesh has its own agenda.

All the books on infertility say it's better if the female climaxes, she reminds herself, rationalizing for the umpteenth time as Bucky reaches down between her legs until she's moaning, writhing, gasping with endorphin-soaked ecstasy. They all say the uterine contractions help guide the sperm where they need to go. They all . . . they all . . . they all say . . . But she can't finish the thought. Her mind has been relegated to the fringes of Cloverdom, shunted aside by forces several thousand tons more potent.

Fifteen minutes later, alone in the shower and plagued with guilt over the continuing rushes of pleasure still pulsing within, she scrubs the soapy washcloth over her limbs, torso, and face with the vigor of an eraser on a chalkboard, convincing herself that by surrendering to her body's desires, by allowing it that perfect swan dive of release, she was simply engaging in her first act as a good mother: giving her child, whom she prays now begins life's journey inside her, its best chance at survival.

• • •

Mia wakes up next to Jonathan and immediately tells him about Gunner's outburst at the police station. " 'Those fucking Jews,' " she whispers, so as not to wake up Zoe. "Can you believe it? He said, 'Those fucking Jews,' even though technically he should have been cursing out his parents' hedge fund manager for not doing due diligence on Madoff." Her back feels stiff from sleeping on Jane's air mattress. Their Kluft mattress at home, made with a blend of cashmere, silk, wool, horsehair, organic cotton, and all-natural latex, was an indulgence, she thinks, well worth the forty-four grand. *We spend a third of our lives sleeping*, she'd said, when Jonathan laughed at the price tag. *How 'bout if we spend one quarter of our lives sleeping and find a bed half as expensive?*

he'd replied, handing over his black AmEx to the mattress vendor with a defeated smile and a what-can-you-do shrug.

"Oh, Mia," he now says, the whisperer of reason as usual, "I mean, as far as Madoff's concerned, he's just saying what everyone else is thinking. Even I think *that fucking Jew* when I hear his name—more because he gives us all a bad name, but still. Cut Gunner some slack. His family just lost their entire nest egg. Or at least what they assumed was their nest egg. His wife's in *jail*. He's allowed a politically incorrect epithet or two."

"He's a dickhead." She hears Zoe stirring in the Pack 'n Play and lowers her voice back down again. "No, worse. He's an entitled, anti-Semitic dickhead."

"I'm not saying he's not an entitled, anti-Semitic dickhead. In many ways he is. In other ways he isn't. I actually have a bit of a soft spot for him—"

"Oh, please. You have a soft spot for everyone." Almost immediately, she regrets the tone of her voice. *When did I become this angry?* she wonders. *This uncharitable? I used to be able to see the good in everyone.*

Jonathan, hearing the same tone, raises his left eyebrow, a trick he uses often and to excellent effect both at home and on his film sets. Without uttering a word, he is able not only to point out the fallacy or incivility of the insult/tired truism/complaint one has muttered, but also to urge its mutterer toward a more Zen-like acceptance of human frailty and fallibility.

"Sorry," Mia says, chastened, grateful, once more, for having married a mensch, as her mother always called him. "Go on."

"No, I'm just saying, I mean, come on. Here's a guy who's been 'working' "—Jonathan forms air quotes with his fingers—"on the same frigging novel for ten whole years, and yet not even Addison has read a page, right?"

"Right."

"So for all we know, he hasn't tapped out a bloody word in *years*."

"Okay, so?"

"So on one hand, that's the laziest fucking thing in the world. On the other, I mean, come on, that's *got* to be painful. Soul crushing. He lost a decade of the normally most productive, satisfying years of one's life, and now, at the age of, what is he, forty-two?"

"Forty-three, I think. He was one of those guys who had to take an extra year of prep school to get into college."

"Is that even allowed?"

"Apparently, yes. Not only is it allowed, it happens all the time. In Gunner's case, I think the admissions director at Yale, where there's an entire Griswold wing of some science or physics building, I can't remember, told his father that they'd be happy to accept him if he could just spend an extra year bringing his grades up from Cs to B+s. Half the kids I met at Harvard with both buildings named after them and unimpressive report cards had to repeat their senior year at those Grotony schools—they used to call it something else, PG, I think, anyway it doesn't matter—in order to reserve a future slot that might have gone to a more qualified, harder-working, building-less student."

"Okay, so fine. He's forty-three. And he stole a spot at Yale from some poor tuba-playing math genius from Dubuque, and he's always gotten exactly what he wanted: the hip loft in Williamsburg, the beautiful wife—"

"She's a piece of work, too."

"I'm not saying she isn't." Jonathan is growing frustrated, she can tell. Sometimes his goodwill toward mankind can be its own form of torture, if only because she ends up feeling like such a petty schmuck by comparison. People are always telling her what a great husband she has, but sometimes she wonders whether their commentary is less about his greatness than about her lack thereof. One time, at the fall cocktail party at her kids' school, she overheard one mother say to another, both of them glancing at her still-handsome saint of a husband, "I mean, really, how the hell did *she* land *him*?," not realizing that the "she" in question was within earshot, trying to ease her husband's existential angst over bicycle locks. ("It just makes me so sad," he'd said. "Every single time I lock my bike to a pole I'm thinking, why? Why must we live in a world of bicycle thievery?") "I'm just saying Addison fits the image Gunner probably pictured for himself when he looked up *wife* in his mind's eye's dictionary. I'm just saying, I mean, hell, the guy's never had to worry about working a day in his life, and now, suddenly, he has nothing. Have some pity."

The phrase *never had to worry about working a day in his life* touches a raw nerve in Mia. "He has the loft his parents bought for them," she says sharply. "He can sell it. I hear Williamsburg real estate is booming, even in this shitty climate."

"Okay, fine, but then where do they live?"

"They rent."

"And what exactly does he do to pay the rent after he uses up the proceeds from the sale of his apartment?"

"I don't know, Jonathan. He finds a job, like everyone else. Or Addison finds a job." What kind of job would she find, she wonders, if ever she were forced to do so? She immediately shoos the terrifying thought out of her mind.

The spike in her tone wakes the baby, whom Jonathan, being Jonathan, swoops up from the Pack 'n Play and cradles in his arms. "Oh, come on, Mia! You should know better than most that that's easier said than done. Neither of them have ever held an actual nine-to-five job in their lives. Where are the diapers?"

"In my suitcase."

Jonathan finds the diaper-changing supplies and gets to work, an act that, when witnessed by Mia's girlfriends, causes either their jaws to drop or their husbands' ribs to get surreptitiously poked.

Mia, however, is focused on Jonathan's pre-diaper-query statements. "I should know 'better than most'? What's *that* supposed to mean?" She wishes she could raise a single eyebrow, but her facial muscles, like her job-seeking muscles, are not built that way.

"Nothing, forget I even said it." He leans over to hand her the baby. "Left or right?"

Mia feels her breasts, both of them equally engorged. "It doesn't matter. Right I guess."

Jonathan flips the baby around in his arms and places her under the crook of Mia's right arm. She knows she should be grateful for this, for him, for everything she has in such abundance, she *knows*. But she can't help herself. "Are you saying I wouldn't be able to find a job if I had to? Is that what you're saying?" Of course that's what he's saying, she thinks. And she can't really blame him, but she does.

"No, of course not."

"Then what *are* you saying?"

"Let's just drop it, please. I'm sorry I even brought it up. Of course you could find a job, if you had to. And I should never have implied otherwise." Jonathan, whose mother was so quick to anger that he lived on edge for each of the eighteen years he was sentenced to her care, has such an aversion to conflict that Mia has sometimes witnessed him taking the blame for crimes he didn't commit—a spilled soda, a minor fender bender, the submerging of their son Eli's iPhone into the swimming pool—just to keep the peace. This has served him extraordinarily well on set. As a joke, his crew once bought him a director's chair that said MY BAD, his signature phrase, in the place of his name. But it could make living with him a bit of a challenge. Sometimes, Mia once screamed at him, you just *need* a good fight. To which, maddeningly, he agreed.

"Our assets are safe, right?" Mia says, shoving her nipple into Zoe's eager mouth. She is both embarrassed by how little she knows about their financial situation and relieved she doesn't have to think about it: a fair trade-off, she thinks, staring down at Zoe's beatific expression, for everything she does for the family.

"Relatively, yes," said Jonathan, rifling through his suitcase for an item he can't seem to find.

"Relatively?" She rubs the thumb of her right hand over the soft flesh of Zoe's knuckles. "Relative to what? To whom?"

"Well, in case you haven't heard," he says with a smile, "there's a bit of a recession going on right now. Have you seen my running shorts?" Though he's managed, even at his age, to keep the normal midlife paunch at bay, Jonathan's cholesterol numbers were not up to snuff at his last checkup. His doctor told him if he didn't add a few hours a week of aerobic exercise, he was putting his arteries at risk.

"Yes, you left them on our bed when we were packing. I put them in my suitcase. Check under the T-shirts."

"What would I do without you?" he says, finding them, slipping them on.

"You'd manage," says Mia. The more salient question, she thinks, is what would she do without him? "So how bad have we been hit?" she asks. "By the recession, I mean."

"You are not to even think about these things," he says, kissing her on the forehead. "We're fine, don't worry. I'm this close"—he holds his thumb and forefinger up, less than an inch apart—"to getting *Remembering Richard* financed." *Remembering Richard*, Jonathan's latest script, takes place in New York, in the hours after 9/11, when a young artist, Franny, who's engaged to be married, hears that her old boyfriend Richard—the inspiration for the series of paintings she is coincidentally hanging for her first big show—was on the plane that hit the North Tower. Grief stricken over this second loss of her ex (she lost him first to heroin), she falls, over the course of the next twenty-four hours, into the arms of Stefan, the happily married but painfully empathic gallery owner, whose wife and kids are stranded in the south of France until the FAA lifts its ban on incoming flights and whose older, wiser heart bleeds for the poor, distraught Franny after he overhears her talking on the phone with her normally patient fiancé, whom he can tell, without even hearing his side of the conversation, has had just about enough of Franny's complicated feelings for Richard.

It's a beautiful love story, his best to date, but because Franny gets married to her intended and Stefan stays with his wife, it's also so unlike his other scripts, he's been having a hard time finding financing, especially in the new climate of austerity. Sony said they'd do it if he could change the script to make Stefan's wife a heartless bitch and Franny's fiancé a cheating fool. Fox said they'd be happy to look at it again if Stefan weren't already married, and Franny were engaged to be married to a heroin-addicted Richard instead of her fiancé. New Line said the audience would be confused by the fact that Franny's paintings were expressions of love for her ex rather than for her husband-to-be. Miramax felt it would only work if Stefan were a widower.

But Jonathan has remained unusually adamant, for Jonathan, about keeping the plot as is: messy, loose ended, irrational. "Fuck these Prada-clad twenty-five-year-olds and their ridiculous script notes," she heard him say to Shari, his producing partner, one night from his home office. "They haven't lived long enough to understand that sometimes shit just *happens*. That even 'good' people are fallible."

"Well, what if *Remembering Richard* doesn't get made?" Mia now asks. Jonathan has built an entire career—hell, an entire life!—on happy endings. She admires him for wanting to knock down some fences, but perhaps a national housing crisis might not be the most judicious time in which to start taking an axe to the white picket ones.

"Then we'll cross that bridge when we get there," says Jonathan. "Please don't worry, sweetheart, really. We're fine." He laces up his sneakers, climbs the basement stairs, and opens the door, quietly, so as not to wake the rest of the house. "I'll be back in forty-five minutes, and I'll pick up some chocolate chips and bananas on the way back, if I can find them, so we can make pancakes for the gang," he whispers from the doorframe, before turning around and bumping into an exotic-looking creature clad in black pajamas. "Oh, sorry Trilby," he says. "I didn't see you."

Trilby, momentarily disarmed by direct, physical interaction with her crime's victim, blurts out, "You left your wallet in the office. I mean, I think it's yours. It could be someone else's, I don't know. I just thought you should know, so yeah, okay," before slinking down the hallway to the bathroom.

· · ·

Jane glances down at her watch, in the midst of all the breakfast hubbub, and wonders whether it's still too early to call Bruno. 9:15 A.M. Boston. That means 3:15 P.M. Paris. He's still at the office, *en permanence*. She'll wait. No point bothering him when he's editing seven different stories streaming in from around the globe. She wonders if there's an equivalent American phrase for *en permanence*. "Weekend duty"? Maybe. "On call" could work, too, but isn't that more for doctors? She wants to tell Bruno about her conversation with Jonathan, about her mother's letter to Lodge Waldman. She feels not unlike the last monogamist standing.

Max Zane, at seventeen looking every inch the scruffy-teen, male version of Mia, is busy cracking open eggs while Jane's daughter, Sophie, who can never get enough of Max, whisks them inexpertly. Eli and Josh have been given the task of setting the table. "How many are we?" says Eli, who must have grown a foot taller and six inches broader since Jane saw him last summer. He definitely got the best of both Mia and Jonathan in the genetic lottery. A good-looking kid, and nice, too.

All the Zane boys, in fact, are nice. Mia may have squandered the best years of her life shuttling them back and forth to school and soccer, but Jane has to hand it to her: She raised three thoughtful, well-adjusted, polite kids. That being said, Jane was a bit shocked when she heard that Mia was pregnant with Zoe. The night she received the e-mail from Mia, with the subject header "Zane train to get new caboose!" Jane told Bruno she thought the whole thing was less about wanting a girl, as Mia maintained ("We spun sperm!" she wrote in the e-mail, in her typical ebullient, candid way. "I know, totally nuts and embarrassing, but I wanted to be sure . . ."), than it was about avoidance. Plus, four kids? She'd heard that four was the new three in America, but still, even the wealthiest American families had to feel the strain of four.

Jane experiences a tiny jolt of self-righteous smugness for having chosen to raise Sophie abroad, in a country with a social safety net. The idea of being bankrupted by child care and medical expenses runs counter to everything the French believe. Then she's reminded, once again, that her immersion in the land of *liberté, egalité, fraternité* might be coming to an end. She'll have to buy medical insurance, figure out how not to get caught in its complicated web. She'll have to hire someone to pick up Sophie from school. So crazy, dismissing kids at 3 P.M.! As if parents still required their progeny home midday to milk the cows and harvest the wheat, when what they actually need is to have them somewhere safe and stimulating until dinner. An old phrase bubbles up, from the one class she ever took in Latin: "*Cessante ratione legis, cessat ipsa lex.*" When the reason ceases, so too shall the rule.

(She wonders if that was the same phrase that bubbled up into Bruno's mind when she was off caring for her dying mother.)

(She doubts it. She imagines his brain was pretty much turned off at that point.)

(Why can't she just forgive him?)

(Everything would be so much easier if she could just forgive him.)

(She can't. She just can't. And so she'll buy medical insurance. Hire a sitter for Sophie.)

"How many are we?" Jane counts on her fingers. "Let's see. Well, there's your family, that's six."

Josh Zane, whose decade-long stranglehold on the position of baby in the Zane family was grievously usurped the day Zoe was born, corrects her. "Zoe doesn't count," he says, unaware of his transparency. "She'll sit on Mom's lap."

"Right," says Jane. "Okay, so you guys are five, then there's Sophie and me, that makes seven, then Clover said she might bring Bucky, depending, so that's nine—"

"Depending on what?" says Mia, ramming another half orange onto the automatic juicer with perhaps more force than necessary.

"On whether he can face our firing squad?" says Jane, shooting Mia a wink that goes unnoticed by everyone else.

"I think twenty-plus years since having broken our dear Clover's heart is a long enough period of penance, don't you? Call her back. Tell her to tell him we won't bite."

Trilby, who sits slumped in the window seat in her black pajamas, texting furiously, says, with a touching meekness belying her nail-hard exterior, "What about my mom? When is she coming back?"

"Oh, sweetie," Mia says, taking a breather on her manic juicing to walk over to the window seat and put her hand on Trilby's knee, which retracts like a snail to the touch. "They said the judge will see her at eleven. I'll drive you over there as soon as Zoe wakes up from her nap. But I promise, they'll let her out, maybe even earlier than that. An old friend of your mom's is heading over there right now to try to sort it out." It was Mia who'd called Bennie Watanabe, earlier in the morning, to tell her about Addison's past catching up with her. She had no idea how Bennie would react to the news of her ex's incarceration, but Mia figured she might as well inform the one person she knew in their class for whom lending a hundred grand would not feel like a hardship and who, coincidentally, once loved Addison.

"Whatever," says Trilby, shrugging. "I don't really give a shit."

"Trilby, I know this is hard," says Mia, trying to rise above her distaste for her roommate's child. Some of it was dumb luck, she knew, pulling the short straw of a difficult child. Her brother's youngest, whom everyone else in the family secretly called Pinball, was recently diagnosed with ADD, but not before that whirling dervish wreaked havoc on both her brother's two older kids and his marriage. But Mia had met Trilby when the girl was a giggling, towheaded toddler, full of optimism and life thirst. This cloud-covered Trilby before her seems much more the product of nurture, not nature.

"So how many are you guys then, without your mom?" Eli asks Trilby. "Four, right?"

"No, three. Just me, Houghton, and Thatcher." (The latter two who are, at this very moment, watching a man ejaculate all over a woman's face on Jane's late mother's computer, forever altering, to the detriment of future relationships, their understanding of what constitutes fun for most females.)

"Three? Where's your *dad*?" says Mia.

"He said he was going into town to the library to write before Mom's judge thing," says Trilby. "He has to get his five hundred words in every day. Like Graham Greene."

Jane and Mia exchange another shared, knowing glance. He's at the *library*? When his wife's in *jail*? If nothing else, Gunner's sense of timing, Jane thinks, has been consistent in its insensitivity. Two weeks after Trilby was born, Gunner and his childhood friend Barrett decided to renovate an antique schooner, built in 1935, that the friend, whose trust fund was significantly larger, purchased that summer on Block Island. So while Addison was busy nursing, changing, and caring for her new infant, never sleeping more than two hours at a time, as Gunner refused on principle to lift a finger—"You wanted a baby, you got a baby"—Gunner spent all day, every day, sanding this and repairing that, punctuated by short breaks to smoke weed, until by September the vessel was seaworthy enough, or so he and Barrett decided while high, to sail through the Panama Canal. So he packed a small bag and left the rest of his clothing and gear in the car his wife and infant child would have to drive back to New York alone, in Labor Day traffic, while he and Barrett spent the next three months overstaying their welcome in various ports up and down the eastern seaboard, repairing more holes, trying to save the hull, running out of dope, until the schooner finally sank off the coast of Florida the day before Thanksgiving, and the Coast Guard charged them thousands of dollars—fines that Barrett insisted they split—for violations too numerous to mention.

"Graham Greene wrote five hundred words a day?" says Jane. Since *You poor thing, having a father like that* seems imprudent, under the circumstances.

"I guess."

"Has he let you guys read any of his novel yet?" says Mia, with a knowing sidelong glance at Jane.

"No, not yet," says Trilby, rubbing her spiky tongue ring back and forth across her teeth. (How can that be comfortable? Mia wonders. Does food get caught under it? Does she impale the roof of the mouth when she chews?)

Mia's son Eli is still focused on his numbers. "Okay, so that's five of us, Jane and Sophie, three Griswolds, one Clover, and maybe an extra, right? That makes twelve." Eli steals a glance at the bowl full of unadorned batter sitting next to the empty griddle. "Wait. What about the bananas and chocolate chips?"

"Got 'em!" says Jonathan, bursting through the door, a charismatic blur of sweat and spent energy hovering above a pair of brand-new Nike Roadsters. Under one arm he clutches a perfect bunch of bananas, stickered over with the word ORGANIC; with the other he holds aloft what looks like a dark brown brick. "Can you believe it? They had Scharffen Berger at your little local deli! I can't even get our local deli to stock Nestlé's."

Jane takes the chocolate brick from him and looks at the price tag. "Fourteen dollars? You could have bought the Tollhouse for three bucks."

"Jane Streeter, you will be eating those words when you taste my pancakes."

"No, I'll be eating your pancakes when I taste your pancakes."

"Oh my God, always such a rationalist." He winks. "God, what a gorgeous morning, isn't it?" Now he turns to Mia, who notices the slight flirtation between Jane and Jonathan with bemused detachment. He would never touch another woman in a million years. Of this she is certain. "Did you make the batter with a dash of lemon like I told you?" he asks.

"Yes, Mr. Control Freak, I did." Mia says this, Jane notes, without a trace of annoyance. She clearly loves both her husband and his idiosyncrasies. And Jonathan doesn't flinch at the sugar-coated insult. A lucky accident of compatible temperaments, so rare, Jane thinks, as to be almost shocking.

And yet he's an adulterer. An adulterer who smiles and loves his wife (who doesn't know he's an adulterer), and loves his kids (who think he's God), and makes twenty-dollar pancakes (because he can).

How is it that she's just learning about the vagaries of human nature at this late juncture in her life? Her entire career, the accolades she has received, have been based on her innate understanding of the human drama simmering just below the surface of violence and war, and yet in her own personal life, in the lives of her friends and their spouses, she's an imbecile.

Jonathan gets to work, shaving the chocolate with a cheese grater while Mia slices the bananas into thin slivers. "No, no, throw them in the Cuisinart or mash them with one of those thingamajigs, so they get nice and mushy," says Jonathan.

"Yes, sir," says Mia, smiling, rolling her eyes in mock frustration.

Eli sets the table for twelve.

Trilby texts.

Max and Sophie beat the eggs.

Houghton and Thatcher watch a woman pretend to like licking the cum off her philtrum.

Gunner stands at the new fiction shelf in the library, scanning the spines of productivity.

Clover kisses a sleeping Bucky chastely on the forehead and texts "it'll just be me" to Jane's phone.

Eli resets the table for eleven.

Bucky sighs, turns over, and dreams about boats, aware neither that Clover has quietly snuck out of the room nor that there's any probability, let alone a high one, that one of his sperm might be boring its way into her egg.

Addison arrives at Jane's late mother's house, leaning heavily on Bennie.

Bennie carries two dozen bagels, a pint of cream cheese, and a pound of nova for the bereaved.

Eli resets the table for thirteen.

Zoe wakes up from her nap and starts to scream.

Jane takes it all in, the part she can see, the part she imagines, and finds it mind-bending, overwhelming. What does it mean, all these tiny actions, these hidden secrets, these fragile humans with their hardships and friendships and fuckships that survive the slog-sprint through time? *Don't you all realize?* she feels like shouting. *We all end up dust.* Instead she wipes her wet hands on her late mother's kitchen towel, gives Addison a bear hug, and says, in the best American argot she can affect, "Okay, guys, time's a-wasting. Let's get a move on with those pancakes."

ELLEN ELISE GRANDY. *Home Address:* 34 Mount Pleasant Street, Cambridge, MA (617-497-9676). *Occupation:* Physician. *E-mail:* hgrandy@cambridgefamilymedical.com. *Graduate Degrees:* M.D., Stanford '93. *Children:* Eleanor Frances, 2002.

After a decade spent overseas as a physician with Médecins Sans Frontières, I moved back to the States a few years after my daughter Nell was born, joining a wonderful family medical practice started by my freshman roommate, Andrea Lebenthal. There are seven of us in the practice now, all women, which means we each take call just once a week, a godsend for the two of us who are single moms.

I still hold out hope that there's a life partner out there for me, a father figure for Nell, but the older I get, the less likely this seems. I can't complain: I've had my fair share of love, and for this and especially for Nell I will always be grateful, but because of the itinerant nature of my work in the past, none of these often already complicated relationships were able to withstand the pressures of so much time and distance apart. Since moving back to Cambridge and settling down with my daughter, I've tried the online dating thing, and let's just say I've now also had my fair share of creeps, stalkers, and men who think posting a photo of themselves fifteen years younger and forty pounds lighter won't make me immediately dislike them when I spot them at the bar, beer-bellied, sweating, and bald.

Okay, so fine. I guess what I'm saying is if you're reading this right now, and you either happen to be or happen to know a decent, kind, intelligent, and relatively attractive (unsweaty, please; bald's fine) middle-aged man in the greater Boston area who is either divorced or coming out of a long-term relationship or a widower— I've tried dating men my own age who've never cohabitated, and let's just say there's invariably a good and often disquieting reason they've remained unhitched for so long—I would gladly entertain the idea of being set up on a date the old-fashioned, nonvirtual way.

Shameless, I know, to write this here, but what the hell. I figured you're as good a population to ask as any, and I'm getting too old for pride.

GEORGE RAWLINS CROWLEY. *Home Address:* 2385 Walcott Street, Pawtucket, RI 02861. *Occupation:* Owner, Rawlins Subaru. *E-mail:* gwc@rawlinssubaru.com. *Graduate Degrees:* Ph.D., Oxford '96. *Spouse/Partner:* Sarah Blake Crowley (Boston University '93). *Children:* Finn Jessup, 1999; John Andrew, 2001; Lilly Phelan, 2003.

What can I say? Did I ever imagine as I was spending all those years in Oxford writing my doctoral thesis on the conception of love in the poems of Edna St. Vincent Millay that, years later, I'd own a Subaru dealership in Pawtucket? No, I did not. What I can say is that what St. Vincent Millay taught me about love wormed its way into me in some lasting, profound way, and when I met my wife Sarah, and we decided to start a family together, I realized I didn't have to choose between love and food. I could choose both, so long as I was realistic about what was possible, given my area of expertise, and what was not.

I tried taking the academic route, but doctors of poetry, suffice it to say, are a dime a dozen, especially these days, and after years of adjuncting here and there and fighting for the scraps of a tenure-track slot somewhere, anywhere, my desire for stability, for the ability to take a vacation now and then, for a decent home for my family and good schools for my kids won out, in the end, over poverty and poetry. Or, rather, the poetry is still in me, and I will always be an avid reader, and sometimes writer, and forever admirer of the form, but the minute I stopped depending on it as a means of putting food on my table, I found a sense of peace and well-being I never realized existed.

Do I love my work? Some days I do, and some days I don't, but what I do love, always, is that owning my own business allows me immense freedom to attend the kids' soccer games and parent-teacher conferences, and it pays the bills, and for now and maybe forever, that seems to be enough. Plus, every night, before bed, I allow each child to fish out a book of poetry from the shelf, and we open it up to a random page, and we read. A few weeks ago, my eldest, Finn, happened upon my favorite St. Vincent Millay poem, "Love is Not All." He's ten now, old enough to parse the meaning of the words with some help from Dad, so after we read it, we had a lively discussion about the poet's intentions.

It was one of the happiest half hours of my life.

CLAYTON JESSUP COLLINS. *Home Address:* 5408 Brooklyn Avenue NE, Seattle, WA 98105 (206-283-8017). *Occupation & Office Address:* Artistic Director, the Fourth Wallers, 4512 University Way NE, Seattle, WA 98105 (206-283-3200, x664). *E-mail:* clay@ fourthwallers.org. *Spouse/Partner:* Anthony DeRosa (Tulane '97). *Children:* Koby DeRosa-Collins, 2005.

For years my father, a part-time carpenter and full-time drunk, was furious with me for not having studied medicine after college. I was the first in my family, hell, in my entire hometown, to go to college, and I was the only child of a widower, and there was no way I could have lived up to those expectations. "But you graduated *Harvard!*" he kept saying, as if that meant I should have magically taken an interest in slicing open humans. Trust me, people, you would *not* want me dissecting a frog much less performing an arterial bypass on poor Uncle Fred.

On the other hand, I do know a little bit about taking an emotional knife to the human heart, and I'll be damned if the little theater group I founded in an abandoned milk bottle factory seventeen years ago, the Fourth Wallers, hasn't had its best run this past year. For starters, we finally built our own space "on the Ave" (as we refer to the main drag here in the University District), in an old Tower Records store that was scheduled for demolition. We

actually kept one of the plate glass windows of the previous structure intact, turning it into a one-way mirror for the folks seated
on the inside, so that some poor kid passing by on the outside—
some poor kid, say, from Marietta, Mississippi, whose father
might have told him that only fairies go see any kind of theater
aside from a passion play—might be able to press his face against
the glass to watch the magic. Meanwhile, one of the works I com-
missioned last fall, *Mister Sister*, a musical about a nun who gets a
sex change, is making its debut at the Manhattan Theatre Club. I
know, just in time for the recession, but whatever, right? It's still
exciting, and two of our original cast members will be in it, and
this brings me bucketloads of joy.

Mister Sister was also a breakthrough in other ways. My aforementioned father—who stopped speaking to me a few years ago
after I came out to him and told him my partner Anthony and I
were adopting a son—just up and decided one day, after I e-mailed
him a review from the *Post-Intelligencer*, to hop on a plane to catch
closing night and meet his grandchild. The next morning, after
he'd stayed up until 2 A.M. helping my cast and crew strike the set,
we were sitting there drinking our coffees in my kitchen when he
said, "You done good, son," giving me a quick pat on the back
while Koby slurped his Cheerios and Anthony scrambled some
eggs, and I had no idea if he was referring to the play or my kid or
my life in general, but damn if I didn't cry like a baby into my
coffee mug.

A couple of months after that, I got a call from Pop's neighbor,
telling me my father had passed. His liver just gave out one day, as
I suspected it would. The neighbor then asked for my home address, so he could ship us the rocking horse Pop had been carving
for Koby in his wood shop. It just needed to be sanded down a bit,
the neighbor said, but he'd take care of that.

Koby and Anthony will be staying in Seattle when I head back
east for reunion, but if you ask nicely, I'll show ya'll a photo I re-

cently shot of my son rocking on that hand-carved wooden horse. He named it Jessup, after my father. He says he wants to be either a cowboy or a doctor or both when he grows up, so he can ride wood horses and fix broken livers. I told him, hell, Koby, you can be whatever the heck you want to be.

LYTTON WALLINGFORD HEPWORTH. *Last Known Address:* 960 Fifth Avenue, New York, NY 10021.

6

Afternoon

"Where the fuck have you been?" says Addison, not unloudly, when Gunner saunters into the family picnic, clutching Belmont Public Library's sole copy of *Moby Dick*, which he will neglect to return, an hour late. She's so used to hiding their marital discord from the outside world that the question, a tossed dagger, feels both shameful and liberating.

She and her children (*his* children, too, she thinks) are seated under the Class of '89 tent near the edge of the Soldiers Field athletic complex at a large round table with Bennie, Bennie's partner Katrina, and their sons Lucien and Dante, who are quietly sketching one another's faces on Lenox rag paper with charcoal. ("To express the soul on paper is for our sons we try to encourage," Katrina explained, both her heavy accent and her subject/verb placement often indecipherably Teutonic.) Blue-eyed Lucien, born to half-Japanese/half-American Bennie, absorbed, ironically, more of Katrina's family's Aryan genes, while brown-eyed Dante, born to fair-skinned Katrina, is darker, more Asian-looking; but it is undeniable that their mothers' experiment in genetic engineering—one egg from each woman, a cup of sperm from each of their brothers—has been a rousing success: The boys definitely look like blood brothers. In fact, from certain angles, and if you overlook the differences in coloring, they could be twins.

Throughout the previous hour, as Addison fruitlessly texted Gunner ("where r u?" leading to "picnics @ soldiers field, we r here" to "hi its ur wife. just out of jail. perhaps u would like to come see me?"), she studied, with a mixture of veneration and melancholy, the generosity of spirit of Bennie's family, its partner/parents acting so seamlessly in concert as to render the complicated footwork of the tango invisible: Bennie fetching the food while Katrina set up the boys at the table with their art supplies; Katrina accompanying Dante to the Jiffy John while Bennie stayed back at the table with Lucien; Bennie running off to fetch a new lemonade for Lucien while Katrina helped him mop up the one he spilled all over his lap. All this while Addison sat alone with her kids. Not that at this age they need help finding the bathroom or carrying their plates of food, but still, she feels Gunner's absence, as usual, deeply. How could Bennie have had such faith in her own convictions, back in the mid-1980s, when the whole idea of a same-sex partnership seemed not only an absurd, even utopian, aspiration but also one destined to plunge said family, especially its children, into a life of endless ostracism and grief?

And yet here are Bennie's polite, sunny kids, creating lovely charcoal drawings, while her goth daughter sits sullenly, irritably, looking as if she'd rather be anywhere else, and her sons stare down, glassy-eyed, at whatever nonsense flits across a two-by-three-inch screen.

"I was at the library," says Gunner, with an unapologetic shrug. Not understanding that his wife's question was more of a cri du coeur than a simple request for his whereabouts: Where. The. FUCK. Have. You. *Been*?

Trilby, clutching a half-eaten chicken leg, knowing how these things usually go down behind closed doors, slouches in her plastic chair, trying to will herself into invisibility. These days, it doesn't seem to matter how much black she dons; on the self-eraser front, the cloak fails.

She doubts her parents are even having sex anymore. She used to hear them, when she was younger, through her bedroom wall, and while the idea of her parents getting it on grossed her out, it also usually meant that the rest of the apartment would be peaceful for a few hours afterward, or sometimes even for a day or two. Now, for a longer period of time than she would have ever thought possible, there has been only silence on the other side of her wall, while the rest of their home has been filled with more recrimination and misery than a child should ever have to endure. Boarding school, she thinks (not knowing, yet, of her grandparents' inability to foot that bill), cannot come soon enough. She's done with those two. Forever.

Houghton and Thatcher, the former wearing a Dead Kennedys T-shirt, the latter wearing a dark blue number with a green Gumby on it, both purchased by their mother and packed into their suitcases as public signifiers of the Hunt/Griswold family's refusal to buy into the usual signs of their tribe—though, truth be told, two polo shirts would have probably cost less—are hiding under their calculatedly messy mops of dirty blond hair and sharing a pair of earbuds. They are pretending to be playing yet another game on Addison's iPhone, but they are actually knee-deep into another youporn video, this one showing a black man inserting his freakishly large penis into a white woman's vagina at the request of said woman's husband, who makes strange little cuckoldy sighing noises behind the camera as his proxy, simultaneously copulating and staring straight into the lens, says stuff like, "That is some badass pussy you got there, brother," while the lady in question periodically emits her own passionate *pensées* in a thick Long Island accent. "Oh my God, honey, oh my God, did you see his cock, Frank? It is *so fucking big*," she says, followed by "Fuck me harder!" and, "Are you getting this, Frank? Is the camera turned on?" Thatcher is on the verge of giggling until Houghton kicks him under the table. This one's too good to risk getting caught.

"The library," repeats Addison. Her tone instantly transforms Gunner's words from a place into an accusation.

Bennie's and Katrina's eyes meet and relay a telepathic message, after which Katrina whispers something to their sons, which makes them gather up their art supplies and quietly leave with a polite but distinctive *nice-to-meet-you* from each boy. "Ice cream, then, to fetch?" says Katrina to the boys, taking her leave. Addison chides herself for bickering in public. Despite Katrina's difficult-to-unravel verbal skills,

Addison was enjoying talking to her about her latest installation at the Guggenheim in Bilbao, a ten-foot-tall Medusa of giant clitorises stretching skyward, as well as about the public school system in Berkeley where (she was surprised to learn, considering the family's means) Lucien and Dante have been happily ensconced since kindergarten.

"Jesus, Ad, what's the big deal?"

She considers, for a brief second, keeping her mouth shut, but it suddenly feels too late for her usual silent brooding. "What's the big deal? What's the *big deal*?" Bennie, in whom she's just confided, not three hours earlier, the width of her marital rift, silently urges Addison on with tiny isometric movements of the sinew in her neck and eyebrows. ("If you're that miserable, Ad," she'd said, "you need to be explicit with him about what it is he's not providing in the way of emotional support.") "The big deal, Gunner, is that, Jesus Christ, I just spent the night in jail! Jail, okay? As in one of the worst fucking places in the greater metropolitan Boston area where I might have spent an evening, even if they hadn't put me on suicide watch, which, by the way, they did, which meant I slept in shackles, yes, shackles! Not that you even thought to ask how my night was. And when I texted you at the library—where I was more than a bit shocked to hear you'd escaped, considering your wife was *in jail* when you chose to go, leaving our kids with poor Jane, who already had a house full of people and let's not forget a *dead mother* to mourn—to tell you that Bennie here"—she motions to Bennie, and Bennie raises her hand slightly, in a noncommittal greeting of hello—"had paid my fine—*my one-hundred-thousand-dollar fine*—you replied, and I quote, 'cool.' That's it. Just *c-o-o-l*, as if I'd just texted you, I don't know, that I was bringing burritos home for dinner. Tasty Mexican food for dinner, now that deserves a one-word response. Wife's outrageous fines paid by old friend who *sprung her from jail*, where she was chained and deprived of even her tampons—although God knows how one would actually hang oneself with a tampon—that deserves something a little more sweeping, don't you think? I mean, I'm not the writer, and far be it from me to put words in your mouth, but maybe a 'holy shit, Ad, that's amazing, can't wait to see you!' or, who knows, maybe you could have gone all out and written 'I love you. I'm so sorry you're going through this.' Or maybe, just maybe, you could have *picked up the fucking phone* and called me!"

"But I was in the library."

"I'm sorry?"

"You can't use a cell phone in a library."

Bennie's face is unable to contain its shock at what she assumes is Gunner's willful ignorance. Or is it actual ignorance?

Addison doesn't even focus on such questions anymore. She stopped trying to figure out the motivations behind Gunner's lack of a gray scale years ago. "Well, here's an idea, *honey.*" The acidity of the sweet word on her tongue spews forth like snake venom. "Next time you happen to be in the library? And your wife texts you to say her old friend sprang her from jail? Why don't you try *WALKING OUTSIDE TO GIVE HER A FUCKING CALL, huh*?"

Houghton and Thatcher have pressed "pause" on their iPhone sex video. Trilby cannot take it a minute longer. She excuses herself to go to the bathroom, where, overcome by the uric stink and piles of Jiffy John turds, she adds slimy chunks of her regurgitated chicken into the bounteous hole.

"I'm out of here," Gunner says. And with that, he turns to leave.

"Where the fuck do you think you're going?" Addison calls after him.

"That's okay, Ad. Let him go," says Bennie.

Luckily, the noise of idle chatter in the tent has drowned out most of this angry exchange. Only a few of the people seated at surrounding tables have stopped gnawing on their chicken bones long enough to have borne witness to the short spectacle of marital combustion.

Gunner hears his wife's question, but he pretends not to, and anyway he is too furious at her for withholding sex from him for over a year now to answer.

• • •

Jane and Clover are standing on the perimeter of the moon bounce, watching Sophie careen from wall to wall, her pigtails contrails. "She's having more fun than a girl should ever be allowed to have," Clover shouts over the din of the compressor, wondering how all those children manage to avoid knocking out one another's teeth. Moon bounces were not a part of her childhood. Neither were school picnics, Girl Scout cookies, ballet lessons, or curfews. She wonders whether raising a child will be as easy to learn on the fly as trading mortgage-backed securities, or will parenthood be more of a continual stumbling around in the dark without ever locating the light switch, like arriving at Harvard after having been homeschooled on a commune? Probably the latter, she thinks, with the hindsight of having seen so many of her friends—even those with proper wellsprings of exposure to decent parenting upon which to draw—plunge into that moonless pond only to emerge several hundred dawns later on the opposite bank, shell-shocked, muddy, and panting.

"I know," says Jane, "it's almost criminal that level of happiness." She recalls, with the type of vividness triggered by life-changing events, the thump and torque of the jump rope Harold gave her in Saigon; the joy of jumping in a safe place. "Wouldn't it be great if there were a moon bounce for grown-ups?"

Clover laughs. "It's called sex, Jane." The words burst out of her before her internal scold can contain them. She's dying to tell someone about last night's adventure, but if her ruse is to work, not a soul other than herself can know. She vows to take the information to her grave. But maybe, she reconsiders, she should tell *someone*, in case she should die of a brain aneurysm or in a tragic car accident, and then one day her kid gets a compound tibia fracture on a moon bounce and needs a transfusion of O-negative blood, or, wait, what type of blood does she have anyway? It's one of those things she knows she should know, but doesn't. Pediatrician appointments weren't a part of her childhood ei-

ther, nor were vaccinations or dentists, and if she ever had a birth certificate, which she sincerely doubts (having been born at home in her
parents' bed), it most likely was burned in the commune's last fire.
What about Danny? She must have a copy of the results of their marital blood test somewhere in her files. She should ask Bucky if he knows
his blood type. She wonders how one goes about asking an old boyfriend from whom one secretly stole sperm to reveal that kind of information in an offhand manner. It's not like you can easily segue from
"What's your sign?" to "So, are you Rh-negative or -positive?"

"Ah yes, sex," Jane says, mock-wistfully. "Remind me. What's that
again?" It's been months since the errant e-mail, since she's allowed
Bruno to touch her. In her most honest moments, she misses it and
him—or at least what they used to have, before her mother's illness,
before he succumbed to his baser desires—profoundly.

Her sexual history has been plagued with regret: not doing it when
she should have, doing it when she shouldn't, missing key opportunities for bliss when they arose. Anders, her college boyfriend, waited
patiently for her to step off the precipice of virginity, until he could
wait no longer. She was so angry at herself for sticking to some moral
code she could no longer defend, she wound up losing it two weeks
later in the Spee Club bathroom, to some jerk named Lars she'd met at
the pajama party and never spoke to again.

Even the night before Hervé left for Afghanistan was tarnished
with regret. She'd hired a babysitter for Sophie, and the two of them
had gone out for dinner at their favorite restaurant on the rue Vieille
du Temple, but the wait for a table had lasted well over an hour, despite the hostess insisting they'd be seated toute de suite. So they
wound up downing three kirs each before sitting down, and then it
took another hour for her *canard au raisin* to arrive, during which she
and Hervé consumed an entire bottle of pinot noir and began to argue,
in their agitated, famished state, about the relative merits and safety of
his trip. "You're a father now!" Jane had said. "You have to think
about these things." Afterward, they stumbled home down the rue des

Francs-Bourgeois, too angry, tired, and soused to get it on. It was the echo of this failure that first pierced her, with vivid intensity, when she heard he'd been killed, how she'd neglected to give her husband a proper, loving send-off.

"You want some water?" Clover asks, thirsty on the one hand, worried on the other that if she stands there one more second she will confess last night's indiscretion. Everyone always ends up spilling their darkest secrets to Jane, even politicians who should know better. Clover can't figure out whether it's Jane's guilelessness, the tragedies of her past, or the pure, undistracted manner in which she sits still and leans in to listen. Whatever its roots, Jane's seemingly endless reserves of patience have made her an excellent journalist and an even better friend. Maybe she should just tell her. It's killing her not to confess.

"Yeah, sure, a water would be great," says Jane. "Oh, and if you happen to see one? A Popsicle for Sophie. She likes red and orange. Purple will do in a pinch. But no green. She doesn't do green."

"Got it. Water for you, Popsicle for Soph, no green. I'll be right back." On her way to the food tables, she nearly bumps into Gunner, who's clutching a copy of *Moby Dick* as if it were a lifeboat. "Gunner!" she says. "What's shaking?" but either he doesn't hear her or he's too lost in a tunnel of his own thoughts to register the sound of his name. Huh, thinks Clover. That's weird. She could have sworn she'd seen tears in his eyes.

Something's going on between Addison and him, no question. Anger visibly, if silently, pinballs between them. And poor Trilby has no elasticity left in her bumper to deflect it.

Back at the moon bounce, Jane hears, "Jane? Jane Streeter?" and turns to face a once-pretty but now somewhat weather-beaten brunette with a name tag bearing a moniker she only vaguely recognizes. "Ellen Grandy. We were in that Stanley Cavell class together?" Ellen Grandy, Jane deduces, must have a child on the moon bounce as well because she's unable to focus on Jane's face without doing that back-and-forth eye twitch endemic to all women whose attention is torn between the exchange of adult information and the overseeing of a child's safety and welfare.

"Oh, right, the comedies of remarriage," Jane says, surprised at how quickly she pulled that ace out of the hole while Ellen Grandy, standing before her in the flesh, triggers not a single retrievable memory. Then again, Cavell's class had been memorable. Probably her favorite of all the classes she'd ever taken at Harvard. They'd spent the whole semester studying black-and-white films from the late 1930s and early 1940s and reading relevant selections from Kant and Wittgenstein on the subject of happiness, filial and otherwise.

Kant (with whom Jane felt an instantaneous and long-lasting affinity) believed in complete moral virtue as a prerequisite to happiness, while undercutting his own argument by acknowledging that not only are human beings incapable of being wholly virtuous but that, oftentimes, virtue might even stand in the way of happiness. Wittgenstein was more concerned with the impossibility of defining the word *happiness* in a subjective world while experiencing it in a temporal one. The only person who can be truly happy, Wittgenstein felt, is the one able to live solely in the present moment, for time—memory of the past, anticipation of the future, therefore death—is happy's enemy.

"I loved that class," says Jane, catching another glimpse of ecstatically bouncing Sophie, wondering whether, outside the boundaries of moon bounces and sex, people are ever capable of living solely in the moment. It occurs to her, in ironic Wittgensteinian retrospect, how happy hearing those lectures and pondering life's questions had once made her. Maybe not as happy as the moon bounce makes Sophie, but happy enough to identify it.

"Yeah, me, too," says Ellen. "Loved it. One of my favorite classes ever."

"It was so . . ." Jane, whose words usually never fail her, can't produce a noncliché adjective. *Relevant* pops into her head, but she realizes it's only her present-day self who feels this way.

"Interesting," Ellen says, filling in the blank adequately, if meaninglessly. She waves to the moon bounce. "Over here, Nell! Mommy's right here." A striking dark-haired girl, who looks to be around Sophie's age, jumps and waves. Now she and Sophie are holding hands and jumping together, fast friends. "I mean, I just loved how all those couples had to get divorced so they could mess around on the side without audiences rioting. So last century, right?"

"I'm sorry?" Jane's memories of the precise details of each remarriage are fuzzy.

"Remember? I think it was like illegal or something back then to make a film depicting adultery. So they got around it by having the couple officially broken up or divorced or whatever."

"Oh, right," Jane says, but either she'd completely blocked out that part or she'd been sick on that day. She makes a mental note to dig up her notes. They must be somewhere in that mess in the attic in Belmont, not far from her mother's Dear John letter to Lodge Waldman.

"Such a nice day today," says Ellen. "We really got lucky. Can you imagine if we'd been here last weekend during the monsoon?"

"I know, right?" says Jane, using a newish-sounding phrase she'd heard Addison's daughter Trilby use a bunch of times that morning, hoping English-speaking American adults now use it as well. After an awkward pause, during which Jane gives Ellen Grandy adequate mental and physical space to take her leave, should she so desire, Jane takes a stab at small talk. "So what do you do? I mean when you're not watching your kid jump up and down on a moon bounce."

Ellen smiles. "I treat all those kids who bump into one another jumping up and down on moon bounces."

"Emergency room doctor?"

"Pediatrician."

"Oh, cool. My father was a doctor. And please don't tell me how many kids hurt themselves on these things every year. I don't want to know. Okay, fine. I do want to know. How many?"

"Let's just say fewer than you might think and more than you would like and leave it at that," says Ellen. "I mean, what are you going to do? Forbid them from *that*?" She gestures to the colorful inflated structure. "Sometimes, in the name of fun, you just have to throw caution to the wind."

"Absolutely," says Jane, wishing she could incorporate such a seemingly simple hypothesis into her daily life, which has, of late, been anything but fun. How strange that she's always been able to throw caution to the wind when it comes to work but hardly ever when it comes to play. It's as if she can't allow herself the joy of . . . joy. For fear of losing it.

"You write for the *Globe*, right? I read your stuff all the time."

"That makes you and three others," says Jane.

"Oh, come on. I can't believe that."

"Believe it. Apparently nobody's interested in foreign news stories anymore. I mean, except for you. And those three others, though by now we've probably already lost them to Drudge." She's enjoying chit-chatting with Ellen Grandy, despite herself.

"Well, I guess it's not actually fair to use me as a litmus test. I'm not your average foreign news reader. I spent years with Médecins Sans Frontières before opening my practice," says Ellen. "So, you know—"

"You're kidding me!" says Jane, now feeling that frisson of instant affinity she feels whenever her path crosses with others who've seen, up close, the grisly results of mixing politics with gunpowder. She's reminded, as she so often is, that one can never judge a book by its cover. By the look of Ellen Grandy—the sensible leather flats, the headband— she'd pegged her as more conventional. "Where were you based?"

"Um, well, I was in Sarajevo in the early nineties, and then I did a few years in the Congo and Liberia, and then my last posting, before I had Nell and started doing more administrative stuff in the Paris bureau, was in Afghanistan."

"No way! Which part?"

Here Ellen Grandy seems to hesitate. "Um, Jalalabad?" Her cheeks redden.

"Oh my God! Did you ever meet my husband, Hervé? Dirty blond hair, about six foot one, reddish beard when he grew it in?"

Ellen's lips disappear between her teeth, and she scrunches her eyebrows, as if trying to conjure his face. "I don't *think* so—"

"He was back and forth to Jalalabad, oh, at least a half a dozen times. Wrote for *Libé*? I mean, *Libération*." She pronounces the whole word, remembering that Americans usually have no conception of the French press aside from *Le Monde* and *Paris Match*. "Wait, when did you say you were there?"

"I moved there in 1998 and stayed until '02."

"And you never met Hervé? That seems almost impossible. I'm sure he told me he stayed in that clinic several times during that period, unless there were two clinics or something, or I'm wrong, and it was Médecins du Monde, but I'm sure he said MSF. I know it. He even joked that it was the only three-star hotel in the Hindu Kush. The MSF Hindu Kush."

Ellen smiles. "Oh, wait, was his last name Duclos? Hervé Duclos?" she says, but without nearly the same level of enthusiasm at the found coincidence as Jane.

"Yes! He was my husband! Holy shit, I knew you had to have met him. That's so crazy, isn't it?"

"Definitely. I mean, I remember him. Sure. Nice guy, as I recall. Tall . . ." Her voice trails off. "I was so sorry to hear what happened to him, Jane. I mean, I heard about it back then, and then I read your entry in the red book, which, wow, I thought was really beautiful. You really have a way with words."

"Thanks. I mean, oh my God, I can't believe you knew Hervé—" Now Jane is confused. If Ellen had read her red book entry, and she knew Hervé, and she knew the two of them had been married, then why make her jump through all those conversational hoops? She chalks it up to yet another one of those weird things people do when dealing with the bereaved.

"And your mother?" says Ellen. "You wrote about her illness. Is she still . . . ?"

"No. She died this past winter. But—"

"Oh, Jane, I'm so sorry. I lost my mother a few years ago. Also to cancer. It's such a blow, isn't it? Even when you have all that time to prepare. Especially when you have all that time to prepare. I mean, I always wonder what's worse, instant death or that long, drawn-out battle."

"I guess they both have their advantages and disadvantages," says Jane, as if they were discussing the choice of one ice cream flavor over another, rather than the deaths of two of the people she loved most in the world. "But—" She's dying to return to the topic of Hervé, to reminisce with someone who knew him in his natural habitat. Why did Ellen let that strand of the conversation drop? Is she worried about upsetting her? If so, Jane thinks, she should figure out a way to let Ellen know it's okay to talk about her dead husband. She *wants* to talk about her dead husband.

"Stand up, sweetie!" Ellen has now essentially turned her back on Jane and is focused intently on the mouth of the moon bounce, watching Nell being somewhat trampled by the bigger kids. "Just push him off of you. You can do it. I know you can." Now she addresses Jane with a slight turn of her left cheek, still keeping her gaze firmly on her daughter. "It's so hard to know when to say something and when not."

Was that an opening? Jane wonders. Or just a stock commentary on parenting? *Say something!* Jane wants to shout. Instead, in a mangled attempt to repeat Trilby's throwaway response—"I know, right?"—she says, "I know, all right."

Now Ellen turns to face her, biting her bottom lip with what looks like enough force to draw blood. "You *do*? So Hervé *told* you? Oh my God, why didn't you just say so? I mean, I know I haven't been exactly forthcoming here either, but Jesus, what a relief! I had no idea! I mean, I guess I was just assuming he would never say a word—"

"Ellen. I'm sorry, what are you talking about?"

"But . . . I thought you just said you knew. Isn't that what you just said? 'I know, all right'?"

"I meant to say, 'I know, right.' Isn't that the expression the kids use these days? 'I know . . . right?'"

"Oh shit," says Ellen. "I'm sorry. I thought—"

Jane can feel her heart racing, her mind rapidly tying loose strings and fragments together. All those trips Hervé took to Jalalabad. Even when the world's attention had moved elsewhere. With a burst of fury that surprises her, her hands adamantly on her waist, she says, "*You thought what?*"

"Nothing." Ellen is fighting hard to keep her expression in shut-down mode, but her quivering bottom lip refuses to yield. "Forget I even said anything."

Sophie and Nell erupt from the moon bounce, tumbling out of its yellow and red mouth hand in hand, overflowing with ecstasy and exclamation: "That was so fun!"; "Let's do it again!"; "Did you see me do a somersault?"; "It made my tummy feel funny!"

Jane scans Nell's exotic, almost Asian-looking face for any trace of Hervé and sees none, thank God, although at this point, nothing would surprise her. "Mom!" says Nell. "This is my new best friend. Sophie! Can we go on again?"

Before Ellen has a chance to answer, Jane shouts "No!" and yanks Sophie's hand away from Nell's with such force that her daughter starts crying. Nell runs to the safety of Ellen's arms. Jane's not sure where to throw the flaming arrow of her anger, at Ellen, Hervé, or at her own willful naïveté. The only thing she knows for certain is that if she stands in that spot next to the moon bounce *one more second* she will start hurling epithets in front of both Nell and Sophie.

She sweeps Sophie up into her arms and runs to the edge of Soldiers Field, her brain exploding with ghosts and smoke. A doctor once warned her, back when a four-year-old Sophie was admitted to the hospital with meningitis just as Jane was stricken with heart palpitations so severe she thought the two of them would be dead by morning, that PTSD can be triggered by anything traumatic—not just war's violence but also a critically ill child, bad news, the death of a loved one—but she refused to acknowledge that her heart and mind were in any way connected. "*Je n'ai pas le syndrome de stress post-traumatique!*"—"I do not have post-traumatic stress!"—she shouted at the physician on call that weekend, gripping her chest, certain she was having a heart attack, even after her echocardiogram and EKG came back normal.

"There's no shame in admitting your pain," said the doctor, trying to reason with her.

"I'm *fine*," said Jane.

She searches the horizon for a place—anyplace—to exhale her pent-up fumes. The few reunion-goers who happen to be standing in Jane's direct path assume, from the look of shock on the mother's face and the speed with which she runs, cradling such a large, limby child, that the girl must be hurt. They immediately and instinctively give Jane wide berth. "You okay?" one of them shouts. "Can I call an ambulance?" Jane nearly laughs at the idea of an ambulance offering her succor. "No, no, I'm fine," she shouts over her shoulder, her biggest lie to date *because I don't cheat and I don't lie!* she thinks, running past a large sign pointing the way to the class of 2004's picnic, emblazoned with the Harvard seal, Veritas. Truth: the temple at which she has always worshipped with a fealty bordering on zealotry. Could she be its sole remaining congregant, its last loyal supplicant? She spots an open gate underneath the Harvard stadium and slips inside the cool shade, her body shaking.

In the safety of the dark, under the large archway, she places Sophie gently on the ground, her own back against a dank wall, then she leans over her stomach, her arms wrapped tightly around her waist, in hopes of curbing the hyperventilating. She tries to focus on her surroundings, to bring herself back into the present. She spots a filthy Utz potato chip bag, ripped of its contents long ago; a dirty sneaker print on a program from the 2008 Harvard/Yale game; a plastic Coke bottle housing an old cigarette butt. The past is everywhere, she thinks. You can't escape it. Though she hasn't smoked since she was pregnant with Sophie, she would kill for a cigarette right now.

"What's wrong, Mommy?" Sophie says, and if Jane is holding it together at all, she is doing so now only for the sake of her child.

"Nothing, sweetie. It's silly really. Remember when you got bronchitis, and you had to use that nebulizer to breathe?" *Breathe!* she tells herself. One breath after the other. Nice and steady. Pull yourself together.

"Yes."

"Well, I'm feeling a little bit like that right now. Out of breath, okay?"

"Okay," says Sophie, still looking somewhat concerned. "Do you need a nebulizer?"

No, thinks Jane. I need a fucking tranquilizer. Or a lobotomizer. I need some fertilizer with a large side of nitromethane. I need a scrutinizer: someone to look at my life and dig under the veneer of normalcy to expose what's really going on, because clearly I've been falling down on the job *for years*. I need, it suddenly hits her, a sympathizer. "I have to make a quick phone call, and then I'll take you over to the Coop to buy you that Harvard sweatshirt I promised, okay?"

"Okay. And we'll get one for Papi, too?" Sophie had begun calling Bruno Papi, to differentiate him from Hervé, whom she called Papa, during Jane's frequent absences to care for her mother. And in every way that counts, except biologically and legally, Bruno *is* her father. In fact, he is probably a better father to Sophie than Hervé could have ever been. And it's about time, Jane thinks, she finally laid to rest not only the ghost of Hervé but the phantom of his perfection. Of anyone's perfection.

"Sure. We'll get one for Papi as well. He wanted a blue one, right?"

"*Non, gris.*" Sophie was constantly slipping back and forth from English to French whenever the topic turned to her beloved Papi.

"Gray? You sure?"

"*Absolument.*"

"Fine, gray it is." Jane takes her cell phone. Starts to dial 911 before remembering it's 411 she actually needs. "Cambridge, Massachusetts," she says, speaking slowly into the voice-recognition software, somewhere in the ether. "The phone number please for a Dr. Lodge Waldman. That's *W-A-L-D-M-A-N*."

• • •

After all six Zanes have pushed down paper plates into overflowing bins, and Zoe has fallen into a postsuckling stupor in her stroller, Jonathan volunteers to take the kids into Harvard Square so Mia can catch up with her friends in peace. Max, whose science fair project on melatonin and sleep cycles won him third place in the California Intel Science Talent Search, will be applying to Harvard in a few months, and he wants a chance to stroll through the Science Center labs unencumbered—Jonathan explains this with a wink to the assembled group—by a mother who can't tell her Ohms from her oms.

"Look who's talking," says Mia.

"I know," says Jonathan. "How the hell did you and I make a kid who's into science?" He leaves Mia sitting at a chicken-bone-strewn, fruit-punch-stained table in the company of Clover, who said it's so weird, she went to get a water for Jane and a Popsicle for Sophie, but when she got back to the moon bounce, they'd vanished; George Crowley, who lived across the hall from Mia and her roommates' Adams House A-entry suite and had once sold one of his poems to the *New Yorker* but now sells Subarus to Rhode Island; George's wife, Sarah, who will not shut up about scrapbooking; Lytton Hepworth, George Crowley's roommate, with whom none of them have exchanged more than a few sentences (though not for lack of trying) during the twenty years-plus he's been doing battle with schizophrenia, but who nevertheless showed up at the reunion picnic on a whim after George found him playing three simultaneous games of chess outside Au Bon Pain, and Lytton realized, to his surprise, that his most recent cocktail of meds seemed to be working well enough for him to engage in an actual conversation with an old friend; and Mia's once-boyfriend Clay Collins, who played Trigorin to her Nina in *The*

Seagull and who is today, though it's hard for his classmates to fathom the unfairness of genetics, even more handsome, winsome, and everything-else-some than he'd been back in college, when he was trying to cure himself of his yen for men by serially dating female cast members who showed interest. (There were, Clay had been surprised to realize, many a young woman who wanted to date a man who listened to her stories, was raised as a southern gentleman, had a knack for finding the perfect suede jacket in a vintage clothing store, and spent enough hours pirouetting in a dance studio to have the abs of the Calvin Klein models after whom he secretly lusted.)

"I mean, you would not *believe* the things you can do with a glue gun, some felt, and a little lace," Sarah drones on, which causes Clay to choke bitchily on his Diet Coke.

"Buttercup," he says, his southern twang still raw if somewhat tempered by two decades in northern climes, "whatever you're doing with your scrapbookin' lady friends in Pawtucket, trust me, there's a tranny right now in New York City who is making things with a glue gun and felt you would never in a million years *dream* possible."

The rest of the group laughs, grateful that Clay has taken the lead to put a halt to Sarah's endless, pointless monologue, but Sarah takes his statement at face value. "Really?" she says, sounding intrigued. "Like what kinds of things?"

Mia rolls her eyes at Clover, who looks at her watch and pretends to have a hair appointment in Harvard Square. "Oh my, will you look at the time?" she says. "It's just flying by. Gotta run! I'll see you all tonight." And like that, she kisses Mia good-bye on each cheek, pulls out her BlackBerry, pretends to look up an address, and is gone. (1 missed call, she sees on the screen. Her heart drops into her stomach at the sight of her husband's name, as she flashes back to Bucky's cock thrusting inside her. She decides to find a quiet place to compartmentalize and call Danny back.)

"Like I was at Jackie 60 for a New Year's Eve party years ago, back when I lived in New York," Clay says to Sarah, "and the Meatpacking

District actually smelled of raw meat and dried spunk. So anyway this pre-op transvestite had stuck his penis through a bunch of petals he'd fashioned out of chicken wire and orange felt, to make it stick out in the middle like one of the stamens of a tiger lily."

"Oh?" says Sarah, trying and failing to not look shocked. "Now that's something you don't see every day."

"No, darlin', you sure don't. Unfortunately, he had to be taken to the hospital afterward when he decided to glue-gun some Nestlé Quik to the tip of his dick, and wouldn't you know it, the dang glue got stuck. Wouldn't come off."

"Oh my God," Sarah says. "What was he thinking?"

"He was thinking, wouldn't it be great if the tip of my dick looked like pollen."

Lytton, who has remained stonily silent, clamps his lips between his teeth, as if to keep himself from laughing, and stares down into his lap at the paper napkin he's shredded.

"Was he wearing anything else?" says Sarah.

"Nope, not a stitch. Just the dick flower."

Sarah fiddles with the collar on her pink oxford blouse. "He must have been pretty cold, considering it was New Year's Eve." Then she turns to her husband. "Sweetheart, have you seen the kids lately? I think I'll go check up on them." She quickly excuses herself from the table.

"Sorry, George, didn't mean to chase your wife away," says Clay, feeling mildly contrite. Sometimes he just can't help himself. But really, she had it coming.

"No worries," says George, clearing his throat, knowing that either later today or sometime in the near future, Sarah will suddenly drop whatever it is she's doing to remark that the gay man at the reunion picnic with the story about the glue-gunned penis was *so rude*. Then she'll either get angry at George for not defending her or she'll make up some other excuse as to why she'd rather not have sex. "So tell me about your theater group," George says, purposely changing the subject.

"I mean, aside from what I read in the red book, which, by the way, I thought was just great, Clay, just great, and I'm sorry to hear about your dad."

"Well, thank you, George," says Clay, "but his death was a long time comin', if you know what I mean."

"Yes, tell us about your theater," says Mia. What she wants to ask is, *How does anyone earn a living running a nonprofit theater group?* What comes out is, "How did it all come about?"

So Clay tells the assembled group about the Fourth Wallers, how they started in an abandoned space with no walls, let alone three, hence the name; how they struggled for years to make a name for themselves, with everyone working as waiters and bartenders and, in one case, as an escort on the side; how they were able to get the old Tower Records building for a song, but then everyone had to help do the renovations with their own hands; how that bonded them even closer together; how they used to rely on ticket sales and corporate sponsorship from local companies like Microsoft and Amazon to make ends meet, but now, with the recession, they're thinking about putting all of their fund-raising efforts into courting individual donors; how they have a regular troupe of players, directors, and playwrights, who get paid nominal stipends, but most of the troupe, except for Clay and a few others, have day jobs to bridge the financial gaps. "The one perk we do offer all of our actors is health insurance," he says proudly. "But it costs us. Dearly. I'm waiting for Obama to get his butt in gear on that front."

"Tell me about it," pipes up Lytton, for the first time since having sat down at the table, addressing no one in particular and staring off into the mid-distance. His mother, who named him for Lytton Strachey, still shells out thousands of her late husband's real-estate-generated dollars each quarter, both to the health insurance companies and to three shrinks—one to treat his illness, one with whom he talks five times a week, the third who is constantly tweaking his cocktail of medications, depending upon his symptoms—to keep her forty-two-year-old schizophrenic offspring from offing himself.

The rest of them wait several long seconds for Lytton to elaborate. When he doesn't, Mia picks up the thread. "How are you doing these days, Lytton?" she says, placing her hand on his, which he immediately removes. "Medically, I mean." The qualifier is redundant, as Lytton hasn't been able to hold down either a steady job or a love relationship ever, no matter how many drugs are pumped into him. She remembers when Lytton invited her to shoot pool at the Spee Club one night their senior year, during the start of what his shrinks would later pinpoint as the first signs of his mental decline. She was about to excuse herself from the billiard room, whispering into his ear something benign like, "I'm going to the bathroom, Lytton, I'll be right back"—she doesn't remember the exact words she used—but what she does remember, nearly word for word, was his response, which Lytton bellowed, seemingly loud enough to shake the portraits of dead Spee men off the wall, "Mia! Please! Keep your excremental undertakings to yourself! I loathe being reminded of the putrid peregrinations of human digestion. All that shit and piss. What a revolting system. And please don't come back here unless you've thoroughly washed your hands. None of us needs E. coli on top of chlamydia and herpes."

The dozen or so other club members in the room that night lost it, some of them actually clutching their stomachs and falling on the ground or onto various leather sofas from laughing so hard, all of them assuming Lytton was either drunk or high or making a deadpan joke. Only Mia had seen the darkness in his eyes, his genuine disgust at the idea of human effluence.

"How am I doing," he speaks into his lap in a monotone, repeating Mia's question as a statement. Then, for the first time that afternoon, he looks straight into Mia's eyes. "Surviving," he says, without even the hint of a smile to temper it.

"That's better than the converse," says George, trying to keep it light.

"I'm not so sure," says Lytton, now looking searingly into the eyes of his former roommate. "Did you ever become a poet, George? Please tell me you became a poet. I need to hear that right now."

"Well, Lytton, do you want the simple answer or the complicated answer?"

"The simple one."

"Then, no, I did not become a poet. I own a car dealership."

"That's so sad," says Lytton. "What about you, Mia. Did you become an actress?"

Mia thinks of all the times she's ever answered "actor" when she's asked what she does for a living. Now, she realizes, is not the time to do so. "No," she says. "I tried, but no. I pretty much just keep the home running and take care of my kids."

"What a fucking joke," says Lytton, again into his lap, and so softly that each of them tries to convince themselves he hasn't said it, isn't going there. Now he looks up at Mia, accusatorily, leaving no doubt as to his feelings. "You were so good. I can still remember you in that play about the housewife who goes into debt."

"*A Doll's House*," says Mia.

"Exactly. When you slammed that door at the end, man, that was a scene I'll never forget. I remember thinking, fuck, I wish my mother were here to see this." He turns to George. "And you. All those hours you spent, hunched over the dictionary, hunting for obscure words, crafting perfect phrases that made me cry. You just . . . stopped doing that? What the hell's wrong with you? All of you! You went to Harvard, for fuck's sake! You had every opportunity in the world laid out on a silver platter at your goddamned feet. You've got intact minds. Impulse control. You can get out of bed every morning without the voices in your head telling you to kill squirrels or rape virgins. What the hell's keeping you two from doing what you're meant to do, huh? Look at Clay. He followed his dreams. Good for you, Clay. Really, I mean that. High five." He sticks out his hand for Clay to slap, but Clay is—they all are—too shocked to move. "You're a tribute to your alma mater. Although I'll always wonder what you could have done on Broadway, but still, you're following the dream, and that's worth something. I mean, holy shit, if I could be healthy for one day, just one fucking day, do you know what I'd do?" He pauses, glancing around the tent now at all that lost potential, all that promise now shrouded in middle-aged fat and khaki. "I'd be sitting in a lab, with my eye glued to a microscope, trying to improve the world just one tiny bit. I was going to find a cure for cancer. Or AIDS. Or multiple sclerosis or any one of a thousand ailments that fucks up human lives. That's what I wanted to do, ever since I was a little kid. To cure people of their misery. And I used to be more than smart enough to do it, and you know that, George, you know it. Who always helped you with your science homework, huh? Who taught you about nucleic acids and dendrites and black holes and punctuated equilibrium, huh? Ironic, isn't it? Because now I'm stuck inside this fucking head of mine, wishing someone else was sitting in a lab, trying to come up with a cure for me.

"You know what they engraved on the wall of my high school? It was a quote by Horace Mann, and they must have it tattooed on my skull as well, because I see those words every goddamned day of my pathetic, bullshit life. 'Be ashamed to die until you have won some victory for humanity' it said. Be *ashamed* to die. Me, I like to think I have an excuse. If I die tomorrow, I can just say to God, fuck you for doing what he did to me, not letting me keep up with my end of life's bargain. You? You should all be ashamed of yourselves. Cop-outs, all of you. Except you, Clay. High five." He holds up his hand again for Clay to hit it, but Clay pauses just long enough to infuriate Lytton, who takes his suspended, un-high-fived hand and uses it to flip the table violently onto its side. Plates, plastic utensils, soda cans, a digital camera, someone's iPhone, and a bunch of half-eaten hot dog buns and half-gnawed chicken bones go flying, distracting the attention of nearly the entire tent. All gossiping stops. Children start asking questions of their parents. Those who once knew Lytton, before he grew the scraggly beard and started talking to himself, strain to place a name with the face.

"Is that . . . Lytton Hepworth?" one former classmate whispers to another.

"Nah," says the other. "Can't be. Must be some homeless guy who just got lost."

And with that, Lytton Hepworth turns on his worn heels and walks away.

For a moment his three former classmates stand mutely, stunned, each wondering what—if anything—to say. Mia picks up Sarah's digital camera off the floor, the one she uses to scrapbook, and hands it to George for safekeeping. Clay finally breaks the silence with an "Okay, so that's something you don't get to see every day either."

"I think I would have preferred a chocolate-covered penis," says Mia.

"Ditto," says George. Then he turns to Clay. "Don't get any ideas."

"Oh, don't you worry about me," says Clay. "I got all the penis I can handle." He stares back down at the turned-over table, still processing the outburst. "You gotta admit, that was pretty great theater. Speaking of which, Mia, you still up for a quick fly-by visit to the Loeb? I'm dying to get over there before we leave tomorrow."

"Nothing right now would make me happier," says Mia, feeling suddenly desperate to revisit the place where she once shined. She links her arm into Clay's.

"George? You feel like joining?" says Clay, knowing the answer but feeling obligated to extend the invitation anyway.

"Nah, that's okay," says George. "I'll just go find a piece a rope and hang myself." He delivers this last part deadpan, with a wink, even though part of him is so stung by Lytton's diatribe, he'll spend the next two weeks trying, and failing, to translate his ambivalence into verse.

• • •

Lodge Waldman was not surprised when Jane Streeter called him, out of the blue, to ask if she could come see him. In one sense, he'd been expecting her call for years. But in quite another, the fact of her blushing arrival in his office, the effect of her finally sitting across from him, a middle-aged woman now, with faint lines around her eyes and her own daughter ensconced with a Pinocchio video in the waiting room, has rustled up so many simultaneously conflicting emotions, he's having a hard time sorting and naming them. Not surprise, no, but some other buzzy, dopamine-soaked sensation resembling anxiety, mixed with love, and also grief, and also relief, all braided together into leather reins that yank him back, almost violently, to a cascade of images starring Jane's mother, Claire: her younger, taut body on the fold-out couch in his old office, the outline of her breasts phosphorescent with afternoon sunlight; her softer middle-aged body, adrift on its widow's bed, uninhibited and often adamant in its ravenous needs and desires; her cancer-ravaged older body, all sharp angles and ropey veins, wanting nothing more than a gentle touch, the repetitive caress of a windshield-wiper thumb. "So you found the letter, then?" he says to Jane, for want of a better opening.

"I did," she says.

"I kind of begged your mother to get rid of it, but she pulled a Claire and—"

"Listened to you intently, but did exactly what she wanted anyway?"

Lodge smiles. "You do know your mother."

"I thought I did." Jane stares out the window of Lodge's office at the new leaves on his maple tree, still translucent. She imagines them red. Then brown. Then gone. "I'm glad she kept the letter. Why shouldn't I be allowed to know my mother completely?"

"That was her exact response. That you'd want to know her."

"And what was your response to her response?"

"That you already knew her. Look, there's a reason there's a door on the master bedroom. The facts and details of your mother's private life had no bearing on the truth of her life, or on the bond you two shared."

"I'm sorry, but I don't buy that." Her eye catches on the spine of a book on his shelf: *Fetish and the Modern Man*. A friend in Paris recently separated from her husband over his inability to give up bondage. Jane was floored when the woman confessed this; she simply couldn't imagine the husband, a quiet and thoughtful neurosurgeon, tying his wife, night after night, to the bed.

Perhaps her problem, apart from a certain blindness to reality, Jane thinks, is a simple failure of the imagination. And yet she had no trouble at all, out there by the moon bounce, picturing Hervé and Ellen going at it. In fact, it was this image of the two of them, naked, fucking—an image she never actually saw with her own eyes but was nevertheless able to project onto her mind's eye as clearly as if she'd been there in the room—that made her flee from the picnic and has been haunting her ever since.

"What my mother did, what you two did together," she continues, "seems completely out of character. Or at least out of the character I knew. It changes my entire perception of her."

"Well, if you really think about it—about your mother's exuberance, say, or her heart—it shouldn't, but I understand why you would think it would. That's what makes morality both relative and interesting." He leans back in his chair and fiddles with a paper clip.

"I wouldn't necessarily use the word *morality* here."

"Oh? What word would you use?" Now he's back at the desk, leaning in. He lets the paper clip drop.

"I don't know. Immorality?"

Lodge nods his head into his tented fingers, ever the shrink, listening for dropped crumbs, clues.

"I'm sorry," says Jane. "That came out wrong." She pauses to gather her thoughts. "Look, I'm not here to cast stones. I just . . . want to know my mother better. Okay?"

"Of course okay. So. What would you like to know?"

"Everything," says Jane. Did they do it in this room? she wonders. In hotels, cars, public parks? Where does one carry on an affair exactly?

"That's a pretty big umbrella. Can you break it down into smaller pieces?"

"Fine. Here, in no particular order, are the questions I'd like answered." Jane pulls out a reporter's notebook from her purse, clears her throat, and reads down a list she composed while Sophie was trying on souvenir sweatshirts. "How did your affair with my mother begin? How did you react when you read her letter? What happened after my dad died, did you start seeing one another again? If not, why didn't you two wind up together after Dad was no longer in the picture? Did you love her? Did she love you? When was the last time you spoke to her? Did your wife ever find out? What about your kids?" Now Jane looks up from her notebook. "I can keep going, if you'd like."

Lodge smiles. "No, that's okay. I get it." Jane really is her mother's daughter, he thinks, despite their absence of genetic ties. He is reminded of her dogged pursuit of facts at all costs, as Claire once described her to him, both proudly and warily, the day the Pulitzers were announced. Jane's prize-winning series had been about a girls' school in Kandahar, illegal under the Taliban but functioning nonetheless, in a private home where the girls pretended to spend their hours learning to weave and bake nan, to hide the fact that they were actually learning to read books and parse the sentences of Virginia Woolf, Henry Miller, James Joyce. Then the sad aftermath, when one of the braver teachers, whom Jane was extremely careful not to identify by face or name, was nevertheless pinpointed as the author of the infamous and oft-republished quote: "For too long, we have been silenced, whether through lack of education, fear of violence, rape. We do not care what ridiculous organs or laws these men try to force down our throats. We will not be gagged by them." As Lodge remembers, a week after these words hit the newsstand, the teacher was stoned to death.

He's always wanted to ask Jane whether she thought about the consequences of using that quote before submitting her story. But now, he thinks, is not really the time or venue in which to do so.

It's hardly ever truth *or* consequences, he tells his patients, especially those who grew up in that TV era and get the reference. It's usually truth *then* consequences, as many a politician has found out the
hard way. Not every statement that erupts from one's mouth should be
printed. Not every thought need be turned into language. Not every
complaint should be levied out loud. Not every secret demands revelation, especially if the impulse to tell arises solely out of a desire for
guilt expiation. He's seen perfectly good marriages crumble under the
weight of unnecessary confession. He advises discretion, whenever
feasible.

But in this particular instance, with Jane seated directly in front of
him, asking point-blank for information about his relationship with
her mother, the lie of omission would be a type of withholding bordering on callous. And so, with a sigh, he begins. "Your mother and I, as
you know, were colleagues," he says. "Our old offices were down the hall
from one another, and sometimes we'd take our lunch break at the same
time. Both of us had patients between noon and two P.M.—these were
popular hours for all those professionals who could only get out during
their lunch periods—so by the time we'd wind up ordering our sand-
wiches in the diner downstairs, we were famished.

"Your mom almost always had a grilled cheese with tomato on
toasted rye, two pickles on the side, and an apple juice. An apple juice!
As if she were still a little kid in her elementary school lunchroom. I
don't know why, but I just loved that about her."

"Me, too," says Jane, the smell of the apple juice and cookies her
mother left out for her after school, whether she had office hours or
not, almost palpable.

"Anyway, our conversations veered almost immediately from col-
legial to intimate, even before your father left for Vietnam. We just, I
don't know, got along. Understood one another on this deep, underlying level. Had a conversational shorthand from the start. Both of us
were going through various marital issues at the time—hers less severe
than mine, but still, there were issues, like I said, even before your dad

left. Those lunches, at least for me, were the only thing that got me through that period, and I know if your mother were sitting here right now she'd say the same thing. We were each other's life rafts. The physical intimacy became just an extension of that, and I know that sounds completely self-justifying, but we could no more stay away from one another than a thirsty person can keep himself from drinking. What's important for you to understand is that it wasn't just a physical attraction between us, although of course there was that. Attraction on its own I could have handled. Or at least sublimated. This was love. And it felt more powerful than either of us or our marriages, which is why I proposed to your mother and why she, rejecting my proposal for her own various—although I felt at the time misguided— reasons, ultimately had to move her office across town just to put a physical barrier between us . . ."

Jane fixates on the cleft in Lodge's chin, watching this indentation— this absence of chin—become an animated presence as he talks. She thinks of the hole in which her mother was buried; the months-long vacuums Hervé's work left in his daughter's life, such that it took Sophie almost a year to understand that her father was actually gone for good and not just somewhere else that wasn't home.

". . . I was bereft after she sent me that letter. Completely bereft, as if she'd died. No, worse than if she'd died, because if she were dead, I remember thinking, I could have at least mourned the loss and moved on. Knowing she was still out there, that she still loved me but was unavailable to me? It was, well, some days, it was all I could do just to crawl out of bed in the morning and drive to my office. I was so distracted, I even lost a couple of patients. The more sensitive ones, who could tell their shrink was incapable, at the moment, of listening."

Lodge remembers the anger with which an elderly widower he'd been treating for nearly a decade stormed out of his office, never to return. "The only thing I've ever asked of you, the only thing I pay you for, is your presence," he'd said. "I have enough walls in my house I can talk to for free."

"So what happened after my dad died?" says Jane. She remembers the funeral more vividly than her father himself; it was the first and probably only time she saw her mother break down.

"All bets were off," says Lodge. "We started seeing one another again a few months later, tentatively at first, and then whenever and wherever we could, often in the evening at your house, after you'd gone to sleep. I'd make up some excuse to my wife as to where I was going, which wasn't hard, since she didn't really seem to care whether or not I was around anyway. She may have even been having her own affair at the time, I have no idea, and I never asked, though I'm pretty sure my wife was simply incapable of real physical intimacy. It was during this period when I proposed to your mother once again, and this time she seemed game, although still slightly wary about what people would think and how my sons would react and of course how *you* would react, although at that point she seemed willing to throw caution to the wind. She even came around to the idea of the benefits of you having my sons as your part-time siblings and me in your life as a father figure, just to have a little more raucousness and chaos around you. You were such a serious child, always doing your homework days before it was due; always cleaning your room, as if you didn't want to leave any traces of life behind. Your mother told me you were an obsessive pencil sharpener?"

"Guilty as charged," says Jane, remembering the unique pleasure of that first electric pencil sharpener her mother bought. How she diligently dumped out the shavings whenever the trap was edging toward full. "Dull pencils made me nuts. They still do. I know. It's not normal. It's just who I am."

"Totally natural reaction to your circumstances," says Lodge. "But back then your mother was worried about you. For almost a year after your father died—maybe you'll remember this—you refused to sleep anywhere but in her bed, because you wanted to make sure she was still breathing. I told her I thought you'd actually benefit from having more people in your life. That it was hard for a child who'd already lost so much to be left with only one person standing between her and yet another upheaval. And let's face it. My sons weren't learning anything about modeling a love relationship by living in our house. If anything, they were learning a bunch of really bad habits, which of course I'm now seeing repeated in my eldest son's marriage, and it kills me. *Kills* me." Zithromax, he thinks. He promised his eldest he would call in a prescription for Zithromax for his grandson. He scribbles a *Z* on a notepad as a reminder. "Anyway, I gradually wore your mother down. She finally accepted my proposal contingent on my divorce. But just as I was getting ready to open the floodgates on all of this with my wife, literally that same week I was trying to compose in my head how I would word my 'I want a divorce' speech, Kiki was diagnosed with Parkinson's. Your mother was adamant: For me to divorce her under such circumstances would be heartless. Even cruel."

"What about the affair itself?" Jane all but snaps. "Wasn't that heartless and cruel to your wife?"

"No, Jane, under the circumstances, it wasn't," Lodge says gently, accustomed and acutely sensitive to quick and often violent shifts in emotional temperature in his cozy office. "My wife gave up on our marriage years before I did. If anything, my affair with your mother allowed me to be a kinder, less angry person at home, both to Kiki and my kids." Lodge pauses for a moment, studying Jane's body language, the way she seems to be curled into herself. "If you don't mind my asking . . . what else is going on with you right now?"

"Nothing," Jane says. "Just sometimes I think men are pigs."

"Men are pigs. Okay. Would you care to elaborate?"

After some prodding, Jane tells Lodge Waldman about Bruno's affair with his Irish assistant; about finding out, not two hours earlier, that her late husband Hervé, whom she, in her own words, had "held on a fucking pedestal" since his early demise, had had a lover as well.

"Is that when you called me?" says Lodge. "After finding out?"

"Yes," says Jane, picking a cuticle.

"Janie . . . do you mind if I call you Janie? It's what I used to call you, remember, that summer we spent in Nantucket?"

Jane recalls the photos of Lodge and her mother, framed so expertly by her father, the light haloing their hair just so. Her dad must have seen it. He must have understood that he was on the outside, looking in. She wishes he were alive today to compare notes. "It's Jane," she says. "Please call me Jane."

"Okay, Jane," says Lodge. "Look, I don't know what to tell you other than that what happened between your mother and me, while not uncommon, is its own unique story, with its own specific set of circumstances and absurdities, and to try to draw any overarching conclusions about the nature of man, marriage, or even monogamy, for that matter, from this one story or from any individual story is to miss the point. Narrative is much less about the facts of the tale itself—who did what where, when, and why, which I know are the tools of your trade—than it is about how the narrator frames the story, what she feels about the story, when she chooses to tell it, where and why she tells it, in whom does she confide. Now, from the little you just told me, it sounds like your current partner—Bernard, is it?"

"Bruno."

"Fine, Bruno. I mean, I don't have his e-mail in front of me to draw upon, but from your description of it, it sounds as if Bruno was simply reacting to your being gone. I know how much time you spent here while your mother was dying, because I had to make myself scarce whenever you were around."

"You did? That's so weird. Why didn't Mom just tell me about you at the end? What did she have to lose?"

"Your respect," he says. "She feared losing your respect as she lay dying. She thought you would judge her."

"That's crazy! I wouldn't have judged her."

"You're judging her right now."

"I am not. That's totally unfair." Jane steals a glimpse at her watch. She should really be going soon if she's going to feed all those kids dinner and get to tonight's festivities on time. There's never enough time.

"Look," says Lodge, trying to deflect Jane's defensiveness. "No one knew. Not my wife and certainly not my sons, and we were intent on keeping it that way. It was our private pact. Your mother did tell a couple of her more discreet friends, and I confided in my brother and in a fraternity buddy from college, but as far as everyone else was concerned? We kept our love a secret for more than thirty years."

"So, what, you just stayed inside our house and never went out?"

"When we were here, yes. Mostly. Sometimes we'd drive a few towns over to have dinner out. And we managed to take a few vacations together over the years, which was nice." He sees Jane shaking her head in disbelief. "Look, Jane, it's not as strange as it might sound. I loved being in your house with your mother. And after you left for college, well, we didn't have to sneak around so much anymore."

"That just seems . . . I don't know, crazy. I mean, you're the shrink. *Is* it crazy?"

"It is what it is. Or what it was. And I don't think it's useful to try to label it. I loved your mother. She loved me. I am grateful for every moment we were able to have together. It makes me sick that I wasn't able to be with her on her last day. Not that she was cogent, as you know, but—"

"*I* was with her," says Jane, cutting him off.

"I know you were. And that was important to her. I'm just being selfish here. I had plenty of time and space to say good-bye when you were back in Paris. I'm not angry about not being with her the day she died, I'm just . . . what I'm saying is that the circumstances of our situation prescribed the boundaries of our love. Not a day went by when I didn't wake up in the morning and wish I could be waking up in your mother's arms instead. But I had a wife who couldn't get out of bed by herself, let alone scramble her own eggs. By the end, she was totally dependent on me. In retrospect? Yes, the whole arrangement was probably foolish. I should have just put my foot down and hired a full-time nurse for my wife and married your mother and dealt with the consequences and social reprobation, end of story. But we don't live our lives in retrospect. We live them minute to minute, and sometimes something that *seems* like the right thing to do at the time turns out to be misguided. Short-sighted."

"Is she . . . still alive? Your wife?"

"No, she died three weeks after your mother."

"Wow. I'm sorry."

"It's been a rough year. Two funerals within the span of three weeks."

"Wait. You were at Mom's funeral? I didn't see you there."

"Jane, there were five hundred people at your mother's funeral. I was there, in the last row, suffering silently. You gave a beautiful eulogy, by the way."

"Thanks."

"I loved your description of going from door to door with your father's clothes. As if they were Girl Scout cookies. That was so Claire . . ." Lodge feels the lump in his throat enlarge. He tries, in vain, to swallow it. "Look, if there's anything worthwhile that you can take away from your mother's and my story it is that humans *need* love. It's not a luxury. It's a necessity. And they'll endure extraordinary circumstances in order to get it. That being said, they also need sex, and though the two are often intertwined—love and sex, I mean—they're just as often if not more often not, which is what I was getting at before vis-à-vis your husband Bruno."

"Partner. He's my partner," she says, thinking, he really *is* my partner. She has no doubt that, given those games of trust she used to play in summer camp, when you fall back and hope your unseen partner will catch you, Bruno would be standing right there at her back to break her fall. Hervé, on the other hand, offered support sporadically, making it very difficult to know when it was safe to collapse and when it wasn't. She solved that particular problem simply and cleanly, by never collapsing.

"Husband, partner, you share a bed and a home, that's all I care about. Look, all I'm saying is that people—and let's not forget, women included—seek solace outside a monogamous dyad for all sorts of reasons that have nothing to do with falling in love. They're bored. They're lonely. Maybe they're trying to get back at a spouse who in some way wronged them. Maybe the sex with their current partner leaves them unsatisfied: There's not enough of it, or the practices of one partner are distasteful to the other, or one partner's body is no longer attractive to the other, which is something I hear in this room all the time. 'My husband's body repulses me.' 'My wife has put on fifty pounds.' Recently, I've been treating a whole spate of women who married for money, but now, with their husbands out of work or going bankrupt, well, let's just say they're finding out that there's not much else holding the marriage together. There really are so many distinct, individual reasons why an infidelity occurs that it's a fool's errand to draw any conclusions about one instance and apply it to another.

"As for your late husband, I can only conjecture here, because I never met him, nor would it be prudent for me to draw any conclusions about his reasons for seeking sex outside the marriage, but I will say that I have treated several patients, in this very room, whose jobs frequently put them in harm's way, whether overtly or obliquely, and the one universal thing I can say about such people is that part of them gets off on the danger, or else they wouldn't be doing the jobs they're doing. One of my colleagues is even researching a thrill-seeking genetic marker, not that we are all necessarily victims of our genes, but you know what I mean."

"I know what you mean." Jane sighs. "I get it. But I guess I thought Hervé was above all that. I mean, you think you know somebody, and then . . ."

"You don't?" says Lodge.

"Yeah," says Jane. "I guess it sounds really naïve when you put it that way."

"It's not so much naïve as it is simplifying something that's a bit more complicated than: You think you know someone, but then you don't. I think we *do* know people, better than we think we do, but our brains choose to create a cleaned-up version of the person that fits our own narrow worldview. Did you honestly think your mother wasn't having sex these past thirty years? Did it never occur to you that Hervé would be tempted by others during his months on the road? Is it really all that shocking that Bruno got lonely while your mind and body were checked out?"

"Of course not, it's just . . . God, how could I have been so naïve? It seems like willful ignorance on my part. As if part of me refused to, I don't know, grow up or something."

"Well, you did have to grow up pretty quickly, didn't you?"

"Sure, but . . . that seems a little facile, doesn't it? My childhood was cut short, so I try to elongate it through obliviousness?"

"Sometimes the most facile, obvious interpretations hit the closest to the mark," says Lodge.

"Or maybe I'm just stupid."

"Come on, Jane. You're not stupid. We're all guilty of willful ignorance. You can't graduate from Harvard and call yourself stupid."

"Oh yeah?" Jane says, standing up. "Watch me." She walks over to the mirror hanging on the far wall of the office and points at herself. "Stupid," she says. "*Estúpida. Imbécile* . . ." She looks over her shoulder at Lodge. "Got any other languages up your sleeve?"

"Just a couple of years of high school Greek."

"I'll take 'em."

"Um, *lollo*? I think. Yes. *Lollo*."

"*Lollo*. I like it." She points at herself once more. "*Lollo*," she says.

Lodge laughs. "Feel better?"

"Much."

"Great. That'll be two hundred and fifty dollars please." For a split second, Jane wonders whether he's serious until Lodge steps around his desk and, seeing Jane's expression, starts to laugh. "Oh, come on. *Now* you're being stupid."

"See? I told you," she says, pointing to her head. "*Estúpida!*"

"Actually," says Lodge, "I was just thinking that I'm the stupid one."

"Why?"

"For not forcing your mother to marry me. For not getting the privilege of being your stepfather." He sighs, and in that sigh, Jane sees the ravages of time and regret.

"No one could force Mom to do anything," she says. "If you knew her at all, you knew that."

"I know. Believe me, I know. But maybe I could have tried a little harder. Listen, speaking of your mother, I meant to ask: What are you going to do about her house? She was worried about leaving you with that burden."

"I don't know. The *Globe* wants me back here, but Bruno wouldn't be able to work here, even if he had a green card. His English is passable, but it's not like there are a lot of editing jobs just waiting to be filled. I mean, first I have to decide if we're even going to stay together. Sophie is young enough that a move won't be that hard, but, well, it's complicated. To say the least."

"I'll tell you what," says Lodge. "I know this is out of left field, but if you end up deciding to sell the house, I'd like to be first on your list of potential buyers. I'm thinking of selling my own house, starting afresh. It hasn't really been a happy home, if you know what I mean, and I don't like the constant reminder, plus your mother's house has more bedrooms, and at the rate my sons are going, I'll have six grandkids by next Christmas. Plus I guess I figure if I were in your mother's house, I'd be, you know . . ."

"Happy?"

Lodge shrugs. "Something like that."

Jane smiles. "You really did love her, didn't you?"

"Yeah," he says, his glasses misting slightly. "I really did."

"Would I be allowed to come back and visit?"

"Oh, Janie, are you kidding me? You and your daughter could have your own wing. It's just me now."

"I'll think about it," says Jane, exiting the office without correcting her name. It's fine, she thinks. Let him call me Janie. Then she gently tears Sophie away from the DVD and tries to answer the many questions provoked by the elongation of Pinocchio's nose.

• • •

"**Y**ou're here for the A.R.T. auditions?" says the young, bespectacled pit bull in a floral miniskirt guarding the entrance to the Loeb Drama Center. She holds the one unlocked door ajar just a crack with the tip of her combat boot, a signal to any student still on campus, any random passerby, any person not here for the express purpose of trying out for the 2009–2010 season of the American Repertory Theater that trespassers will not be tolerated. But before Mia can laugh nervously and say oh my God, no, sorry, we're just alumni poking around, we'll come back another time, Clay is already assuming a character.

"Why yes we are," he says, scanning the clipboard and seeing SATURDAY, JUNE 6/FEMALES splashed in 48-point Helvetica across the top, with numbered blank spaces beneath it, a few already scribbled in with the names and contact numbers of the hopefuls. "My lady here's trying out, and I'm here to root her on."

Clay's enthusiasm, his spontaneity, his ability to role-play both on the stage and off used to rub off on everyone, Mia included. There are people in the world, she thinks, who make you a better version of yourself. Or at least a more authentic, less-inhibited version. When Clay left her for Luba way back when, her heart was crushed, but what she missed most was their melding of minds, not bodies. In fact, Clay was fairly hesitant in the bedroom department, for what are now—and were back then, for anyone paying attention—obvious reasons. "Always gotta bring the cheering section," says Mia, jumping into the role of Clay's "lady," replete with southern drawl. She feels a giddiness she hasn't felt in years. "I hope we're not too late."

She wonders if the girl's nose ring ever gets snagged in the moth holes of her sweater. What is it with this new generation of young women? Trilby's tongue ring this morning; Max's friend from pre-school (or so she'd learned through Facebook) with her pierced labia. When Mia recently ran into labia girl and her boyfriend, she couldn't help wondering about mechanics. Did she remove the hoop before sex? Was she even having sex yet? Not something you can really ask, although getting one's labia pierced, like the colorful flags put up by the shop owners of new businesses, seems as good an indicator as any that the store's open for business. Standing in line behind the couple at a Peet's coffee on Sunset, seeing the boy rub his thumb over the viper tattoo at the small of the girl's back, Mia had to mentally will herself not to picture his penis getting scraped by the backing.

When did mutilation come to signify female boldness? she won-ders. Or, if all of them are getting pierced and tattooed, is it less about boldness and more about the kind of conformity that had her sitting in that Woodmere salon, circa 1982, getting an ill-considered perm? At least the perm grew out. She imagines Max's preschool friend many years hence, removing the hoop to give birth. She fast-forwards a few years after that, as the new mother's toddler discovers the snake above his mother's ass. "What's that, Mommy?" "Oh, that? That's my viper."

"You're right on time," says the nose-pierced clipboard wielder, opening the door its full width. "Even a bit early. Here, sign your name on the next blank line, then you can go have a seat in the house. They'll be starting in about, oh"—she pulls her cell phone out of a hidden pocket in her skirt to check the time. (No one wears watches anymore, thinks Mia. When did that happen? And how do these white girls grow dreadlocks? The world sped by while she was driving carpools and stuffing goody bags with landfill. Girls who weren't even born when she was graduating college now have dreadlocks, nose rings, jobs, *sex* . . .)—"seven minutes or so. Did you bring your head shot and résumé?"

"Oh, Jiminy," says Clay, ad-libbing. "I think we left them on the desk back at home. You want me to run back and—"

"That's okay," says the gatekeeper. "You can just drop them by after the audition. They'll be here until ten. Then tomorrow they're casting the males from two until eight. Here . . ." She hands Mia a photocopy of a monologue from the pile of papers stacked under the audition list. Mia sees the character's name and the first few lines of dialogue and recognizes the passage immediately: It's the climax of *A Doll's House*, toward the end of Act III, after Torvald reveals his true self, and Nora suddenly realizes she's been raising three children with a stranger. "It's the first play of the season. The director says you don't have to be off book. Just familiarize yourself with the lines before you go up."

"Oh, she's been off book on that one for *years*," says Clay, with a wink. Then he grabs Mia by the arm. "Come on, darlin'. Your destiny awaits."

"Such a drama queen, isn't he?" Mia mock-confides to the clipboard girl, rolling her eyes, really getting into the part.

"As if," says Clay, in the queeniest faux-outburst he can muster.

"I just guard the door," says Clipboard Girl, uninterested. "But I'm sure if you say she'll be great, she'll be great." She plops down on her sad metal stool and reopens the paperback she'd been reading before they interrupted her. "Oh, and I'd drop the drawl before you go up there, if I were you," she calls out over her shoulder, with what sounds to Mia's sensitive ear like condescension. "The play takes place in Norway, not Nashville."

To which Mia, switching seamlessly to the Long Island accent she's worked hard to erase, flings it right back: "Oh my Gawd. Of course. I would never dream of doing Nora as a southern belle," which throws Clipboard Girl for a loop she quickly chalks up to the absurdity of old people and actors. She wants to be a director when she graduates. Or maybe a political activist. Guarding this door is her penance for having parents who were more concerned with gold faucets than they were about paying their daughter's tuition. She's reading Simone de Beauvoir for the first time, which, she'll later tell her musician boyfriend, is rocking her world even harder than Weber. It will be years before she's able to look back on this period from her small, cluttered cubicle at WomenWork International and realize how exciting it all was, how full of new ideas and promise, despite the lost hours guarding doors.

"You are bad," Clay whispers in Mia's ear.

"You are worse," she whispers back. Then she breathes in, deeply. "Oh my God, take a whiff," she says. The lobby of the Loeb smells exactly as Mia remembers: slightly musty, like violin rosin mixed with charcoal ash and baked muffin. But the somewhat drab aesthetic of the building itself, though well maintained with Harvard dollars, surprises her. In her mind, over the years, the Loeb transmogrified from dark, austere minimalism into glowing, rococo nirvana. Or maybe that's just the feeling she gets whenever she remembers being inside it. Or maybe she's confusing one of the more gilded sets for the actual architecture of the building. Anyway, she thinks, it was never the brick and mortar of the place that sucked her in. It was the stage. "Let's shmy around for a little while," she says to Clay, "but we better get out of here before they call my name."

"Excuse me, 'shmy'?"

"It's Yiddish for, well, I think some sort of a combination of checking things out and snooping. My grandmother would know for sure, but she's dead."

"Ah, yes. Death. *So* inconvenient. I like shmy. I'll steal it. How do I use it in a sentence? Can I say, 'Lady, let's shmy!'?"

"No. You can't just shmy. You shmy *around*. And no offense, but it sounds wrong in that accent."

"Oh yeah? How 'bout old English? My Lady, doth thou wish to shmy? Or wilt thou be having thy bagel with a shmear?"

Mia has to work hard to keep a straight face. "Oy gevalt, my Lord. You are incorrigible."

"Forsooth!" Clay takes Mia's arm and links it in his. Then he bends his knees down, then up, down then up. "Schlemiel! Schlimazel! Hasenpfeffer Incorporated!" He hums the first few bars of the *Laverne &*

Shirley theme song then pushes open the house doors, and Mia lets loose her giggles, but then the two grow instantly silent the moment they enter the theater. They stand there in the aisle, taking in the empty stage, the ghosts of productions past, the sloping vista of spring-loaded seats, all resting in the up position save for those pushed down by the rear ends of Nora hopefuls and by a handful of those wielding the power to choose one over the others. A few heads turn when they make their way down the aisle and claim two seats in one of the back rows, but most of the women are intently studying their monologues, mouthing the words to themselves, gesturing to invisible Torvalds.

"Wow," whispers Mia, for lack of the proper language to describe that rush of emotion she imagines one is supposed to feel upon entering a house of worship, which has only ever struck her in this place. Clay grabs her hand over the armrest; she laces her fingers into his and gives them a small squeeze.

"I know," says Clay. "Back in the belly of the beast. Awesome, isn't it? Plus I'm going to get to see you do Nora again. How cool is that?"

"Right," Mia whispers to him. "As if I'd ever go up there."

"You will if I make you." Clay smiles mischievously, his gaze resting on the stage, already imagining it.

"Clay, whatever you're scheming, you better stop it right now. Seriously. I haven't auditioned in years. It's not even an option."

"Come on, Mia, I bet you still know that monologue cold. Just do it. For shits and giggles."

"Let me see, how do I put this politely? No fucking way. Not for shits and giggles, not for them, and not for you." She says this with the adamancy of a woman who cannot only conjure, as if it were yesterday, the painful sting of professional rejection but also one whose breasts are growing heavier with milk by the second. She wishes she'd thought to stick the manual pump in her purse. "Anyway, I have to go back to Jane's to feed Zoe before I explode. I mean, look at me. I'm like Barbarella here."

"And here I was thinking you went and got yourself a boob job," says Clay, unselfconsciously reaching out to cop a feel of Mia's breasts in the way only a gay man or a close girlfriend is allowed to do. "Hot dang, lady, those are some crazy big tits."

"Tell me about it," she says. "I told Jonathan he should enjoy them while he can because they'll shrink back down to nothing after I'm done nursing." Then she suddenly thinks: and so will I. Followed by: this was a bad idea, coming here. And then: crazy schizophrenic Lytton was right. I had all the tools, and I didn't use them. When she actually stops to think about these things, it plunges her into despair. She's trained herself, over the years, to relegate such feelings of failure into the back corners of her mind, but sometimes they find a secret passageway around the wall and spill out along the edges, like smoke. "Look, let's just sit here and watch one or two of the auditions, and then we're out of here, okay? I have to get back."

"Okay," says Clay. "I won't push it."

"Thank you." She squeezes his hand once more as the first woman is called up onstage.

"Too young." Clay dismisses her immediately, before a word even exits her mouth.

He's right, Mia thinks. She looks way too young and inexperienced to play Nora. Plus she reads the lines as if they were invective, not inner thought transformed into outward epiphany. Nora is disappointed with her husband, but she's not as angry at him as she is furious at herself for blindly, unquestioningly accepting his worldview as her own. When she tells her husband "*It is your fault that I have made nothing of my life,*" she is both accusing Torvald of malfeasance as well as castigating herself. The monologue demands subtlety as well as an understanding of the historical context in which it was written, when women could not sign for loans, when slamming the door on one's family was so shocking for certain audiences, Ibsen was forced to provide an alternative ending when the play was staged in Germany. The monologue also requires at least a passing grasp of the sometimes untenable and universal compromises of marriage, no matter the era.

Mia understood all this back in college, despite her own youth and inexperience, simply by virtue of having gestated in the acid womb of Stella Mandelbaum. She and her brother were continually sucking from the tit of their mother's malaise. Mia vowed to be a different kind of maternal presence in the lives of her own children, and in most respects she upheld those vows with aplomb. Okay, so sometimes she loses her temper and sounds eerily like her mother, but unlike her mother, she immediately regrets her bad behavior and begs her children and husband for forgiveness. No one's perfect. At the very least, she's done an excellent job at hiding her own failures and disappointments from her sons.

When Max recently asked her, point-blank, whether she regretted giving up her career after he was born, she gave the boilerplate answer she gives to everyone: "Max, I just had to face the fact that I was not beautiful enough to be a movie star. Plus I didn't want to miss a single moment with you." Both of these statements were true, and yet taken together, they were also little better than a bad fib. Had she been offered good parts, she has no doubt she would have taken them. And while she originally *thought* she didn't want to miss out on a single moment with her children, the minute they were all off in school, she was relieved to have a piece of herself back, even if that "self" found itself filling the hours not in front of an audience but shopping for food, going to the gym, volunteering at her sons' school, running errands, straightening the house, stuffing envelopes for various causes, and reading the paper from end to end.

But now that Zoe is here, a convenient chapter two, she finds herself back in the trenches of hands-on mothering, which leaves her too busy, too tired, and too emotionally frazzled to imagine what the next chapter of her life's saga might look like, although she's certain it will not include more babies. For one, her knees and back couldn't take it. For another, she's not enjoying full-time motherhood as much this time around. Or rather, she is enjoying her time alone with baby Zoe a thousand times more than she did with her first three (painfully aware, with the benefit of hindsight, both of how ephemeral it all is and of how little she actually needs to worry about first steps, first teeth, first carrots and peas), but whereas she once gleefully sought out the company of other mothers like a magnet to paper clips, she has now become the kind of mother who repels the others with her utter indifference. In fact, when it came time to sign up Zoe for Gymboree, Mia couldn't pull the trigger. The thought of sitting shoeless in a circle of sleep-deprived sybarites while some failed actress blew thousands of tiny and perversely unpoppable bubbles into their single-process-treated hair made Mia so depressed, she broke her 6 P.M. rule and had a glass of Chardonnay with lunch.

The most grounded women she knows—not the happiest, she's not naïve enough to buy into the notion of steady, continual happiness, since "happy" describes a state that is unpredictable and evanescent for every-one, no matter how comfortable they are in their own skin, but she digresses—have careers that allow them to have a steady foot in both worlds, work and home, on a sliding scale and ratio set according to their individual emotional and financial needs. Before she had a daughter, she didn't really worry much about the fact that her sons never saw her earning a paycheck. But ever since Zoe was born, she's felt a nagging responsibility to set a good example. Never mind that she's worried, for the first time in her married life, about her family's finances.

She has no idea what the actual numbers are—Jonathan handles everything money-related, including taking out the weekly wads of cash from the ATM for the housekeeper and the gardeners and the nanny—but recently, when the monthly AmEx bill came lumbering in at well over $78,000 (she'd replaced the lawn furniture and the boys' laptops and bought a new sofa and a couple of light fixtures and a few cashmere sweaters for the baby and an espresso machine, nothing major, but still, it added up), Jonathan had, unusually, thrown a fit. "Cashmere? For a six-month-old? Jesus Christ, Mia, we can't keep bleeding cash like this!" he'd snapped. But every time she asks him for a clearer picture of their financial health, especially now with their portfolio in what she overheard their accountant Stan Shipley describe as "a fucking tailspin," Jonathan always says, "Don't worry. I've got it covered. We're fine."

It's crazy! Mia thinks. I have the right to sign a loan, the right to earn money, and yet here I am in 2009, no better off than Nora. She decides she will bring this up with Jonathan tonight, after the reunion dinner. And she will no longer accept "I've got it covered" for an answer. It's absurd for her not to know the most basic facts about their financial well-being. No, worse than that. It's wrong, and it's embarrassing, and if Jonathan balks, she'll call Shipley herself.

The director interrupts Nora #1 in the middle of the monologue with a "thank you very much," which is never a good sign. Nora #2 is called up onstage, and she does a much better job with the tone of the material, except she's not believable. She doesn't inhabit the role; the effort of the acting, the nuts and bolts of it are too visible. Also, her sense of timing is off. The words flow out of her mouth with a syncopation that feels jarring, such that when she recites the line "*I have existed merely to perform tricks for you,*" she places odd pauses after both *existed* and *merely*, which makes her sound less like a human and more like those computer programs that mimic the human voice.

"Next," whispers Clay as the director says, "Thank you very much," nearly simultaneously.

Mia's breasts have become rock hard. She'll have to pump an ounce or two before Zoe nurses, just to allow the nipple to have a bit of give and elasticity for the latch. At the mere thought of her daughter, she feels her milk letting down and, yup (she fixes her gaze on the two nipple-size, nipple-located stains on her blouse, shit), leaking out. When Jonathan once asked her what letdown feels like, she told him it's the chest-area equivalent to the onset of crying, when you can feel the liquid pooling behind the eyes before they emerge. "Come on," Mia says to Clay, about to stand up. "Look at me. I'm a frigging mess here. I've got to get back."

He stares at the stains on her blouse, unfazed. "Oh, please, you know what they say."

"Huh?"

"Don't cry over spilt milk." Clay grabs hold of her arm, urging her to sit back down. "I'm loving this. Aren't you loving this? Isn't this fun? Stay a few more minutes with me. Pretty please?"

Yes, she thinks, it is fun. I am loving it. I want to stay. "I should go." The third Nora is called, but no one stirs or appears on stage. "Andrea Krull?" the director shouts a second time, and then another voice shouts out, "I think she just went to the bathroom," and before it dawns on Mia that hers was the next name on that list, the director is now shouting, "Mia? Mia Zane?"

"Go!" whispers Clay. "Come on, just do it."

"No way!" Mia says, a little too loudly, and now everyone is turned in their direction.

"Ms. Zane?" says the director. "Please, everyone, we don't have all day." Now he stands up and addresses the theater at large. "Look, this is an open call. Our new A.D. wanted it this way, to shake things up around here, but it also means we've got a tight schedule and many Noras to see between now and this evening, so when your name is called, please be ready, and for God's sake, if you have to use the ladies' room, please do so now, not three minutes before your audition. Ms. Zane? Are you ready to go up?"

And here's where Mia Zane's sense of guilt, shame, and propriety prove, once again, victors over rationality. Why can't she just say, *No, I'm sorry, there's been a big mistake*? Because she can't. And because, yes, she has to admit, a tiny or maybe even a medium-size part of her might actually *want* to go up there and show these young Noras how it's done, never mind her age, postpartum jelly roll of a stomach, and milk-stained blouse. In fact, Clay's right. To hell with the stains. There's never been any use in crying over spilt milk. And there's no use lamenting the lost years. "Yes," she says, standing up. "I'm ready." She turns to Clay and mouths, "I'm going to kill you," but she doesn't really mean it, and he knows it.

Clay stands up and hugs her, hard. Her breasts feel like giant boulders between them. Then he whispers in her ear, "Zane, go show these bitches how it's done."

Mia walks down the aisle toward the stage completely lost in her head, in the type of memory and deliberation that wipe out peripheral vision. If there were a camera following her—being married to a director, she often imagines her life as a film, albeit one that, until just this minute, has been more boring than she imagined it would have been, given the previews—it would be mounted on a dolly, shooting one of those long tracking shots where the focal length and background change dramatically while the human figure stays the same size. She forces herself to concentrate on her breathing, on getting into character. It's been two decades since she slammed the door on that stage.

It's about fucking time she opened it.

Now she's finally standing on the proscenium, sweating under the lights, the harsh white spot blinding her to any one person or object in the audience. Good, she thinks. She doesn't want to see anyone. She imagines Clay in the back row, cheering her on. She pictures him as Torvald, pathetic Torvald, standing in front of her twenty years earlier. She's about to begin when she hears the director yell, "Wait, where are your sides?" Then to the room at large, once more, the frustration in his voice palpable as he says, "Please, people, before you step up on that stage, make sure you have your sides with you."

"That's okay, I'm fine without them," says Mia. An earlier glance at the monologue was all she needed to realize the sentences are in her, as clear as they were the day she first performed them. Certain passages are just like that, permanently etched into her memory: the balcony scene from *Romeo and Juliet*; Hedda Gabler's line about courage, how if only one had it, then "life might be livable, in spite of everything." She closes her eyes for a brief moment and begins. "*It is perfectly true, Torvald,*" she says. "*When I was at home with Papa, he told me his opinion about everything, and so I had the same opinions; and if I differed from him, I concealed the fact, because he would not have liked it. He called me his doll child . . ."* She feels the words rushing out of her now with the same inevitable insistence as the milk now surging out of her breasts in thick rivulets, the thrill of the former wiping out the shame of the latter. It is a scene the director will describe in the coming years, with ever in-creasing exaggeration, again and again: the middle-aged woman, he can't remember her name, some alum at her twentieth reunion who snuck into the audition, clearly too old for the part but so damned good and so impassioned in her delivery that "her breasts were, like, spraying milk all over the fucking stage, and I mean: All. Over. The fucking stage."

"I have existed merely to perform tricks for you, Torvald," Mia continues, slumping down on a wooden block that's been painted black, the only prop on the stage. Then, with growing strength and conviction, she stands up once more to deliver the final sting of words with the perfect mix of potency and defeat. ". . . *it was then that it dawned upon me that for eight years I had been living here with a strange man, and had borne him three children."* A few gasps can be heard in the audience, and Mia knows she has them in her grip, and now she sees her way free and clear to the finale. Taking a small but deliberate step forward, addressing an empty spot on the horizon—herself; God; the audience; whomever—she holds one hand to her heart and lets it rip: *"Oh! I can't bear to think of it! I could tear myself into little bits!"*

Clay jumps up out of his seat and begins to clap wildly, which causes a few others to clap along with him. "Now that's what I'm talk-ing about!" he says. "Brava, Mia! Way to knock it out of the fucking ballpark."

Mia shushes him with a finger to her lips and rolls her eyes at his show of enthusiasm, but she also knows the outburst was not false. She deserves it. All of it. Or at least more of it. Jesus, what was she think-ing? So she'll never be a Hollywood star. Who gives a shit? There are plenty of opportunities in LA to do theater. Why hasn't she taken them? Dear God, she thinks. I've lost so many years.

(She can't bear to think of it. She could tear herself into little bits.)

The director stands up and addresses Mia. "Excellent job, Ms."—he looks down at his list for her name—"Zane, truly excellent. But if you don't mind my asking, since I don't have a copy of your résumé here, what stage were you last on?"

"Um, this one?" she says hesitantly. "For a student production. My senior year of college."

"And that was . . . ?"

"Uh, 1989." She can hear a smattering of stifled chuckles. That's okay, she thinks. Let them laugh. They'll be old someday, too, and then it'll be less funny. She imagines the director doing the math: twenty years plus a Harvard senior. . . .

"Ah, got it. So you haven't done anything since then?"

She pictures the homey set of the Preparation-H commercial she landed a few months out of college; the satin-lined coffin in which she played dead, for ten hours straight, for that CBS pilot that never aired. "No, not onstage." She blocks the harsher rays of the spotlight with a palm to her forehead. She can just make out the faint outline of the director, scribbling God-only-knows-what onto his clipboard. "Look, I'm sorry for wasting your time. I just . . ." She's not really sorry, but apologizing has become such a habit, she can't help it.

"No need to apologize," he says. "In fact, you've raised the bar in here, which is good, but just so we're clear . . ." He pauses. Lets loose a nervous cough. "The character of Nora Helmer really should be played by an actor in her late twenties to early thirties. At the most."

"Of course," says Mia. "I totally get it." She's middle-aged now. Which means she can't play Nora anymore, or Juliet or probably even Hedda, but if she's lucky, she still has another half of her life to traverse and at least a dozen or so excellent characters she can still play: Mary in *A Long Day's Journey into Night*; Blanche in *A Streetcar Named Desire*; Martha in *Who's Afraid of Virginia Woolf?* Great roles, each one of them, and then she can graduate to the cranky grandmothers, like Violet in

August: Osage County, a part that any actress worth her salt would kill to play. All is not lost. It never was. She feels the cavity behind her eyes now filling, her breasts overflowing, sweat now dripping from every pore. "Thank you," she says.

Then she exits stage left.

LUDWIG GERHART VON ARNHEM. *Home Address:* 14 Jubilee Place, London SW3 1AW. *Additional Home Address:* Untere Tuftra 11, Zermatt 3920, Switzerland; *Additional Home Address:* 12 Via G. Orlandi, 80071 Anacapri, Isle of Capri. *Occupation and Office Address:* Partner, Aurora Partners. *E-mail:* lgvonarnhem@aurorapartners .com. *Graduate Degrees:* M.B.A., Wharton '95. *Spouse/Partner:* Eloise Marder Von Arnhem (A.B., Oxford '97). *Children:* Ernst Foxhall, 2001; Delphinia Cleo, 2003; Ossian Arthur, 2005.

Life is busy and rich. I run a hedge fund in London, where I live with my wife and three children. We spend our winters skiing at our house in Zermat, our summers in Capri, or rather, my wife goes down to Capri with the children, and I do the weekend commute back and forth. Exhausting, but worth it! Stop by if you're ever in one of our cities!

STEVEN JOSHUA KRAMER. *Home Address:* 8220 Lincoln Terrace, Los Angeles, CA 90069 (310-754-0078). *Occupation and Office Address:* Writer, *Superdigger*, NBC Studios, 3000 West Alameda Avenue, Burbank 91523. *E-mail:* sjkramer12@gmail.com. *Spouse/ Partner:* Lisa Renfrow Kramer (A.B., Harvard '91). *Spouse/Partner Occupation:* Writer, *The Goonies*. *Children:* Riley Renfrow, 2003; Angus Renfrow, 2006.

After a brief stint as a faith healer in Nepal, I realized I was the son of God and spent the next seven years wandering the globe in search of disciples and a skilled plastic surgeon. When those plans fell through—I only found two disciples, and neither of them knew how to crush noses—I decided to embark on a secret mission to Pluto. Problem was? By the time I got my rocket ship all gussied up and loaded with all the latest doodads (iPod dock, hamburger grill, condom dispenser), Pluto was taken off the list of planets. Scientists! That's when I decided to open up a combination bikini wax/grilled cheese emporium, until the health department had to go and shut us down for reasons I'm not at liberty to disclose. Somewhere in there I met my wife and spawned a couple of kids, and they are way smarter, cooler, and more perfect than all of your spouses and kids combined. How do I know this? Easy. I am the son of God. Anyone want to buy a used rocket ship? I'll throw in forty pounds of cheddar and a tweezer.

CHARLES RANDALL POOLE. *Home Address:* 602 North Locust Street, Muncie, IN 47303 (765-908-7745). *Occupation and Office Address:* Assistant professor, Ball State University, 2000 West University Avenue, Muncie, IN 47306. *E-mail:* crp@ballstate.edu; *Graduate Degree:* Ph.D., Duke '96.

Here's the crazy thing: I love what I do. I teach classics at a small university in Indiana, and I wake up every day loving my job, my students, my life. The problem is I don't really care about publishing scholarly work or completing all the administrative tasks that go along with being a college professor, so I've spent the past twenty years hopping from school to school, never getting tenure. I feel like a bit of a gypsy, and it hasn't been great for my love life either. Most of the women I date end up deciding that my lack of ambition is appalling, but I feel like I *do* have ambition, just not in the traditional sense of the word. My ambition is to teach the classics to students eager to learn, and from all accounts, I do an admirable job of this. After my stint at Ball State is up, I'm thinking about leaving Indiana and taking an on-campus, free-housing position at one of the northeastern prep schools. It's probably what I should have been doing all along, but I'm stubborn. I thought I could carve out my own little niche in the university system, which frankly seems kind of broken to me. Isn't the point of being a teacher . . . to teach?

I have some hobbies, which keep me sane. I'm an avid biker until the first snowfall; I love to ski, and I'm now learning how to snowboard; I've been getting into rock climbing; I read a ton of fiction and nonfiction; and I love going out to see movies, music, plays, anything that moves me. Obviously, I get particularly excited when a play by Aeschylus or Euripides comes to town. This happens often enough, and I always turn it into an event, inviting my whole class to the performance. I get letters every now and then from former students, who tell me I was the one who made them love the classics or become a classics professor or write modern-day versions of classic plays. These letters are, to my mind, life's true currency.

Still no kids, although I'd like to have a couple one day. Until then, it's just me and my golden retriever, Antigone.

GITA SENGUPTA-JONES. *Home Address:* 1442 Hampton Ridge Drive, McLean, VA 22101 (703-556-2265). *Occupation and Office Address*: Mom. *E-mail:* gitasj@aol.com. *Spouse/Partner:* Alex Jones (A.B., Princeton '87; M.B.A., Wharton '91). *Spouse/Partner Occupation:* Marketing Director, AOL; *Children*: Sumina Frances, 2004; Sanjay Graham, 2006.

My husband Alex and I met when we were both working at AOL. We were always the last two people in the office, and one day he invited me to share a yogurt with him in the cafeteria, and the rest, as they say, is history.

I kept working after each of my children was born, but last year our daughter Sumina was diagnosed with a brain tumor, and I took a leave of absence to care for her full-time. I know other things must have transpired during these last five years, but really it's Sumina's illness that occupies all of the space inside our brains and heart. As of this writing, her prognosis is not great, but we are trying to keep a positive attitude. Sumina is old enough to understand that she's sick, but not old enough to understand the ramifications of her illness, so we try to keep it light, both for her sake and for the sake of her little brother, who's gotten a bit of a raw deal being the younger sibling of a critically ill child. I know this experience will make him stronger, eventually, but right now he just seems confused and a bit lonely, since he's always being left with a sitter when Alex and I are at the hospital with Sumina.

I don't understand why God makes a world in which children get so sick, and yet I pray to whatever gods I can, every day, for her survival. If any of you are in the habit of saying prayers, no matter your denomination, no matter your beliefs, please add Sumina to your list.

THOMAS ALLEN WOLFF. *Home Address:* 1121 Alice Street, Oakland, CA 94612 (510-445-0787). *Occupation and Office Address*: Teacher, Oakland Unity High School, 6038 Brann Street, Oakland, CA 94605. *E-mail*: twolff@unityhigh.org. *Graduate Degree:* J.D., Harvard '93; *Children*: Bruce Jared, 1999; Drew Emmons, 2001.

I got divorced, left New York, and quit my job as a partner at Davis Polk, where I'd been toiling away miserably since law school, to start a new career as a high school history teacher. Both the job and the climate in Oakland suit me much better. My boys spend their summers and holiday breaks with me, which isn't ideal, but that's what I got in the settlement.

I keep up with some of my former roommates from Leverett House, and I look forward to seeing everyone else at reunion.

JANICE ELAINE HOWARD. *Home Address:* 1401 Northwest 15th Avenue, Miami, FL 33125 (305-325-6675). *Occupation and Office Address*: Physician, Internal Medicine, University of Miami Hospital, 1400 Northwest 12th Avenue, Miami, FL 33125. *E-mail*: janice howard@umh.org. *Graduate Degree:* M.D., University of Chicago '95. *Spouse/Partner*: Malcolm Alvarez (B.A., University of Michigan '87; M.D., University of Miami '92). *Spouse/Partner Occupation*: Oncologist. *Children:* Timothy Howard, 2005.

I consider myself lucky to be one of the few blind doctors in the U.S. It was definitely challenging learning how to intubate, locate an aorta, and diagnose a rash without the use of my eyes, but I had a lot of wonderful teachers who believed in showing rather than telling, to the point where sometimes it takes my patients a few minutes to realize I cannot see.

That being said, I mostly do lab work and lobbying these days, trying to convince the U.S. government to support stem cell research, which I feel is the key to curing so many illnesses—Parkinson's, MS, amyotrophic lateral sclerosis, spinal cord injury, burns, heart disease, diabetes, and arthritis, just to name a few—it's nearly criminal not to move forward on that front.

In 2005, my husband Malcolm and I became the proud parents of little Timmy, who was born uneventfully and brings us untold joy every day. Miami, where we live, is warm and lovely, and I try to take a swim every morning.

Three years ago, I was diagnosed with multiple sclerosis. I have good days and bad days, but mostly I try just not to dwell on it. If I've learned anything in these past twenty years it's that life never works out as you planned, but you take what you're given, and you run with it.

Can't wait to meet up with everyone at reunion!

Evening

It was Addison, feeling restless and untethered without Gunner, who suggested they all leave the boring dinner dance and head to the Spee Club, and then Bennie said, "You know what? It's about time I saw the inside of a Final Club," checking first with her wife (who was chatting up some curator from the Tate) before calling the hotel babysitter to say they'd be back probably closer to midnight, not eleven, and then Bucky, who'd initially suggested the Fly Club garden until he was told it's now a Hillel, said he'd get the key from Ludwig Von Arnhem, who used to be in the Spee and was itching to ditch the dance, too, after his girlfriend of three months, a former Victoria's Secret model with whom he took up—officially, that is—after separating from his second wife, complained she was bored and no one speaks Russian and aren't there *any* drugs around here, and then Clover joined in because some unhinged husband of a classmate she could barely remember tried to blame her for the recent foreclosure of his home ("You should be ashamed of yourself!" he'd said, drunkenly spilling a drop of seven-dollar Merlot on the tip of her $800 Manolo, and for a flash she thought he'd somehow found out about her having misappropriated Bucky's sperm, not the American dream), and then Jonathan and Mia, who were glad to have an excuse to get away from motor-mouthed Luba, who'd cornered them by the dessert trays to tell them more about her latest trial than they'd ever care to know, even if they'd been judge and jury both, said yes, please, get us the fuck out of here, and then Jane was located off in the far corner, away from the blare of the DJ and his speakers, spinning 1980s nostalgia in the form of Chaka

Khan, Estefan, and "Too Turned On," Simple Minds, "Red Red Wine," and "Sweet Child O' Mine," having an intense conversation with Ellen Grandy, whom she barely knew back in college, but man, from the outside looking in (thought Addison), the two might as well have been lovers tearfully reuniting after years spent apart, and Jane said sure, she'd love to come, as long as Ellen, who was also crying—Jesus, what the hell could those two have been yammering on about?—could join, and then Mia went to find Clay, who wondered aloud whether his hillbilly pansy ass would even be allowed inside the Spee, to which Mia said c'mon, all those friggin' Final Clubs—Finals Clubs, whatever they're called, she could never remember if there was an *s* or not—are paeans to latent homoeroticism, and before they knew it, the four ex-roommates, Addison, Clover, Mia, and Jane, along with a dozen or so hangers-on, were making their way up Dunster Street in their natty dresses and suits, the women trying to avoid catching their heels in the cobblestones, the men anticipating cigars, yanking ties loose, and for the first time that weekend, it finally felt like old times: the flash mob, the random destination, the anticipation of youthful debauchery.

"In a weird way, I'm actually glad you let it slip," Jane says to Ellen, keeping themselves several paces behind the rest of the group. "Canonizing him, as I've been doing, hasn't served anyone well. Know what I mean?"

Ellen is blown away by the mature, acrimony-free manner in which Jane has chosen to handle the news. She feels like putting an arm around her but doesn't risk it. Yet. "I know exactly what you mean, but it was still wrong of me," she says. "I'm sorry. Really sorry."

"It's . . ." says Jane. She spots a homeless man off in the distance, fishing a half-eaten sandwich out of a public trash can. She's struck by the same sense of pathos she frequently encounters when bearing witness to similar scenes: We are all one minuscule step away, she thinks, from sifting through trash. How many kids had she seen over the years, climbing mountains of rotting refuse in their bare feet, fighting for scraps with the dump birds? How many families had she seen, squatting over open sewers on the borderlands of conflict, who once had private places to relieve themselves, however humble? Hell, how many Americans who bought trustingly into the dream were now bathing in public restrooms, sleeping in cars? Jane stops in her tracks ten feet from the homeless man. "Wait," she whispers to Ellen, "isn't that . . . ?"

"Lytton Hepworth," says Ellen. "Yeah. I think it is. Stay here. I'll be right back."

Ellen runs across the street into a convenience store and emerges, a minute or so later, with a bagful of food: a bunch of bananas, three cheeses, a couple of apples, a loaf of bread, and two boxes of granola bars, which she casually slips to Lytton. He takes the groceries with a quick nod; Ellen crosses back over Mount Auburn Street to catch up with Jane and the group. "Right. So, where were we?" she says.

"You were apologizing for having sex with my late husband," says Jane.

"I really am—"

Jane cuts her off. She doesn't need to hear the apology twice. "And I was about to forgive you."

"You were?"

"I was. I do."

"Thank you," says Ellen. "I've been feeling guilty about it. For a long time."

"Good. You should feel guilty. Now let's move on." Within the first half hour of her now three-hour chatathon with Ellen, Jane immediately understood what Hervé must have found irresistible about her: an unaffected intensity, a sharp intellect utterly indifferent to its sharpness, an ability to laugh at herself, a passion without pedantry. Not that the betrayal feels any less painful than it did during the moment of its discovery, or during Jane's hour of hyperventilating shock afterward—if anything, now that the jolt of the revelation has worn off, she feels the sting of it even deeper—but with Hervé dead, any anger she feels toward Ellen seems beside the point. Or at least not worthy of the energy needed to stoke it. Hate, as she knows only too well, requires not only a depersonalized object of one's hatred but also constant fuel and kindling, creating nothing tangible, nothing enduring aside from a pile of ash and the need for a broom. Plus (and this surprises Jane) she finds it oddly comforting to reminisce about Hervé with someone else who once loved him. Their shared affection reanimates him.

When she covered Mitterand's funeral back in 1996, the year after she and Hervé were married, she was simultaneously appalled and fascinated by the stoic image of Mitterand's grieving widow Danielle, standing side by side with his mistress Anne Pingeot, and the illegitimate daughter of that union, Mazarine. "I don't get it," she'd said to Hervé when she arrived home that night. "If this were an American president, there'd be screaming pundits. Riots!" (In two years, Bill Clinton's extracurricular activities with a certain stained-dress-saving intern would prove her prescient.) "How can she just stand there like that, next to her husband's mistress? At his *funeral?*"

"*Qu'est-ce qu'il y a à comprendre?*" Hervé had said with a shrug. What's there to understand? "Mitterand loved his mistress and his daughter, and he loved his wife, and he wanted them all to be at his gravesite, so they were all there together. No big deal." Jane accused Hervé of being callous and insensitive that evening, of not understanding how bonkers it all seemed, but the next morning she scoured every single French newspaper in search of the adulterous outrage she was certain would help prove her point before realizing the entirety of France—left, right, center, it didn't matter one's political affiliation, age, or religious beliefs—felt the same yawny way about the public juxtaposition of wife, mistress, and illegitimate daughter as her husband: big shrug; no big deal.

She grew to accept the reaction, culturally, but she never really understood it on a visceral level. Until today. At this very moment. Chatting with her late husband's mistress. Maybe France has rubbed off on her more than she realizes. "Don't leave just because I fucked up," Bruno keeps telling her. "This is your home. You two are my life. I *love* you." This last phrase he always delivers using the formal *vous* rather than the familiar *tu*: "*Je vous aime*," he says, with deliberate deference and politesse, because he thinks it sounds more beautiful.

She wonders how Bruno is coping with her and Sophie gone. He called last night and left a message on her cell, telling her how much he misses them both, how much he wants to be here with her, how, if she'll just say the word, he'll be on the next flight to Boston. She pictures him in their wood-beamed apartment on the rue Vieille du Temple, sleeping on their low-to-the-ground bed on the sloped oak parquet, hugging Jane's pillow to him, as he always does when she's away or when she arrives home late after he's already gone to bed. Even in his sleep, he'll sense her crawling under the covers, and he'll release his tight grip on her down-filled substitute and pull the real thing toward him, breathing in the scent of her neck. "*Je vous aime*," he'll whisper in her ear, and she'll assume he's awake, but she's always wrong. It's become instinctual by now. He just says it, subconsciously, without even opening his eyes. And she'll lie there, enveloped, drifting off, and it will remind her of her earliest years in Nha Trang, all of her siblings snuggled up next to one another on two thin mats pushed together on the floor, the ocean air masking the stench of chemical deforestation, the chorus of crickets drowning out the occasional burst of gunfire outside their open window until neither breeze nor chirps could mask nor drown it out any longer. It will remind her of the year after Harold died, when Claire, thank God, refused to listen to all those people who told her she shouldn't let a mourning nine-year-old sleep in her bed. It will remind her of her weekend mornings with Hervé on the rue Monge, on those rare occasions when they were both in town between assignments, and she'd wake up with the sun to buy some cheese and pâté on the rue Mouffetard, and when she'd get back, he'd still be sleeping—Hervé could sleep through anything, on anything, a trick that served him well when his bed was a ditch in a mine-strewn desert or the icy floor of an unheated, ethnically cleansed house—so she would put the groceries in the refrigerator and crawl back into his arms to wait for him to wake up and make love. It will remind her—quite simply and for lack of an actual place to visit, either physically or mentally—of home.

If she's still awake at 2 A.M., she decides—and at this rate she will be—she'll call Bruno in Paris, just as he's getting up, to tell him she's decided to sell her mother's house. If the *Globe* can no longer afford its foreign correspondents, so be it. She has no desire to move back to Boston. To begin life from scratch for the fourth time in as many decades in a country where income disparity between the wealthiest one percent and everyone else outrivals that of even traditional banana republics. Her standard of living as a working journalist in America, versus France, would plummet to the point where she and Sophie might have to choose between going to the dentist and buying groceries, and really, what kind of a life is that?

Amazing the middle class isn't rioting at this point. Where is the outrage? Or is everyone just too busy surviving on scraps from the trash heap and looking for work? She should do a story on that. The invisible bleeding. But for whom? Does anyone even still read the *Globe*? If you'd told her when she was graduating college that, twenty years later, journalism would be a dying industry, she wouldn't have believed you. Newspapers stand at the very foundations of a democracy. Or at least they used to. Or at least they should.

The British papers are still surviving, Jane thinks, covering news both foreign and domestic. Maybe she'll go to London and meet with editors at the *Guardian* or the *Financial Times*. Plus her French is fluent enough now that she can probably write for a French newspaper or a magazine or an online something-or-other if she can find an open position. Or she could translate English books into French, like her friend Sabine, who makes a decent living at it. Sophie would love that, having her mother home more often; she herself might even love it, too: a regular life with regular hours. Or maybe she can get a job in the press office at the American Embassy. Or, it suddenly hits her, she can skim off some of the proceeds of the sale of her mother's house and trade it for the chance to stop making excuses (*I can't, I couldn't, I shouldn't*) and write something totally her own. Something long, meaty, worthy of that most precious of commodities: a reader's time.

"I have an idea," she says to Ellen. "Why don't you and Nell come for a visit to Paris? She and Sophie seemed to really hit it off today." Sophie, in fact, was furious at her mother for having pulled her away from Nell, the one American girl at the whole reunion, she'd stated with the requisite melodrama of a seven-year-old, whom she actually liked.

"That would be amazing," says Ellen. "Nell is crazy about all things *Madeline*."

"Sophie's a *Madeline* freak, too," says Jane. "She even went so far one night as to pretend she had appendicitis, just to get the toys."

"Tell me about it," says Ellen. "I just rushed Nell to the hospital last month with a *Madeline*-inspired appendicitis."

"You did not."

Ellen smiles. "I did so. You'd think being a pediatrician I might have known better, but no. The doctor on call that night said they even have a name for it: Madelineicitis."

"I love it."

A few blocks ahead, Clay is yucking it up with Jonathan and Mia. "You should have seen your wife this afternoon," Clay says to Jonathan. "She blew those other ladies out of the Charles River."

The deep flush of Mia's cheeks had been so noticeable when she came rushing back from Harvard Square to feed Zoe that afternoon, Jonathan had wondered whether Clay was, in fact, a closet heterosexual until Mia told him what had happened at the Loeb. "I felt alive again up there," she said, "vital." After Zoe passed out, she'd yanked down her husband's jeans and taken him in her mouth with more passion than she'd exhibited in years, before throwing him down on Jane's Aerobed.

"Sweetheart," says Jonathan, reaching proprietarily for Mia's hand, "why didn't you ever tell me you missed being on the stage?"

"I didn't realize I did until this afternoon," says Mia. Sometimes, she thinks, it takes someone who knew you back when to illuminate the missing you here and now, a black light beamed over invisible ink, a fresh set of eyes that haven't witnessed the decades of self-deception, a new set of ears that were not privy to the steady, insistent drumbeat: *I'm fine, I'm fine, I'm fine.*

A few paces behind, Bucky drapes a proprietary arm around Clover. "Shall we go for another round tonight?" he whispers in her ear, but now that she has the two things she wanted from him (proof of past love; grade-A sperm), she finds herself not only indifferent to his overtures but slightly concerned by them.

"Bucky," she says, gently but firmly removing his arm, "I had a great time, don't get me wrong, but you're married. And I'm married. Happily at that." She knows how odd this must sound, in light of the events of the past twenty-four hours, but she needs to make it clear that last night was a one-off. Or a two-off, if you count this morning, which she's already transformed in her head—and therefore in the future biographical record of Clover Love, circa 2009—from something deeply arousing and enjoyable into a necessary semievil whose sights, smells, and details she will either try to erase from her memory or take with her to her grave, although the former, she realizes, might be difficult, considering the product of that event might be (God willing) a daily presence in her life. After talking to Danny this afternoon, listening with spousal pride, admiration, and love to his tales of Guantánamo and gastronomical woe—his prisoner was still imprisoned; the only place to eat within walking distance of the prison was a Subway sandwich shop—she felt so queasy with guilt or perhaps pregnancy hormones that she called Zabar's and had them overnight two gift baskets, one for his client, Abdullah, the other for Danny and his legal team.

Not that a chocolate babka, two dozen bagels, and a pound of coffee beans could ever erase the stain of her infidelity, but they sure went a long way toward appeasing Clover's guilt over it.

"Got it," says Bucky, who'd spent the whole afternoon thinking he should divorce Arabella and marry Clover, the one person, if he's being honest with himself, he ever truly loved. "Say no more," he says, finding it suddenly difficult to swallow. He'll never understand women, he decides. Really. Never.

Addison watches this brief exchange between Bucky and Clover from five feet back and thinks, oh my God, they totally did it last night, and now she's blowing him off, but because Bennie and Katrina are simultaneously giving her the third degree about Gunner's whereabouts, she files the information away for future pondering. When Clover's blue-eyed, dark-haired baby boy, Frank, is born nine months later, the spitting image of Danny, but also, let's be honest, Bucky, with a perfect dash of Clover's caramel melanin and Giacometti limbs, Addison will be the only one of Clover's friends to question, albeit privately, little Frankie's paternity. She will not judge her for this, nor will she ever confront her with her suspicions, and, in fact, her ability to process the ambiguity without either gossip or resorting to its binary categorization as either good or bad, right or wrong, will help give her the strength of conviction and acceptance of life's deckled edges she will soon need to process not only her marriage to Gunner but also the inauthenticity of her own path.

"So vait," says Katrina to Addison, her accent turning the *w* in *wait* to a *v*. "Since lunch you have not seen him? But then vere did he go?"

"Back to New York," says Addison, trying her best to sound blasé. "He sent me a text." She pulls out her iPhone and locates Gunner's most recent text—"on bus to nyc"—which hovers in a gray iPhone conversation bubble under another pithy nugget—"can't make it"—which he'd sent the previous Monday, without further explanation, when he decided on a whim to catch a Russ Meyer film at the Film Forum he claimed was tangentially related to his novel instead of coming to hear Thatcher's end-of-the-year choral presentation, as promised.

("It's just a friggin' choral concert," he'd said, in response to Addison's fury over his missing it. "He'll do another one at Christmas." To which she'd countered, spit flying, "You could have Netflixed *Beyond the Valley of the Dolls*, you fucking asshole.")

"That's it?" says Bennie. " 'on bus to nyc'?"

"Yup, that's it." Gunner's first novel had been praised by a number of male critics for the emotional barrenness of its language, as if that were an asset. Female readers, on the other hand, were unmoved by the book, one of them going so far as to give it the ultimate insult on a well-trafficked book blog: She "flung it across the room." ("Bullshit," Gunner had said when he read this. "No one actually flings a book across a room. Who are all these people flinging books across rooms?" Addison, who at that very minute was holding in her hands 320 bound pages of self-indulgent lad lit she was berating herself for having been duped by the hype into buying, flung it across the length of their bedroom.)

She told him if he ever wanted to have a larger audience, or at least an audience of the great unpenised, he'd have to give his readers the subtextual nuance—pain, joy, fear, love, *feelings* for heaven's sake— underlying his characters' physical traits, actions, and words, as opposed to just the traits, actions, and words themselves devoid of emotional context. That didn't mean he had to resort to mawkish sentimentality, but a quick glimpse, now and then, inside the multilayered morass of his characters' hearts—being a visual artist, she really didn't care about his page-long descriptions of moles, eyelashes, nose widths, and lip dimensions, preferring to imagine all those minute physical details on her own, as part of the fun—would do his writing (and him, for Christ's sake) a world of good. "Well, what if their hearts are empty?" he'd said.

"Then show me that emptiness," said Addison. "Make the reader *feel* it."

Incredible, she thinks, that she ended up not only with a man but with a man whose I-love-yous she can count on one hand. "I don't believe in saying 'I love you,'" Gunner frequently responds, whenever Addison begs him for some small scrap of affection. "It's become a cliché. You know I love you, so why should I have to say it?"

But she doesn't know he loves her. She can't even be sure that he likes her. Or if she likes him.

Bennie wants to ask Addison many more questions, to probe deeper into the seemingly sadistic dynamics of her ex-lover's marriage, but they've arrived at the door of the Spee Club, and she can already see Addison shutting down, stepping into her phone booth, turning into SuperAddison, untouchable and unflappable. "Little pigs, little pigs, let me come in," says Addison, tap-tap-tapping the brass bear-shaped knocker against the door, not realizing Ludwig Von Arnhem is right behind her, key in hand.

"Shouldn't that be 'Little bears, little bears'?" says Ludwig, cracking only himself up as usual. In college, his sense of humor was so legendary for its lack of humor that the *Lampoon* had published a six-panel cartoon entitled "The Biting Wit of Ludwig Von Arnhem," each frame containing an increasingly hysterical Ludwig spouting non sequitur nonsense ("I have one word for you: aluminum!"; "Who's afraid of Virginia ham?") to a silent, unchangingly blank-faced listener. Ludwig, still laughing at his unjoke, is about to stick his key into the red Spee Club door when it swings open, revealing three undergraduate club members, still on campus for whatever reason (summer school? summer jobs? reunion workers?), standing defensively in the vestibule in their studiedly unstudied rumpled oxfords and jeans.

"I don't know," says Addison, staring at the barely postpubescent young men, with nary a hair on their chinny-chin-chins. "Do these dudes look like bears to you? They're more like puppies. *Saplings.*" She downed three gin and tonics at the party. She's feeling right at that perfect, unbridled peak between sobriety and social embarrassment.

"Excuse me, but can we help you?" says one of the students, a tawny-haired, green-eyed, dazzling-toothed specimen of youthful zest, utilizing every one of his well-trained vocal and facial muscles of politesse while blocking the door with his get-the-fuck-out-of-here stance.

The two groups stand face-to-face, mirror images of one another distorted by a gulf of two decades, each feeling superior to their time-warped counterpart for reasons only the older group can fathom. The current students see the pasty alumni and think poor, sad, balding sacks, trying to relive their long-gone youth. The alumni—who know exactly what the young 'uns are thinking, thank you very much, giving them the ironic advantage in this hall of mirrors standoff—see the current students both as they appear today and as they will one day become, as if witnessing it all in stop-motion flash forward: the disappointments, the broken vows, the friends and family laid to rest; the loves lost, the pounds gained, the compromises and the sad surprises and the football-size lemons swallowed whole.

"Ludwig Von Arnhem, class of '89," says Ludwig, holding up his key in his left hand while offering his right for a sturdy handshake. "Don't worry. We'll stay out of your hair."

"Oh, sorry, dude, didn't realize you were a member," says the student, who shakes Ludwig's hand before taking a deferential step back with his young compatriots.

"Jay-sus!" says Clay—loudly, for kicks, with as much southern twang as he can muster without sounding like an extra in *Deliverance*—as the group passes through the vestibule into the formal foyer, presided over by a massive, taxidermied bear. "So this is where all the haves dug into their beef tenderloins while us have-nots were chowing down on chickwiches in the cafeteria. Not that I don't love me a good chickwich now and then, but dang, check this place out." He stares down at the marble floor, up at the chandelier. "I hope ya'll appreciate what you got here."

He addresses this last statement, rhetorically—they can't hear him, The National is cranked up too loud—to the small group of students in the billiards room across from the bear, where a young woman holding a pool cue leans slowly over the table, spilling cleavage onto green felt. Mia stares at her chest—I mean, really, it's *impossible* not to, and the girl knows it—and thinks, good lord, if only I'd been that beautiful at her age, my life would have turned out so differently. Not better, necessarily, just different.

Clover looks at her and sees the effortlessness of her movements, her comfort with the phallic pole, no doubt the result of having grown up in wood-paneled rooms just like this one. She wonders if it's possible to get a pool table up the stairs of her brownstone, or will it have to be hoisted through the window? She wonders how much longer she can afford the mortgage on that window or even the staff to clean it without gainful employment. Seven months she's been out of a job. Seven months! At her level, managing director, in her area of expertise, mortgage-backed securities, there are simply no openings, nor will there be, she fears, for years. But what else can she do? She's never done anything else, never worked anywhere else aside from Lehman. Maybe Danny's right. Maybe they should suck up the loss of having bought at the height of the market—the irony of her own house being underwater is not lost on her—and sell the nearly fully renovated brownstone in Carnegie Hill to buy something cheaper, using the difference as a cushion against the dismal economy while she tries to figure out chapter two of her life, plus how much does a nanny cost anyway, $700 a week minimum, right? And then of course yearly private school tuitions, or so her friends with kids tell her, are now inching their way up to forty grand: more than twice what her own tuition at Harvard would have been, had she not received financial aid. How do people who aren't in her field even do it? It's unfathomable.

Addison looks at the young woman and thinks, I used to be you. Taut. Unlined. Entitled. Certain that the combination of my pedigree and a Harvard diploma would lead me to greatness without effort, and yet this morning I woke up naked and bleeding in jail, with nothing to show for the past two decades aside from some mediocre paintings of my hairbrush, a husband who loathes me, and three kids whom I've unquestionably already fucked up.

Jane stares at the display of cleavage and wonders how many men, aside from her husband, will be privy—after she's married, before she's dead—to those tits.

In fact, the girl's heaving chest has captivated nearly all of them, some of the men to the point of tumescence. One, pretending to check e-mail, surreptitiously snaps a photo of the milky mounds with his iPhone, which he will longingly stare at that night, after his wife passes out, while pleasuring himself in the bathroom.

Jonathan decides the only solution is to look elsewhere. Bucky is remembering, with intense relish, last night's spectacular romp with Clover. Ludwig Von Arnhem is wondering if there's any way he can ditch the Russian chick he brought with him, more as a conversation piece and ego buttress than as good company, to try his hand at seducing the breasts' owner. It's becoming harder for him to bed the younger ones these days, but he's got enough going on in the bone structure and wallet department that he's still able to close the deal on occasion. This newest object of his seemingly bottomless desire is about to knock the eight ball into the far left corner pocket when one of the young men grabs hold of the purple thong sticking out the back of her low-slung jeans, and the cue ball goes flying. "Fucking hell, Antonio," she says, playfully. "You are *such* a douchebag."

"All the better to clean that nasty shit out," says her tormentor, who now lifts up the girl with a single hand to her crotch, flings her over his shoulder, and starts spinning her around to the tom-heavy beat of "Brainy," a show of deliberate bravado meant to dissuade the old leches drooling over his occasional score from even trying.

"Put me down, Antonio! Oh my God, put me down!" she says laughing, gripping the back of the boy's Brooks Brothers shirt for dear life.

Ludwig, thinking better of his plans, turns to Clay. "You've really never been in here?" he says. It had never occurred to him that there were people at Harvard who'd never stepped foot in a Final Club.

"Nope, never," says Clay.

"Me neither," says Bennie, and then a few others chime in with similar responses, and within minutes Ludwig is giving his former classmates the nickel tour.

"And here's President Kennedy," says Ludwig, pointing to the tiny oval of JFK's head on the wall of the long crimson hallway hung with a century's worth of Spee group photos.

"Look at that," says Clay, reading the fine print. "1939 to 1940. Now that's awesome."

Soon they are all making their way up the grand staircase to the enormous expanse of couches and Oriental rugs on the second floor, the site of so many blurry evenings. Mia, who'd spent a couple of evenings in the Spee as a freshman and enough as a sophomore to grow weary, by her junior year, of its ethos of exclusion, even if it meant having no real place to hang out after hours—Harvard having been woefully short of such venues for those not in Final Clubs, meaning all of its women and most of its men—finds herself actually enjoying this unplanned instant of melting pot populism.

Here they all are, no matter where they prepped or summered or not, no matter their lineage or physical attractiveness or the depths of their family's pockets: Gay Clay from Marietta, Mississippi, the first in his family to go to college, let alone an Ivy League one; Bennie and Katrina, the class of '89's first official single-sex married couple, living a nuclear-family fantasy unimaginable, when they were students, in its utter normalcy; and (now more alumni are streaming through the once perennially shut door, having heard via texts from those inside that it had been flung wide open) there's that dude who grew up in Queens, what's-his-name, the one who once went streaking down Mount Auburn Street during an ice storm, after a night spent eating acid and smashing plates and dancing on tables in the *Lampoon*'s Great Hall, who now makes top dollar writing for that NBC sitcom about the gravedigger with superpowers; and there's that classics professor from Indiana, who hasn't made tenure for lack of published scholarship but is nevertheless beloved by his students and doesn't really give a shit, and who back in the day wore those Coke bottle glasses and left Lamont Library only to eat; and that woman from Jaipur, who'd grown up without a rupee but now lives with her excruciatingly boring husband in a split-level four-bedroom in McLean, Virginia, purchased with AOL stock options (back when they were worth something), whose five-year-old daughter is apparently quite sick, and who once stood outside Weld Hall during that first snowstorm freshman year and cried, tongue out, from the sheer joy of flakes tasted; and look, that geeky kid from the town near Mia's in Long Island, whose mother used to visit him in Cambridge every other weekend, who recently left both a partnership position at Davis Polk and a castrating, depressed wife to teach ninth-grade American history at a struggling high school in Oakland; and that blind woman who went off to medical school and then on to testify before Congress on the importance of stem-cell research, who's apparently now suffering from multiple sclerosis as well, because life's unfair like that.

There they all are, pushing the couches back at the first notes of the Jackson Five's "ABC," which some minor genius decided to blast through the Spee's sound system and which, unlike the late 1980s drivel the DJ was spinning at the dance, actually hits these revelers in some deep Proustian place: a song that came into being just as they were turning three or some of them four, a sugar-coated-candy anthem of their earliest years, when they were maestros of the alphabet, dutiful counters of dandelions, singers of major key songs; when they asked thousands of questions—"Where does the universe end?"; "Why do people stop growing?"; "Does your brain talk to you, too?"—of their exhausted parents, who were slowly waking up to the realization that learning, for such children, would come easily, while other things (social acceptance, an ability to blend in, days unmarked by boredom) might not.

Freaks, they were! Nearly every single one of them, with their gifted ghettos and their gold stars, their perfect SATs and their yellow Honor Society shawls, though many of them hid their freakish selves well. Until they arrived at Harvard. And then they were just one of the crowd. Halle-fucking-lujah.

"ABC!" they all sing at the top of their lungs, "easy as one-two-three," as a few expertly rolled joints, which appear out of nowhere, are passed around the room, and the tops of Red Stripes are popped open, and the loose flesh on those upper arms is flapping like crazy now, fingers snapping, hips and chests thrusting, knees bending, never mind the torn menisci or the doctor's orders or the intensity of the cannibis compared to the oregano dime bags of their teendom, and fuck those nubile hotties downstairs, look at these old-timers go, each caught in the act of remembering, collectively, that era of wing testing—pre-Harvard, pre-adolescence, pre-kindergarten even—when they believed not only that they could fly but that they'd remain aloft forever.

• • •

"This isn't your first time, is it?" Addison's daughter Trilby asks Mia's son Max, who is hovering above her, supercharged and naked but for his socks, on the Aerobed in the basement rec room of Jane's dead mother's house.

"No, of course not," he lies. "Is it yours?" He can't remember how old Trilby is. Fifteen? Sixteen? She seems ageless. And a thousand times more worldly than he'll ever be.

She was the one who chided *him* for being a pussy for not coming out with her and her sailing camp friends (her sailing camp friends!) to hear that horrid band, Vaginal Discharge, whose name, improbably, turned out to be less offensive than their music. And because Max didn't want Trilby to think him a pussy—because, in fact, he'd been imagining this precise tenterhooky moment of turgidity from the minute he arrived at the house Friday night and saw a completely transformed Trilby, pouting pink-haired in the window seat in her black jeggings and low-cut black tank, looking ripe, wise, injured, and willing—he threw away seventeen years of his mother's careful training and dire warnings about "fast" girls (the whole notion of which, he decided, was an absurd relic from Mia's adolescence) and left eleven-year-old Josh, whom he swore to secrecy, in charge of the little kids. "No way!" Josh had said at first, when he found out Eli, their fifteen-year-old brother, who was equally if secretly fascinated by Trilby, would be sneaking off to the concert as well, until Max promised Josh to buy him *and two friends* three tickets to whatever R-rated movies were coming out that summer, no questions asked.

Houghton and Thatcher, twelve and eleven years old, respectively, were staying behind as well, but Max didn't trust two kids who spent eight hours a day watching youporn to entertain Jane's seven-year-old daughter Sophie or to listen for the cries of his baby sister Zoe for whom, granted, Max would responsibly thaw a frozen yellow sac of breast milk his mother left behind before they left, in case she woke up, but still.

He wishes he could live up to everyone's lofty expectations of him, he really does, but he wants to be inside Trilby more than he's wanted anything in his entire seventeen years, and this need has clouded any claim he may have once had to better judgment. Evangeline Sorrensen, Max's girlfriend back in LA, refuses to go all the way with him, even though his tongue and fingers have explored every contour of the soft flesh between her legs, and her mouth seems to spend more time on his cock than it does eating food, although she claims not to be anorexic, just ectomorphic, which he began to doubt the day she told him she doesn't swallow because each teaspoon of sperm contains five to seven calories. "Why can't we just do it the normal way?" he'd asked her recently, for he really can't understand the difference between penetrating her anus, as she's several times allowed him to do, and missionary sex. In fact, he finds the distinction absurd, like entering a house—into which you've been invited!—through a broken window on the second floor when the front door is just waiting there, fully functional and convenient. He realizes gay men do it that way all the time, because what other choice do they have, but in the context of a now six-month, exclusive heterosexual relationship, the back door feels somehow raunchier, dirtier, *wronger*—for lack of a better or more grammatically correct term—than he imagines normal sex might feel.

"I made a promise," Evangeline had said, holding up the gold purity ring she wears on her left ring finger, which she received gratis at a fancy father/daughter dinner dance financed by government grants to high school abstinence programs. Max finds the whole idea of a purity ring creepy, like a chastity belt but somehow less honest, since at least a chastity belt declares its intentions out loud, while a gold band given to you by your father and worn on one's ring finger, for heaven's sake, feels like a whole other Humbert Humbert–level of pretense and smut. Especially when worn by a daughter who has no compunction about taking it up the ass.

"That's ridiculous!" Trilby had shouted over the din of the atonal music, when Max had answered, in response to her "So are you and your girlfriend having sex or not?" that they did anal but not vaginal.

"I know, right?" Max had said, but by then Trilby was sucking on a joint passed to her by fair-haired Finn, who looked every inch the sailing camp counselor-in-training, and then Trilby passed it on to Max—his first one ever, though he blithely pretended otherwise—and the whole Evangeline hypocrisy went up, so to speak, in smoke.

For her part, if you'd asked her just a few hours ago, Trilby would have said she'd rather lose her virginity to Finn Angstrom, who drove them to the show, or even to Linus, Finn's little brother who was her age, but Finn wouldn't give her the time of day—he made fun of her tongue ring, even after she'd removed it, and wouldn't even drive them home; they had to call a taxi to make it back by eleven, jerk—and the jury's still out on whether Linus has even gone through puberty yet. But being with Max tonight has surprised her, and not in a bad way. For one, he doesn't play games. He's pretty much who he appears to be on the surface, and he doesn't try to hide his true intentions, though she has a hunch that he's lying about his loss of virginity,

although who wouldn't if you were seventeen? I mean, really. For another, even though he's kind of a dweeb, he's not the type of dweeb
who's awkward so much as he's the type of dweeb who is unaware of
the underlying coolness just waiting for expression. He genuinely
seems to care about grades and following the rules and public opinion,
sure, but also, quite demonstrably, about his loved ones and feelings
and kindness and doing the right thing, traits her mother constantly
berates her father for not having. She wonders if that kind of stuff
could ever rub off on you, were you to spend enough time in the presence of someone who possessed it. She imagines—no, she's sure—it
could.

That night, when Eli had wandered off to the bathroom without
telling anyone, Max looked shell-shocked, genuinely upset to have lost
track of his little brother. Before running off to search for him, he
grabbed Trilby by the hand and said, "Please, stick with me, Trilby. I
don't want to lose anyone else I love in this crowd." Then he immediately blushed, realizing he'd just shown his hand, hoping she hadn't
heard him above all that noise, and his blush made her blush, and she
said, "Max Zane, did you just say you loved me?" to which he
answered—and this killed her, it's the reason she's naked with him
right now—"Trilby, if you help me find my little brother, I will not
only give you my undying love, I will worship at the altar of Trilby
Griswold until the end of time." Then he grabbed her face and kissed
her, quite passionately, on the lips, which is when Eli suddenly reap-
peared, and Max could tell Eli was upset by their embrace, so he
texted Trilby—he texted her! while standing next to her! just to
make sure she understood where he stood—"oops i think we just
hurt Eli's feelings. wd like 2 kiss u again but not in front of little bro,
ok?"

"Ok," she'd responded, feeling weak-kneed as she hit "send," then
she squeezed his hand surreptitiously, and he squeezed back, and it was
as if Finn and Linus Angstrom no longer existed, and the band's music
was just noise, and the people around them were just barriers to her

destiny, and the only place she wanted to be was alone and unclothed with Max, as swiftly as possible.

"Of *course* it's not my first time," she lies to him, hyped up on expectation and the sight of his erection. To prove her lie, she pulls out the condom she purchased that afternoon at the Store-24 in Harvard Square, as a precautionary measure against Finn's rumored experience, and rips it open with her teeth. "Do you want to put it on, or should I?" she says, praying for the former.

Max, ever the gentleman, says, "Oh my God, I'm so glad you have that. I totally forgot to bring one," and offers (thank God, thinks Trilby) to slide it on himself, having practiced numerous times on unwitting bananas.

It turns out, however, that because of many factors, including but by no means limited to trembling hands and youthful embarrassment and surging adrenaline, it's a bit harder to unroll a condom onto your own technically still-virgin penis in the heat of the moment than it is to unfurl one onto the head of a health-class banana. Trilby ends up having to help him, and they both giggle self-consciously as she does so, and then she stares into Max's eyes, and he stares into hers, and everything else drops away, and then, without any fanfare, without any of the pain or bleeding she's heard can accompany such maiden voyages, he's deep inside her, and the ease of his entry surprises her, since she's never ridden a horse or done gymnastics. In fact, Trilby is so consumed and moved by what's occurring at the perfect jigsaw nexus between her and Max, she starts to cry. The sensation surpasses, by factors too great to name or count, any previous pleasure she's ever known, including riding the Kingda Ka at Six Flags, listening to certain Death Cab for Cutie songs on her iPod, or eating freshly steamed lobsters on the porch of her grandparents' house in Maine. Not that she would ever publicly admit to enjoying "I Will Follow You into the Dark," but it has, on occasion, moved her to tears.

It occurs to Trilby that she has no means for contextualizing this new experience, no way of wholly expressing it in a way that doesn't sound vulgar, crass, or sentimental. "Love" comes close, which is ridiculous, she knows, considering she and Max have met less than a handful of times over the years, *through their mothers*—there are even photos in a predigital album somewhere of the two of them taking a bath together back in the late 1990s—but she decides to own this feeling and to respect its awesomeness, and no, she doesn't mean awesome in the way her classmates have overused the word to the point of meaninglessness but awesome in its original incarnation, i.e., (a thing) worthy of awe.

Max, though similarly moved by the act of missionary lovemaking, which—fuck! he knew it!—is so much more pleasurable than the absurd burlesque he enacts with Evangeline, has lost any intellectual capacity to ponder its meaning or his feelings or to give them a name. Or to even worry about giving them a name. His one and only thought right now is really an antithought set on automatic repeat, like when his dad's old record player does that thing where the needle can't move beyond the second chorus on "You Can't Always Get What You Want," except instead of, "can't always, can't always, can't always," his refrain goes like this: *don't come, don't come, don't come.*

He is able to heed this inner voice and remain in a blissful state of full-masted attention for all of 139 seconds before the official deflowering is over. "I'm sorry," he says, collapsing onto Trilby's chest, winded, yanking off the condom immediately, as per his health teacher's instructions. But where to put it? For the time being, he simply drops it onto the floor next to the Aerobed and covers it up with the Vaginal Discharge T-shirt he bought at the show on a kitschy whim. Over the next decade, whenever this T-shirt reappears at the top of his drawer, it will remind him of this moment, and he'll involuntarily smile.

"Sorry for what?" says Trilby, breathing equally as hard.

"For . . . you know . . ."

But having nothing with which to compare Max's short-lived performance, she doesn't know. All she does know is that they just spent nearly an hour together, exploring one another from head to toe, the latter which she never dreamed could feel so good inside someone else's mouth. In fact, Max touched and licked and caressed her in corners of her body she didn't even realize she possessed before tonight. He brought her to the lofty brink of heights that made her sweat and shudder on the freefall down. Hell, she just lost her virginity, it suddenly occurs to her, to someone with whom she's not ashamed to have lost it. Really, for all she knows, Max could become the next president of the United States. Or a brain surgeon. Or one of those super-smart movie directors, like Jean-Luc Godard. He's totally that kind of guy, with limitless potential—in a little over a year from now, he'll no doubt be in a freshman dorm in Harvard Yard, she's sure of it—and when he's up there many years from now on whatever dais is lucky enough to support him, she can point to the TV and turn to her kids and say, "I loved that guy once." Maybe those kids will even be his kids, who knows? Max's dad made a whole career out of happily ever after. It has to be possible, if people aspire to it, right?

For once in her life, she has made a good choice: a choice based on something instinctive and unnamable deep inside her, rather than on some nebulous force or antiforce outside herself. To thine own self be true: a life-altering epiphany for a fourteen-year-old, when the words finally click in, one to which she will soon cling during her parents' messy divorce, and during the next four years of high school, and even years later, as she navigates the shoals of early adulthood. "Stop," she says. "That was the best thing that's ever happened to me. Don't ruin it with an apology."

"Sorry. I mean I'm not sorry. I mean, that was the best thing that ever happened to me, too," Max says, flipping onto his back and pulling Trilby's warm body toward him until her head is resting in the crook of his arm, and this is when he finally notices the tears streaking down her face, as her cheeks catch the light of a moonbeam now striking the small basement window. "Wait, why are you crying? Did I hurt you?" He props himself up on his elbows, inspecting her for injury.

"No, silly. Not at all." She pulls him back down.

"Are you upset?" he asks.

"Are you kidding? I'm happy. It's a rare feeling. Quit your yakking so I can soak in it for a little while, okay?"

"Oh, sure. Okay. No problem." He tries to remain silent, but he bites his tongue for about as long as he maintained his erection. "I'm really happy, too," he says, and not just to make her feel good. He means it. He's frigging *happy*.

"Yeah, but you're happy all the time."

"No, I'm not. Why would you say that?"

"I dunno. I just see your family, the way you all treat each other. I just assumed people like you are always happy."

"That's ridiculous," says Max. "No one's always happy. Most of the time I just . . . am. I exist. I go to school, I do my homework, I eat dinner, I brush my teeth, I go to sleep."

"Yeah, but your parents like each other. That has to count for something."

"I guess. Don't your parents like each other?"

Trilby stares at him and shakes her head at his ignorance of the world. "Are you kidding? They can barely stand to be in the same room."

"So why do they stay together?"

"God knows. To torture us?"

"Well, would you rather they get divorced?"

"I don't know. Some days I think it would just be . . . easier. On all of us."

"Really?"

"Yes, really. Is that so shocking to your innocent ears?"

"No." Max laughs. "It's just, you're the first person I know who *wants* her parents to get divorced. I mean, don't parents usually stay together"—here he makes air quotes—"'for the sake of the children.'"

"Yeah. Of course. And I'm sure in many cases that's the right choice. And I know it'll suck if I have to keep packing an overnight

bag like half of my friends already do, shuttling between two apart-
ments, but I just think, in my parents' case . . ." She turns her back to
Max, eases into his spoon. "I don't know. I just want to believe in
love." Her voice cracks. "I want to believe that it's possible."

"Hey, Trilby," he says, pulling her toward him until all parts of his
chest and stomach are contiguous with her spine. They really couldn't
get any closer if they tried. "Trust me. It is possible. I've actually seen
it. On an MRI." During the school year, because his mother thought
it would look good on his college applications, Max worked as an assistant to a couple of researchers at UCLA who were testing the
growth of cancer cells in mice exposed to the fumes of Teflon when
superheated, but just down the hallway were superheated fumes that
were of far greater interest to a teenage boy: a biology professor, whom
Max befriended by going on coffee runs for her to Starbucks, who was
mapping the areas of the brain that are stimulated when a person sees
either the object of his affection or a photograph of that person, or if he
hears the sound of her name or her voice, or if he is simply told to
think about her on his own, without any visual or aural cues. "Turns
out?" he tells Trilby. "All of them light up the same areas of the brain
in the exact same way. It doesn't matter if the physical person is there
or not. The love . . . *exists*. Regardless. How cool is that? And there's
this other professor she was telling me about, at Syracuse," he says, his
voice getting animated, "whose thesis is that it takes only a fifth of a
second for a human being to fall in love. Think about that: one fifth of
one second. Mind-blowing, right?"

"Totally mind-blowing," says Trilby, thinking that she might be
falling in love with Max right now, but that they should probably get
dressed and off the Aerobed pronto, as her mom called to say they'd all
be home around midnight, and it was already eleven-fifteen. But she
feels so comfortable in Max's arms, and her body feels so warm enveloped in his, and anyway Eli promised he'd text them as soon as he saw
the parental headlights appear in the driveway, that the two of them
drift off to sleep, entwined.

• • •

Eli Zane is too busy watching Houghton Griswold's favorite book-marked clip—the tattooed German lady who skillfully handles three penises simultaneously—to notice the beams of his parents' headlights approaching. In fact, because he and his younger brother Josh and Houghton all are wearing noise-canceling headphones (Josh's and Houghton's are plugged into a splitter on Thatcher's laptop, so they can better hear the wet, slurpy sounds of coital quintuplings on gangbang.com), and because Thatcher is passed out on the couch, after having devoured nearly an entire box of Oreos, and because Eli is simply mesmerized by the dexterity with which the German lady transforms herself into a human power strip, providing three distinct points of entry without losing either rhythm or concentration, not one of the boys notice their parents' arrival in the house until well after all of the adults have been standing behind them for several long seconds, speechless. "Josh, Eli, what do you think you're doing?" says Mia, removing her sons' headphones and shutting down both computer screens with, it must be said, some violence.

Addison, who normally doesn't yell at Houghton if she catches him watching porn—not because she supports the idea of a twelve-year-old boy watching videos of random couples or groups having sex but because she figures that the watching of such videos is both inevitable and within the realm of normal for a pubescent boy—decides to show some peer-pressure-induced backbone. "Houghton, what the fuck?" she says. She realizes, only after the fact, that her word choice may not have been the most prudent.

"You guys went through an entire box of Oreos?" says Jonathan, picking his battles and the empty wrapper, which he could have sworn was full when they left, up off the floor. He actually finds it a feat of superhuman restraint and courage that any boy growing up in today's world manages to *not* watch porn 24/7. Oreos, on the other hand, are another story. "Trans fats will kill you." He, like so many men of his generation, learned this lesson too late, before the research came out and the arteriosclerosis set in. It pains him, literally, to think of all the Oreos and Ritz Crackers and frosted Pop-Tarts his mother left out on the kitchen table for him every day after school. For years.

"Thatcher ate 'em. Me and Josh only had one," says Houghton.

"Josh and I," says Addison.

Thatcher lifts his head off the couch's pillow and opens one eye long enough to say, "Liar! You both had two." Then he passes out again.

Clover—who's invited herself over tonight both to be with the rest of the gang and to avoid having to deal with a possible reappearance of Bucky in her hotel room—can't help but giggle at the boys' antics. Then she thinks to herself, oh my God, I have no idea how to raise children. No wonder it's taken her this long to settle down. If her ex-roommates think eating Oreos and watching porn on a computer are harmful to kids, what would they have made of all the pot brownies and live orgies that took place in the living room and garden of her family's commune? Sometimes, triggered by the sight of a beard or a macramé vest, or by the opening notes of certain songs on classic radio, a memory of one of those primal scenes will hit her, and she will have to stop whatever she's doing to walk it off.

"Where's Sophie?" says Jane.

"Thatcher put her to sleep," says Houghton.

"*Thatcher* put her to sleep?" says Mia. "What about Max?"

"I'll go check on her," says Jane. She rushes down the hallway to her daughter's room. When she sees her fast asleep, snuggling Ga, her stuffed bear, still wearing her grass-stained clothes from the afternoon picnic but otherwise fine, she chokes back a handful of tears. She can survive just about anything, but not something happening to Sophie.

That's when she spots Ga on the floor and realizes Sophie is not snuggling her stuffed bear but rather an infant child. Tightly. On a single bed off of which Zoe could have easily plunged if she weren't first crushed or suffocated. Jesus, she thinks, prying her daughter's

fingers from the baby, who thankfully remains sleeping once reposi-
tioned in the crook of Jane's arm.

Meanwhile in the living room, Eli is equivocating as fast as his
withering erection will allow. "Max couldn't put Sophie to bed. He
was busy."

"Doing what?" says Mia.

"Studying for the SATs." Eli mentally pats himself on the back for
quickly coming up with the one fail-safe excuse she won't question.
Mia even forced Max to take the Barron's book with him this weekend, even though the last practice test Max took yielded him a more
than adequate enough score to put him within spitting distance of his
mother's alma mater.

"Okay, then what about you? Why didn't you take the reins and
put her to bed?"

"I was busy, too," says Eli.

"I'm sorry, but watching a woman degrade herself with three men
does not count as 'busy.'"

Eli, in his utter embarrassment at being caught—not literally, thank
God, but still—with his pants down, and harboring unconscious anger
toward his older brother for getting it on with Trilby, whom he'd been
dreaming about *for years*, or at least since two summers ago, when
Trilby and Addison showed up unexpectedly at their house in Antibes
at the end of a mother/daughter European tour, and he and Trilby
were forced to share a room for two glorious nights, one of which had
her lying on her stomach, propped up on her elbows, rereading the
British version of the first *Harry Potter* in her strawberry-print pajamas,
whose top's neckline hung down from the sharp jut of Trilby's collar-
bone just low enough for Eli to catch a mind-blowing glimpse of her
budding breasts that will haunt him well into middle age—says, "Jesus,
Mom, it's not like I was *having* sex like *some* people I know in this
house. I was just watching it."

Jonathan, who incorrectly assumes his son is referring to the clan-
destine quickie he and Mia shared on the Aerobed after she came back

from the Loeb, all flushed, says, "Eli Zane, were you spying on your mother and me this afternoon?"

"Oh my God, no, Dad. No! Ugh, TMI!"

"TMI?" says Jane, stepping back into the living room. Argot changes so fast, she thinks. It's impossible to keep up in one language, let alone two. Which was it again, *I know, right*, or *I know, all right*? Funny how slipping up on that one had led to Ellen's much more revelatory slipup. A gift, that knowledge, as painful as it still feels to process.

"Too much information," says Mia, noticing her infant in Jane's arms. Her sleeping, quiet infant, who should have been in the Pack 'n Play downstairs. "Why do you have Zoe?"

"Sophie was using her as a transitional object, but otherwise she's fine. Although you might want to check her diaper."

"Jesus, Eli! How could you let this happen?" says Jonathan as Mia takes the baby in her arms, sniffs her rear end, and smells the crusted feces in which she's been marinating for God knows how long. "And what sex were you referring to before when you said . . . ?" Jonathan suddenly notices the absence of both Max and Trilby and, duh, finally puts two and two together. Oh, God, he thinks. Please let Mia not have come to the same conclusion. She won't handle it well in her lactating, pissed-off, hormonally altered state.

"Eli, where are Max and Trilby?" says Mia. Her voice has a sharp bite to it.

Too late, thinks Jonathan. She's too smart. Always has been, sometimes to her detriment. There is no way for this to end well. He'd seen Max eyeing Trilby when they first walked into Jane's house on Friday night. He'd mentioned their son's painfully obvious crush to Mia, after she came home from the police station, but she'd been so tired and bedraggled and angry at Gunner for the "Those fucking Jews" comment, she said, "Trilby? Are you kidding me? That girl is trouble with a capital *T*. And besides, Max is so not there yet, emotionally." Jonathan disagreed with both of her assertions, but for the sake of marital accord, he kept his mouth shut, a talent he credits with the longevity and harmony of their union. Although now that she's asking all sorts of questions about their finances (which are in such a shambles right now, he's missed two mortgage payments on the house in Antibes), he's not sure how much longer he can keep up the cheery facade. He'll level with her tomorrow, he thinks. Before the memorial service. No, after. She's always in a more forgiving state after a good cry over untimely deaths.

Addison starts to laugh, nervously. "Oh my God, Max and Trilby? I didn't see *that* one coming." Oops, she thinks. Indelicate word choice again. But wait, fourteen? Isn't that a little young to be messing around? Actually no, she reckons, remembering the first time she and Gunner had sex in his room at Foster, when his roommate was off in Concord having dinner with his parents. Addison's and Gunner's folks both claimed some last-minute illnesses meant to mask the fact that they were actually too drunk to show up, so the two of them decided to take advantage of the nearly empty campus to soothe their feelings of abandonment and loneliness together: a terrible premise for a relationship, in retrospect. She and her future husband were only a few months older than Trilby is now, if that, since Trilby is one of the oldest in her class. Jesus. How does that even happen? One day, she's a baby sucking milk from her mother's breasts, the next she's a young woman stuffing her own breasts into—and now out of, in all likelihood—a push-up bra. Nothing like a daughter's budding sexuality to make one feel like a dried-up crone. Where did the years go?

"Where are they?" says Mia.

"Nowhere," says Eli.

"Eli Zane, that's enough," says Mia. "I demand to know where your brother and Trilby are right now." Zoe, sensing her mother's stress, wakes up, alarmed, and begins to pout.

"Give me the baby," says Jonathan, knowing Mia's inclination for going from zero to sixty in a baby-dropping instant. "I'll deal with her." He takes Zoe from his wife and heads to the door leading down to the basement, only to be blocked by Eli, who jumps in front of him.

"Don't go down there!" says Eli, standing in front of the door and startling Zoe with the panicked timber of his voice to the point where her pout turns into a full-throttled wail.

"I have to," says Jonathan. "Her diapers are down there."

"Actually, I moved them up here," says Mia, picking the diaper bag up off the floor. "*So the boys could change her if she shat herself.*"

Zoe hears the seething rage in her mother's voice and goes straight from crying to DEFCON 1.

"Let me have the baby," says Clover, who's never changed or soothed a screaming infant in her life but figures she should probably start somewhere. Despite Mia's and Jonathan's protestations, she grabs the diaper bag from the former, the baby from the latter, and carries an apoplectic Zoe into the back of the house, in search of quiet and dark.

"Just use my mom's bed," says Jane, remembering the first Christmas when she brought infant Sophie home to Boston, and Claire insisted on changing her grandchild's diapers on a purple towel she'd set up at the foot of her bed.

Eli, feeling guilty for outing Max and Trilby, opens the door to the basement and shouts down the stairs. "Max! Mom and Dad are here!"

Trilby wakes up first, with a start. "Shit," she says, rubbing her eyes. "Wasn't he supposed to text us?"

Max, who's still unraveling the threads of consciousness, stares into the face of his cell phone, as if searching for the answers to the universe: nothing. No text, no note, *nothing*. "I'm going to fucking kill him," he says.

"Dress first, kill later," says Trilby, tossing him his boxer shorts and quickly donning her own undies and pulling up the left strap of her bra just as Mia storms down the stairs, followed closely on the heels by Addison and Jonathan, both of whom tried but failed to convince Mia to give the kids a few minutes to pull themselves together before confronting them with their real crime, leaving children unattended.

Jane stands at the top of the basement stairs, half in, half out, wondering whether to intervene, thinking she should probably get Mia and Jonathan a new set of sheets. Best to stand up here for now, she thinks, unless it gets all Capulet and Montaguey, which it could, knowing those two. Back when they were roommates, Mia and Addison had the most volatile of all of their individual relationships, starting from that time sophomore year when Mia found out that Addison had kept her from joining the Signet with her one-word description of Jane and Mia as *suburbanites*. Jane couldn't have cared less, but Mia had been crushed to the point where she still mentions it, on occasion, albeit in an ostensibly self-deprecating way.

"Max Zane, you are *grounded for life!*" Mia yells, momentarily shocked into silence at the sight of Trilby's right breast. "And you, young lady," she says curtly, after the pause, "put on some clothes." She picks up off the ground and tosses to Trilby the Vaginal Discharge T-shirt containing Max's used condom, the latter which lands with a messy splat on Mia's open-toed sandal.

A week later, IMing over Facebook, Trilby and Max will refer to this moment as the "splat heard 'round the world." But for now, everyone in the room—at least for the next few seconds—has chosen to ignore it.

"Excuse me, Mia," Addison says, "but what gives you the right to speak to my daughter that way?"

Trilby pulls up her right bra strap and puts on the T-shirt, which thankfully is a men's large and reaches all the way down to her knees.

"I have every right to speak to your daughter that way," says Mia, picking the condom up off her shoe and holding it aloft. "She *seduced my son!*"

Max's face turns bright crimson. "Oh my God, Mom, please!"

Mia checks to make sure the nearby trash can is lined before tossing the condom in.

At this point, Trilby is keeping her eyes firmly fixed on her toes while Max, Jonathan, and Addison all yell at once.

Max: "She didn't seduce me! It was totally mutual!"

Jonathan: "Oh, come on, Mia, lay off the poor kids, this is embarrassing enough as is!"

Addison: "For Christ's sake, Mia, she's *fourteen*!"

The *fourteen* rises above the chorus of anger and hangs there, midair.

"You're fourteen?" says Max.

"I thought you knew," says Trilby.

"She was also a virgin before tonight," says Addison. "Not that a girl's past sexual experience should even figure in the realm of finger-pointing, but—"

"Mom! Oh my God!" Trilby is mortified. "I told you that in confidence!"

"You were a virgin?" Max takes Trilby's hand tenderly in his.

"Yes," she says, feeling on the verge of tears for the second time tonight, not because she's sad but because of all the reactions a teenage boy could have had to this revelation under trying circumstances, Max's grabbing her hand with such compassion and—dare she even imagine it—*love* would have been the last response she would have ever expected. She was right this morning, watching him stir the pancake batter with Sophie. Max truly is special. With him, she could do *anything*. Or at least be the best version of herself possible. She vows to earn enough money babysitting this fall to return the cash she stole from Jonathan's wallet.

"Well, that makes two of us," says Max. He now has his entire arm around Trilby, a united postvirginal front against the adults. The Post-Virgins, he thinks. An excellent name for a band. Or at least a hell of a lot better than Vaginal Discharge, two truly unfortunate words to be abutted together and plastered in gigantic scarlet letters across Trilby's chest at this particular juncture.

"Max, for heaven's sake," says Mia. "You're applying to college this year! You can't afford to screw up like this!"

"Screw up like what?" says Max. His mother saw the condom. Clearly she realizes they were being smart about protection.

"My question exactly," says Addison. "How does what went on in this room have anything to do with Max's chances of getting into college?"

"Addison, let's not forget you were in *jail* last night! Okay? *Jail!*"

Jane starts walking down the basement stairs, quickly.

"For parking tickets, Mia! That I didn't pay twenty years ago! Who knew they even kept records of such things, and besides, what does my being in jail have to do with my daughter? Or Max's college applications? What's gotten into you, Mia? Why do you always have to be so fucking judgmental?"

"Oh, please. You've been judging me ever since the day you met me. '*Suburbanite*'? Remember that?"

"Mia, you're not in your right mind," says Jonathan, trying to calm his wife down.

"Come on, guys," says Clover, heading down the stairs. She lays a clean, changed, blissfully sleeping Zoe into the Pack 'n Play. It took her a ton of wipes and elbow grease, but in the end, when the baby was finally free of the crusted-on poop, Clover started making funny faces, really meeting Zoe's gaze, and Zoe started to giggle, and then Clover sang "Amazing Grace" into the baby's ear, the song her mother used to sing into her ear, and Zoe collapsed into a fragrant heap in Clover's arms. Magical, she thought, that moment when the baby goes from being a wriggly mass of sound and sinew to silent dead weight. She silently prays to whichever fertility gods happen to be on weekend duty to bless her with her own. "What's going on here?"

"Oh, same old, same old," says Jane. "Addison and Mia are having a tiff."

"Oh boy," says Clover.

Addison looks as if she might explode, but the presence of a sleeping baby tempers her volume. "Oh my God, Mia!" she shout-whispers. "I said I was sorry about that stupid suburbanite thing *years* ago! Yes, okay, I was a haughty, entitled twit in college. We were all twits in college. Clover with her inferiority complex—"

"Gee, thanks," says Clover.

"Jane with her inability to let loose and have fun—"

"I let loose and have fun," says Jane, trying and failing to disinter from memory a single example.

"And you with your provinciality, your constant need for adulation—"

"Hey, that's not fair—"

"I'm not saying it's fair, and it's certainly not an accurate description of you now, but that was my impression of you back then. Look, none of us was perfect, and for heaven's sake, none of us is perfect now. Why do you keep bringing up the same shit, over and over again? It's done, Mia. It's in the past. Let's move on already. And I will ask you once again: What does any of this have to do with my daughter and your son?"

Max and Trilby, who will soon discover over the course of their Skype-enabled relationship that they share a love of all things Harry Potter, are staring down at their toes, wishing for an invisibility cloak.

"It's just . . . I don't want Max to have any unnecessary distractions this year, okay? He has to stay focused on getting into a good college."

"Mom!" Max clenches his fist and is about to speak up when Addison lets loose.

"Jesus Christ, Mia," says Addison, "you've got to be kidding me! What, so he can get into Harvard? For all the good it's done both of us, you'd think you'd be a little more dubious about the Ivy League arms race. It means nothing, Mia. Nothing! Some of the most successful people I know never even went to college!"

Jane physically places herself between Addison and Mia, as if twenty years haven't passed and they're all back in the womb of the Adams House dining hall, their aggrieved gestures trailing sunlit swirls of cigarette smoke across the arched windows along Bow Street. "Come on, you two, this is crazy. Addison, she's allowed to worry about Max getting into college. Her worry is misplaced in this particular instance, as it has nothing to do with poor Max and Trilby here, but for argument's sake, you can't actually claim that having Harvard on a résumé isn't an asset, especially in this crap economy."

"It was life altering for me," says Clover.

"I wouldn't say it was life altering for me," says Jane, "but it definitely helped me land my first job, which is not insignificant. On the other hand, I might have actually learned more about journalism in a school where it was a concentration rather than an extracurricular, but that's beside the—"

"Concentration?" says Jonathan.

"Harvard's fancy word for major," says Addison, who still finds herself having to take short mental beats to translate "sixth form" into "twelfth grade" whenever she tells stories about her senior year in high school, or "I concentrated in Visual and Environmental Studies" into "I majored in art."

"Can we please stay on topic?" says Jane, who wastes precious hours every week trying to figure out which word or phrase to use in which Babel-towered context. *College*, in French, means "middle school." For years, until a confused colleague corrected her, she'd been telling people she went to middle school at Harvard. She turns to face Mia. "Please, Mia, you've got to stop bringing up an offhand comment Addison made over twenty years ago. I mean, really. Let it go. Have some compassion. Show some forgiveness."

Jonathan shoots Jane a raised eyebrow, a gesture she reads more clearly than any lecture he could have delivered on the topic of clemency. Yes, she shrugs. I know. Practice what you preach. I'll try to forgive Bruno, I will.

Max, a bubbling geyser, finally erupts. "For fuck's sake, Mom!" he says, angrier than either of his parents have ever seen him. "My entire life, I've done exactly what you told me to do. I brought home all As. Never a B on any report card. Never! I do all these stupid extracurricular activities, stuff I don't even enjoy doing, just so it will look good on my college application. Truth be told, I don't even know if I want to go to Harvard, but I'm applying because of you and Dad. In fact, I have no idea who I am or what I want, outside of what you want for me. It's like my whole life's been programmed toward a single outcome, and veering off that path is a failure. Which it's *not*! As for what happened tonight, don't think I didn't see that smug little look you gave me, when you asked about that stupid thing Evangeline wrote on my Facebook wall, and I said it was about her decision to save herself for marriage. You were *relieved*! As if what Trilby and I did tonight was wrong, while the weird shit my supposed girlfriend makes me do for the sake of her 'purity' is just, well, forget it. I don't even want to go there. You want to know something ironic? Up until five minutes ago, this was the best night of my life."

"Mine, too," says Trilby, emboldened by Max's passion.

"In fact, when I get back to LA, I'm going to break up with Evangeline," says Max, throwing it out there. He doesn't dare look Trilby in the eye, for fear of blushing. "I've had it up to here with her hypocrisy."

"Really?" says Trilby, squeezing Max's hand even tighter.

He finally looks her in the eye. Who cares if he blushes? He's in love! "Yes. Really."

"Max, all I was trying to say is you have to think of your future," says Mia.

"I'm always thinking about my future, Mom!" says Max. "I think about my future so often, I feel like I've missed out on *years* of the present!"

He has a point, thinks Jane. Regardless of the actual value of a Harvard diploma, this whole obsession with getting your kids into a good college, slave driving them through high school until they can't see straight, only to toss them out at the end of four ivy-covered years so they can work eighty hours a week for some U.S. corporate megaentity seems just plain (a smile creeps across her face as she recalls her outburst in front of the mirror of Lodge Waldman's office) *stupid*.

Addison feels the sinew in her neck tightening, her hands clenching. *You have to think of your future?* How does Mia get off, insinuating that my daughter would in any way be a blemish on Max's future? Trilby may have inherited a bit of her mother's rebellious streak, but she's also the most genuinely cool and interesting person Addison knows. In fact, if she had to choose to spend a day alone with anyone on earth, it would be with Trilby. No question. And if Mia spent even an hour with her, without judging her for the way she looks or the clothes she wears or the bands she likes, she would realize that.

Jonathan notices today's date on Trilby's concert T-shirt and chooses not to bring it up. He'll scold Max privately about ditching his babysitting responsibilities to sneak off to a rock concert, but for now he's actually secretly relieved by his son's rebellion. Good for Max, he thinks. He had to gnaw his way through those apron strings at some point, but man oh man, how is it that Max is leaving for college in a year? A year! A year at Jonathan's age passes by in an instant. He pictures Max's spot at the dining room table, empty. The absence of Max. The image slices into him, oozing blood. "I think we should call it a night," he says. "I'm exhausted."

"Good idea," says Jane, who's magically stripped the Aerobed and remade it with clean, hospital-cornered sheets without anyone being the wiser. In such moments, she feels the essence of both of her mothers coursing deep within her.

" 'They fuck you up, your mum and dad . . .' " Max starts to whisper into Trilby's ear.

She finishes the stanza out loud: " 'They may not mean to, but they do.' I love that poem," says Trilby. "I wrote my English term paper on Larkin."

"You did?" says Max. He didn't think it was even possible for his love to expand any further. Larkin is his favorite poet. (For now. Later he'll discover Wislawa Szymborska, whose poems he will read and reread into old age.)

"You did?" says Addison. "You never showed me that paper."

"Not true. I asked you to sign it when I got my grade back. You told me to just forge your signature. Besides, there's a lot of stuff I don't show you. Or tell you about." Trilby turns to Mia. "Actually, Mrs. Zane?" (Addison is a lenient mother with one exception: She insists that her children address all adults, no matter how well known, with a proper prefix and last name, a habit that was so firmly ingrained in her as a child, she never even thought to challenge or amend it when she had kids of her own.) "Some of tonight . . . *is* my fault. I mean, Max and Eli wouldn't have left Josh in charge if I hadn't, you know, made them come to the Roxy with me."

"What?" says Mia. "You went to a—"

Jonathan quiets his wife with his signature raised eyebrow. It's enough for the girl to publicly admit her wrong. There's no need for Mia to rub it in.

"Oh, Trilby," says Addison, "is that where that awful T-shirt comes from?"

"Yeah. We went to hear them. Finn Angstrom drove us."

"Finn? From sailing camp?"

"Yeah."

"Oh, baby." Addison hugs her daughter. "Don't worry. I under-stand. It's okay. I used to sneak out and go to Dead shows when I was your—"

Trilby pulls away. "No, Mom, it's not okay. Like, it's *really* not okay. You should totally ground me for sneaking out. Like other moms. That's what I wrote my term paper about."

And like that, Mia's distaste for her roommate's child disintegrates. In fact, she might really be starting to like Trilby.

"Wait a minute," says Addison. "You . . . *want* to be grounded?"

"If I do something wrong, yes. So go ahead. Ground me."

"Okay," says Addison. "You're grounded." The words feel like tiny aliens in her mouth.

"Cool," says Trilby. "For how long?"

"Well, how long were you thinking?"

"I don't know. I guess a week for sneaking out and leaving the me-dium kids in charge of the little ones and another week for hacking

Mr. Zane's Facebook." She turns to Jonathan. "Sorry, Mr. Zane. You left your profile open. I couldn't help myself." When she'd admitted what she'd written to Max earlier in the evening, he'd spit out his beer laughing, assuring Trilby that his dad, who was used to the sometimes elaborate pranks pulled by film crews on set, might be slightly annoyed but he would not be angry.

Jonathan, tipping his neck to the side, seems more bemused by the revelation than annoyed, as if he might want to use it as a plot point in his next script. Trilby knows that twinkle-eyed head tilt well. It's the same one that overcomes her father before he pulls out his Moleskine to steal pieces of her life. "I was wondering how that happened," says Jonathan. "So if I don't log out, you can just type stuff into my status update?"

"Yes."

"Who knew? What about—"

Trilby cuts him off. "I also took two hundred and twenty dollars from your wallet to pay for the tickets, but I'll pay you back with my babysitting money. I promise. Wait, here . . ." She digs into her purse until she finds and hands over the $120 she didn't spend. "So now I just owe you a hundred." The relief she feels at her unburdening, from the partial repayment of ill-gained spoils, is palpable. Her shoulders feel lighter, her neck less cricked. Who knew the truth could be so liberating? Certainly not her mother, whose lies, both to herself and otherwise, are so ingrained into her being, they've become their own form of truth, like a banker's.

She wishes she better understood what people like her mom's friend Clover does, but even her parents haven't been able to properly explain how one day everyone was living in big houses and buying lots of stuff, and the next day they weren't. Something about a collective delusion. Whatever that means.

"Okay, two weeks," says Addison. "That sounds totally fair. Trilby Griswold, I hereby pronounce you grounded for the next two weekends." Ironic parenting, Addison realizes, will be a difficult habit to break.

"Awesome. Can I still talk on the phone and go online?"

Addison has no idea how to answer. "I don't know. Can you?"

"Sure," says Trilby. "I think that would be okay, considering the crime. I mean, if I'd, you know, bullied someone online—which I haven't done, don't worry—then you'd have to think about taking away online privileges from me, but in this case I think just the physical grounding should be fine."

"Okay, then. You are grounded with benefits."

"Mom. Ugh. It's 'friends with benefits.' And it has nothing to do with—"

The doorbell rings. Jane looks at her watch. "It's after midnight," she says. "Who on earth . . ." Oh my God, she thinks, understanding exactly who it is. He came anyway, even though she told him not to. She pulls her cell phone out of her pocket and sees eleven missed calls, all of them from Bruno. Of course. She turned off her cell phone when she went to meet with Lodge Waldman. Then the rest of the day got away from her.

"Bruno?" says Jonathan, looking over Jane's shoulder at the face of her cell phone.

"I'm assuming," says Jane.

"Jane," says Jonathan, "I'm sorry, lady, but if you do not marry him after a move like that, then someone made a big mistake letting you into Harvard." He bounds up the basement stairs two by two.

The rest of the gang are halfway to the front door when they hear Jonathan's elated voice. "Bruno! *Mon dieu!* What the fuck man! I can't believe you're here. You don't know how bad I've needed you. I'm outnumbered four to one."

"I have been trying to reach Jane all day. She is here?"

Jane feels her heart pounding at the sound of Bruno's deep-timbered, soothing voice. A radio voice, everyone tells him, but he has no interest in doing anything but editing. "I like being the support," he always answers. "The buttress, not the wall."

"*Oui,*" calls Jane, rounding the corner. "*Je suis là.*" When she sees

Bruno standing in the doorway clutching his suitcase, his clothes rumpled from the flight, she runs to greet him, and—Jane being all of five feet, Bruno scraping the ceiling at a solid six-foot-three—is lifted up off the floor and into his arms. Bruno buries his head in her neck. "*Mais t'es fou*," Jane says, holding his head in her hands and kissing him somewhat chastely. "*Je t'ai dit de ne pas venir.*" You are nuts. I told you not to come.

Jonathan, the only one in the house fluent in both French and the latest on Jane and Bruno's relationship, shoos everyone else into the kitchen.

Bruno places Jane gently back on the ground and switches to English, the native tongue for neither of them, but one he's determined to use more often for the sake of parity: "I know you did tell me not to come, but I also know you enough to comprehend when you say one thing but mean a different. Thing. And so I think it to myself, even if you decide you do not want that I am here, I will still help to clean the closet of Claire, like I promise you when she die, and then I go."

"Like I said. *T'es fou.*"

"I'm the crazy one? Who is the crazy one still awake, huh? I decide to drive by, when I can't reach you on the phone, just to, you know, how do you say '*jeter un coup d'oeil*,' 'throw an eye blow'?"

"Check things out." Jane has always adored the way Bruno mangles the English language, translating French idioms word by word. She once heard him yelling into the phone, to an Iraqi fixer who'd failed, once again, to meet his reporter at the appointed time and place, "I've had it up to the level of my head!" Jane had to gently explain to him that "*J'en ai ras-le-bol*" would be better expressed as "I've had it up to here."

"*Ah, oui*, check things out," says Bruno. "So, yes, I see the many cars in the alley—"

"Driveway."

"Yes, driveway. But I do not expect to see the lights illuminated. Why you did not answer your *portable*? Are you still angry to me about—"

"No, no. Sorry. There was no malice in my not answering the phone at all. At *all*! I turned off the ringer when I went to meet . . . oh, God, I have so much to tell you, Bruno. You'll never believe it. My mother. She had . . . a lover. For thirty *years*. I haven't even been able to wrap my head around it yet." She shuts the front door, grabs Bruno's bag, and rolls it into the entryway, where they sit down on a hard-backed bench.

"I know this," says Bruno. "She confess it to me last Noël. Before she die. You were out doing something with Sophie, I don't remember, maybe, how you say *faire le patinage*?"

"Ice-skating."

"Yes. Ice-skating. But Claire made me promise not to tell you until after she die. She had fear you would judge her, because her lover is married."

"You're joking."

"Why would I joke about this?"

"Am I really that much of a killjoy that my own mother had to keep a secret from me?"

"What is this word, *killjoy*?"

"That one you can translate directly. A killer of joy."

"Yes. Sometimes you do this. Kill the joy. But this is of no worry of me. I love every part of you. Even the part that shakes her finger no-no-no." He takes Jane's small hand in his and kisses her fingers. "Please, Jane. Do not kill the joy because I make a fuck-up."

"No, you don't 'make' a fuck-up. You fuck up."

"Oh, but I did. I make an immense fuck-up."

"Fine. Okay. You *made*—past tense—an immense fuck-up." She rubs his palm with her thumb. "Speaking of which, I met this woman today, Ellen Grandy . . ."

"Wait, I know this name," says Bruno, screwing up his face trying to place it. "Ah, *oui*. She is the doctor with Médecins Sans Frontières, yes?"

"Was."

"Huh?"

"She *was* a doctor with Médecins Sans Frontières. Now she works in private practice here in the States, but wait, how do you know her name? Did you edit a story on her or something?"

"No," says Bruno, suddenly feeling entrapped, once again, by the lie of omission. No more, he thinks. He will be as honest as he can without compromising Hervé's confession. "She was an ancient friend of Hervé's."

"Old, you mean."

"No, she must be only, I do not know, in her early forties? Your age, I think. This is not old."

"No, I meant old as in not ancient. We don't say 'ancient friend' in English. She was his *old* friend. And she was more than that, is what I actually found out. She had an affair with him. Can you believe it?"

Bruno shrugs. "Yes, of course I can believe this." He feels relieved, like when a blocked ear finally pops as the plane soars skyward.

Jane is floored by Bruno's lack of reaction to the news. Which could only mean . . . "Wait. So you *knew* about Ellen?"

"Yes, for a long time."

"So what the fuck, Bruno? Why didn't you say anything?"

"To you?"

"Yes, to me? Who else would I be talking about?"

"Wait, is it not *whom* else? *Whom* else would I be talking about?"

"Bruno! Who, whom, whatever! Why didn't you tell me?"

"Why would I tell you such a thing? You were married to him. He tell me this in confidence many years ago. Then, when he die, I see no point in killing him twice. It would only cause you hurt."

Jane's head feels heavy with dissonance, discovery. "But I was screaming at you when I found that e-mail! Saying Hervé would have never cheated on me! You didn't once consider setting me straight, if only to put yourself in a better light?"

Bruno seems shocked that Jane would even consider he could do such a thing. "No. Never. I made a promise to Hervé to rest silent, and I keep it."

"Wow." Jane contemplates the enormity of this omission. She, like Bruno, is often the trusted friend in whom others confide, but given the same set of circumstances—the same accusations from a partner, the same ill-informed lionizations of the deceased—she's not sure she would have had the same moral rectitude and dutiful devotion to the kept secret as Bruno to let the myth stand. Morality, in her mind, has always wanted to be a binary entity—good on one side, bad on the other, sturdy guardrails between the two marked by well-lit signs—when, in reality, the moral path rarely offers itself up so tidily. Most of the time, trying to do the right thing feels much more slippery, haphazard, and comical, like crawling around on the bathroom floor with two playing cards, trying to retrieve drops of mercury from a broken thermometer.

Truisms her younger self held so dear have not held up to the scrutiny of time and circumstance. Military intervention is always wrong, she was convinced—she even wrote her senior thesis on it, with regard to Vietnam—until she saw what was happening on the ground in Kosovo. Lying is bad, she always thought, until her mother lay on her deathbed, fretting over the way she must appear to the steady stream of visitors who kept showing up with roast chickens and pies.

"Don't be silly, Mom," Jane would say. "You look great." Claire knew she was lying. Jane knew Claire knew she was lying. But they both kept up the pretense because the truth—that her mother looked like a skeleton stretched with a thin canvas of skin—was too painful. By the end, it became a private joke between them. A guest would ring the doorbell, Claire would say, "How do I look?" and Jane would reply, cheerily, "Breathtaking." It wasn't a lie exactly—there is a weird, undeniable splendor in the face of the doomed—but the word and its verb root allowed them the open-to-interpretation elasticity that less malleable adjectives (*beautiful, lovely*) could not provide. Claire did cause those who showed up at her deathbed to lose their breath, gasp. Just not in the usual manner.

Sophie, awakened by the bass undertones of Bruno's voice, bounds into the entryway, the back hem of her nightgown fluttering behind her calves. "Papi!" she says, leaping into his arms, squishing herself expertly between Bruno and Jane.

"Oh my little cabbage," he says, kissing her forehead, "what are you doing on the outside of bed?"

"What are *you* doing speaking English?" she says, looking at him askance.

"Practicing. You will to help your Papi?"

"Okay," she says, with a shrug of her narrow shoulders. "But you're going to have to work really hard. No one says 'little cabbage' in English. That's just silly. And they also don't say 'on the outside of bed.' They say 'out of bed' or just 'awake.' Did you bring me a bear?"

"But of course." Bruno pulls a purple stuffed bear out of the top of his suitcase, one of many he has purchased here and there since the death of her father. It's become such a habit, the entire foot of her bed is covered with a rainbow of ursine fur. "But I will only give it to you if you promise to take him directly back into the bed, okay?"

Sophie hesitates a moment before agreeing to the deal. Taking the new bear into her arms, she hugs and kisses Bruno, then her mother, and heads back to bed. "*Je t'aime*, Papi," she says, once they've tucked her in. "*Et je suis ravie que t'es venu!*"

"I'm happy I came, too," says Bruno, kissing her forehead. "And I love you right back."

"Bruno," says Jane, flicking off the light in Sophie's room and shutting the door. "What if you'd shown up here, and I'd said, I'm sorry, you can't stay?"

"I imagined such an event. I tried reserving a hotel, *en cas ou*, but do you realize there's not a single hotel room in a twenty-kilometer radius of this city?"

"Tell me about it," says Jonathan, appearing in the hallway, on his way to the bathroom. "Reunion weekend. Apparently, although I did not know this until last night, people book a whole year in advance.

Bruno, I have an excellent bottle of cognac in the kitchen if you'd like to *prendre un verre* with us."

"I would love to take a glass with you," says Bruno, "but right now I have a promise to Jane I must to fulfill." He walks into the kitchen, where the adults are gathered around a bowl of microwave popcorn, and greets them with hearty two-cheek kisses and *h*-less *hellos*. Then he heads directly to the lower cabinet where he remembers Claire having kept her ample supply of used shopping bags, organized by size (large/small) and material (paper/plastic). He pulls out a dozen or so of the large paper ones. "So," he says, handing a brown grocery bag to each person, "who will help me to paint the fence?"

"What?" says Clover. They're all used to Bruno's creative interpretation of the English language by now, but that doesn't mean they actually understand him.

"He's been reading *Tom Sawyer* to Sophie," says Jane.

"Come," says Bruno. "We will, how do you say *vider*?"

"Empty," says Jonathan.

"Ah yes. We will to empty the closet of Claire."

Jane thinks to herself, *The Closet of Claire*: a good title for a book about a mother with a secret life. Then she frets over what to do with her mother's underwear. She can't give it away. But throwing it out seems wrong. Too final.

Addison has a visceral reaction to the word *closet*.

Mia, who saved every playbill and review from her thespian half-life, wonders which of her kids will get stuck emptying out her drawers when she is gone. All that useless, well-organized paper will have to go. Why does she even hold on to it? To remind herself of who she once was? Yes. And so what? There are worse reasons to hold on to scraps.

Clover, who has decided that her recent crimes—sperm theft, aiding and abetting in the collapse of the housing market—require some serious counterbalancing with good deeds, grabs three bags from Bruno. "I'll help you paint your fence," she says. "Come on. Let's do this. Who needs sleep?"

"Not me," says Addison. Some of her favorite memories from college sprang from all-nighters. They also sprang from copious amounts of drugs, but that was back when her body could handle the affront. She and Gunner, hoping to rekindle some minor spark of the couple they used to be, popped some Ecstasy last New Year's Eve after the kids had gone to bed, and though she did wind up feeling some sort of chemically enhanced version of spousal love, the spell lasted only eight hours while it took her body until mid-January to feel like itself again.

"Me, too," says Mia, grabbing two bags, one for her, one for Jonathan. No doubt Zoe will be up in a few hours anyway, fish-lipped and hungry.

Ten minutes later, at a hair before 1 A.M., Clover, Addison, Mia, Jonathan, Bruno, and Jane have all changed out of their formal clothes and into their pajamas, standing back to back in Jane's mother's walk-in closet, their eyes busily scanning the jam-packed if well-organized racks and shelves, trying to figure out where to begin. Bruno takes charge. "Okay, Jane, what, if anything, do you want to guard?"

"Keep," says Jane. "*Garder* means to keep. You guard an entrance. You keep objects."

"You can keep people, too," says Jonathan, raising his second eyebrow of the night in Jane's direction.

Jane grabs Bruno's hand and squeezes it, tightly.

"And secrets," says Clover.

"Not Jonathan," says Mia, remembering the surprise fortieth birthday party he tried to throw for her, accidentally cc'ing her on the Evite. "He can't keep a secret worth shit. It's like he's constitutionally unable to lie."

Jane catches Jonathan's eye and has to look away. She feels both cursed by the burden of his story and grateful for his having shared it.

"You can also keep appointments, keep up appearances, keep breathing, and keep friends," says Addison, putting her arm around Mia. "Even if your friend's son and your daughter just, well . . ."

"Good lord," says Mia, "did that just happen or did we dream it?"

The two of them shake their heads, not knowing how to approach this new chapter to their story, but then Jonathan's nervous laughter bubbles up to the surface, and this gives everyone else permission to lose it, and it becomes a chucklehead free-for-all ("Oh my God, the condom, the *condom!*"; "The poor girl, standing there in that T-shirt") despite the impetus and the venue. Mia literally has to steady herself by holding on to the edge of a shelf. The laughter feels vital, like food.

Only Bruno is confused, but Jane says, "Trilby and Max . . . ," without finishing the sentence, and Bruno adds, "*ont baisé?*," and when Jane nods yes, he, too, is now smiling, if still slightly baffled. He would have been more surprised had Max and Trilby *not* jumped into bed together, *mais bon.* He just finished editing a three-part series on the abject failures of U.S. teen abstinence programs, whose very existence so appalled *Libé*'s readers, they shut down the paper's servers for over an hour with their comments.

"Well, at least it wasn't Max having sex with *you*," says Mia to Addison, still clinging to the shelf. "Remember Lizzie Wainwright?"

"Oh my God, *yes!*" says Addison. Lizzie Wainwright, or so the story went, had gone out to the Hong Kong one night in the fall of freshman year with her roommate Bree and Bree's newly divorced father, Fred. After several rounds of Scorpion bowls—large vessels of alcohol-laced punch, drunk communally around a table through elongated straws—Lizzie and Fred had to help a well-lit Bree back to her room in Wigglesworth, the freshman dorm where Fred, twenty-five years earlier, had also regurgitated Scorpion bowls into his bedsheets. Upon his arrival in his daughter's room, Fred felt overpowering rushes of both nostalgia and abject fear as he suddenly remembered he had a package from Bree's mother back in his hotel room containing a six-month supply of his asthmatic daughter's inhalers he was supposed to have delivered upon penalty of death and/or higher alimony payments, the latter his ex would have made sure to levy were he to neglect to do so, but he had a 6 A.M. flight he had to catch the next morning, so Lizzie, who'd been more or less moderate in her Scorpion bowl consumption, volunteered to go back to Fred's hotel room to fetch it. The next morning, around 5 A.M., Lizzie slunk home, carrying the package and wearing, as a buttress against an overnight drop in temperature of twenty degrees, Fred's vintage Harvard crimson-and-white-striped scarf. At first everyone couldn't believe it: Lizzie Wainwright and Bree's *father?* Oh my God, gross. No way. Then, when the shock of it wore off, the story became just another crack in a long line of we're-not-children-anymore potholes that would keep cropping up along the roads of their lives. "I hear she's now the brand manager for that adult diaper company, what's-it-called," says Addison.

"Clearly she's doing an excellent job on brand recognition," says Jonathan.

"You mean these?" says Jane, pulling out, from under a well-hidden shelf, an unused package of Depends her mother was forced to wear in her final weeks. Of all the indignities she had to endure, Claire maintained that that one was the worst. Jane feels a fresh stab of sadness, the pain radiating outward. How could her mother—her beautiful mother!—be gone while these cartoon diapers remain?

"Yes, that's them," says Addison, grabbing the Depends and tossing them, without fanfare, into a bag. "There, one object down, seven thousand more to go. What about these tennis shoes, keep or chuck?"

"I don't want to keep anything," says Jane. Each object is a land mine. She looks at her friends and imagines them each in the protective, mine-sweeping gear from that movie about Iraq she finally just forced herself to see when it played at the UGC Odéon. Bruno had wanted to go with her—"It will bring up stuff," he'd said, in his typical compassionate if oblique way—but she'd said no, she wanted to go by herself, which was stupid (there's that word again) in retrospect. Half the things we do, she thinks, even those of us who consider ourselves pretty darned smart, are stupid in retrospect. In fact, some of the smartest people she knows have made the dumbest errors, granting more weight to intellectualized reasoning than to their (oft contradictory) baser impulses. Look at Addison, she thinks. She's gay! Married to a man!

"Nothing?" says Addison. She's been secretly eyeing a pair of white vintage Courrèges go-go boots she would kill to guard/keep/whatever verb you want to call taking them into her home and pairing them with the three vintage Pucci dresses also in her direct line of vision.

Clover spots the dresses, too, perfectly maintained, along with what looks like an original Mary Quant miniskirt. They'd be too big on Jane's size-two frame and probably too small to fit over Mia's ample hips, but on Addison and her, man-oh-man. The thought of giving such treasures away is too much for Clover to bear. "Jane, be smart about this. I know it's hard, and this would all be easier if you could just shove everything into bags and be done with it, but your mother had amazing taste. I mean, look at this skirt!" She pulls out the brown leather treasure, in mint condition, and checks the label. "Yup, just what I thought. Mary Quant. Do you know how much you could get for this on eBay?"

Jane remembers her mother wearing that skirt to a party at, wait, of course, the Waldmans'. Her first winter in the United States. She'd never heard of Hannukah before and was therefore surprised when everyone started dancing the hora around the dining room table, holding hands and singing in yet another language she didn't understand. Did her mother hold Lodge's hand that night? Yes, she did. Definitely. Or, wait, maybe no. Jane can't remember. It's all so fuzzy now. Only individual frames remain of the film of her life: the skirt swaying, a feeling of closeness, the flickering flames of the menorah. "I have no idea how much I could get for it on eBay," she says. "I can't even bear the thought of dealing with it."

When Hervé died, it was her mother who flew over and dealt with the removal of his clothes so quickly and with such magical efficiency, to this day Jane couldn't tell you how the bags made it out of the apartment.

"I'll sell it for you," says Clover. "Well, maybe not this one. I'd like to keep this one, but believe me, we can set up a college fund for Sophie with the proceeds from this closet. I mean, shit, if I can bundle a bunch of bad mortgages and sell them to people who should have known better, I can definitely sell valuable vintage to people who know a pair of awesome boots when they see them. Just look at this stuff!" She picks up a black suede boot and checks the label. "Biba. Amazing."

"I'll help you," says Addison. "But if it's okay with Jane, I'd like to claim a few pieces, too, since these are all my size, and apparently I'm now too poor to buy new clothes forever."

"Take anything you'd like," says Jane. "Seriously. You know my mom. Knew, I mean. Past tense, shit. I'm not used to that yet. Whatever. You *knew* her. She would have been thrilled to know the clothes, at least, would have had a second life."

Jane remembers the day—Sophie must have been no more than four—when her daughter understood not only that she but that *everyone she knew and loved* would one day die. Jane feared it was because of Hervé's untimely demise, but a child shrink she consulted about it said no, most children figure out mortality sometime in their early-to-mid childhood, whether or not a person close to them dies.

"But I get a second life, right?" Sophie had asked.

"No, sweetie, you only get one," Jane told her.

"Just one?" Sophie's mouth dropped open.

Jane had felt a small lump in her throat, despite herself, as if she, too, were learning the one great truth about life for the first time again: that it ends. "Yes, sweetheart, just one."

"But what about heaven?"

Jane considered dissuading her daughter of the whole heaven juggernaut, but children, she knew, need the comfort of the fantasy. So she did what any good parent who doesn't want to lie outright does: She stalled. "If anyone is special enough for heaven," she said, "it's you."

"Okay," says Clover, taking charge. "Here's what we're going to do . . ." On Claire's bed, she creates four piles: one for the Salvation Army, another for her, a third for Addison, and a fourth for clothes to be sold on eBay, which she organizes meticulously and with drill sergeant efficiency. Jane is put to work stuffing the finished piles into bags and labeling them with a Sharpie. Mia and Bruno stand in the closet itself, stripping dresses of their hangers, shelves of their sweaters, drawers of their contents. Addison is put on aesthetic duty, separating the wheat from the chaff; this results in periodic squeals of delight, such as, "Holy shit, look at *these*!" and "They just don't *make* them like this anymore." Meanwhile, Jonathan plugs in his portable iPod speaker dock and sets Pandora to Radio Jonathan, a carefully honed blend of minor-chord-driven bands like R.E.M., Aimee Mann, Nirvana, and Radiohead he's been nurturing on its path to perfection by pressing thumbs-down whenever something too hard-core, soft-core, or major-chord pops up, or thumbs-up when the algorithm treats him to "Man on the Moon" or "You Can't Always Get What You Want" or something equally as stirring; no matter whether he's heard it before or not, it just has to hit him in the gut within the first twenty notes.

He's been hoping to find the perfect sound track for *Remembering Richard*, a soulful mix of songs about settling for imperfection, in time for a meeting with his agent Wes and an indy financier who's shown passing interest in the script if they can "*Garden State* it up," in the financier's words, with a killer iTunes list. "This is it. Our last-ditch effort," Wes had said, when he called Jonathan last week to tell him about the meeting. "No one's funding independent films right now. The wells are all dry. If he doesn't bite, I'm saying yes to that Cameron Diaz thing."

"No, please, anything but *Unwedded Bliss*," Jonathan had said. The script, by some hot twenty-three-year-old, concerns a wedding dress designer who falls for the bride whose dress he's designing. "It's totally inane."

"It's Paramount," Wes said. "It'll get you out of that sinkhole you've been complaining about."

"I'd rather be homeless than direct that piece of shit. I mean, come on, who ever heard of a straight wedding dress designer anyway? The whole premise is bogus."

"Beggars can't be choosers," said Wes.

Jonathan feels his chest tightening at the memory of that conversation. "Beggars?" he'd said. "Since when have I become a beggar?" In retrospect, he wishes he'd said, "Fuck you, Wes. Find another client to insult." But he was too worried that at his age, it might be hard to find a new agent.

Addison tosses a blur of fabric to Clover. "If you want the wrap dress, take it," she says. "It'll look better on you anyway."

"Everything looks better on her," says Mia with a mock sigh. "Bitch."

"Sweetheart, you look beautiful in everything," says Jonathan, his sincerity heartbreaking as he comes up behind Mia and kisses her on the neck. This elicits, from the others, a howl of groans and a throaty "Get a fucking room!" as Jonathan wonders, once again, when and how to tell his wife they'll have to sell the house in Antibes.

"What does this mean, 'Get a fucking room'?" says Bruno.

Clover feels an embarrassing rush of pleasure, as fresh memories of her recent interactions in the Charles Hotel surge up from the depths. She'll have to figure out a way to keep these images of Bucky moving inside her from bubbling up and sullying her conscious thought. "It means get a hotel room," she says.

"Excuse me?" says Bruno, still confused. "But why to get this hotel room?"

Whenever he's with Bruno, Jonathan can't help picturing Peter Sellers as Inspector Clouseau. He literally has to suppress his desire to say *minkey*. "It's just a rallying cry against public displays of affection," he says. "In case you haven't noticed, we are a nation of Puritans and prudes."

"Yes, I have noticed this," says Bruno, shaking his head and smiling.

Clover wraps the wrap dress over her other dress. The sleeves are an inch short, but no matter. It will be useful if her belly expands. Thank God maternity clothes have become better-looking since the demure tents and clown overalls Addison and Mia had to endure. Incredible that her child, should she be carrying one, will be nearly a whole generation younger than her roommates'. Max leaves for college in a year, when Mia's forty-one. Clover's child, God willing (she does the math in her head), will leave for college when she is sixty-one. Sixty-one! Had she known that, in the end result, she wouldn't even use her husband's sperm, she might have taken the procreative plunge years earlier. She wishes she could tell her younger self this. She takes off the dress, folds it as neatly as possible, and sticks it on top of her pile of stuff to keep.

"What about these?" Mia says, holding up a pair of rainbow suspenders. "Ebay or donate?"

"Oh my God," says Jane, standing up from her bag-labeling position on the floor and walking over to Mia to grab the suspenders. "The *Mork & Mindy* suspenders. I can't believe she kept them. I remember buying these for her for Christmas." Mork was the first American TV character who made sense to Jane: an alien, trying to figure out the rules of his new environment. In general her mother was against TV consumption, but for *Mork & Mindy* Claire made an exception, sitting on the couch once a week with her daughter and laughing together at the absurdities. "Nanoo, nanoo," she took to saying when she'd wake Jane up for school, which she never failed to follow up with a "Rise and shine, Sunshine! It's another glorious day of life," as she thrust open the curtains.

"These I'll keep," says Jane. She clips them to her pajama bottoms without fanfare and gets to work stuffing another bag.

By 4 A.M., Mia, Addison, Clover, and Jonathan have collapsed together on the king-size bed, forty-three bags of clothes have been lined up against the wall, two vacuum cleaner liners have been stuffed and tossed, and Claire's closet is now completely empty aside from a few lone hangers and Jane and Bruno, who stand, cross-armed, in its center. "So that's it," says Jane. *"Fini."*

"*Oui*," says Bruno. "*Fini.*"

"*Incroyable*," says Jane. "It feels so . . . empty." In the end, though Jane won't know this until later, it was Addison who dealt with her mother's underwear, tossing them into a green trash bag, which she immediately took out to the curb.

"You already know this, but I will to say it anyway, because it would be useful, this repeating," says Bruno, who'd already lost both of his parents to cancer and Alzheimer's several years earlier. He takes Jane's hand in his. "It will ameliorate, your sadness. Two years from now, three years from now, you will be doing something that will remind you of your mother, or you will hear a song she loved, or you will see something you desire to show her, and instead of feeling despondent that she's not here, you will catch yourself smiling. Really. Happens to me all the time."

"I know." Jane has only vague memories of her birth family, but certain odors—the Vietnamese restaurant on the rue Bastille in the fourth, the smell of rhododendrons—are capable of exhuming intense feelings not of loss but of grace, comfort, well-being. As for Hervé, she sees him every day in the planes of her daughter's face, which doesn't provoke sadness anymore so much as a deep-seated if melancholic joy. "But right now I'm just not there yet."

"Of course you are not." He turns to face her, now holding both of her hands in his. "The grief is too new. And she was your *mother*. The mothers are the hardest. There's that great letter by Proust to his friend whose mother had just died. Do you know it?"

Jane shakes her head no.

"Wait, I will to find it." He removes the phone from his pocket and Googles, in French, the words *Proust inert henceforth* and *broken*, without quotes, hoping these four little words will lead him to the half-remembered phrase within a letter, hazily recalled, whose recipient's name escapes him. "*Et le voilà!*" he says, still amazed by the ease and instantaneity of information, the minimal effort now required to disinter it. One need not remember anything anymore. The entire human population of Earth can fall victim to Alzheimer's, and one would still be able to locate the full lyrics to "Tangled Up in Blue" or to Lady Macbeth's cri du coeur with only the vaguest recalled fragments: "rain falling on my shoes"; "unsex me now." He takes curious comfort in this.

He reads off the tiny screen:

Now there is one thing I can tell you: You will enjoy certain pleasures you would not fathom now. When you still had your mother you often thought of the days when you would have her no longer. Now you will often think of days past when you had her. When you are used to this horrible thing that will forever be cast into the past, then you will gently feel her revive, returning to take her place, her entire place, beside you. At the present time, this is not yet possible. Let yourself be inert, wait till the incomprehensible power . . . that has broken you restores you a little, I say a little, for henceforth you will always keep something broken about you. Tell yourself this, too, for it is a kind of pleasure to know that you will never love less, that you will never be consoled, that you will constantly remember more and more.

"I love this idea," Bruno says. "Of being broken but finding pleasure in it."

Jane smiles. She is struck, as she often was, even when she and Hervé were married, at Bruno's quiet reservoirs of intellect and compassion. "The gentle giant," Hervé used to call him, using the English phrase, for it was surprising, in a person so large, so physically intimidating and unwieldy, to see the inner child so clearly. Bruno's need for love had a childlike innocence in it, too, both in its vastness and in its conspicuity. It must have been painful, Jane thinks, to have been abandoned by her—for nearly a year—as her mother lay dying. And like that, without further thought, she forgives his transgression. "Bruno," she says, turning around, pressing her body next to his, "I know it's late but . . . please. Make love to me."

"Now?" he says, somewhat shocked, for it has been at least six months since their last congress, maybe longer, he's lost track. "Here?" He looks behind him at the tableau of bodies on Claire's bed. What could she possibly mean?

Jane stands up and skims off, from the top of a nearby bag, an old sheepskin rug that had been replaced, in the 1990s, with sisal. Claire had kept it for sentimental reasons—it was the first joint purchase of her marriage to Harold—but then found herself hauling it out for functional purposes one Christmas when her granddaughter was seven months old and still unsteady in her sitting. Jane places it now in the center of the closet floor and gently shuts the door. "Yes, here," she says. "Right now."

"But what about, you know—"

"You know" are Jane's birth control pills. She'd run out during one of her trips to care for her mother but couldn't stomach paying the exorbitant monthly cost to refill the prescription Stateside. "Forty-eight dollars!" she'd said to Bruno. "Can you believe it?" In France, they were essentially free. Since she and Bruno weren't having sex anyway, she decided not to waste the money. She'd meant to start taking them again when she got back to Paris, but grief and the endless paperwork of the dead got in the way, plus she wonders if there's even any point in going back on the pill at her age. "I don't care," she says. "I want you. Right now." She pulls down her rainbow suspenders and lets her pajama bottoms sink, without ceremony, to the ground. Then she yanks off her T-shirt until she's standing in her underwear.

Bruno stares at Jane's nearly naked torso, its lines and curves as stirring to him as the first time he laid eyes on them. He feels himself stiffen, his jeans constricting. Dropping to his knees, removing what he can of his own clothes while Jane dispenses haphazardly with the rest, he devours the sharp jut of her hip bones, the swell of her breasts, the concave triangle between her neck and clavicle. Then he yanks off her underwear and buries his face in the musty tangle until she, unable to remain standing any longer, crumbles to her knees and falls on her back, feeling the softness of the rug on her skin, then the downy friction, in 2/2 time, between her shoulder blades.

Their movements and muffled moans fill that barren room with the only logical repudiation of its vacant racks and empty shelves. In nine months time, five days after Clover goes into labor in New York with little Frankie, Jane, Bruno, and Sophie will welcome Claire Streeter Saint-Pierre into their sunny home on the rue Vieille du Temple.

The birth will be uncomplicated; the infant healthy and easy; the father, as Jane will write on her Facebook wall, atop a photograph of a three-hour-old baby Claire, "over the moon." Jane will initially mourn the fact that her mother will never get to meet her namesake, but that dense cream of sadness will be aerated with time's whisk, mulled with memory's sugar, until one day Jane will taste only sweetness at the utterance of her daughter's name.

And once a year, without fail until his death, she will send a Christmas card to Lodge Waldman at her old Belmont address, so he can watch the new Claire grow.

Sunday, June 7, 2009

In Memoriam

Indicates reported deceased since last Anniversary Report

    Elizabeth Frances Abernathy
*   Jonathan Hatch Brownmiller
    Anthony John DiCarlo
    Jasmine *Fulton* Randal
    Delia Anne Harrison
    Carl Ronald Lefevre
    Asher Thomas Monk
    Pearce Snowdon Northrop III
    Cynthia *Nussbaum* Franklin
    Michael Edward O'Hara
*   Bill Sunshine Pelton
    Penelope Jane Schiff
    Leonid Yegorovich Shirvin
*   Sharon *Spivak* Warren
    Orly *Weinberg* Axelrod
    Allison Dunworth Young

Obituaries

JONATHAN HATCH BROWNMILLER died on December 27, 2008, in Boulder, Colorado. He was born on January 23, 1967, and graduated from the Lincoln School in Ash Fork, Arizona. Brownmiller was a resident of North House and received an A.B. *summa cum laude* in biology. He studied medicine at the UC San Francisco and worked as an orthopedic surgeon at the Hospital for Special Surgery in New York until 2004, when he moved to Denver to start a bicycle business. He is survived by his parents, Helene and Bud Brownmiller.

BILL SUNSHINE PELTON died on September 11, 2007, in Northampton, Massachusetts. He was born on September 12, 1967, and was prepared at the Phillips Exeter Academy, where he was captain of the women's field hockey team. Pelton was a resident of Adams House, a member of Phi Beta Kappa, and graduated *cum laude* in computer science. After graduating, he completed his Ph.D. at MIT in Artificial Intelligence before moving to Northampton, Massachusetts, to work on the Theodora Project. He is survived by his partner, Felicia Herrera, and by his parents, Lou and Betty Pelton.

SHARON SPIVAK WARREN died on February 14, 2006, in Washington, D.C. She was born on May 13, 1967. Graduating first in her class at the Dwight D. Eisenhower School in Coral Gables, Florida, she received an A.B., *magna cum laude* with highest honors, with our class. Warren was a history of science major at Harvard and a resident of Dunster House. After graduation, she worked as a public advocate for breast cancer research in Washington, D.C.

She was also a gifted flutist who played in a local chamber orchestra. She is survived by her father, Harold Spivak, her husband, Whit Warren, and by her three children, Eleanor, Adam, and Daisy.

ANGUS ARTHUR FROELICH. *Home Address:* 2600 Cook Street, Denver, CO 80205 (303-587-9496). *Occupation:* CEO and founder, The Orpheus Group. *E-mail:* afroelich@orpheusgroup.com. *Spouse/ Partner:* Lily Busby Froelich (B.A., University of Colorado '90). *Children:* Kelly Jane, 1999; Luke Randolph, 2001; Allen Brock, 2004.

I started the Orpheus Group, a consulting firm specializing in arts, sports, and ecological/green organizations, after a decade spent locked in the golden handcuffs of McKinsey. We set up shop here in Denver and moved the family from our former home base in Chicago to be nearer to my wife Lily's parents and to take greater advantage of the great outdoors. We were followed almost a year to the day later by my old roommate and best friend, Hatch Brownmiller, who left a thriving career in orthopedic surgery to pursue his actual passion, biking. With my firm's help, he opened up Heaven on Wheels, a high-end bike shop frequented by none other than the bicycle-loving mayor of Denver himself, John Hickenlooper. (Who, if we're all lucky, will one day be the governor of Colorado and then maybe even the president of the United States, mark my word. Helluva guy. Watch him carefully.)

Anyway, when Hatch wasn't running the business like an old pro, shaking hands with the mayor and whatnot, he was running me into the ground like a sadist, insisting that I lose fifty pounds by reunion. He had me on my bike four mornings a week, come rain or shine, and on snow days and the other three days he made me do yoga—no, that was not a typo, I actually took up yoga, people—and damned if I didn't lose those fifty pounds Hatch ordered (for health reasons) and then some (for my own vanity), along with a bucketful of stress and most of my hair, not that the latter had anything to do with the former, I just thought it was worth mentioning that, though I now have the body of—well, not exactly Michelangelo's *David*, but maybe *David*'s slightly flabbier, older cousin, Irv—I am also now completely bald. That's right, *b-a-l-d* bald. Haven't any of you chem majors come up with a secret formula yet? You're Harvard grads, for Christ's sake. Start inventing!

My kids are my joy; my wife still loves me, despite my lack of hair and the fact that I *refuse* to root for the Broncos; and I thank God for the gift of my life every friggin' day.

The Memorial Service

J ane, Clover, Addison, and Mia, all four of them pumped full of Nespresso pod run-off, generic ibuprofen, and Au Bon Pain croissants hastily procured and masticated in Harvard Square, take their seats in the Kirkland House common room at a hair past ten, just as the first eulogist, Angus Froelich, approaches the podium. The crowd seems small, although considering the early hour and the thousands of offspring and last night's debauchery, not unexpectedly so, and anyway they have nothing with which to compare it. None of them have ever been to one of these reunion weekend memorial services before, but Bill Pelton, back when he was Belinda, had been their housemate in Adams House; and Addison had slept with Hatch Brownmiller's other roommate, what's-his-name, Griffin, that one time freshman year; and Clover, who'd held yearly fund-raisers for Sharon Spivak's breast cancer organization at her house in the Hamptons, had been asked to give a short eulogy on her behalf; so they roused themselves from the slumber of the dead to pay their respects to the literal dead.

"Oh my God, is that Angus Froelich?" whispers Addison to Clover, and when Clover nods yes, she says, "Holy shit. He must have lost sixty pounds."

"Seventy-five," says Mia. "I asked him last night." Mia is determined to drop the last twenty pounds of extra baby weight if it kills her. Well, not really if it kills her—she has no intention of being eulogized at the twenty-fifth for pulling a Karen Carpenter—but she has made an appointment with both the nutritionist and the trainer to whom Jonathan sends all of his actors who show up on set with a jiggle, however slight.

"How'd he do it?" says Jane, who's never needed to lose a pound in her life but found herself nevertheless riveted, when she was in Belmont caring for her mother, to the seemingly endless array of weight-loss reality shows.

"Yoga, biking, no white bread," whispers Mia.

"That's it?" says Addison, who for many years believed her life would be better minus three to five pounds. Maybe six. Until recently it finally occurred to her that the few extra pounds were the least of her burdens.

"That's what he told me," says Mia, suddenly feeling a bit rude, considering the occasion and venue, discussing the vicissitudes of flesh and bone.

"Shhh!" says someone sitting behind them, and they all fall guiltily silent as Angus begins.

"I didn't like Hatch when we first met . . ."

"Hell of an opener," whispers Addison to Clover. "I hope yours is as good," but she is shushed again by the scold and falls silent.

". . . I thought he was a bit aloof, cold." Angus glances down where his notes should be, if he'd had them, then up at the seated crowd, clearly at ease with extemporaneous speaking but not with the subject matter. "The first thing he said to me when I arrived in our dorm room in Weld was 'Dude, don't touch my bike.' Not 'Hello, nice to meet you' or 'Hey, so here we are, roommates!' or even 'Please dude, don't touch my bike,' but simply 'Dude, don't touch my bike.' Hatch always claimed he added a *please* at the end, and since he's gone I'll give him the benefit of the doubt, but in my memory, there was no *please*. Great, I thought. I have to spend my entire freshman year with this bozo? The only thing he had going for him, as far as I could tell in those first few seconds of snap judgment, were his looks. Meaning, or so I imagined, it was only a matter of time before beautiful women would show up in our room, and when they couldn't find Hatch or our other roommate Griffin—who, no joke, turned down an offer to be on the cover of the 1985 Men of the Ivy League calendar—maybe every once in a blue moon they'd settle for me.

"How wrong I was. On all counts. Except for the part about the pretty girls showing up in our room, which they did in droves. But not once—not once!—did any of them ever settle for me, as pathetically as I might have tried to sway them otherwise. As for Hatch's opening salvo—'Don't touch my bike'—it was, I later realized, uttered from a place of fear and insecurity, not nastiness. That bike was his baby. The one steady passion of his life. He later told me that purchasing it had taken him four years of working nights and weekends at the local pizza parlor in Ash Fork, and he was simply afraid of anything happening to it. Like the time his father, on a bender at the time, drove it into a tree.

"Hatch and I ended up rooming together all four years of college. And despite my first impressions of him, Hatch Brownmiller turned out to be the most warm and caring human being I've ever met. My best friend until the day he died.

"There are literally thousands of examples of what made him so special, but to give you just one, I'll take you back to freshman year. The three of us—Hatch, Griffin, and I—were all punched for the Delphic, Griffin because his dad had been a member, Hatch no doubt on account of his bone structure, and me because, well, God only knows. A clerical error, let's assume. Griffin and Hatch were invited to join; I wasn't. Griffin accepted, Hatch declined. Why? He said my not getting in had nothing to do with it, but I never believed him. Finally, twenty years later, after I lost seventy-five pounds in no small part due to Hatch's fear, ironically, that I would die an early death from excessive Dorito consumption, he admitted the truth. At a cocktail party during punching season, one of the members had said to him, pointing behind my back, 'You live with that fat fuck? You poor bastard.'

"'I couldn't be with the kind of people who would say that kind of stuff behind your back,' he told me.

"A few years ago, when Hatch's marriage was foundering—he wanted kids, she didn't, we'll just leave it at that—I invited him to come stay with us until he could figure out his next move. He'd been talking about leaving medicine for years—not that he didn't like it, he just didn't love it or the hours, and frankly I was tired of hearing him complain about both his wife and his job—so when he separated from his wife he also took a leave of absence from orthopedic surgery, from New York, from the entire infrastructure of the life he'd so carefully constructed. His 'false self' he called it, though I sometimes accused him of revisionist history. I think he simply outgrew what he once thought he wanted. Happens to the best of us. Anyway, he lived in our spare bedroom for several months, trying to figure out whether he liked Denver, whether opening a bike shop was a viable option, whether it was possible to completely reinvent himself on the brink of middle age.

"Those months with Hatch in our house were some of my favorite months of my life. Even my wife says so, and that's saying a lot, having your husband's college buddy living under your roof for so long. Because he'd been deprived of having children of his own, he took to playing uncle to my kids like a fish to water. I'd come home from work and find them knee-deep in some crazy project he'd invented, like turning the living room into a spiderweb or making a volcano out of baking soda and vinegar. Anyway, cut to three years later, Hatch's business is thriving, he's got all the time in the world to ride his bike, and he meets Jill, who's dying to have kids, like, yesterday.

"So the four of us—Hatch, Jill, me, and my wife—we decide to go to Boulder for the weekend over Christmas break. It's the end of December, and it's cold, but the roads are completely clear and plowed, so Hatch suggests we go biking for an hour or so while the ladies go for massages. So we bundle up, snap our shoes in place, and we're off. While we're out riding, Hatch tells me he's thinking of asking Jill to marry him, but he's afraid of making that kind of commitment again, what did I think? I say, 'Buddy, are you fucking kidding me? If you don't marry that woman, you're a fool.' 'Okay, fine,' he says, 'I'll do it.'"

Angus takes a breath, sputters. "Fifteen minutes later . . ." Several long seconds pass as he attempts to regain composure, but his eyes are too full now to contain their contents any longer. The surface tension breaks. Tears fall. "Fifteen minutes later, I'm holding Hatch's body in my arms. It all happened so fast. One minute we were riding, the next he was down. A simple sideswipe. The driver was completely sober. It was just . . . an accident. I tried to will him back into existence, I really did. I gave him CPR, tied off the bleeding, I held him next to my body to keep him warm. But he went limp before the paramedics even showed up.

"I wish there was a lesson to draw from this, some piece of wisdom I could give you to make his death mean something. But I've got nothing, folks. Not a single truth or pithy aphorism or comforting thought. Other than to say I loved Hatch. And my wife loved him. And my kids loved him. And his girlfriend loved him. And I bet some of you here loved him, too. And now he's gone."

Angus steps down from the podium and retakes his seat, where he is comforted, with a gentle arm around his shoulder, by his wife.

Mia, who never met Hatch, is crying, thinking about the proposal that never happened. Addison, who met Hatch once briefly, on her way from Griffin's bedroom to the bathroom, is crying, thinking about how you can transform your life completely—really take stock, figure out what works and what doesn't, even midstream—and then one day, boom! None of it matters. Clover, who can't remember whether or not she ever met Hatch, is crying, thinking about the children he'd wanted to have but never had. And Jane, who thinks she might have taken a Civil War class with Hatch their junior year, is crying not because she knew or didn't know Hatch but because no matter how many people close to her have died, no matter how much grief has been piled on and endured, the fact of death itself still has the power to shock her, every single time, with its indifference.

. . .

Jonathan leans up against the kitchen wall, stretching first his left hamstring, then his right. "You sure you're okay watching all of them?"

he says to Bruno. His older kids and the Griswold kids are all still sleeping, but Zoe woke up at the crack of dawn, as usual, and Sophie has been zoned out in the family room, indulging in her favorite verboten (or at least verboten when her mother's around) pastime: watching American cartoons. Mia said she'd cart Zoe along to the memorial service, so Jonathan could go on his run, but Bruno had jumped at the opportunity to babysit.

"But of course," says Bruno, who has the baby strapped to his chest in the BabyBjörn as he tries to figure out which color pod to place in the Nespresso machine. "*Putain, mais quelle couleur c'est la plus forte? C'est nul, ce système,*" he mumbles to himself, searching for some indication on the pod itself of its strength, forgetting for a moment that Jonathan has a few years of high school French under his belt.

"*Système*'s masculine?" says Jonathan.

"What?"

"You said, 'It's hopeless, this system.' <u>*Ce*</u> *système*. *Ce*. Masculine. But it ends with an *e*, right?"

"Yes, but every rule is made to be broken, no? *Vagin* is masculine as well. So are, how you say"—he holds his hands, palms up, to his chest, cupping the air in front of it—"*les seins?*"

"Breasts."

"Yes, breasts are masculine as well. Makes no sense."

"Or *seins*, as the case may be."

"Huh?" says Bruno.

"Never mind. Bad joke. Makes no sense. Makes no *seins?*"

"Oh yes, ha-ha. Good one." Bruno smiles.

"No, bad one." Jonathan looks puzzled. "Wait, vaginas and breasts are masculine? That seems so . . . wrong."

"Yes, and *figure-toi*, bomb is feminine. *Une bombe. Bizarre*, no? But please, Jonathan. Tell me what color I must to use. I am in need of the caffeine immediately."

"Black's the strongest. But I think purple tastes the best. What about penis, masculine or feminine?"

"*Un pénis*, but of course. Masculine."

"Well at least there's that."

"Yes, although I once had an Australian girlfriend, there is a long time ago, who could never say it right. '*Je veux sucer ta pénis*,' she would say. Ta *pénis*, as if the penis were feminine. It amused me so much. But I did not correct her."

"Yes, well, considering that the grammatical error was expressed within a request to give you a blow job, I think you can be forgiven your pedagogical failings."

"*Pardon?*"

"Call it 'situational incapacity.'"

"I'm sorry, I do not understand these words what you say. Situational what?"

"Never mind." He sees Bruno still struggling to choose the right pod. "Dude, it's not rocket science. Just pick the purple one. It tastes good."

"No. I must to choose the most strong," says Bruno, pulling a black pod out of the Tupperware container Claire bought to store them. It was he himself who'd bought the machine for Jane's mother, the last Christmas they were all here together, after he realized he would otherwise have to spend another holiday week drinking the swill from an American drip machine. Some of his colleagues had bought one for the office, the French being early adopters of pod systems, and they seemed to tolerate it well enough, but he settled for it only when he was too busy to leave his desk, since a perfectly brewed, crema-rich espresso could be purchased for less than a euro downstairs at the café. He felt the same way about the pod system as he felt about dating other women back when Hervé was still alive and married to Jane: Until he could find a woman like Jane, all other women he bedded were just a lesser version, fulfilling a need (sex/caffeine) but not a desire (love/a perfect cup of coffee).

With the smell of Jane still lingering on his fingers, and the memory of last night's coupling still fresh in his head, he vows to remember, from now on, the difference between the two. The universe handed him an opportunity when Hervé died, and he must not trample on it ever again. He felt guilty at first, for feeling euphoria on top of his grief that night he got the call saying Hervé had been killed, but that guilt has long been replaced by feelings of well-being and gratitude so profound that every year, on the anniversary of Hervé's death, he looks up at the sky, for lack of a more compelling focal point, and says, *"Merci, mon pote"*: Thanks, mate.

"I'll be back in less than an hour," says Jonathan, standing half in, half out the front door. Speaking of breasts and vaginas, he thinks, he could have sworn he heard Jane and Bruno getting it on in the closet last night, an act for which he takes whatever credit he's due. He hopes the revelation of his own indiscretion allowed her, in some small way, to begin the process of forgiveness. Those two belong together, he thinks. More than she ever belonged with Hervé, as much as Jonathan admired the guy's bravery. But after Sophie was born, well, it wasn't that he judged Hervé for returning, again and again, to the battlefields of Afghanistan and Iraq, but, as a fellow parent, he couldn't abide by it. Jane dialed it back, way back, and still wrote meaningful stories; why couldn't Hervé have done the same when they offered him that position covering the *Élysée*?

One had to forgo certain things as a father, he felt. This was the pact one made with one's children upon their conception: to do everything within one's power, within reason, to stay alive long enough to see them through to adulthood. This had been his primary concern vis-à-vis Zoe, when Mia begged him to have one more child: He'd just turned sixty; he was sixty-one when she was born, and he'll be seventy-nine when she graduates high school. And that's if he's lucky.

And so he runs. And runs. Hoping to stave off the inevitable for as long as possible.

"Take your time," says Bruno. The weight, warmth, and fragrance of the baby asleep on his chest feels comforting in a way he has never experienced. He wonders what it would be like to breast-feed. Is it arousing? Jane once told him it was, but not in a sexual way. "In a *sensual* way," she said. At the time he did not understand the difference between the two—sexual, sensual, it was all the same to him, whether in French, English, or Esperanto—but now, with Zoe ruffling his chest hairs with her tiny baby breaths, he gets it. Despite all of their past chitchat about not having children together—Sophie is, for all intents and purposes, his child, even if French law doesn't technically see it that way— he makes his second and third vows of the morning: to marry Jane, if she'll still have him, and to make a baby with her, if at all still possible. Yes, she's forty-two, but she's a young forty-two, with no signs yet of menopause. He will plant the seed with her tonight, after everyone heads home. That is, if the seed hasn't already been planted.

Jonathan takes off, making his way toward Fresh Pond through the sun-dappled streets of Belmont, feeling the first welcome rush of endorphins surging through him. He's been fairly religious about his exercise schedule, running every morning, with rare exceptions, since the day his doctor told him his cholesterol numbers were charting through the roof, but the early weeks of the new regime were brutal. His body fought him with every step. *No-no-no-no,* it seemed to be whispering, as each foot—*clomp-clomp-clomp-clomp*—fell. Psychologically, however, it's been a no-brainer: run and live or sit on your ass and die. Never mind little Zoe, who (and this kills him, *kills* him) will most likely not have a father to walk her down the aisle, no matter how many miles or how often he runs; he has three nearly fully baked children to take into consideration as well, and they deserve an intact father for as long as humanly possible.

He always knew, marrying and fathering children as late as he did, that he would probably deprive his children of a father earlier than they (or he) would like. He holds out hope that he will one day get to meet a grandchild or two, but even if Max manages to have kids in his early thirties, Jonathan will be in his seventies by then. And unless Zoe becomes a teen mom, there's little to no chance of him getting the chance to meet her children.

Some part of him—the part that waited so long to get married—has always wanted his films to be a catalyst, however sappy, for young love, young marriage, for having babies early enough to really enjoy them both as children and adults. He sees how much harder it is for Mia to mother Zoe at forty-two, when, in her twenties and early thirties, she had enough energy and stamina to handle all three boys effortlessly. Thank God for that, too, since he was in his early forties when the boys were born, already feeling the physical strains of age. It seems to him the whole career first/babies second model favored by a certain subset of East Coast educated intellectuals, whether men or women, puts the cart before the horse.

On the other hand, had he married and had babies with Charlene, the dancer he was seeing in his early twenties, there's no doubt they'd now be divorced. She recently friended him on Facebook, and he could tell how incompatible they'd be simply by scrolling through her exclamation-point riddled, irony-starved updates: *Mani-pedi at Pixie Nails: awesome!*; *Off to the gym!*; *Ugh, stuck in traffic. So annoying!* It's so hard to find the correct balance, he thinks, between career, love, sex, money, children, freedom, responsibility, fulfillment, physical health, mental health, and vitality. Most people are lucky if they get one or two right. That he has so many of them under control, at least for now—with the looming exception of their finances—seems nothing short of a miracle.

But the vitality issue is intractable. At sixty-one, he is old. There is no other euphemism for it.

Holy shit, he thinks (forgetting his age for just a moment), look at that stunning light, the way it pixellates through the trees as he moves through space, hitting the side of his face like the beam from a film projector. We are all stars of our own movies, he tells his children, but we are also its writer, creator, and narrator. ("Yeah, yeah, yeah," Max will interrupt, playfully, "and it's our God-given duty to make it interesting. Got it, Dad. Check on the life well spent. Now can we clear our plates and have dessert?") Jonathan imagines the tracking shot of this scene, the camera on a dolly following him down the road, the human figure kept consistently center frame until the last possible moment, when the rig should fly up on a jib for a more bird's-eye view as the man slips out of the frame. A medium shot would be best, the body in profile, backlit, such that the sun keeps peeking around the shadowy figure, hitting the camera's lens as it runs. And of course the sounds of huffing and puffing, the psychological struggle made aural and physical, would have to be added into the mix by his favorite Foley artist, Ben.

Voice-over would be a cop-out in this instance, he thinks—not always, but in this instance yes—and the man's precise *pensées* themselves shouldn't really matter to the scene, so the music should really be the mouthpiece of the inner noise without the character having to narrate it. But what music? Always tricky, music. How about something slow and ballady, by the Stones, both as a counterpoint to his movements and because it is the music of his late adolescence and thus the most visceral to him, and anyway this isn't a real film, of course, just an imagined one, so he doesn't have to consider things like cost and rights to a Rolling Stones song, which would be prohibitive.

He stops for a minute to run in place, spinning the dial on his iPod until "As Tears Go By" is playing. He starts to run again, imagining the scene. The song—composed in a kitchen by Mick and Keith, under duress, they were literally not allowed out by their manager, even to piss, until the song was fully baked—is as stirring as always, stoking the deepest fires of his limbic core, but no, it wouldn't be right for the scene. For one, the melody's too on-the-nose. For another, the lyrics would get in the way. What's needed, really, is something somber and classical, an adagio, maybe, that could slowly build to an allegro, creating a contrapuntal dissonance, at first, between image and melody until the two could meet somewhere in the middle: an acceptance of the older self, the melancholy of the doomed. He stops again and turns the dial until he reaches Chopin's Ballade No. 1, Op. 23 in G minor, recorded by

Arthur Rubinstein in 1959. A perfect performance, really, and a perfect counterbalance to the modern-day image of a man, a father, on the cusp of old age, running for his life.

Amazing, he thinks, how we all so willingly participate in the charade, stumbling along year after year, decade after decade, knowing from the minute we're curious enough to ask that not only are we marked with an expiration date, but that this date—this crucial piece of information!—is unknown to us. Cannot be known to us, unless we take matters into our own hands, which several of his friends over the years have done, with varying degrees of success. It's hard for Jonathan to imagine having nothing to live for, no hope, but he also realizes he's in the minority. So much sadness cloaks the lives of so many, and yet even the sad ones muddle on, flocking en masse to churches and mosques, to bars and whores, to Cinderella on Ice and to his candy-coated films, because there in the dark, surrounded by the damned, they can participate in the mutual delusion of happily ever after.

It's only recently, as he heads into his seventh decade, that he's been feeling slightly guilty about this, his small role in the continual propagation of the untenable fantasy.

The Chopin flows through his veins like the opiates he once briefly allowed therein, back when he had long hair, a draft card, and a dog-eared copy of Kerouac in his back pocket—man, he was lucky not to have been called up, and all because he was born on June 24, number 358 in that ridiculous lottery-by-birthday drawing—until there's only him, the Earth, the sun, the notes on the piano and two little tears forming (to his embarrassment, really, but what can he do?) at the corners of his eyes. That his story, like all stories, must end; that the world will go on without him; that these trees, this road, that dirt, those rays, such notes, his *children* will all exist without him, it's . . . it's . . . he can't even come up with a proper description. *Unfathomable* comes close, but no, it's more than that. *Mind-boggling*, yes, but it doesn't feel specific enough. History is mind-boggling. Birth is mind-boggling.

The Milky Way is mind-boggling. Hell, everything related to life, if you break it down, is mind-boggling. *Melancholy* does a decent job, but it leaves out the concomitant joy over the accumulation of years and wisdom, experience and love.

Mia: his love. They talked their way around it when they first met, the vast gulf between their ages. "I don't care," she said. "I love you. That's all that matters."

"But I'll abandon you one day," he said. "It's a near certainty."

"Nothing's certain," she said. But she must have known, somewhere in that giant heart of hers, that the possibility of spending a good chunk of the final third of her life without him was quite high. Now, at forty, she is still young enough to be in the apex of her story, to make some grand reversal that will forever affect her narrative arc. A part of him is jealous of this, her youth relative to his, the years she has left. He is at arc's end, looking back with awe and appreciation yet wondering whether he has one more reversal left. He'll find financing for his screenplay yet, if he has to get down on his knees himself to beg every wealthy person he knows to help him. It'll be a good movie, he's sure of it. Maybe even his best. The one his kids will be able to show their grandkids with pride. Look what your grandfather *did*!

Not that he isn't proud of his romantic comedies, with all of those wedding photos under the closing credits, but as an artifact of life—his life, any life—well, they don't tell the whole story. Life gets messy. For everyone. And weddings are hardly happy endings. They are the most fragile of beginnings.

He spots, in the distance, a moving van, parked in front of a house. As he approaches, a young couple comes into view. The new owners, no doubt, as the woman is standing as close to the man as she can with that enormous belly—she must be at least eight or nine months pregnant—while the man holds a small digital camera out in front of them, the lens facing inward, trying to get both their faces, his wife's belly, and the new house in the shot.

Impossible, thinks Jonathan. He stops to help them, as usual.

"Here, let me take that for you," he tells the young couple. "I'm a professional."

• • •

Felicia Herrera, Bill Pelton's widow, steps up to the podium, looking every inch the female she was born and remained, even as her partner started taking the hormones that would transform her into a he and their lesbian relationship into a heterosexual one. She is slightly stocky, compact, with spiky hair dyed an unnatural shade of red, but she works the assets she does have well, wearing a low-cut dress and cranberry-colored lipstick, her eyes heavily outlined in black. "I lived with Bill for a decade, until his suicide two years ago," she reads from her notes, without looking up.

Mia and Jane exchange glances. Addison pokes Mia in the ribs. Clover raises her eyebrows. They'd all suspected Belinda had killed herself, or rather that Bill had killed himself—it was so hard to refer to Belinda as Bill when they'd all known him as a woman—but Jane had heard from someone, she can't remember whom, that Bill had died in a car crash.

"Really?" Mia had said. "I heard it was a suicide."

Addison had heard the same thing, and Clover had no solid information one way or the other, though she was admittedly curious to find out how Bill had died, which was always the first piece of information she'd try to extract from her parents whenever someone on the commune went off the rails, never to return. (She was the only one of her roommates in college never to try LSD or anything stronger than pot, since "acid freak-out" and "overdose" were frequently the answers.) She, too, suspected from having read the obituaries in both *Harvard Magazine* and the red book that Bill had killed himself, but the monthly alumni magazine hardly ever bothers to mention the cause of death in their back-of-the-book memorials, and the red book has always remained consistently vague on the topic: just the date of birth and the date of death and a few innocuous biographical tidbits in between.

"Unlike some of the Harvard grads I've met over the years," Felicia continues, "whom, if you ask 'Where did you go to college?,' will answer, 'In the Boston area,' or 'In Cambridge, Mass.,' Bill had no use for false modesty. He was so proud of having gone to school here that he hung his Class of '89 banner in our home office, above his Veritas chair and his Adams House mug . . ."

Adams House, thinks Mia—picturing streaks of blue hair and vintage cocktail dresses and boys in fuchsia lipstick blowing smoke rings into patchouli air—was years ahead of its time, offering not only safe harbor to gay students but also a celebration of their sexuality by their peers, of all persuasions, in an era before the abutment of those two words, *gay* and *student*, had become culturally acceptable. It was a kind of utopia, in fact, the only house at Harvard with an annual Halloween drag night in which everyone—straight, gay, bi, it didn't matter your orientation, you felt like a spoilsport if you didn't show up in drag—participated. Sure, there was a lot of posing and posturing as well: The clothing was often black; the cigarettes often clove; and the orgies in Greta Suskind's room in B-entry, though Mia never had the courage to attend one, often legendary. But at its heart, Adams House was a rare escape from the shackles of conformity.

Too bad, she thought, upon hearing that the student lottery to the Harvard houses was randomized in the mid-1990s. In her era, you were allowed to list your top three choices, and then hopefully you got one of the three if you weren't "quadded": exiled, a good fifteen-minute walk in good weather, to one of the houses in the old Radcliffe quad.

Sure, it was nerve-racking at the end of freshman year, trying to squeeze one's entire persona into a cultural stereotype: Were you, say, an Eliot House prep, a Kirkland House jock, a Lowell House egghead, a Dunster House hipster, a Winthrop House high schooler, or an Adams House *artiste*? But there was also something uniquely comforting, at the end of a long day spent learning with and debating other students with radically differing opinions on, say, Nicaragua, abortion, and gay rights, to come home to a place where the Contras were human rights violators; a woman's right to choose was sacrosanct; and homosexuality was just one other way, among many, of loving.

That first Halloween drag night of their sophomore year, as Mia remembers it, Belinda had showed up in the dining hall dressed in a Brooks Brothers suit she'd borrowed from the house tutor. She'd just cut her hair short, or at least much shorter than usual, and she'd painstakingly glued, with spirit gum to her upper lip, a mustache Mia had nabbed for her in the costume shop at the Loeb. At first Mia didn't recognize her housemate. Unlike everyone else in the dining hall, who seemed to be cross-dressing more for comedic kicks—the men in particular went totally over the top, wearing dark red lipstick, overstuffed bras, outrageous ball gowns, and feather boas—Belinda just looked, and quite convincingly so, like a man.

"Wow, look at you!" Mia had said to Belinda, when she finally saw the woman under the man, but it was striking how much more confident, more at home in her skin Belinda seemed as a man than she had as a woman. Instead of hunching over, hiding her breasts under crossed arms, she stood up so straight and tall, Mia was shocked by the difference in their height, which hadn't been apparent to her before.

"I know," Belinda had said. "I took one look at myself in the mirror and thought, dude, look at you. I'm never wearing a dress again." From then on, Belinda wore only men's clothing and searched, in vain, for a woman to love, until—or so she'd beamingly told Mia at the last reunion—she met Felicia at a lesbian bookstore in Northampton.

"After I'd heard Bill's car had flipped over a nearby embankment, I knew it wasn't an accident, even before I came home and found the note." Felicia is winding up, after describing Bill's addiction to painkillers in the wake of his second reassignment surgery, which ran into grafting complications that became intractable. "It's a really long note, and it's really personal, but I know Bill wouldn't have minded if I read the last section of it here." She clears her throat and places one piece of paper behind the other. "So here goes. 'I need you and everyone else to understand that becoming a man did not drive me to kill myself. I wanted, more than anything, to live a regular life, to be your husband, to travel with you and hold your hand and laugh at life's absurdities together, and had the surgery not gone wrong, I have no doubt I would have lived to a ripe old age by your side. But this life I've been left with—endless days and nights of constant pain, where pleasure has been completely eliminated, where I can't work or socialize or enjoy a spring day—is no life at all. You know that. And I can't see it changing. And I hope one day you can forgive me.

"'I love you, Fizzy. I really do.'" Felicia pauses, catches her breath. "That's what he called me, Fizzy. 'And I'm so sorry to leave you . . .'"

Clover reaches into her purse to grab a tissue for Addison, who seems particularly shaken by Bill's story. The screen of her silenced BlackBerry comes alive, as if it had been waiting for her to peek inside. "look 2 ur right," says the text. It's from Bucky.

• • •

Jonathan carefully frames the young couple in the viewfinder of their crap camera so that both the new house and the moving van are visible in the background. He wishes he had his Nikon D80. This will be one of those keepers, he knows, a shot for the couple to hang on the wall or to revisit after an argument or to nostalgically gaze upon toward the end of their lives: a simple, vivid, visual reminder of the day the buds were first blooming, the fruit ripe, the horizon so far off in the distance it was as yet undetected. An awesome responsibility, getting a shot like that just right.

"You're kidding," says the woman, rubbing her swollen belly. "*You're* the director of *Movers and Quakers?*"

"I am indeed," says Jonathan, going for a different angle to block out the reflection of the sun in the dormer window.

"How crazy!" says the man. "That was our first date."

"Then this must be kismet. From *Movers and Quakers* to movers and . . ." He tries to come up with a word that rhymes with *shakers* and means pregnant or married or new homeowners or some such thing. He quickly zooms through the whole alphabet in his head. Nothing. ". . . a new home."

The husband squinches his eyebrows, wondering if such an analogy requires his laughter. Jonathan holds his hand up as if to say, *Don't bother. My bad. Couldn't come up with the right pun.* He wonders, in fact, whether he isn't suddenly losing his knack for the comeback: troubling, in his line of work, to say the least.

Movers and Quakers, a tale of star-crossed love between a poor Quaker minister and the Orthodox heiress to an Israeli moving company, was the first of Jonathan's romcoms not to recoup its initial investment at the box office. In fact, as far as Sony was concerned, it bombed, both domestically, where it was pilloried and boycotted by both liberal and conservative Jewish groups alike, for its endorsement of the "Second Silent Holocaust" of intermarriage, as well as abroad, where the whole friction between a Quaker man and a Jewish woman didn't translate well, if at all. He'd made a terrible mistake with that contract, forgoing a large director's fee for back-end points that never materialized.

Mia, expecting a large windfall from the film—everyone did, it wasn't just her—had already hired the team that would knock down the far wall of their house to build a new extension, a place apart for the boys where they could play their music and entertain their friends in peace. But both she and the architect had gotten carried away, creating a soundproof music studio, where the kids could not only play but record their music; a home gym; a twenty-seat movie theater with digital surround sound; and a games/entertainment room, with enough space for a Ping-Pong table, an air hockey table, and a full wall of vintage games from the 1970s, like Pac-Man and Asteroids, and a couple of pinball machines. Mia had always wanted a room filled with such things when she was a teenager, and now her boys, who would have been just as happy playing Xbox, had one.

The renovation had cost them close to two million dollars, part of which they ended up financing with a home equity loan. A few months after the construction was completed, the market tanked, and they lost what little remained of their savings. Not that Mia is aware of any of this. Yet.

Today, Jonathan thinks. Today on the plane home, I will tell her we're in deep shit. That we have to sell the house in Antibes, at the very least. Probably some art as well, and most likely . . . oh God, he can't even think about it. He will remind her that these are rich people's problems, completely solvable via asset liquidation.

Not that this makes him any less stressed-out about their situation. In fact, these days, money—or rather his sudden lack thereof—is all he can think about. The shame of debt feels bottomless, an indictment.

"You guys work fast," Jonathan says to the couple, gesturing to the woman's belly with his eyes. "That film only came out, gosh, what was it? A year and a half ago, right?" Was it really only a year and a half ago? Jesus, he thinks. How quickly the whole thing can tailspin. One minute you're flying high, full speed ahead, the next a pocket of air catches your wing just as a lightning storm hits. He feels his chest tightening at the mere thought of it. If the U.S. housing market weren't so deep in the toilet . . . but no, that's ridiculous. Part of the reason he's in the pickle he's in is because the U.S. housing market tanked, taking everything and everyone down with it. How could all those lenders, bankers, quants, and brokers have been so blind? How does an entire country enter into a common state of denial?

He wonders how much the young couple paid for their charming center-hall Colonial. Probably got it for a steal. Lucky them. Timing's everything.

"Our first date was in January of '08," says the man. "So yeah, very recently."

"We moved in together a month later," says the woman, squeezing her husband's hand.

"We just knew, right away," says the husband. He turns to face his glowing, fecund bride, and she turns to face him, and Jonathan, jolted by the bright spark of that electrical current, has instincts well honed enough to capture it. He crouches down. *Click!* He snaps the perfectly composed shot that will sit in a silver frame on their new mantel for the next eight years, until the husband can no longer stand the sight of his wife's sagging breasts, nor her nightly refusals of ardor, nor being apart from his colleague, Vivian, and so another moving truck will come to haul away his vinyl record collection and his first edition Updikes and the liquor cabinet and flat-screen TV into which he'll so often escape, while his wife stands at the threshold, comforting their three children, who will shout at the van backing out of the only home they've ever known, "Daddy! Don't go! Daddy, please don't go!" while behind them, unseen from the van, the photograph that Jonathan so painstakingly composed will be smashed to bits on the slate hearth.

"Blindsided," the wife will lie to her friends. "I was completely blindsided."

"Well, here you go," says Jonathan, handing the camera back to his subjects, pleased that he was able to play a minor role in their recorded history. Nice couple, he thinks. Visibly in love.

And with the notes of Chopin reinserted back into his ears, off he runs to Fresh Pond, heart pounding.

· · ·

A few of the former members of the college chamber orchestra with whom Sharon Warren, née Sharon Spivak, used to perform have begun tuning their instruments as Clover searches over her left shoulder, in vain, for Bucky. Violin bows stroke an assortment of A, D, G, and E strings, all of them searching for that perfect nexus between sharp and flat; the cellist repositions his chair; and the flutist runs a bunch of lightning quick scales as a new text appears on the screen of Clover's BlackBerry. "No, ur other right, knucklehead. :)" Of course. Bucky wrote "look 2 ur right," not her left. Right and left: two concepts children are usually taught in school early enough for it to sink in, but Clover had been deprived of this and other equally useful pieces of information her parents had deemed unnecessary to her education— names of trees, capitals of the U.S. states, rules of English grammar and punctuation—until it was too late for them to be subsumed, second nature, into her being. Even now, though her facility with numbers (innate, she's convinced) is legendary in certain circles, she confuses maples with oaks, Dallas with Austin, verbs with gerunds, commas with semicolons, and left with right, although recently her husband, who was getting fed up with her always turning right when the GPS lady said left, taught her that the thumb and forefinger on the left hand make the correct-facing L, so she's getting better on that front.

Danny. Jesus Christ, why isn't he here with her? Flutterings of love at the conjuring of his lesson give way to suppressed anger, which slowly radiates out from her chest into her extremities, surprising her. She told him about this weekend a *year* ago. She kept reminding him, every month or so, that it was coming up. "This is important to me," she'd recently told him, when she found out he still hadn't booked his plane ticket. "I have to give Sharon's eulogy. I'd like you to be there for moral support." He'd promised to try. Which technically, she pointed out, wasn't a promise. What will happen when it's a parent-teacher conference? A birthday party? Will he promise to try to get to those, too, or will he promise to actually go? He'd promised to try to get over his squeamishness with regard to leaving a sperm sample in a cup at the fertility clinic, and look how well that turned out. A promise to try, at heart, is meaningless; it's just a well-crafted cop-out.

Danny, his colleagues always tell her, is a brilliant lawyer. Never shows his cards. Always wins.

Not this hand, buddy, she suddenly thinks, rubbing her belly, willing it to expand. She turns to her right and spots Bucky up against the wall, clutching his BlackBerry. Clover catches his eye, and he gives a slight, almost embarrassed wave as the piano player stands up to speak.

"We'd like to dedicate this piece to Sharon's memory," says the pianist, clearing his throat. "It was her favorite. Everyone ready?" They all nod. He lifts up his hand, as if holding an invisible conductor's baton, then lets it drop, scrawling the anchor of 4/4 time into the air: "And one-two-three-four, two-two-three-four . . ."

The first doleful notes glide off bows, whistle through openings. Bucky's thumbs peck at his BlackBerry. Clover's screen lights up. "wow. stunning. what's it called again?"

"pachelbel's canon," she writes back. "he forgot to say the name of it." She'd walked down the aisle to that piece the day she got married. She didn't care if it was almost as old, tired, and clichéd as the Wedding March. It was and remains, to her mind, one of the most lovely pieces of music ever composed. Plus it reminded her of Sharon, with whom she'd become friendly several years after college, and then quite close after she got sick. Sharon had lived long enough to have met Danny, but not long enough to have made it to the wedding. She was the only one of Clover's friends to have expressed any reservations about the relationship, however slight, based on a minor interaction she had with him in the hospital room, a few days before she was sent home to die.

"Doesn't your husband's firm need him?" Danny had asked Sharon, after Whit and Clover had both stepped out into the hallway to take calls from their offices. Whit, like Danny, was a litigator, but he'd reassigned most of his cases when the cancer that first appeared in Sharon's left breast was found to have metastasized throughout the rest of her body. When Danny and he became acquainted, Whit was spending the bulk of his days rushing back and forth between the hospital and home, calling into the office to consult on various cases only when absolutely necessary.

To which Sharon, slightly taken aback, said, "Well, yes, they do need him at the office, but right now the kids and I need him more."

"It's amazing they allow him to take off that much time," said Danny. "It can't be good for his career."

"I'm sure it's not," said Sharon. "But that's kind of beside the point right now, don't you think?" She asked him what he would do, say, if it were Clover in her place, dying.

"Clover's strong," he'd answered, unable (Sharon could tell, she later told Clover) to even imagine such a scenario. "She'd be fine."

"Strong and fine have nothing to do with it," Sharon said.

"He's just young," said Clover, by way of excuse, when Sharon told her about the exchange. "His career means everything to him right now. You know that phase. We all went through it."

"Just make sure, before you marry him," Sharon said, her terminal status stripping her of any obligation for euphemism or niceties, "that he will be there when you need him. That's all I'm saying. Have that discussion. Now. Before it's too late." Clover and Sharon were lying side by side in Sharon's hospice bed in her living room when she said this, the two of them listening to Pachelbel's Canon and staring out at the falling snow that had stranded Clover on a business trip overnight, much to her delight, since she was able to spend some unexpected quality time with Sharon. DC schools had been canceled for the day, so Whit was in the kitchen with the kids, making cookies and hot chocolate and playing air guitar to Green Day after an afternoon spent sledding. He was good at that. Keeping the party going, no matter the circumstances.

Three weeks later, Whit sent out the e-mail saying Sharon was gone. The funeral, as per Jewish law, was to be held the next morning at Washington Hebrew. Clover begged Danny to take the train with her down to DC, but he had a massive case pending. "She was more your friend anyway," he said, not understanding that what Clover needed at that moment wasn't a friend of Sharon's, but rather a friend. Period.

Clover types into her BlackBerry: "giving next eulogy. v nervous."

"don't be," writes Bucky. "u'll be gr8."

"doubtful. don't love my speech. too clinical, too much about her work. wish i could rewrite." Danny, whose oratory skills have been known to change the paths of his clients' lives, had promised to help her, but he never actually found a pocket of time to sit down and do it.

"fuck the speech. speak from the heart," types Bucky.

"i think i've forgotten how to do that."

"no time like the present."

"as if i needed reminding of that right now."

"i know. so sad. people our age. poof. gone."

"kills me. i loved sharon."

"carpe diem, lady."

"no shit."

"i mean it."

"mean what?"

"carpe diem. u and me."

"wtf are you talking about?"

"run away with me, pace."

"ha ha. very funny."

"not joking."

"don't understand."

"yes u do. i know u felt it. maybe not fri night. but definitely sat morning."

"felt what????? u r being obtuse."

"oh, come on. u'r going to make me say it?"

"say WHAT?" She looks over her right shoulder at Bucky, beseech-ingly.

He pauses for a moment before typing, "LOVE!" without losing eye contact.

The word combined with his expression feels like a shot of adrena-line straight to the heart, like that scene in *Pulp Fiction* where Uma Thurman is revived out of a drug-induced coma.

"am MARRIED," she types.

"me 2."

"happily."

"yeah, right."

"what's THAT supposed to mean?"

"ur actions speak otherwise."

"that was NOSTALGIA, ok? nothing more."

Addison is watching this entire exchange, riveted, trying desperately to sneak a peek at the words being typed. With the few glances she manages to steal, she understands most of it. Addison likes Danny, but it's not as if he's been in the picture long enough for her to really know him. Hell, her husband's been in the picture forever, and she still doesn't know parts of Gunner the way she knows Clover. Or Bucky. Or Jane or Mia or even Bennie, who was an open book from day one.

Some people put up walls. Others don't. Addison's finally understanding this, twenty years too late. When she bumped into Gunner at that bar in Eressos, the Berlin Wall was being hacked to bits on the small TV behind the bar. "Isn't that amazing?" she'd said, with tears in her eyes. He'd shrugged, dry-eyed, and said, "Yeah, I guess." *Yeah, I guess?* What kind of person says, "Yeah, I guess," while watching a man take a sledgehammer to the Berlin Wall? The signs were there from the beginning, but she willfully filtered them out.

Mia is listening to the music, moved to tears by its beauty. She would like to move people again, to have her name listed in a playbill once more before it appears in the program for a memorial service. She feels as if she's finally waking up from a decades-long hibernation. There has to be a way for her to get back onstage.

Jane recalls the simple fragments from Proust Bruno showed her last night—"Let yourself be inert"; "henceforth you will always keep something broken about you"—and makes a mental note to e-mail the full passage to Lodge Waldman, along with an offer for him to have first dibs on her mother's house. They are perfect, as words of condolence go. So simple, so direct, so explicit in their scope and feeling. She wonders if she's capable of ever writing sentences one-tenth as good, of stringing together a bunch of nouns, verbs, and adjectives that don't just tell a story but describe Life with a capital *L*. She gets distracted by a stray hair on the woman's sweater in front of her and has to sit on her hands so as not to be tempted to remove it.

"not nostalgia," types Bucky. "love."

"u calling me a liar?"

"maybe."

"u confuse lust for love."

"negative." Bucky's now typing furiously, his thumbs pecking away at warp speed. Finally, the treatise lands on the face of Clover's phone. "i know what i felt, pace. that shit doesn't just go away because 20 yrs have passed or because i was too stupid to understand what i gave up back then. i love u, pace. i've always loved you. you've been living inside me since 1985."

The words, in their nakedness, make Clover gasp. "stop it! u don't love me. u don't even know me!"

"yes. i do. and i do. i probably even know u better than u know yourself."

The notes of the canon build to a crescendo. Its melody—her wedding march—combined with Bucky's texts and Sharon's absence and the possibility of new life forming inside her rattle Clover to the point where her stomach tightens, her eyes mist. What the fuck is wrong with him? Why does he have to bring love into it? "i'm serious," she writes back, shooting him an angry glance. "stop. now."

"am being dead serious. i love u. run away with me, lady. we'll go sailing off together into the sunset. what do u have to lose?"

"MY MARRIAGE!"

"to a big baby who won't get his sperm tested?"

"bucky! jesus! stop it. u don't understand the parameters." She doesn't really understand them either, but that's not the issue. The issue is that Danny is her husband, 'til death do them part. She made a vow. A solemn vow! Of course, part of that vow was not to sleep with anyone else, either, but in the grand scheme of vow keeping versus baby making, the baby won. Chubby hands down.

Bucky refuses to give up: "i<3 u," he writes. "i want to spend the rest of my life with you. i want to make this clear, in case there was any doubt. i don't want to regret not saying it. i love u i love u I LOVE U!"

"u don't love me! u love the IDEA of me. of righting a past wrong. of reuniting after so many years. u'd be bored of me in 5 minutes. i don't even have a job right now. am pathetic."

"so not true!"

"so true."

"tell me something."

"what?"

"what do YOU think happened between us yesterday AM? and don't tell me it was just sex. i've had 'just sex.' this was something else." After he woke up to an empty bed, Bucky stumbled into the shower and mentally ran through the events of the night and morning more thoroughly, still basking in the astounding glow of it. Crazy, really, to find himself in bed with Clover Love! And yet not so crazy either. In fact beautiful, on so many levels. He hadn't felt his heart beat with such rhythm or purpose for years. But it was only while he was washing the caked-on sperm off the shaft of his penis that he suddenly realized he hadn't used a condom with a desperate-to-get-pregnant woman whose husband, in all likelihood, was sterile. So there was method in her madness? Everybody wants something. (His heart fell.) But reexamining the memory once again, it struck him, profoundly, that their lovemaking Saturday morning could not have been just about babymaking, even if it might have started out that way. It was, unless his memory has completely failed him, the most profound and mutual act of love he's ever experienced.

"it was just sex," Clover types.

"bullshit."

"enough, bucky. the song's almost over. i have to concentrate on my eulogy. too nervous."

"ok ok. don't be nervous. i'll be here. pretend it's just u & me and u r telling me a story. forget everyone else. pretend they r not even here."

"easier said than done."

"just promise me one thing, b4 i never see u again."

"don't say that. we'll see each other again."

"no. it'll be too painful for me."

"stop exaggerating."

"not exaggerating. at all. but i need you to promise me 1 thing."

"sure. what?"

Bucky types out his request, hesitating a few seconds before pressing send, his heart beating wildly. "if my hunch correct, put me on your xmas card list. allow me at least that."

But before Clover can respond, in the midst of her shock at seeing what she thought was her hidden deed spelled out so baldly on her tiny screen, the canon ends and she hears the pianist say, "And now Clover Love will say a few words on Sharon's behalf."

The thump-thumpings in her chest make her feel faint. Her limbs feel de-boned, filled with sand. She should have known it was no use trying to hide something as enormous as a blastula from Bucky Gardner. He's seen through her since the day they met.

Authenticity. The word, or more precisely her lack of it, hits her, propels her forward, a determined hand at her back, until she's standing at the podium. She lays her speech on the lectern and reads the first sentence silently, to herself: "Sharon Warren worked tirelessly on behalf of her organization, the Lila Fund, raising over twelve million dollars annually in support of breast cancer research." What a terrible opening! More of an introduction to the keynote speaker at a corporate luncheon, not a proper eulogy. She stares out at the audience and catches Bucky's eye. He's nodding his head and urging her on. He mimes crumpling up a piece of paper and tossing it over his shoulder. She realizes that this is what she must do. Throw it away. Toss it. All the plans, the belabored effort, the well-intentioned something that turned out to be nothing. Speak from the heart. Starting right now.

"So I wrote this eulogy the other day." She holds up the speech for her audience to see. "But now that I'm standing here in front of you, it seems totally wrong. Inauthentic. Not worthy of anyone's life, let alone Sharon's."

Bucky makes okay signs with both of his forefingers and thumbs and smiles. Then he mimes what she's seen a thousand mothers miming every morning to the windows of the yellow school buses that clog the streets of her neighborhood, snarling traffic and making her ache for her own shadowed figure in a school bus window. It's a three-part sign: first a pointed finger to the middle of his chest, for *I*; then the forearms crossed over the heart, for *love*; then the finger pointed out at the object of affection, for *you*.

She folds the speech and places it on the slant of the lectern. "I didn't really know Sharon all that well in college. We ran in different crowds. Mine was fast and furious, and hers was . . . well, I guess you could say human-paced and kind. Anyway, though our paths rarely crossed here, I did recognize her, when I bumped into her one night after work at the Harvard Club, from a freshman seminar we both took called Illness as Metaphor. Ironic, isn't it? It was based on Susan Sontag's treatise by the same name, but we read lots of other writers on the topic as well. Tolstoy, as I recall. Chekhov. Kafka. William Carlos Williams. A bunch of others I'm forgetting, but always in the context of Sontag's words. I'm sure some of you know them well. The rest of you, like me, read the CliffsNotes." A few chuckles.

Clover feels the audience's support, their kinetic energy. It's so unlike the often bored or sometimes even hostile response she used to get to the PowerPoint presentations she had to give, day in and day out, in her life as a banker, especially toward the end, when she started to worry. "The centre cannot hold," she'd typed onto one of the slides, giving proper credit to Yeats. One of the derivatives traders in the room had shouted—*shouted!*—"We get it, smartypants, you went to Hah-vahd. But that doesn't mean you know shit about the health of the credit default swap market. And you spelled *center* wrong."

"I was taking the seminar because I was fiddling around with the idea of becoming a shrink," she says, "until I decided banking would be a much more stable, giving, noble career." She infuses this last line with enough irony and self-mocking that people laugh. Bucky once again holds up his hand in the okay sign, urging her on. "Sharon was taking it because she'd just lost her mother to breast cancer, and she was trying to sort out her understandably complicated feelings about that.

"I remember we all had to read our final papers to the class, and most of ours were kind of boring and theoretical about the language of illness, the linguistics of it. As if we were all budding Noam Chomskys or pathetically trying to be. Sontag's theory, if you'll recall—and I hope I'm remembering this right—is all about how the sick person is often blamed, at least linguistically, as if they'd brought on their disease themselves. But Sharon found it odd that Sontag never mentioned, not once in her text, that she herself was a breast cancer survivor. So Sharon's paper, in stark contrast to all of ours and Sontag's, was a firsthand account of her mother's decline, from the day of diagnosis to her last breath, and it was . . . heartbreaking. By the time she finished reading it, we were all blubbering. Even the beefy football player, whose name now escapes me but who, swear to God, never said a single word in class or changed his expression from a kind of neutral look of sheer boredom, even *he* was crying.

"Anyway, fast-forward to our little chance encounter at the Harvard Club in New York many years later, where Sharon was hosting her first fund-raiser for the Lila Fund. She called it the Lila Fund after her mother, Lila, because she couldn't very well call it the Sharon Fund, now could she, if she didn't want people to know she'd been recently diagnosed with breast cancer herself? For five years, no one other than her husband had any idea she was sick. She didn't want it to interfere with people's perception of the organization or its mandate or its viability as a long-term, *healthy* organization, which, by God, it is and remains, thanks to her husband, Whit, who took over all of the legal and CFO responsibilities, and her copresident, Jean, who deals with the day-to-day operations. I know. I've seen the books. They're rock solid.

"But enough about the Lila Fund. That's what I wrote about in here"—she holds up her discarded eulogy—"and I urge you all to go to their Web site, www.thelilafund.com, and send in a donation in Sharon's memory if you can, or click on the link to buy a ticket to the annual fund-raiser at my house in East Hampton—it's fun, I promise, we hire a DJ, the food's good, and you can come in your jeans or even a bathing suit, we don't care—but what I do care about right now, deeply, is telling you about Sharon Warren the person. Or rather, I guess, and more specifically about what Sharon represented to me, to her husband, to her children, to all of us who knew her, really, and that is, if I could sum it up in one word . . . *authenticity*. She was the most guileless, authentic person I've ever met, and we're all old enough now to know how rare that is.

"Yes, she kept this big secret, for five years, about her illness, but that was part of her quest for authenticity as well, having seen what her mother went through. She wanted people to respond to her, not to her illness. She wanted to protect her children from pitying stares, especially since she was convinced she would beat this thing and move on, and no one would be any the wiser. She wanted to live as authentic a life as she possibly could while she still had it, given the parameters she'd been given, and for her a life that was authentic was a life that had no time or patience for self-pity.

"In fact, when I think about it? Sharon never did anything, at any point in her life, because it would look good on a résumé, or because it would make her fabulously rich, or because it would somehow show her in a better light, or because it would bring her fame or awards or give her an in with a better crowd. I remember this one time, a fairly well-known film director, who shall remain nameless, had kind of stumbled into our fund-raiser in the Hamptons as a guest of Billy Joel's, and after talking with Sharon for only five minutes, this director decided he wanted to make a movie about her life. You know, a kind of Norma Rae who has breast cancer, who's also on the front lines fighting the establishment. Anyway, this was a year and a half before she died, when she and everyone else knew she was dying, but she was still well enough to take a meeting with this guy, which she left feeling really excited, thinking that the film would bring great publicity and maybe even greater funds into the organization after she was gone. But somehow the director felt there wasn't enough conflict in Sharon's life—as if having a mother who died of breast cancer and then dying of breast cancer herself and leaving three kids behind, weren't dramatic enough—so he asked the writer he hired to change certain biographical elements of the story.

"In the script she was shown, she had an expensive shoe fetish. And a weird tic where she could never remember any of her underlings' names. And one child who was reacting to her mother's cancer by becoming a kleptomaniac while the other became a cutter. And a husband who was off drowning his grief in an affair. None of these were of course implausible reactions to a woman's illness, but they certainly weren't Sharon and her family's reaction to her illness. Far from it. That family faced cancer with more courage—and I know if Sharon were standing here right now she'd say, 'Fuck courage, we did what we had to do'—but I don't know what else to call the way she faced her illness other than courageous, so let's just leave it at that.

"Anyway, she called me after she read the script, not crying, as I would have been, but laughing. Hysterically. 'Well,' she said. 'I guess I'll just have to die anonymously then. Too bad. I was looking forward to wearing a dress to the premiere that would really emphasize my hacked-off tits.'

"I mean, even on that front—so to speak—Sharon refused to be inauthentic. After her mastectomy, she had these beautiful black-and-white photos taken of her and Whit. In one of my favorites, she's completely naked, totally unashamed, with Whit lying next to her fully clothed, hugging her around the rib cage with his nose buried in her neck. She called it her John and Yoko photo, only, as she said, 'I'm John and Whit's Yoko, because I'm naked, flat-chested, and doomed to die early, and Whit can't hold a tune to save his life.'"

The audience laughs again, some of them through tears. Clover keeps her eyes trained directly on Bucky, who, with subtle movements of his head, mouth, and hands, is as present and supportive as anyone could be from twenty feet away.

"I mean, how great is that, right? The woman *never* lost her sense of humor, even toward the end. With one great exception. She could not talk about her kids' future—could not even contemplate it—without tearing up. Sharon's children, I should probably note, were four, three, and five months when she was diagnosed. They were ten, nine, and six when she died.

"I really, truly, desperately hope none of you ever has to go to a funeral where three little kids are walking behind their mother's coffin crying, 'Mommy! Mommy!' because it is the saddest image I have ever seen. Ever. And . . ."

Clover starts to lose a bit of control, her eyes seeing the scene as if it were still unfolding right in front of her. "And . . ." She has to take her glasses off, for they are being covered in a salty residue. "And . . ." Shit, she thinks, I can't finish. But she has an important closing thought that just occurred to her, and she wants to say it.

Suddenly, as if he's heard her telepathically, Bucky is standing next to her, propping her up. "It's okay," he whispers, using the excuse of handing her a tissue to lean over and squeeze her hand. "Just breathe deeply. No one cares. You're doing great, Pace. Just great. Take your time." He cleans off her glasses with the corner of his shirt and places them on the lectern.

After a minute or so, Clover gathers her composure and says, "Sorry. I just . . . I just want to say one more thing about Sharon, and that is this." She feels Bucky standing behind her, just off to the side—left, right, it doesn't matter, he's there—and there's a warmth to his presence, an electrical charge between their bodies she can feel. It's not sexual at the moment. Not at all. It's . . . oh, shit, he was right. Okay, fine. It is love. "I don't believe a beautiful, young mother's early demise teaches us anything constructive. It's one of those things that makes us shake our hands at the gods and say, 'Really? *Why?*' But I do think we can all learn something, not from Sharon's death, but from her life. How many of us here can honestly say we're living the most authentic life that we can lead? How many of us are being true to ourselves, true to our ideals, true to that eighteen-year-old kid who first walked into the Yard, filled with dreams? We're all given one life. One. And we're all marching toward the same miserable end. The question is this: How will you fill the rest of your days? How will you live a life that's authentic? I'm not saying it has to be particularly 'meaningful' or that we should all run off to become Mother Teresas or anything like that, but I know, deep in my gut, that if I can live out the rest of my days being half as genuine as Sharon Warren was, every single second of every single day of her life, then her legacy is not lost. She is not lost."

And at the exact moment Clover feels she will crumble to the ground, Bucky is there to catch her.

· · ·

Jonathan's feet run as if trying to escape a predator nipping his heels, which he realizes is a ridiculous image, but he can't help conjuring it. He knows he's luckier than 99.99 percent of all the other recession-hit families to even have an exit strategy, but still. Last night, unable to sleep, he went online and reexamined all of the accounts and credit card statements, realizing, to his horror, that it is worse than he thought. If things don't improve over the next year or so, they'll have to sell both houses.

And so he runs.

Cowardly, he knows, this running. Hiding the truth from Mia. But she's turned the house in Antibes into a veritable Shangri-la, a place apart where their family—torn asunder in every direction by adolescence, afterschool activities, homework, faraway film sets, and the minute-by-minute minutiae of caring for an infant—has an opportunity, for a few weeks every summer, to be a family. To spend time with friends. Without interruptions. Of any kind.

There in the Mediterranean hills, over which their stone house is cantilevered, meals replete with stinky-cheese endings are consumed slowly; the boys, on the brink of manhood, still find joy in hiding out in and building onto the tree house left for them by the previous owners; Frisbees are tossed; outings are planned to the ocean floor where phosphorescent fish are marveled over. There, too, he and Mia are able to finally talk, to exchange real thoughts and feelings and information, without the constant interruptions that so frequently befall them. Cell phones work sporadically if at all, and surfing the Web is severely limited by the constraints of dial-up.

He knows this kind of disconnection will come to an inevitable end soon enough. Being able to untether oneself from the data stream will become less and less of an option as the availability of enablers—cell towers, free Wi-Fi signals, some future data-facilitating invention as of yet uninvented—becomes more and more ubiquitous. But for now Antibes is the place they go to remember who they were, both as individuals and as a family unit, before their limbs bore 3G-ponic fruit; before human-to-human interaction uninterrupted by dings, rings, chirps, and slide whistle whoops ceased, overnight, to exist.

But while Mia will probably be more upset about the Antibes house than their house in LA, for Jonathan the ego blow of selling off their primary residence will strike deeply. They will have to sell at a price far below what they might have asked for it just a year earlier—that is, if there's anyone left out there able to casually drop several million dollars on a property that, until very recently, was worth twice that. Yes, yes, of course, he and Mia can make up some story about how the offer was too good to refuse, how the buyer walked in off the street, how they wanted to move closer to the ocean/Brentwood/the Sony lot/whatever, but there's something fundamentally crushing about the need-based selling off of a home where one raised one's children which, Jonathan fears, he won't survive.

He has a photo of the type he just shot for that young couple, of him and Mia, pregnant with Max, standing in front of the house on

San Remo Lane the day they moved in. (He can't remember who took it. One of the movers? A neighbor? So many of the trivial tidbits get lost.) The fact is, no matter how much success life has granted him, he will feel like an utter failure if they sell that house. It's not just a primary residence. It's his home.

Every night on the news it's another family out on the street. He can't watch it anymore. He turns it off as soon as he sees the inevitable FOR SALE sign topped with an all-caps FORECLOSURE. As if a sign could ever possibly signify the real suffering happening just offscreen: marriages torn apart; families left homeless; psyches damaged; lives wrecked. Not to mention all the secondary insults: a drop in health, a rise in shame, an increased risk of suicide.

He knows—he *knows*—one shouldn't get attached to a physical structure, but people do! Rich, poor, somewhere in between, it doesn't matter, they can't help it. It's in their blood, deep within their temporal lobe, the place where memory lives. They say the heart feels what it wants to feel, though at the present moment the only thing Jonathan's heart feels is a now not-unfamiliar sharp stab that strikes him straight between his ribs. Shit, not again, he thinks. "Meditate," his doctor suggested, when he went in last month complaining of these new chest pains on top of the old ones. "All studies point to a significant decrease in the gray-matter density in the amygdala, which we know moderates stress."

So Jonathan, hoping to lighten the load on his amygdala, met with a meditation coach. He made it through the first few steps—sitting up straight, choosing a mantra, breathing—without a hitch, but when it came time for the next few—detaching himself from his mind, *silencing* his mind—he could not transcend his inner noise. In fact, the harder he tried, the worse his brain spiraled in on itself, until trying to learn how to meditate was stressing him out more than the stress that had brought him to meditation in the first place.

His doctor suggested Wellbutrin, which she said would aid in norepinephrine-dopamine reuptake inhibition. "Nora who?" said

Jonathan, with a smile. "Could you translate that into Endocrinology for Dummies?"

"Stress," said the doctor. "It'll ease your stress." She handed Jonathan a prescription, which he promptly lost. He keeps meaning to call her office for a new one, but his anxiety distracts him until it's too late to call.

As for Jonathan's temporal lobe, it is now bathed in the familiar comfort of Chopin's notes as Fresh Pond moves into the foreground, and his feet step up their already blistering, demon-fleeing pace. When his body finally arrives at pond's edge, and his eyes are peering out at the vista of water, trees, and sky, a smattering of puffy clouds above echoed in the liquid mirror below, his occipital lobe identifies this almost instantaneously as beauty, and his frontal cortex produces two near-simultaneous, competing thoughts. The first, which he experiences as a burst of joy, is this: Holy shit, am I glad to be alive; the second, triggered by a surge of crushing pain, as if an elephant were standing on his chest, is this: Oh my God, I'm dying.

The pain now paralyzing him with its intensity was actually triggered several minutes earlier by an unusually large spasm of stress, which ruptured a piece of the plaque lining his main coronary artery, which in turn formed a blood clot that will, within minutes, if left untreated, deprive Jonathan's heart of the necessary oxygen it needs to survive.

Several minutes behind Jonathan on the running path, Aaron Scharfstein, a Harvard economics professor who'd been sounding the warning bell on the American housing market for years, to the detriment of his career and credibility, is out for a jog with an old friend. Professionally, he tells this friend, he is riding high these days, now that his doomsday theories have been proven sound. The CNN bookers have him on speed dial. His lectures are packed. Personally, however, he feels like a failure for having not been able to make himself heard when his words might have made a difference. The friend says, "Don't be so hard on yourself. No one was listening. They didn't want to hear."

The two are not far, but they are also not close enough yet to see Jonathan's knees buckle under him.

As his shoulder blades hit the dirt, Jonathan's perception of reality, distorted by a dearth of oxygen and a terrifying understanding of the ramifications of that dearth, twists time into a sepulchral slo-mo. His temporal lobe fires indiscriminately, shooting shards of memory straight from its ancient canon: his mother's face in profile, at the wheel of the family Edsel; his father, postwork, removing his hat; his brother tackling him into a dune on the Jersey shore; Mia sashaying into his office, wearing a smile and a polka-dot dress; the umbilical cord that was stuck around Eli's neck until it wasn't; Josh's first steps, on the Santa Monica Pier; Max just last night, taking Trilby's hand; the candles at his fiftieth birthday, melting wax into chocolate ganache; Mia nursing a baby; the visible pulse of a fontanelle.

Zoe! he thinks. My God, Zoe!

The world goes black.

. . .

Mia, Clover, Jane, and Addison are standing outside Kirkland House, saying their good-byes. Promises are made to keep in touch, offers of hospitality exchanged. "Oh my God, totally," says Mia to Clay. "We have more than enough room."

He invites her to see his next show, a commission from a young playwright about a mother in Scarsdale who falls asleep at twenty-five, nursing an infant, only to be woken up fifteen years later by her two surly teenage daughters demanding a ride to the mall. "Ooh, that sounds just up my alley," says Mia. "I'll come. Definitely. Who's playing the part of the mother?"

"I'll tell you what, girl. You figure out a way to get yourself up to Seattle for two months?" says Clay. "That part's yours."

"Very funny," says Mia.

"You think I'm joking?" says Clay. "I ain't joking."

"You know what?" she says. "I'll talk to Jonathan, see if it's even feasible."

Clay smiles. "Now you're talking!"

Clover says to Bucky, "I feel like I'm disintegrating."

"Welcome to the club," says Bucky. He puts an arm around her. Kisses the top of her head. "Just take your time. It's a lot to consider."

"I'm not even talking about your offer," says Clover, disentangling herself from his embrace. "I'm talking about life. Or . . . whatever. I don't even know what I'm talking about. That was rough, that service, wasn't it?"

"Yeah, it was."

"Look, I really appreciate you propping me up, and the tissue and all that—really, I do—but the answer is no, Bucky. I can't just . . . leave my husband. And you're married, too, in case you've forgotten." She's feeling inauthentic already! Speaking soap-operatic platitudes that are appropriate for the situation at hand but are hardly a true measure of her feelings, although she's having a hard time pinpointing exactly what those feelings are. To admit love would be a start, but uttering such words out loud would be to cross the Rubicon over a rickety bridge specifically designed to unmoor itself behind her. She's angry at herself, both for allowing love to enter into the equation and for her inability to quickly identify a solution to the quagmire and implement it. How can she love two men at once? It's ridiculous, the kind of sloppy bookkeeping that would never have been tolerated at her old job, although that's not really true either.

"Look," says Bucky, "I'm not asking for your answer right now. I'm asking you to think about it. Go home to your husband. I'll call you in a few months."

"I really don't think anything's going to change between now and then."

"Pace, I don't know what world you've been living in, but in my world everything can change between now and then."

Addison hugs Bennie. "Lady," she says, "I really, I just . . . I don't know what I would have done without you this weekend. I'll never forget what you did. Never."

"It was nothing," says Bennie.

"Are you kidding me? It was everything," says Addison. "You *sprang me from jail*, if you'll recall. How am I ever going to pay you back?"

"You won't."

"That's ridiculous. Of course I will."

"Addison, please. I'm not trying to brag, but it wasn't financially painful for me to pay that fine, okay? I give away more than that to charities I don't even care about. I'm a sucker when it comes to buying those benefit tables. Save the Pigeons of Poughkeepsie? Okay, sure, just tell me where to send the check. Look, think of it this way: It would be the equivalent of someone else lending you ten bucks. Five even! I don't want to hear another word about it. Ever."

"Okay, okay. I'll stop. Jesus, Bennie, I've missed you. I'm so sorry I've been out of touch."

"So hit 'accept' on my frigging friend request already," says Bennie. "We can start there and move on to a cup of tea whenever one of us is in town, how about that?"

Addison immediately pulls out her cell phone, fiddles around with the buttons, and hits accept. "Done," she says. "When's our next tea?"

Bennie laughs. "I'll be in New York for work at the end of September. I'll call you when I know the exact dates."

"Cool," says Addison. "I'll keep the kettle warm."

Jane is coordinating school vacation schedules with Ellen Grandy, realizing their daughters' spring breaks don't overlap. "Well, why don't you and Nell just come for Christmas then," she says. "I mean, now that my mother's gone, it's not as if we have any reason to come here this year. Nell can sleep with Sophie in her bedroom, and you can stay on the pull-out couch in my office. It'll give us all something to look forward to."

"Really?" says Ellen. "Are you sure? I mean, think about it first before you make that kind of an offer."

"Nothing to think about," says Jane, nevertheless engaged in a swirl of random thought: If you'd asked her, a week ago, whether she would have ever invited her late husband's lover to stay with her in her home, she would have laughed you out of that home. But when faced with the actual person herself—a person to whom she is elusively drawn, she assumes, for the same reasons as Hervé—she can't help wanting to get to know the woman better. "We'd love it. And I won't be working that week anyway, so I won't need the office."

"All right then," says Ellen, albeit tentatively. "Christmas in Paris. I'll see if I can rustle up some cheap tickets. Nell will be thrilled."

"So will Sophie."

Mia's cell phone goes off. A photo of Jonathan and the four kids, snapped a few days after they brought Zoe home from the hospital, appears on the screen of her phone. Max had showed her the "assign to contact" button in her iPhone's picture file, so now every time one of her kids or Jonathan calls, the caller's photo magically—or so it feels to Mia—pops up on her screen: Max on the balcony of their house in Antibes at sunset, his face sunburnt and glowing; Eli sticking his tongue out at the camera on the red carpet of Jonathan's last film; Josh in his orange Tigers uniform, wielding a bat; Jonathan sitting on their bed cradling Zoe, the boys snuggled up with him in their boxer shorts and pajamas on a lazy Sunday morning, marveling over the not-yet-week-old creature. "Hey, sweetie!" she says, reacting each time to the sudden telephonic apparition of her husband and children in the palm of her hand with an almost giddy feeling of shared history, love. "What's up?"

But the voice on the other end, belonging to Aaron Scharfstein, is unfamiliar, panicked, barely audible above the sounds of sirens, the shouts of strangers. "Uh, yes, hello, am I speaking to the wife of Jonathan Zane?" Later Mia won't be able to recall a single word of the rest of this exchange that bifurcated her world into then and now, before and after, just the seven capital letters, broken up into three syllables, upon which her eyes happened to fall the instant she heard the news. Those letters, that word, inscribed on the Harvard shield of Clay Collins's name tag, was this: VERITAS.

There was no accounting for it, she would say to friends later on, the odd details one retains. Her eyes must have alit on that word, that shield, every hour of every day back in college—on chairs, gates, banners, walls, mugs, sweatshirts, flyers, pencils, underwear, you name it, truth was on it. It just took her twenty years and a choked heart to finally see it.

Harvard and Radcliffe

Class of 1989

Twenty-Fifth Anniversary Report

CLOVER PACE LOVE. *Home Address:* 16 Tingum Road, Harbour Island, Bahamas. *Occupation and Office Address:* CEO, Pace Tours Unlimited. *E-mail:* cplove@pacetours.com. *Graduate Degrees:* M.B.A., Harvard '98. *Spouse/Partner:* Archibald Bucknell Gardner IV (B.A., Harvard '89). *Spouse/Partner Occupation:* Captain, Pace Tours Unlimited; *Children:* Frank Love, 2010. *Stepchildren:* Archibald Bucknell V, 1994; Eloise Mason, 1996; Caroline Pearce, 1999; Charles Case, 2001.

These past five years have been such a whirlwind, it's hard to know even where to begin. I think I have to start back at our twentieth reunion, where my son Frank was conceived. That I happened to be married, at the time, to a man who was not at the reunion made things complicated, to say the least. We separated a month after little Frankie was born, when I finally came clean and told him that the child was not his. My ex, understandably, was quite upset. Let's just say it was a real low point, and I don't recommend divorce as a life experience, unless absolutely necessary. Bucky Gardner, my old beau from freshman year and the father of my son, had recently separated from his wife as well, and after our divorces were finalized, we got married in city hall and took the summer off, with Frankie and my new stepchildren in tow, to sail around the Greek Islands.

Being a stepmother is tricky, no doubt, but my stepchildren have made it as easy as they can, under the circumstances. They're good kids, mature beyond their years, and after having been child-less for so long, I'm grateful to have this huge, boisterous brood during school holidays and summers.

On the work front, I tried finding another job in banking equivalent to my former position at Lehman, but my heart wasn't in it, and the job market was still abysmal, so for about a year or so, while Frankie was still in his stroller, I helped Addison set up her vintage clothing shop in Williamsburg, to get some business experience under my belt outside the banking world and because, as you can imagine, it was like going to a party every day working with Addison. Bucky and I were renting an apartment in Tribeca at the time, looking to buy a place big enough for all five kids, but then it suddenly occurred to us that Bucky's youngest, Case, would be heading to boarding school the following fall, so the idea of us staying in New York to be near his children was no longer an issue. That's when we sat down together and really hammered out what each of us wanted from the rest of our lives. I told Bucky I was tired of Wall Street, that I wanted to work at a company that actually produced something tangible—a product I could believe in; a memorable experience. Bucky said he wanted to spend the rest of his life sailing.

Within the Venn diagram overlap of those two desires, Pace Tours Unlimited was born. We found a home in Harbour Island, Bahamas, near enough to the dock that Bucky can walk along the beach to work. It was slow going and rocky at first, trying to build a name and reputation for ourselves, but then Jane flew out from Paris with Bruno and their daughters, and she wrote a story about her trip and old friends and the idea of blended families— hers and ours—for *Travel + Leisure*, and after that we had to turn away clients.

Recently, it struck me that for the first time in my life, I feel a sense of balance and contentment I've never felt before. I love my work. I have enough time with Frankie that I never feel guilty. He goes to a great school within walking distance of our house. I have four bonus children who bring raucous laughter and friends down with them whenever they visit, which is frequently. I'm married to my college sweetheart, whom, as it turns out, I never stopped loving.

There, Bucky, as promised, I just saved you the trouble of writing your own entry. Carry on, Captain Gardner. Everyone else? I'll see you at reunion.

ADDISON CORNWALL HUNT. *Home Address:* 85–101 North 3rd Street, #4, Brooklyn, NY 11211 (718-427-0909). *Occupation:* Owner, Back in the Day Vintage. *E-mail:* acornhunt@gmail.com. *Spouse/Partner:* Esther Grimm (B.A. Brown, 1991; Culinary Institute of America, 2008). *Spouse/Partner Occupation:* Chef, Plum Lane. *Children:* Charlotte Trilby, 1995; William Houghton, 1997; John Thatcher, 1998.

Good lord, people. Really, truly, you gotta believe me, I had every intention of getting this done on time, and yet once again, I put it off until the last minute. You'd think I'd have learned by now. You'd be wrong.

Okay, so, lots of stuff to cover, little time to cover it. I got divorced. It sucked, it's over, moving on. I met my current partner Esther at a boring party neither of us had any intention of attending, and now we share a sock drawer. Amazing. She's a chef, and she cooks like a dream, but my expanding waistline and I are determined to lose some of our girth between now and the reunion. Wish us luck.

So what else? Oh yeah, right. I had some serious liquidity issues back in 2009, and it took a while to sort that stuff out. During this time, I finally had to admit that as much as I love painting, I wasn't ever going to have a solo show at MoMA, but I was going to have to earn a real living if I didn't want my kids to starve. I had no marketable job skills aside from graphic design at that point, and there were no graphic design jobs to be had, so I started out by hawking a bunch of Jane's mother's vintage clothes on eBay, splitting the proceeds with Jane. I realized I not only had a weird knack for it, I actually enjoyed it. A lot. With an initial investment from Bennie Watanabe, who's known around these parts (my apartment, that is) as the Hunt/Grimm family guardian angel, I opened my own vintage clothing shop, Back in the Day, right on Bedford Street near the L train entrance: vintage central, if you know what I mean. Clover was my CEO for a year until she picked up and moved to Paradise. I'm not kidding. The name of one of the islands near hers is Paradise, but hers is even better. You should go there. I'm serious.

Now I'm the CEO. I'm not as good as Clover, but I try.

Anyway, Clover said I should be picky about what we sell, to stick to quality over quantity, which is the best piece of advice anyone has ever given me about life let alone retail, so now I have a loyal clientele who stop in weekly, to see what treasures we've found. Then one day some Japanese travel guide must have written a rave about our wares, because now we get forty to sixty Japanese girls stopping in here every day, and man oh man, those girls can *shop*. If any of you former East Asian studies concentrators out there can still read Japanese and are able to find the mention of my store in that guide, I'd love to know the name of the publisher, so I can personally send them a thank-you note on the exquisite handmade vintage paper I just found in some woman's attic.

My eldest, Trilby, is a sophomore at Bennington, and she's going to kill me if she reads this, but she's been seeing Mia's son Max for a while now, though they've never actually managed to live in the same city for more than a few months at a time. After his dad died, while Gunner and I were separating, Max moved in with us for three months to do a summer internship in the city, which was healing and really nice for everyone. I love that kid. He's now a man. It's crazy how time passes. Houghton leaves for college in a year. Thatcher will go the year after that, if he can just pass chemistry.

I try to stay open, present, grateful for what I have. I could dwell on all the mistakes, the seventeen years spent hiding in a troubled relationship, but I choose to look forward. I'd like to make it to eighty in good health. I'd like to meet my grandchildren. I'd like to stick with Esther for as long as she'll have me. It's nice to finally love and be loved in return. I had no idea what I'd been missing.

JANE NGUYEN STREETER. *Home Address:* 11 bis, rue Vieille du Temple, 75004 Paris, France (33 1 42 53 97 58). *Occupation:* Writer. *E-mail:* jane@janestreeter.com. *Spouse/Partner:* Bruno Saint-Pierre. *Spouse/Partner Occupation:* Editor, *Libération*. *Children:* Sophie Isabelle Duclos, 2002; Claire Streeter Saint-Pierre, 2010.

Five years, it occurs to me, is the perfect amount of time between these entries. A lot can happen in five years. For me the changes were both slight and monumental. Slight in that I still live in the same apartment and fall asleep every night with the same man as before, although now he's officially my husband and legally Sophie's dad. Mia insisted we get married at her house in Antibes after her husband died: one last blowout before the house was sold. The deadline and Mia's pleas worked wonders. We committed ourselves to both the date and to each other, and it was one of the loveliest weekends of our lives. Melancholy, of course, too, as we were all missing Jonathan like crazy, but Mia said planning it gave her something to focus her grief on, instead of the void. Having lost my first husband as well, I understood the compulsion completely.

The monumental changes were the usual—my mother's death from cancer, a new life, a new career. Baby Claire, named for my mother, was born a few months after the wedding, and I gave her a full year of my undivided attention before trying to step back into the working world. This proved to be more difficult than I'd imagined. My services were no longer required at the *Globe*, so I freelanced articles for various British publications and took on a few translation projects. Then, after I sold my mother's house, I had a bit of a cushion, so I took the opportunity to give myself two years to write a novel. *The White Mouse of Nha Trang*, based loosely on my experience as a child in Vietnam, was finally sold to an American publisher last year and will come out this spring, just before our reunion. I'm proud of it, but I also know the realities of the publishing industry these days, so I'm keeping my expectations low. I've never worked harder on anything in my life— every day it felt as if I were slicing open another vein and pouring the contents out onto the page—but I guess the best I can hope for is that the few people who actually find their way to the book and read it will, in whatever small or large way, be moved by it.

Bruno has managed to hold on to his editing job at *Libé*, but it feels very tenuous right now to be a wordsmith. It makes me wonder what kind of wordless world our children will inherit. It's hard to imagine a world without sentences, thoughts, poetry, and prose, and yet every day I see it happening: the shortening of our attention spans, the editors who ask for two hundred words max, the daily fix of small nothings. A YouTube clip of two monkeys humping; Aunt Mildred's status update; baseless rumors; lies that become truth simply for having been typed into somebody's blog. What can one learn in two hundred words or 140 characters or thirty-five seconds about anything? Nothing, it strikes me, that's worth knowing.

MIA *MANDELBAUM* ZANE. *Home Address:* 804 Marco Place, Venice, CA 90291 (310-589-0923). *Occupation and Office Address:* Broker, Venice Beach Properties. *E-mail:* mzane@venicebeach properties.com. *Children:* Max Benjamin, 1992; Eli Samuel, 1994; Joshua Aaron, 1998; Zoe Claire, 2008.

The past five years have been the hardest five years of my life. I was actually going to leave this part blank, but this morning I sat down at my desk and realized I had two full hours between showings, so here goes nothing.

As many of you who were at our Twentieth are aware, my husband Jonathan died of a heart attack the Sunday morning of re-union weekend. Apparently—or so I learned from both his physician and our accountant—he was under a tremendous amount of stress that day, which he hid from both me and the kids for reasons that died with him. Suffice it to say, I wish I had known. Maybe his heart would have failed anyway, but to know that financial worries may have played even a minor role in his demise—and worse, that I was kept in the dark—has been almost too much for me to bear. I understand his desire to protect me, but I can't help thinking that if he'd shared his burden, it would have been lighter, and he would still be here.

That first year after he died was spent in a blurry haze of grief, paperwork, and asset liquidation. We sold our house in Antibes, but not before I made Jane walk down the aisle there with Bruno. We sold our house in LA and moved into a much cozier place in Venice Beach. It's lovely. Don't feel sorry for us. Two of my boys are away at Harvard, both on financial aid—thank you, all of you who give—and the third's nearly out of the house as well, and we couldn't have stayed in that bigger house even if we'd wanted to. It held too many memories in its too-large rooms. We never needed that much space anyway.

Our debt was such that, even with our assets liquidated, I still had to find a job. Quickly. Watching our real estate agents in action, I realized that being a broker was the one potentially well-remunerated job where my acting skills would come in handy while still leaving room for me to be a single mother to a toddler and three grieving teens. So I got my license. I begged for work. I can't say I find my career totally fulfilling, but it's not unfulfilling, either. It feels good to earn a living. I like working with clients. I like selling homes to young couples just getting started. And I'm particularly well suited to dealing with the widows. It's a pleasure, in some weird way, to share grief with a stranger. I've become known for my compassion with the mourners, which serves me well, since a third of my deals involve estate sales.

My children have been incredible throughout this experience. It's impossible to put it into words. Strength? Dignity? It all sounds so clichéd. Suffice it to say that, even though they lost their father, they are my rock, and I'm so grateful for their love.

If and when I ever get truly back on my feet, I'd like to return to the stage one day, in whatever capacity I can. I realize how much I miss the thrill of performing, of creating a character, of moving an audience to laughter and tears. Clay Collins keeps telling me if I can "git my ass on up to Seattle," he'll give me a role, sight unseen. One day, I hope to have the time and means to take him up on this.

I have not found love again, but neither have I given up hope. I believe there could be someone out there, just waiting for me to find him under a rock. But just to hedge my bets? If you happen to know this person or the location of that rock, you're more than welcome to e-mail me the details. Or if you happen to be that person? Meet me at the Twenty-Fifth. I'll be there, with bells on.

If I've learned anything in the twenty-five years that have transpired between graduation and today it is this: I am stronger than I thought I was and weaker than I'd hoped to be, and in between those two extremes is a little thing called life.

ACKNOWLEDGMENTS

This book is a work of fiction. I invented the plot, made up the scenes, crafted each sentence myself. Part of me—let's call her Attila—wanted to skip over this section and take sole credit.

But!

Attila has an alter ego we'll call Eugenie. Eugenie is less of a megalomaniac, more of a team player. She knows that none of us, not even the most hermitic of writers, lives or works in a void. We are inspired, buttressed, moved, informed, and perhaps even loved by others, and it is through this interaction with humanity, in ways both overt and subconscious, that we take a completely fabricated story and transform it, if we're lucky, into something true.

We ask the various humans in our orbit a bunch of annoying questions, even though Google overflows with answers, because Google isn't a person. Oh sure, Google can tell us all about investment banks and the deals they make and where their offices are located on an interactive map, but it can't tell us what it was like to be a female employee of one of those behemoths during the boom years (thank you, Sharon Meers). Or how it felt to be a fourteen-year-old kid at the St. Paul's School in the early eighties (thank you, Michael Karnow). Or to punch the Spee Club as a Harvard sophomore (thank you, Josh Berger). Or to represent an inmate at Guantánamo (thank you, Sarah Havens Cox).

So, while tattooed Attila sits in her corner and sulks, Eugenie would like to step forward in a yellow sundress and pearls to offer sloppy kisses and hugs of gratitude to the aforementioned angels as well as to:

Ellen Archer and Barbara Jones, for believing—accurately, as it turns out—that plying an author with wine would shake out the seeds of a story; Elisabeth Dyssegaard, for providing the hothouse and soil; and Jill Schwartzman, for expert watering and pruning;

Laura Tzelepoglou and Sotiris Chtouris, for swapping their house in Mytilini, with its desk overlooking the Aegean, for our house in Harlem, with its desk overlooking a boarded-up building;

Kammi and Brad Reiss, for donating that snowy week away from my family at the Franklin Hotel, thus providing the time, space, and free cappuccinos to reach the end;

David McCormick, for treating his client to a fancy ham and cheese sandwich at Gramercy Tavern after the manuscript was finished;

Tad Friend, for continuing, year after year, to be my first and shrewdest editor, of both life and words;

Abby Pogrebin, for too many things to mention;

Patrick Dooley, for his insider's view on the joys and hurdles of running a nonprofit theater and for a judicious "break it down!" when I was stymied by plot;

Charles Ferguson, whom I don't know but wish I did, for making the documentary *Inside Job*, which I'd make required viewing, were I king;

The Hyperion/Voice backup singers: Claire McKean, for allowing me to stet an italicized *schtupping*, which, ironically, has to be italicized in this sentence, but never mind; Laura Klynstra, for designing a beautiful jacket for this baby while still recovering from the birth of hers; Karen Minster, for the spot-on look of these pages; Christine Ragasa, for her unflappable hand-holding; Bryan Christian, for sharing both his chocolate chip cookie and his marketing savvy; and Jon Bernstein, for his status updates, tweets, and Instagrams d'Italia;

Eric Alterman, Abigail Asher, Adam Gopnik, Sarah Havens Cox, Marni Gutkin, Paul Kogan, Patty Marx, Sharon Meers, Martha Parker, Robin Pogrebin, Kammi Reiss, Dani Shapiro, Ayelet Waldman, Meg Wolitzer, and Jennifer Copaken Yellin, for early reads and/or offers of blurbs;

Isabel Gillies (as Addison), Julie Metz (as Mia), Susan Fales-Hill (as Clover), and Rebecca Pearsall (as Jane) for agreeing to appear, gratis, in the book trailer; Agustin McCarthy, for making it fun;

The Harvard Class of 1988, for consistently and collectively writing, every five years, the most engrossing book on my nightstand;

Jacob and Sasha Kogan, for rewriting Trilby's IMs into accurate teen shorthand and for putting up with their mother's imperfections; their baby brother Leo Kogan, for being not only the bravest four-year-old in Children's Hospital but also the disco ball around which we dance;

Paul Kogan, again, always, for the two-decade, never-dull ride on love's roller coaster;

And finally, to Attila and Eugenie, for constantly duking it out.

READING GROUP GUIDE

Introduction

Addison, Mia, Clover, and Jane are all graduates of Harvard's class of 1989. Every five years, each class member is asked to write a small essay for inclusion in the red book, a report bound and delivered, just prior to reunion, to alumni from that year.

For the most part, none of these women need the red book to stay up-to-date on each other's lives. Addison, the trust-fund baby–cum–hippie artiste, remains unhappy in her uninspired marriage and unsupported role of parent to three disengaged children. Mia, a mother of four with a husband nearly two decades her senior, is busy relearning what it means to parent an infant while guiding her eldest through the college admissions process, closing her eyes to financial woes her husband is clearly keeping from her. Clover, newly laid off from her lucrative Wall Street job, keeps close tabs on her dwindling bank account but is more concerned with becoming pregnant by her husband, who refuses to acknowledge his apparent infertility. Jane has temporarily returned to the United States, after decades spent overseas, to deal with her mother's estate; she struggles both with her mother's recent death and with the equally fresh pain of her partner's infidelity.

When the four show up in Cambridge, Massachusetts, families in tow, to celebrate their twentieth reunion, the weekend's events result less in reconnecting than in a reevaluation of their lives as they round the corner of middle age. While Harvard's red book regularly highlights what everyone has accomplished, this reunion of classmates reveals much more about what's missing from each of their lives. In the end, it is only by finally recognizing and owning these missing pieces—disappointments, failures, dreams too-long deferred—that these women are able to make the necessary changes to move on with their lives and find, if not happiness, then a close facsimile thereof.

Discussion Questions

1. *The Red Book* is peopled with a broad range of characters. Discuss how successfully you feel the author wrote from the point of view of individuals of so many different social and financial backgrounds, sexual orientations, ethnic identifications, and religious beliefs. Consider, too, that Kogan wrote from the point of view of people of both genders as well as from vastly different generations. Were all of her characters well developed and believable? Was there a character you felt could have been portrayed differently? (And to what purpose?)

2. Both Addison and Mia studied creative arts in college but stopped pursuing their respective fields professionally once they were married and began having kids. Do you feel their stories ring particularly true? Would it have been possible for either one to have led a balanced life while pursuing her passion, and if so, which one(s) and why? Compare their professional trajectories over two decades with those of Jane and Clover, both of whom built successful careers after Harvard. Out of them all, which one, if any, made the wisest decisions and compromises? How large a role did fate, chance, and history (i.e., a massive recession, the shrinking of the newspaper industry) play in each of their narratives, and to that end, how would this book have been different if the author chose to write about the twentieth reunion of the class of 1985? What about the class of 1975?

3. Consider the different biases and aversions these characters have: Bucky's parents' racism; Gunner's anti-Semitism; Mia's prejudice against Trilby's angsty teenage appearance; Addison's aversion to the idea of same-sex couples raising children; Jane's harsh judgment of Bruno and her mother for their respective infidelities. What kind of comment does *The Red Book* make about our worst fears, prejudices, and biases and the ways we let them govern our lives? What does it say about the way (and the reasons) we change?

4. Similarly, examine some of the more morally or ethically ambiguous actions taken by the novel's protagonists: Addison's willful ignorance of/inattention to $100,000 in parking fines; Gunner's rampant narcissism and self-centeredness; Clover's attempt to be impregnated by her married ex-sweetheart; Danny's inability to empathize or sympathize with Clover during emotionally difficult times; Mia's rash spending; Jonathan's one-night stand with his producer; Bruno's infidelity; Jane's relatively unforgiving stance with those she loves (at least for most of the novel). What can we learn from these characters about the role morals and ethics play in our lives?

5. While sex is not the only culprit behind the marital discord in these romantic relationships, it plays a large role in the dynamics of its characters' lives. For instance, Gunner blames much of his distance from Addison on her refusal to sleep with him, while Addison tells herself that she refuses to sleep with him because he won't help with the child-rearing. Is that the whole story? On the opposite end of the spectrum, Mia and Jonathan—while troubled, but not irrevocably so—enjoy a healthy sex life and genuine physical attraction for one another. Consider the way this novel portrays the importance of sex in a long-term relationship, and discuss whether or not the lessons learned by these characters ring particularly true. (And, based on the events in the novel, why?)

6. *The Red Book* also highlights our human tendency to compare ourselves with peers and to judge the ways and means by which we have lived our lives. The characters in the novel do this every five years via Harvard's red book, and also through social Web sites like Facebook. What comment is Kogan making about our compulsion to compare ourselves with others? How much do you, like these characters, keep track of what your peers from high school and/or college are doing/accomplishing? What helpful effects, as well as harmful ones, can come from such comparisons?

7. This novel also explores, to some extent, mother-daughter relationships—through Jane's grief over her mother's recent death, Trilby's dissatisfaction with Addison's permissive parenting, and Mia's recollections of her own frustrated mother. Discuss the ways in which Jane's discovery of her mother's infidelity challenges Jane's perception of her mother and marriage in general; the ways in which the sections narrated from Trilby's point of view avoid typical depictions of teenage rebellion; and the ways in which Mia's life is both a mirror and a foil to that of her mother's. What does each relationship reveal about the power, influence, and pitfalls of the mother-daughter connection?

8. Consider Trilby, Thatcher, and Houghton, as well as Max, Eli, and Joshua, and how they represent the marriages that created them. Discuss how Gunner and Addison have damaged their children by avoiding the problems in their marriage, particularly when compared to Mia and Jonathan's children. Also, think about the ways in which Mia and Jonathan's children are perhaps less prepared for life's harder knocks because of the security and lack of family tension in their upbringing. How do you think Eli and Joshua will be affected once their financial and emotional welfare is threatened by Jonathan's untimely death? In what ways would Trilby, Thatcher, and Houghton be better equipped to handle such tragedy? (Or would they?)

9. While we don't often find ourselves inhabiting the male perspective in this novel, we do get sections narrated by Max, Jonathan, Bucky, and Bruno. What kind of comment does Kogan make on men and their changing roles as spouses and parents in contemporary times? Consider how Danny and Gunner, who are generally unsupportive of their spouses (and, purposely so, underdeveloped as characters), are representative of a "dying breed" of men, as both find themselves ditched by their wives by the novel's end.

10. How does the close friendship of Mia, Clover, Addison, and Jane resemble your own close friendships from college and/or high school? What are the redeeming aspects of each character, and what makes them worth following throughout the novel, despite their faults? What part of their friendship is enviable? Is there any part of their friendship that you found unusual, or maybe even unenviable?

A CONVERSATION WITH
DEBORAH COPAKEN KOGAN

On your Web site, in the piece "About the Author, Unplugged," you touch upon the personal struggles you've had balancing your various careers with raising children—something your characters in *The Red Book* struggle with as well. What rules/guidelines/ advice has helped you to navigate the multiple roles of mother/ writer/spouse/friend? After your experiences, what would you tell your own daughter about leading a balanced life? (Or would you just have her read *The Red Book*?)

Dear lord, if I had any real, quantifiable wisdom to impart on this topic, I'd write a different kind of book on the subject altogether— nonfiction, stuffed with studies—both for my daughter and for my two sons. (Please, let's not leave our sons out of this discussion.) But being as clueless about the secrets of a balanced life as the next person, I resort to well-worn platitudes—"Sharing is caring!"—and to fiction, where I people my book with characters who are stumbling around in the same dark as I am. What I actually tell my children, summarized, is this: The most important decision they can make in life, if they decide they want a traditional two-parent family, is to find an empathetic, loving, mature, responsible partner who is willing to share, 50/50—not 70/30, not 60/40—in the burdens and joys of both child-rearing and home maintenance.

Earning one's own living is also, I believe, crucial in that equation, both for reasons of security (if one partner dies) and self-worth, but each partner cannot be expected to earn exactly the same as the other, especially if they work in different fields, particularly in this wretched economic climate, and certainly when one of them is breastfeeding an infant in the United States, which has pretty much the worst maternal/family benefits of any first-world country I know. (Maybe one of my pieces of advice should be "Move to Sweden.") My husband and I try to do the best we can vis-à-vis income generation, within the professional parameters we're given. I used to outearn him, now he outearns me, but these facts and figures probably say more about the upward trajectory of his industry (tech) and the downward trajectory of mine (media/publishing) than about how dedicated each of us is to paying equal parts of the grocery bill. In other words, thank you for buying this book. Really.

You also note in your bio that male authors receive different treatment from the press than women, particularly with regard to rearing children. How have you dealt with or combated this general misperception or miscasting of your personality?

When my first book, *Shutterbabe*, came out eleven years ago, quite a few reviewers referred to me as a stay-at-home mother, even though my advance had been twice the yearly salary of my previous job, and I happened to write that particular book in an office outside my then toddler-filled home, and the fruits of my labor were more likely than not sitting on the reviewer's desk as he was writing his review. Make no mistake: I enjoy writing books, but it's hard work. And I say that having worked as both a war photographer and a TV producer. In fact, in many ways being a writer is the hardest job I've ever had. It's lonely. It's filled with rejection. The pay is often laughable. It requires discipline to sit down every day, cranking out words, coming up with new plots and ideas, and being willing to sit and listen to the faint rumblings of one's imagination/muse/whatever you want to call it while simultaneously quashing that nasty, red-horned devil of internal doubts, fears, and self-criticism. But that's not answering the question, is it? How do I combat the misperception that I'm not working when I'm working? I have no idea. I wish I did. I guess by answering questions such as these with as much forthright defensiveness as I can. Barring that, I guess I could wear a name tag that says, "Hello! My name is Deb! I'm a writer!"

On the other hand, the older I get, the less I care about the way I'm publicly perceived. I care much, much more about my quality of life, and in that sense, I feel lucky. I have work I enjoy. I make enough money to get by. I am present in my children's lives. That's enough.

Your impetus for writing *Between Here and April* was the image of a dead rat you came across while on a run in Central Park. What was the impetus for writing *The Red Book*? Did the final draft look anything like what you'd envisioned when you first began writing the book?

The impetus for writing *The Red Book* was sparked when I went out for drinks with Barbara Jones, the novel's original editor, and Ellen Archer, Hyperion's publisher. It was 2009, the beginning of the recession, and my life—like many people's I knew—was in a tailspin. My husband had been out of a job for eight months. Our rent had been hiked up so high we had to move. Our older kids were entering adolescence; our then three-year-old, who'd been essentially deaf for that crucial window of language acquisition between twelve and eighteen months, was having trouble speaking. Our marriage was going through painful transitions. I'd just lost my beloved sixty-seven-year-old father to pancreatic cancer before having a nervous breakdown in the middle of his book tour, which I'd promised him, on his deathbed, that I would embark upon in his stead. (He'd been working on that book, his only one, since the early seventies; he died two months short of its publication.)

I'd recently returned from my own twentieth reunion, which took place in the spring of 2008, and I was telling Barbara and Ellen about both it and the red book: how the latter had always made for such fascinating reading that my husband, who did not go to Harvard, would often steal it from my bedside table to immerse himself in the lives of strangers. "It might be interesting," I said, thinking about how different my life seemed at that moment from the version I'd composed just a year earlier, "to do a follow-up. A nonfiction book about my classmates, comparing the life they presented in the red book to the life they're leading now, especially today, in the midst of this financial meltdown, when I bet a lot of their narratives have suddenly diverged from their previous paths."

Suddenly, Ellen's face lit up. "No," she said, "not nonfiction. No one will be honest enough for nonfiction. This is a novel. And you must write it."

"You're right," I said, suddenly energized. "It's a novel." Right then and there, I chose the class below mine—1989, definitely, I said, as they would bridge the abrupt transition from one economy to the next—as well as the reunion year, 2009. A twentieth reunion, I realized, would allow me to have female characters who could theoretically still get pregnant, whereas by the twenty-fifth, issues of having children, at least naturally, would be somewhat moot. Then I ordered another glass of wine and mapped out the bones of the characters.

By then I was drunk, and it was time to go home.

A month later, I'd written the first red book entries and had plotted out the weekend, some threads of which changed over the course of writing the novel, but not by much. The only real structural change was that Clover ends up with Bucky at the end; I'd planned for her to have stayed married to Danny, taking her secret of their son's paternity with her to the grave, but something wasn't working when I actually wrote it out that way. It was my agent, David Mc-

Cormick, who said he really wanted to see the former lovers get together at the end, that it would feel right, on a number of levels; David's usually smart about these things, so I listened to him and rewrote it.

By the time I finally typed "The End," about a year and a half after I started, I realized that writing this book had brought me, no exaggeration, back from the dead, out of my grief, in the same way a more orthodox Jew would have gone to shul to say kaddish every morning. The daily ritual of writing about life—which is, of course, a priori, writing about death, albeit more obliquely—had thrust me back into the land of the living in a way I could not have imagined, when I was focused so intently on the loss of my father. I only wish he were still around to read it, and I just realized now, typing these words, that this will be the first book I've written that he hasn't read.

———————————

Your roles in your professional life have been as diverse as your roles in your personal life. What have you learned through your engagement in so many different fields? How much has your photography influenced your writing? Has your writing or reading life affected your eye as a photographer?

I actually don't see writing and photography as all that different, although obviously they require different skill sets and brain hemispheres. (Don't ask me which hemisphere goes with what, I can never remember. Google it. They know.) Each medium requires really looking, interpreting, translating human experience into something that can be shared with other humans, seeking out metaphors, preserving slices of life within an artificial, limiting framework—in the case of photography, within a rectangle; in the case of writing, within the strictures of narrative and language. I actually think photographers would benefit from forcing themselves to write now and then, in the same way writers would benefit from running around their neighbor-hoods shooting Instagram photos on their cell phones.

In each medium, the key skill is knowing what to leave out. Life throws so much at us, we're literally bombarded with images and words all day long. But it's the job of both the writer and the photographer to filter out all that noise and say, here, look at this, look what I found, focus on what's vital, ignore the rest.

You've also tried dramatic writing: screenplays, a TV pilot, and the beginning of a stage play. In which kind of writing do you feel most at home? Do you imagine you'll try essay writing, or poetry? What are you working on right now?

I feel at home in all writing, though fiction was the hardest nut to crack because of my aversion to lying. Really, I can't even play poker because I feel physically ill if I have to pretend I have a good hand when it's crap. I had to keep telling myself that fiction is a bunch of lies strung together in pursuit of truth, just to get through each day. I still feel somewhat squeamish about it, as if I'm doing something illicit when I write fiction, playing God with all those puppets in my head.

As for poetry, I spent the bulk of my teenage years writing it. Bad poems, mostly, but every once in a while one of them would win a student prize, which just fueled the fire of my teenage narcissism fur-ther. I once got in big trouble with my European History teacher for writing poems instead of listening to him in class, which explains why I can never remember which Mary was beheaded when or why. I was enamored of language back then, loved playing with words and sounds, and I hope my prose has retained some of that delight, as when I real-ized, while writing this book, that many of the songs and groups from the late '80s rhymed: Chaka Khan, Estefan, "Too Turned On"; Simple Minds, "Red Red Wine," "Sweet Child o' Mine." Oh, I can't tell you how excited I was when I stumbled upon this. It's the little things, really.

I am currently writing the screenplay of this book for both mercenary and educational reasons. By educational I mean that the more screenplays I write, the more I learn about the form. Or at least that's the theory. This will be my fourth screenplay. I also wrote a teleplay. None of them have been turned into movies or TV shows. I believe it was Einstein who said the definition of insanity is doing the same thing over and over again and expecting different results. What the hell did he know?

I'm also plotting out a new novel, of which I've written only the first line, and I have this black comedy play that's been marinating in my head for over a year. Hopefully, I'll get it all down on paper one day. I feel the limitations of time acutely. Writing this, for example, means I've spent two fewer days writing something else. And don't even get me started on Facebook and Twitter. I actually have a program on my computer called Freedom that keeps me from going online. My friend Michael bought it for me. Thank you, Michael.

As for essays, I write them all the time. In fact, I wrote a whole book of them, *Hell Is Other Parents*, some of which I've performed live. In fact, I have one I'm supposed to be working on right now, and the laundry situation is out of control, so if you'll excuse me . . .